MY HOME IS ON THE MOUNTAIN

MY HOME IS ON THE MOUNTAIN

CARO CLARKE

SAPPHIRE BOOKS

SALINAS, CALIFORNIA

My Home is on the Mountain

ISBN - 978-1-952270-40-6

Editor - Tara Young
Book Design - LJ Reynolds
Cover Design - Fineline Cover Design

Sapphire Books Publishing, LLC
P.O. Box 8142
Salinas, CA 93912
www.sapphirebooks.com

Printed in the United States of America
First Edition - Saptember 2021

This and other Sapphire Books titles can be found at
www.sapphirebooks.com

Chapter One

How much steam could a radiator give off? Would she be stranded here until she made newspaper headlines? HOPE FADES FOR COLONEL HOWISON'S DAUGHTER. SOCIETY FRIENDS WAIT AND PRAY. She watched a bee fly into the woods. At some point, tragically, FOUND TOO LATE.

No human sound. Only the birds calling, a bee buzzing past her, the hiss of steam. Another bee. Cecilia sat up. Her brother had once told her that bees traveled in straight lines only to water. Water would mean PLUCKY MODERN GIRL RESCUES SELF. And I, thought Cecilia, stripping off her driving gloves, am a very modern girl.

She perched on the Buick's side mount, empty Thermos in hand, and waited. A bee shot by like a bullet. She was up the steep verge after it into the trees, taking an animal track that threaded its way below the towering oaks and yellow birch, hope and attention fixed on the bees zipping past. Ahead, a bright wink—sunlight on water? Yes. Tom was *always* right. Now she heard it trickling and quickened her pace, but she stopped abruptly as she stepped out of the woods. Someone was sprawled by the creek, asleep in the meadow flowers.

Barefoot, in nothing but overalls, wide brimmed hat fallen aside, but here was no country boy. Cecilia drifted across the meadow, breath high in her throat.

Who is this? A local farm girl, long, ragged, rake-thin, and half-buried in the meadow grass. Cecilia saw fox-colored hair, a nose and chin reddened by the sun, one cheekbone even more burned, and a shoulder crisply red. As she moved to cast a shadow, a tanned forearm came into view, a glimpse of white ribs. What had made this sleeping Artemis too tired to sense the sun was burning every exposed inch or that a stranger was standing over her?

Then she did, waking and scudding back, knees up, arms hard across the bib of her overalls, scowling.

"I'm sorry I disturbed you," said Cecilia. "I was looking for water clean enough for a car's radiator. I don't want to turn an innocent Buick into a mud-filled monument to stupidity."

The girl said something unfriendly in a crow voice that Cecilia had to tune her ear to mountain speech to understand: "You might find a monument handy." Cecilia raised puzzled eyebrows. "You could sell folks tickets to see it, save up, and buy a car that works."

"Tickets to whom, on that infernal road? I wouldn't earn enough for shoe leather."

"You're the one who drove it. Nobody else does."

"I've learned that lesson at bitter length. I need cooling down and," her own pointed glance at the girl's sunburn, "so do you."

"I ain't dressed for company."

"I don't mind a bit," Cecilia said truthfully. "You *are* better dressed for wading, if you would?" As the girl hesitated, Cecilia offered her the Thermos and turned away to face a cluster of blue-eyed grass, adding, "While I admire those."

Behind her, sounds of the girl rising, sloshing in

the creek, a dunk, approaching drips.

"Please, you first."

"It's your jug."

"I insist." Cecilia's back remained resolutely turned.

The girl's shadow drank and wiped its mouth. "I'm obliged. I was dry as meat on a spit. Still looking like it, too, at least up one side."

"Have more."

"I'm done. And done talking to the hind end of your hat."

Cecilia turned at once, but the girl was already stooping again to the creek. Cecilia looked at that lean, bare back and thought, I'm in trouble. Then, *if I take that Thermos while I'm on my feet, I'll have to walk away*. She dropped at once to the grass and was arranging herself to appear comfortably settled when the girl straightened and looked down with reluctant admiration. "You staying?"

"I thought we could get acquainted."

"Why?"

Because I need to know who you are. "Because it appears you're the only other person on the mountain." Cecilia took her Thermos and sipped. "You might even pay a penny to see a car."

"You got to do better than a stopped car. I've seen one of them before."

"Then perhaps to stir your pity?"

The girl did not smile. "Yes, ma'am."

"Oh, not *ma'am*. My name's Cecilia. What's yours?"

"Airey." The girl sat cross-legged, apparently absorbed by the grass and flowers.

"An attractive name." Airey. "I've not heard it

before."

"It was my granny's, and her mam's and granny's before her." The girl's attention continued to roam.

"How lovely—like an heirloom. I inherited *my* name from the patron saint of music."

The girl looked up at last. "I like music."

"Do you? So do I."

"I play fiddle. For money."

"You're a professional!"

"Reckon so. Or a monument." The girl's look dropped again, sharpened, and one long arm reached to free a violin bow from the flowers. "Shouldn't never have left it out, but it don't seem to be harmed. I was taking off some busted hairs." She stretched again to rescue an open wooden box, clipped the bow under pegs in its lid, and tucked a flap of quilt over the violin nested inside. "Busted my second-last string, too. My professional days will be laying idle just when so-longs are coming faster than chips off a stump."

"So-longs?"

"So-long-and-farewell parties. Folks selling to land buyers and leaving."

"Land buyers? Oh, the park. You as well?"

"We ain't seeking to."

Cecilia returned to more hopeful territory. "Have you been playing professionally for long?"

"Some years."

"Locally, or do you travel?"

"You don't got to talk to me just 'cause you need my help." Airey began to get to her feet. "Where's your car?"

Not yet. "At the other end of that path, but my brother tells me cold water will crack a hot radiator top to bottom. When I left it, the engine could have baked bread." Airey remained on one knee. "And I'm not actually in need of help. I came here to rescue myself and believe I'm sufficient for the purpose."

"You was just expecting."

"I was just hoping."

Airey looked unblinkingly at her, sat again, leaned back on her arms, and crossed her long legs at the ankle. "Seems I ain't in no rush to clap eyes on a monument."

Cecilia sipped water and said nothing.

"You asked where I play. Every place I can, nearby and as far out as neighbors' wagons or my own feet can take me."

"Are you in a band? Do you play alone?"

"Both. Mostly me."

"I play a little myself—the piano—for pleasure, not as a professional."

"Seeing how you're dressed, you don't got need to."

"I'm fortunate in that."

"It keeps you playing a little?"

"I play a little because I have little talent."

"Plain spoken. You got some other thing you do better?"

"I spend my time, quite a lot of time, in fact, how shall I describe it—flitting among flowers."

"Then you was born a caterpillar." At Cecilia's questioning glance, "'Cause now you're a butterfly. That's all you do? Visit flowers?"

Cecilia plucked a stem of the blue-eyed grass. "You'd be surprised how it fills a day."

"Reckon I would, seeing all things born on earth have been given work to do."

"The lilies of the field toil not."

"Their work is filling our hearts with God's grace."

"Butterflies?"

"To help flowers like bees do and," Airey conceded, "to give us that same grace. You flittered all the way up here for flowers?"

"I took that cursed road to be somewhere new. To do something new. To see something new."

"You got it today."

"As something new, you could not be improved."

Airey considered her. "You want more?"

Of you? "Yes."

"Come again and I'll play for you."

"I'd like that very much—if you won't mind an audience of one."

"I don't. When?"

"Whenever you want, as I flitter at will. How much do you charge?"

"Money?"

"Of course money."

"Your kind don't pay."

"None of us?"

"None I've met so far. Your kind think we like doing things for free for you."

"Then I hope very much they weren't my kind. Or if they were, let me be an interesting surprise. I must pay you or not come."

"I won't take money when it was me who invited you."

"A dilemma! What shall we do? We might—could we—shall we swap? I'll bring you violin strings if you'll play."

"A butterfly that's got some bee in it. You're something new to me." Airey's face lit with a slow, sweet smile.

When she had recovered, Cecilia said, "Oh, entirely a butterfly, but one who believes there's a best of her kind. Tell me where I can find you."

"Up there." Airey nodded behind her.

"The top of the mountain?"

"No soul but cows ever lived on the bald. Our farm's a little way up from here. It's sunnier than down in Fittes Cove and better soil, too. When you come, don't take that road you're on now. It's an old railroad bed that leads to Sankgallon Gap Timber Company land, which means nowhere worth going. Take the other one that runs through Fittes Cove and along Fish Creek to Hinterhouse, then head up the drovers' road. It goes to the bald, but turn left at a little pine killed by lightning. We're at the end of the lane."

"Where would I be going?"

"Our place. The Fitch place."

"So you're Airey Fitch. Fittes and Fitch: relations?"

"Cove and creek was both named for us. Our name's been spelled different from time to time. We used to own every inch of these parts, being pretty much the first ones here. My great-going-back grandsire came over from the Old Country with gold coins sewn in his coat, and he put it on an assayer's scale to buy this mountain. We got the cove later on off the folks who went land hunting down in Seminole territory. We had plenty till the war."

"This mountain is in my family's land grants."

"We gave Applesell Bald its name and most other places besides. We found it, we bought it, we worked it, and it's ours. Everything best round here was or is Fitch. My fiddle playing, too. You'll like it."

"I know I will." Cecilia twirled the blue-eyed grass in her fingers. "I'm taking this home to remind me of the day I met the Fitch of Fitch."

"I don't need a flower to remember *you*."

"You're right. Keepsakes are for things past, while *I* have an invitation." Cecilia tossed the stalk aside. "I won't condemn this to an eternity under cellophane, stifled in a scrapbook."

"All things languish when taken from their rightful place." Airey stopped. "This ain't how I usually talk to lowlanders."

"Are you enjoying it?"

"Seems so."

"I hope it continues when we meet again."

"I got an ambition to see. And to see if you're still wanting something new."

"There's no doubt."

"Then I reckon your monument's ready for water." Airey rose and offered her hand. Cecilia was wafted to her feet. She smoothed her skirt to hide her gasp and looked away in self-protection as Airey bent for the Thermos.

"This all you got? No pail nor bucket?"

"I don't usually drive with one."

Airey slung the violin box across her back and led the way into the forest. Cecilia now had no choice but to look: at the play of muscles across Airey's shoulders as she held aside branches, at her easy stride, at her cropped hair, feeling hurried by more than a fast walk up a narrow path.

Airey whistled when she saw the roadster. "You could have sold tickets for real: penny for one side, two cents for a view eastwest, nickel the round trip."

"It's a beauty, isn't it? My father gave it to me for my birthday."

"He lets you drive all over creation by yourself? He wouldn't like where you are now."

"Why would he mind my being with you?"

"He wouldn't mind that. He'd mind your car being bone-dry."

"It won't be for long."

Airey touched the engine. "Hot, but maybe not too hot." She shielded her fingers with a pocket rag, eased off the inlet cap, flinched back from the rush of steam, and tipped the Thermos of water into the hissing radiator. "No cracking come to ear." She leaped up the verge to return to the creek.

As soon as Airey was gone, Cecilia collapsed against the wing of the Buick. *Golly*. She half-laughed, half-appalled at the torrent of sparks rushing through her. *Control yourself. Think of something else*. The long drive home. How late she would be. How this was not a crush. Of what excuse she might give Mother. How this was not going to become a crush. Airey emerged from the woods, and Cecilia abandoned both lines of thought.

Airey held a birch bark cone of water in one hand, the Thermos in the other. She poured both into the radiator. There was a faint splash.

"You're going to need a lot more." Cecilia did not pretend to regret it.

"Yes, ma'am," said Airey grimly and was gone again.

Cecilia spent the next hour lounging by the car, trying to convince herself that she had been caught by surprise, that she was light-headed from the sun, that she would dismiss this as folly when she got home, but each time Airey appeared from the woods, she felt everything—leaves, birds, her own body—come to attention. She said nothing as Airey emptied her containers, bounded up the bank, and was gone, each time realizing that any resolution to resist her had vanished like silk in a flame.

At last, the radiator's inlet made a clenched gurgle. Airey screwed on the cap. "You're all set for home."

Cecilia remembered unhappily that this was the point. "Thank you, Miss Fitch. I hope you haven't regretted your invitation after all this work. Shall we set a date? Next week? Thursday? No, earlier. Monday?"

Airey flushed as she opened the car door. "I ain't got no engagements Monday. You'll find me home."

The roadster started with a bland purr. Cecilia reversed with precision and turned to wave, but Airey was already fading into the forest.

Down to the cove, down to the turnpike, blinded by images as dazzling as a flash-lamp: that short pale hair, that long arm reaching into the grass, that naked back, those hands dripping water. That smile. *Heaven help me.* She had never been gripped like this before—this frankly and physically hard before. She endured its delicious, painful twist. And now? Nothing. Of course nothing. Since nothing would happen. Nothing *could* happen.

The turnpike unfurled through the hills. At the first empty stretch of road, a voice asked, *Why can't it happen?* She thrust back, *Because there's too much of every kind of distance to cover.* She knew when a girl had to be declined. The memory of Airey lifting her to her feet made every drop of blood in her sing out, *Don't decline.* Absurd. Impossible. Not to be entertained.

The voice said contemptuously, *A Howison of Old Waring refusing a challenge?*

A challenge from whom? There was no one else in the car. Nothing had decided to fling Airey Fitch at her feet like a gauntlet.

But she was, said the voice. *She was at your feet.*

Cecilia gasped. Could she take it as a sign? Or more honestly admit that she was caught on a hook of her own making? *I am, and I don't plan to break free.* Every drop of blood cheered. *It's madness, but I'm going to chance my luck with Airey Fitch.*

The odds were against her. Weren't they always? But—Airey Fitch. She faced certain defeat. Did it matter? Airey Fitch. It did not matter at all.

She parked the roadster in the old stables behind the house and slipped up the backstairs. Mother caught her on the landing. "You're late, Cecy. Did Spencer Wystone meet you on the way?"

Cecilia sighed in spirit as she revived that fiction. "I'm trying *not* to meet him. I'm late because I drove home through the mountains, and my engine overheated."

"Heavens above, anything could have happened to you up there!"

"Oh, Mother." *Anything did.*

"There's no rush to get ready. Mr. McClure is still in with your father, so dinner's delayed again."

Varda picked up her clothes as Cecilia undressed for her bath. "You've grass stains all over your skirt,

Miss Cecy."

Cecilia saw herself in the mirror as she reached for her robe. "Oh, and I've caught the sun, too. How annoying." She remembered Airey Fitch's sunburnt jaw, the red strip down her beaky nose, and quickly bent for her slippers. Alone in her bath, she indulged herself with more: Airey standing over her, looking down, Airey reaching up to a branch, Airey stepping from the forest with leaves in her hair.

Airey Fitch. Unlike any factory or mill girl she knew, yet as tough, unlike any college friend, yet as quick-witted—and barbed as an arrow. Unlike every one of them because she wanted nothing from her and asked for nothing. Except an audience. *Something I'm happy to be.*

Cecilia played piano for the family as they gathered in the summer room for the cool evening breeze. She chose familiar pieces that left her hands free to play while her mind roamed around Airey Fitch. How well did Airey play her fiddle? Enough to earn money from the local farmers, which could mean anything. Cecilia anticipated a diplomatic Monday. *It will be worth it.*

Airey Fitch. No ring. Not a wife, when mountain people went famously young to the altar. Shouldn't she have two or three children by now? Or did a fiddle repel mountain boys? Cecilia's fingers dreamed across the piano keys. Those eyes. Those shoulders. Was Airey Fitch thinking of *her?* How unfair if she wasn't. Grandfather's *tut* brought her back to her music.

At the breakfast table, Trenton said, "I've been told you were stranded at altitude. Anywhere useful?"

"Near that tract of white pine, for instance? Do you think seeing it would change my estimate of either the costs or the benefit?"

"I wish you'd stop encouraging your sister taking an interest in the business," said Mother.

Trenton grinned. "Miss Ruthless already has an interest."

"That great-aunt of yours," Mother began.

Cecilia deflected brightly: "I'm meeting Patmore in town this afternoon. Is there anything you need?"

Mother smiled, saying to Rosamund, "You mentioned wanting to go into Avender."

Cecilia resigned herself to the disposal of her day to her sister-in-law, but Rosamund said, "No thank you, Mama Howison. Cecy hates putting up her car roof." She buttered a roll and said to Cecilia, "Really, honey, you ought to take more care. There's not enough crushed strawberries in the world to save a ruined complexion."

"I hear that mountain wildflowers work wonders."

"Packed in cold cream, yes, but why bother if you insist on driving with the roof down?"

Cecilia drove into Avender with the roof down and parked near the music store. Pennicote and Drake's counter was busy, but Marvin abandoned his customer as she approached. "A pleasure to see you again, Miss Howison. What can I get for you?"

"I'm shopping for someone else." She thought back to the violin students at college. "I need, oh, three sets of violin strings." More would tip the delicate social balance.

"In gut? We're low in E. Will you take some in

steel?"

She would. She also bought herself a book and went across the street to Leaman's drugstore, was almost at its door when she noticed the Drennan sisters about to cross her path. She stopped, dismayed, and prepared herself.

Ethel said, "I'll catch up with you, Louise," and rounded on her. "Well!"

"Hello, Eth."

"Were you going to walk right past me?"

"If I hadn't been concentrating on a cherry phosphate, I would have retreated."

"So you *have* been avoiding me."

"Because you told me you needed time to think and that I wasn't to try to see you or to call or write."

"I didn't say forever."

"We can't have this conversation in the street."

"No one's paying attention. We're safer out here."

"We're never safe."

"Don't you think I knew that? Back then? I was terrified every single minute. If anyone had found out, I'd have been cut to pieces. Cut to pieces."

"If you're feeling safe, we must be over."

Ethel's eyes flashed. "You never take anything seriously, do you? *I* do. We—it was imbecility. Lunacy. I'll never understand myself. But with you disappearing completely and Mama wondering every day why two such good friends weren't speaking and if it was a silly fuss over a boy, I was close to screaming. My nerves were rags!"

"We could go back to being friends. Better friends."

"How can I possibly? I thought, after all this

time, it would feel like a bad dream, but seeing you, I can't help remembering—"

"This isn't a good place for that."

"Not for *you*. I'm honestly mystified why anyone would *choose* to keep being afraid of-of *everything*, even their own *thoughts*."

"Do they frighten you? I wonder why."

"Don't flatter yourself!"

"Difficult, in the circumstance. But please don't be troubled. Let those thoughts evaporate—or bury them in a vault or make them walk the plank."

"I'm aware *you* speak from considerable experience."

"In our particular case, I have no troubling thoughts."

"You *should*. What we were doing was wrong, wrong and sinful and—"

"I'll never agree with you."

"—and I'm only thankful I came to my senses in time." Ethel put a hand to her throat. "My nerves are going again."

"After talking with me for two minutes? Those senses of yours need to get the whip hand."

"You're making fun of me!"

"Yes, at you pretending you don't feel—"

"I feel nothing—*nothing*—but disgust. Disgust. And I'm—"

"Ruined for a life with men? No? I hope not, Eth, for your sake, though I suspect it's true."

"Keep laughing, but you'll find out for yourself soon enough. When your father loses his patience with Flaming Youth, you'll be Mrs. Spencer Wystone—no, you've dispensed with him, haven't you?—Mrs. Patmore Reaveley, before you know where you are."

"Because he'll make me take the curb and bit?"

"You'll have to think of your social position at *some* point. You can't keep roving like a wild girl forever."

"Do you think I'll ever settle down? Settle for less?"

"I have no idea. I've stopped you from destroying *my* life, and I sincerely won't be disturbed if you destroy yours."

"Then I'll get on with it." Cecilia stopped at the wince in Ethel's eyes. "But let's not end like this. We were good pals. Let's at least be civil to each other, if only distantly. I hope one day you'll stop dreading the past."

"You know we can never be friends again," said Ethel doggedly. "Ever."

"Does hating me make it easier?"

"Heavens! I don't hate you. I'm just so tremendously sorry."

"Oh, Ethel. I'm sorry, too."

Cecilia watched her rejoin her sister and went into Leaman's. The soda jerk had seen her through the window and was starting her phosphate. *What else did he see?* Ethel's emotions must have been visible from the courthouse tower. If she were this reckless on the street, it would be wise to duck the Sisterhood of St. Anne luncheons for a while. Cecilia sat with a frown of irritation and regret. It didn't need to be this way. It should never be this way. But if a door kept being closed, you had to stop knocking. Her soda appeared. "Thank you, Curtis." She blew into her straw to open it, took out *The Violin: Its Famous Makers and Players*, and firmly began to read.

At the end of chapter three, she glanced at her

watch. Almost late. She found Patmore standing patiently at the doors of the Rex Theatre. What a nice man he was! What an obliging man he was. She held out both hands to greet him.

He held them a second too long. "You look like a hyacinth in that dress."

"I'm sorry to have made you wait."

"Was that waiting?"

"At least forgive me."

"You're acquitted of everything except having eyes as beautiful as sapphires."

Oh, Pat, don't. She pulled a little face to make him grin. "Were you working today?"

"Completing some depositions in a foreclosure. I like to visit the high moral ground now and then."

"You shouldn't make light of yourself."

Patmore looked ruefully down at his well-filled suit. "Light? After two weeks at my sister's? I've gained ten pounds, despite playing pony for those brats every blessed day. Remember when she wouldn't be anything but a pioneer mother raising her doll babies? Now she's only too happy to abandon the real ones onto their long-suffering uncle."

"I remember insisting on being Ginnie Moon, girl spy."

"And Captain Reaveley always napping—excuse me, hanging by a thread—on your porch swing, waiting for your smuggled medicines. The intrepid and the inert! I hear Spencer's off to Ohio. Will you miss him?"

"When I've other friends who don't prefer Ohio?"

"I'm hoping you might start thinking of me as a—"

An usher opened the doors. Cecilia smiled gratefully at him and asked Patmore, "What are we seeing?"

"*The Good Bad Girl.* If it's too racy, we could—"

"No, no, it's perfection."

After the movie, she negotiated a carefree walk with him around the courthouse square, as gently as possible refusing an invitation for an after-church picnic. She had the only invitation she wanted.

On Monday morning, Cecilia drove sedately through Old Waring's gates. A mile down the road, she stepped hard on the accelerator; two hours later, she was humming through Fittes Cove. She met a mule-drawn wagon piled high with tables, barrels, mattresses, bales of blankets, sideboards, shovels, saws, and brooms, waving cheerfully at the family perched on top. Small kitten clouds were skipping across the sky, and a girl was expecting her.

At the far end of the cove, two whitewashed buildings marked the end of the flat land. Road signs pointed south to Galt's Crossing, north to Heresy. Cecilia considered the third choice: a rocky track rising straight up the mountain. She looked around. On the porch of the closest building, *Hinterhouse General Goods: D. Keller, Prop.*, two men were spitting long brown lines of tobacco juice into the dirt, their attention fixed on her.

There was nothing else. That track had to be the drovers' road. She released the brake. If she disappeared, she was sure her audience would be able to give Daddy a description of her roadster down to its last spoke.

The drovers' road looked and felt like a dry waterfall. She crawled up at six miles an hour until the jouncing had her to four. Beech, black cherry, and red oak met high above her head. Birds, blue, gold, brown, flashed through the open space from one mass of rhododendron to another. At what seemed only yards from the grassy peak, a twist of blackened trunk told her that she had found the lightning-killed pine. An opening in the forest hinted at a lane. She turned cautiously and headed into the wilderness.

Mossy knuckles of stone fence jutted from the underbrush on the right side, edging old fields long abandoned. To the left, she saw terraces of fields behind a screen of birches. Corn, corn, poles covered with bean tendrils, corn. Ahead, to her amazement, half a dozen chestnuts flanked the lane, their majestic crowns taller than any other tree on the slope. *Last of their kind?* She pulled her gaze away from them to a clearing, a farmyard, that appeared to her right. A shabby one-story house stood on the cleared slope. Its whitewash was weathered to scurf, every window held at least one cracked pane, but it was surrounded by banks of peonies, zinnias, and marigolds, and its long porch was festooned with climbing roses. A gaunt, ancient barn sagged in place farther up the slope. Hens wandered by old corn cribs, two tethered mules pricked mild ears at her. Cecilia half-circled the Buick in the yard, ready for a quick retreat.

A woman appeared at the door. She had a handsome square face and the most glorious copper hair Cecilia had ever seen. *What a pity Airey didn't inherit* that. A tiny boy crawled past her and watched round-eyed as Cecilia walked up to the porch.

"Good morning."

"Morning." The woman looked her up and down with the partial recognition that Cecilia had long since given up either liking or disliking and said something that Cecilia, again retuning her ear to mountain speech, heard: "You're the gal Airey told us was coming up today."

"Yes. I'm Cecilia Howison."

"Howison! Lord bless us. Howison. Airey didn't say nothing about you being a Howison. I recall seeing your picture in a place or two. Airey don't pay no mind to such things, otherwise she'd have known your face. If she had, you wouldn't never have got an invite. Been a long time since one of your kin came up this side of the mountain. Back in Airey's grandsire's time, that's when we last had dealings with a Howison."

The car was still warm. It would take a second to be gone. Cecilia reminded herself that she had a swap to honor. "A business deal, yes."

The woman turned her head and spat tobacco juice over the edge of the porch. "What else *is* there with Howisons? Still, no point holding it against you personal."

"Thank you."

"I reckoned Airey was touched in the head 'cause no lowlander would ever come all this way to hear her fiddle, but here you are, big as life and a Howison with it. She headed early to hay in the Big South Acre so she'd be back in time."

"You have a late season," said Cecilia, wondering how much hay the Big South Acre held.

"It's cooler up here than your bottom lands, though we got better soil. It makes for a fine life, but a hard one, Miss Howison, specially if you ain't got a man." The woman sighed. "Airey can be real big-headed, but she's been my tower of strength since her pap went to the Kingdom. I'm glad you've come for her playing. Having folks hear her puts joy in her heart like fire through dry birch. And look—just like she owned a watch and chain."

Cecilia turned, and everything else faded. Airey was striding under the chestnuts through shafts of light, overalled and booted, her hat pushed back, a scythe over her shoulder. Cecilia gripped the porch post for support.

Her mother called, "Airey, you change out those men's clothes before you join company," and scooped up her son as she went inside.

Cecilia walked down the slope. Airey took off her hat as they met. Cecilia absorbed Airey's damp blue shirt, her scratched and bitten arms, the sunburn peeling from her chin and nose, the sheen of sweat on her face, her limp hair, each physical detail a tiny blow that rocked her where she stood. Airey's slow smile nearly toppled her.

"I was expecting you close to now."

"So your mother said."

"I've been thinking about you."

"Have you? I've certainly been thinking of you."

"You look trim as a nuthatch in that dress. Go on inside while I clean up."

"You needn't change for me. You're nice as you are."

Airey glanced at herself. "I look like storm of green came for me and got me square on. Mam will have coffee ready for you."

Cecilia struggled not to brush her down, to straighten her collar, to touch her. "Then I'll see you in a moment." She walked up to the house, paused on the porch to let her ferment subside, and stepped into complete darkness. Something brushed her ankle. She stiffened.

"That's Jabez," said Airey's mother's voice. "I've heated you up some coffee." She picked up a black shape from another black shape and swirled the contents invitingly. "Ain't exactly purely coffee 'cause we grind it up with roast chestnut, but it's good drinking."

"Yes, please," said Cecilia, readying herself. Her eyes adjusted to the gloom. She saw two other people, a girl of about eight, her hair as short as Airey's, standing near her mother, and a young woman about Airey's age sitting by a door at the back of the room, where sunlight fell on her lapful of white cloth. Airey's mother said, "That there's my oldest gal, Merit, and this here's my baby gal, Polynegry."

"How do you do?" said Cecilia generally. She saw that the room was the entire house, stove and kitchen shelves in the far right corner, a patched, darned horsehair settle at the far left, two rows of wooden chairs facing it, and more chairs around a long table that stood in front of the small brick fireplace. Newspaper had been pasted over every wall as tightly and completely as paint. Beside a door that must lead to other rooms, a lithograph of an old-world town was nailed above a puncheon shelf that displayed a pile of rocks and a heavily carved clock. Airey's homemade violin box hung from a peg below. No books, no electricity, no radio, no indoor plumbing. This level of poverty made Cecilia want to drive to every store in Avender and buy and buy until they turned away her money. She brought out her now absurd hostess gift.

"Ma'am, I've brought a little thank you for having me into your home."

"Well, ain't you sweet. We're always pleased when folks come round." Airey's mother opened the box with a perplexed smile.

"They're fondants," said Cecilia. "Soft candy."

"A real fancy treat! I thank you."

Airey appeared through the door by the clock. She had changed into a green and yellow dress that would have been more flattering on her mother and once clearly was. Her hair was slicked back, and her feet were bare. She seemed a creature half of this world, half of another, angular and magical, a griffin.

Airey looked at her, looked sternly at her mother. "She ain't been given a seat. She ain't got nothing to drink."

"Your mother's offered me coffee," said Cecilia, taking the chair Polynegry hurriedly set for her.

"Call me Mrs. Grigg." Airey's mother spit tobacco juice into an old lard can. "That's my late husband's name, the one after Airey's pap. Airey, I've been brung candy in a box. Ain't that real nice and ladylike? Here's your coffee, Miss Howison, good and hot. Yours, too, Airey."

"You're a Howison," said Airey.

"Does it make me unwelcome?"

Airey looked away for longer than Cecilia found comfortable. "I reckon you can't hold a grudge against a person 'cause their grandsire won a game your grandsire should never have played. You drink that down, and I'll give you some music."

Jabez had bumped himself to Airey's feet. She lifted him and settled him on her hip, the first feminine gesture Cecilia had seen from her. "You want coffee,

Jaby? Just a sip. A little one. Now look, you're getting it all over your chin."

"That's cause you ain't giving it from his own cup," said Polynegry from the far side of the table.

Airey cleaned his face with a handkerchief as he squirmed to be free, took his hands, and swung him like a bell, lowering him on each swing while he kicked with delight. She supported him as his feet touched the ground. "See the Amazing Standing Boy. Come one, come all."

Her mother said, "You get doing what you promised, Airey."

"Yes, ma'am." Airey parked him on his rump and went to her violin box.

Cecilia took out the Pennicote and Drake packet. "I've kept my promise, too."

"What's this?" Mrs. Grigg's voice was sharp. "Airey, I hope you ain't pestered this lady to do chores for you!"

"I wanted to hear her," said Cecilia, seeing Airey's stiff rise of chin. "We agreed on a trade: violin strings for her playing."

"As long as Airey ain't bossing folks or taking charity. We don't tolerate charity in this house."

"We've never needed it," said a quiet voice, Merit, from the kitchen door. "We trust the Lord to provide."

"Amen. We do honest work for honest money. Airey's playing brung us eight dollars forty-six cents last fall."

"They passed a hat," said Airey with pride.

Mrs. Grigg nodded. "It was at the biggest fiddle contest in the county, and my gal won. Of course, they couldn't give her first prize over the men, so they made a special ladies' cup, but even so, the folks who came reckoned she was owed more. I never saw so many nickels and dimes collected together in one place."

"The cup's little, but it's silverplate," said Polynegry. "She gave it to Jabez. It's his now. He don't dribble out of it."

Airey had unwrapped the packet and was setting the coiled strings across her hand.

"I bought spares," said Cecilia. "Steel strings are the solution to continual breakage, but you might not care for them, as they alter the quality of the sound."

"I owe you quite a show."

"Come one, come all."

Airey gave her a quick smile. "You're going to hear everything I got." She fixed the new strings to her battered violin. "These will need bedding down. They're good." She tightened her bow, swept the long hairs with a small block of rosin to roughen them, and tuned the strings by ear. "We'll go outside 'cause the fiddle's real loud in here."

"It's loud everywhere," said Polynegry.

"If Airey's putting on a show, let's all go outside," said Mrs. Grigg.

In a minute, chairs were through the back door and on the bare earth of the farmyard, where an old saddleback log cabin, joined at a right angle to the main house, made a sunny corner. Merit gestured for Cecilia to sit beside her. Airey stood inside the kitchen door, rubbing powder into her palms.

"Airey's sanding her hands with grit," said Merit. "She says she can't play all callused up, except she leaves them on ends of her left fingers, so the strings don't cut them."

An involuntary thought of how soft and hard

fingertips might feel on bare skin made Cecilia look away. She saw that Merit was older than Airey, and her face held a docility that Cecilia suspected came of being Airey's sister. Merit smiled at her, showing tobacco-stained teeth, as she took up her embroidery. Mrs. Grigg settled beside them, a handkerchief on her own embroidery hoop. Cecilia could see a spray of lily of the valley delicately growing from one corner. Polynegry cradled a bowl in her lap, picking over tiny beans. Jabez was the only one with idle hands. Aside from herself.

Airey stepped out to the single stair. Her face held a new look: concentrated, alert. She put her violin to her collarbone and played an old, sad song, standing as motionless as a pine tree while the melody wove a gentle dark ribbon through the day.

"That was Airey's pap's favorite," said Mrs. Grigg. "Ain't it nice? He taught it to her when she was a little bug of a thing."

"Play something peppy," said Polynegry.

"Who's deciding this set?" asked Airey, zipping into a jig. The Fitches' toes tapped and soon Cecilia's joined them.

When it ended, she said, "You play very well."

Airey nodded and dashed through another jig, a reel, breakdowns, country waltzes, hornpipes, Tin Pan Alley foxtrots, more jigs, a Hawaiian-style waltz, more reels. Cecilia was impressed: Airey was as good a fiddler as she had said and had clearly deserved her prize.

"If Airey'd been a man," said Mrs. Grigg with a melancholy spit of tobacco juice, "she'd have been off to Atlanta and in a string band fast as mush slicks from the spoon. Even being a girl ain't stopped her getting work, at least not while there was still enough folks round here to hire her. She played for the Nazarite Baptist picnic last month."

"Their last in these parts," said Airey. "They've mostly moved out of the cove. They didn't want a man fiddler who might come with liquor snuck in his case and behave scurrilous."

"She brung home a big turkey pie," said Merit.

"The Nazarites dance 'cause King David did in front of the Lord," said Airey, violin scroll-down against her chest as she retuned her strings. "I got them all on their feet like His spirit had come among them. Now I'll play you something different."

This time, she slid her hand to the end of her bow, raising and fully straightening her arm as she brought the bow to the strings. A fountain of singing notes filled the air, louder, clearer, more lyrical, though as effortlessly played as the jigs and reels, but it was not this that had Cecilia rising from her chair, staring. She knew Airey saw her; still the music sprang and fell like dancing water, endless dappling diamond drops, flinging brightness into the sky until its last joyous flourish.

Airey lowered her violin. "I reckoned you'd know that."

"I…yes, I do." Cecilia was almost unable to speak. "I've-I've heard it before. Where did you learn it?"

"Our neighbor, Mr. Brewken," Mrs. Grigg answered. "He settled down the slope from us a while back."

"Do you know what you played?" Cecilia asked Airey.

"Mr. Brewken told me when I learned it, but I

can't recall exactly."

Cecilia heard the troubled grief in her voice. "It's by Bach. He called it a prelude. *Preludio.*"

Airey's face lit. "I remember now you say it. I thank you for that. It's the start of a whole set of tunes by him. I know them all."

"Play them." Cecilia sat down. "Please. Play them."

Airey lifted her fiddle with an almost replete look. Cecilia listened with fixed attention. Mr. Potz had given his violin students the Bach suites, and Cecilia had heard them played badly for a year. In Airey's hands, this was sun to that darkness: fresh, innocent delight, precise and beautiful as a dancer's steps. Cecilia floated in the shimmering air after Airey lowered her bow.

"Play something else, Airey," said Mrs. Grigg. "Miss Howison don't care for that."

"No, no!" said Cecilia, coming to herself. "Not at all—I enjoyed it intensely. It was...superb. I...it-it was rapturously well played. I'm speechless."

Airey gave her a lordly smile. "I said you'd like it."

"I need to-to, oh, I don't know what I need to do." Cecilia was on her feet again, turning blindly toward her car. "I have to see—find—to go home. Mrs. Grigg, thank you—forgive me."

"Why, surely." Mrs. Grigg did not hide her surprise. "If that's all you want to hear, it makes for a real short visit, though I can't deny there's only so much of Mr. Brewken's sitting-down music a body can take. Airey won't play it no more."

"That's all I want her to—I mean, how kind—I'd love to come again, thank you so much," Cecilia heard herself gabble and rushed down to her car, thoughts flying in every direction.

"Miss Howison."

Cecilia stopped and turned on the slope. Airey stood above her. "If you liked it that much, why are you cutting out?"

"Because I liked it so much. I can't tell you. I'm overwhelmed, I didn't know—how could I know? How could I know there was someone like you up here, totally unknown?"

"I'm plenty known. You was told about the Nazarites' picnic and me winning the cup."

"Not that—that as well—I mean proper music."

"Everything I play is proper. I work hard."

"Yes, I can hear." Cecilia took a breath. "I'm sorry, I've been startled—and now-now I have to *do* something. I don't know what it is, but something. May I come again? I assure you I don't normally react like a startled fawn. May I hear you play again?"

"You never expected that."

"Of course I didn't expect it! How could I? Why would I expect anything like you here or a hundred miles in any direction from here, outside a performance hall?"

"I reckon I'm the best you've ever heard."

Cecilia looked seriously at her. "You're very good."

"I got heaps more I can play." Airey went with her to the car. "Blues, parlor, dance tunes, old-time, Mr. Brewken's, whatever music you want."

"Especially his."

Airey opened the roadster's door. "Then get over being that fawn and come back."

Cecilia drove home in a blur and ran upstairs to the nursery, to find her brother Tom perched on one of the low children's seats, feet on another, a notebook in his lap.

"Gently, my child," he said. "Must you approach with such healthy vigor?"

"What are you doing here?" She tugged off her driving gloves impatiently.

"In no special order, recovering from merry-making in town, avoiding the honored parents, and organizing an informal concert for an illustrious visitor." He flicked cigarette ash against an open bottle on the floor. "You appear to be not so much invigorated as agitated, little one."

"Do I? I've been driving." She looked around. "Where have they put everything that used to be here?"

"My elevation off the floor suggests to me a few chairs remain, I behold your miniature tea set, and I gaze with satisfaction upon my admirable geological collection. Happy, happy boyhood days and the fruit thereof!"

"I meant the Grafonola."

"*That* everything. In the attic, if it still works. We replaced it with one of those newfangled record-playing devices that run on electricity called, if I am correct, as of course I am, a Victrola."

"I want to lend it to someone. I wonder if we have any needles left."

"Whom do you know whose roof shelters not a Victrola of its own?"

Cecilia pirouetted one of the little chairs and sat

beside him. "Tom, what would you do if you stumbled on someone—on someone extraordinary? A, oh, a Scott Fitzgerald, right here."

"I'd clap myself in the nearest bughouse."

"I mean it. If you found someone gifted—really gifted—but unknown outside a small circle of friends and neighbors. Someone who perhaps didn't know *how* gifted he was."

"What would I do?" Tom examined his cigarette. "Nothing, given I lack the Howison impulse to meddle in other people's lives. I'd content myself with envy. It's been a winning strategy since dear old Ruyerford days: surrounded by my betters, yet with a song in my heart."

"I feel as if I've been shot from a cannon. I need the Grafonola, I need to go to Pennicote and Drake, I need to find someone at the conservatory who can help to—"

"This, the first tragic evidence of the fatal Howison tendency, springs forth like Athena, fully formed and ready for mischief. No wonder you're agitated. Come, unburden your girlish heart to your loving brother."

Cecilia twisted her gloves together, seeking a way to tell him about today without too tangled a lie. "I went to tend Great Aunt Ruth's grave last week and took a mountain road home. I met someone who plays the violin."

"How enchanting and how apposite, given what I'm planning! If a mountain road, then a mountaineer, and thus the violin, it being inescapably part of their lives."

"It's certainly part of hers."

His head came up. "A girl, is it?"

Her instinctive caution made her say lightly, "Girls are allowed to play, even up there."

"What could a belle of the wildwoods play to agitate you so?"

"Every sort of popular music and—oh, Tom: Bach. She's a young unknown talent, and it's—"

"Young? We speak of a wee lassie?" He sat back and took a drag of his cigarette. "Observe me intrigued."

"Her playing isn't far short of Mr. Feldstedt's."

"Time for your own trip to the bughouse, sister dear. No country fiddler is within reach of Concertmaster Feldstedt."

"I know what I heard."

"Not to crush your sweet enthusiasm, but you're hardly an expert of that instrument. It doesn't happen, Cecy. Great artists are trained by great artists. They quickly become known, even at a young age. They're sought out. They don't bud and bloom in the backwoods."

"But you haven't heard her—"

"You didn't pay much attention during Feldstedt's concert. Your memory might, dare I say it of a musician, err?"

Cecilia had not been paying attention because she had been passionately, and it turned out pointlessly, watching for Ruby. "I remember enough."

"I remember being submerged in a fragrant sea of the fairest coeds our state has to offer."

"*The Collines Female Academy is pledged to raise in every student's heart the sacred banner of all that is refined, wise, holy, and good, so each may be the bearer of these in the home,*" Cecilia quoted automatically. "Oh, dear. Still with me."

"The bearer of the banner! What refined, wise, holy, and good assistance do you feel you must render this gifted mountain damozel?"

"She needs to be heard by an expert. She should be playing Beethoven, not *Old Dan Tucker*."

"Why?"

Cecilia was taken aback. "For the same reason it's wrong to condemn a born poet to a life of radio jingles. Artists should be helped to ascend to their chosen art."

Tom shifted, easing his hip. "It sounds as if she's ascending all by herself."

"That's not a choice! Not a choice when she can play Bach the way she does."

"Do you think you can give her the choice between a barn dance and the Avender Concert Hall? Is that likely?"

"I want her to see that the concert hall is her only choice."

"Ah. I feel honest compassion welling up within me for this rustic poppet."

"Tom, if you had heard her!"

"Bring her down here, have her audition for Mama's friends, and if she's as good as you say, I'm sure one will introduce her to a teacher and perhaps even fund her education. Still, even after all that, could a hayseed, however talented, be fit to join an orchestra's junior desks?"

"Senior desks," said Cecilia, but her fervor paused. Did she want Airey taken up quite so quickly by Mother's cronies? "She's not eager to please lowlanders."

"Well done, the little prodigy! There speaks the pride of the old mountain stock. Or are you suggesting *she* wouldn't like it because it's thine own self who wouldn't? Will she reflect badly on you? Does she pick her teeth with the tip of her bow? Spit 'baccy on the floor as she tunes?"

"Of course not, but given Daddy's plans, would Mother thank me for bothering them with this right now?"

"Indeed they would. He'd have an opportunity to show benevolence unto the honest poor, and you can bet the newspapers would be there to witness it."

Cecilia could feel the road to Airey washing away before she had driven a single mile.

"Bizarre as it might seem," Tom said to her silence, "it could be that this *puella pagana* doesn't need your assistance. Tell her that concert halls have orchestras, orchestras need violinists, and that she's welcome to audition for them when she's old enough to do so."

"I *will* tell her," said Cecilia. *And right now.* "But first I need to know what she knows, so I can—" She stopped at his sardonic smile. "You really think I shouldn't help?"

He took her hand. "You are your mother's daughter in every shining respect, my dear, which means you must do as your heart dictates." He kissed her fingers. "And I, inspired as ever to rise to your angelic goodness, won't forget to ask Henry to bring down the old wind-up. Oath of a Howison. Are you going to ask to borrow my records? Because I'm going to say no."

"I'll bring my own and buy more."

"Be careful in those mountains. You don't know the roads."

"I will," she said, taking the whole of his warning.

Cecilia had the summer room to herself after dinner. She worked her way through Bach, the inspiration of the day, while she tipped Airey back and forth in her mind like a glass puzzle. *The world needs to know her.* That was beyond doubt. *I need to know her first.* Absolutely beyond doubt. But she would be the greatest Babbitt on earth if she delayed by even a day bringing Airey to the attention of some music grandee. Tom didn't understand. She had come across a pearl of great price. Airey needed more than the address of the nearest orchestra, more than recommendations, she needed to be invested in, she needed a mentor, a guide. *I can do that—I will be that—for her.* And with luck, so much more.

She stopped playing to sort through a sheaf of piano-violin duets. Mr. Brewken's music—sitting-down music! Airey needed to comprehend what she was playing. Her education would start with these. Would start tomorrow.

Tomorrow saw Grandfather in bed with another heart spell. Cecilia spent the day, the next week, reading *Barron's* to him. Finally, he ruffled her dark curls. "I'm back to fighting fit, lambie. Now off you go to your beaus. Don't let an old man keep young men waiting."

"I prefer it here, sir."

Grandfather smiled. "That's why they call."

She drove to Pennicote and Drake and cornered

Marvin. "I want a recording of every type of violin music, and I want the best artists, including any American women you stock."

"We have some old recordings by Mrs. Powell."

Cecilia remembered Maud Powell's photograph on Dardhardt Conservatory's thinly populated American Masters commemoration wall. "Let me see. That's all? I'll take them. For the rest, let's get a good range."

Marvin stacked records on the counter, adding albums to the piles at Cecilia's suggestion. He slipped the records into sleeves until all were filled.

"Now," said Cecilia, "sheet music. I don't know if it's needed, but let's have some study scores. Bach—no, I don't need to bother."

"This one's a little shop-soiled," said Marvin. "Shall I give it to you for half the price?"

"Why not? And phonograph needles, a dozen packets."

"I hope your violinist friend is delighted with all of these, Miss Howison."

"So do I."

She drove across town to the academy. Mr. Potz was not in his office. Cecilia left one of her cards in the net on his door and felt Airey's future beginning to bud.

It rained in the night. Cecilia rose to close her window and paused to listen. A beautiful sound, as the crops needed it. She stayed with her hand on the curtain. The wind was coming from over the mountains. It would be raining in Fittes Cove and across Applesell Bald. It would be raining on Airey's roof. Was Airey awake and listening, too? Cecilia smiled. Airey probably slept as heavily as a field hand. *She is a field hand.* Cecilia imagined her swinging her scythe under the sun, muscles slick with sweat. That—and Bach. Bach! *Lord, send me strength.*

Chapter Two

Varda," Cecilia said after a fast breakfast, "my new crêpe de chine, the postilion cap, and my blue driving gloves." *Fighting fit.*

At Hinterhouse, she smiled at the two men on the porch and gunned the Buick up the drovers' road, braking hard at the blackened pine. The rifle muzzle she had seen was already dipping and the boy holding it blushing. From his foxy hair, Cecilia knew she was looking at a Fitch.

"Sorry, ma'am." He slid down the bank. "You ain't who I thought you was."

"Whom were you hoping to shoot?"

He grinned. "I hoped to stop any passing park man and talk some sense with him." A small white and honey-colored feist dog came out of the brush and began a perimeter sniff of the Buick. "You're the lady who came to hear Airey's music, ain't you?"

"I am. I'm Cecilia Howison."

"My name's Lorimer. I'm Airey's brother. You got a whizz-lightning car. How fast can it go?"

"I once reached fifty-eight miles an hour."

"On the pike." He gazed at it with as much concentration as the men at the general store. "Airey ain't here. She and Polynegry went down to help Mrs. Labhard with her tobacco."

Cecilia almost wailed. "I'm sorry she isn't home. May I leave some things at your house?"

"Mam's sort of expecting company," Lorimer said with a touch of judgment, "but she won't mind you. She likes folks."

"Shall I take you with me?"

Lorimer gave the roadster a longing look. "I got to finish weeding the two-acre. Get on up, Roy."

"Can you watch for land buyers and hoe at the same time?"

"Royal and me do it together, him the watching, me the hoeing." He jumped up the bank to let the Buick go by.

Cecilia met Mrs. Grigg on the farmhouse porch. "I'm sorry I've arrived without notice. I met your son on the lane, and he thought you'd allow me to leave a parcel for Airey."

"You surely can. Come in and set. We got real coffee today. Mrs. Labhard brung it when she came up asking for my gals."

Cecilia lifted her bundle of record albums and sheet music from the car with difficulty. The phonograph would have to await stronger arms. "These are for her music."

"That's a kindness, seeing she don't get no help from nowhere. Warner Jacklin, who plays down as far as Georgia and even on radio with the Melodious Mountaineers—that's his string band—he reckoned Airey was good and better than any man he'd ever heard but said a flat *no* to hiring her 'cause an unmarried gal would raise too much trouble in a traveling band. Said it to her face that neither he nor nobody would take her, and Airey turned white as ash."

"That's a shame."

"I can't find it in my heart to disagree with him. I'd never rest easy with Airey traveling round with a bunch of men and not one married to her. She's still set like a mule to get to Atlanta and find herself another string band 'cause that's how she's built, and I ain't got word to rein her in." Mrs. Grigg spat tobacco juice. "Here's me talking while you're standing holding that big load. Ain't it good Airey's not here to see! I'll get you a cup."

The coffee was ferocious. "Properly brewed," Mrs. Grigg said proudly at Cecilia's gasp. "My first husband, Airey's pap, said he'd have married me for my coffee alone. We prospered when we was young, and I didn't lack for coffee nor sugar. He'd open his eyes wide to see us now. It was the park coming here that killed him, and I'll swear it holding ten Bibles in each hand." She turned toward a faint moan from a back room. "My gal Merit's down with a sick headache."

"I have aspirin." Cecilia offered her small silver pill case. Mrs. Grigg took it to the back rooms. Cecilia looked at the cooking stove, the oilcloth-covered table, the worn rag rug. That Airey—Airey with her talent—was hoeing tobacco when she could be playing in a symphony orchestra made Cecilia broil with rage. She heard Mrs. Grigg returning and steeled herself to finish her coffee.

"May I leave Airey a note?" She used one of her visiting cards and was tucking it under the string of the Pennicote and Drake parcel when they both heard the rumble of an engine down the lane. Mrs. Grigg spat her wad of snuff into the lard can and changed into a fresh, embroidered apron, smoothing it over her hips with both hands.

"No need to go just 'cause someone's come," she said as Cecilia rose. "I reckon that's Pastor Souch. He's a friend of the family."

Cecilia wondered if Lorimer agreed.

Mrs. Grigg went out. "I got coffee the way you like," she called to the truck pulling up. "Merit's in bed feeling poorly, but we got a lady visiting Airey on account of her music."

"From the Siffville School?" asked a man's voice.

"You know I don't welcome their kind here." Mrs. Grigg led him inside and said to Cecilia, "This here is Pastor Souch. Brother Port, this is Miss Howison from down yonder."

The man smiled as he hung up his hat. "I would have recognized you without the introduction, Miss Howison, not that I expected to see one of the family up here."

"How do you do, Pastor Souch?"

"You can ease off the *pastor*. I've been called and do my preaching at His behest, but I don't take a title. Sister Bertha, does Merit need a prayer said over her?"

"She'd be bashful even of a pastor by her bed, which you are, since you speak before the Lord." Mrs. Grigg served him coffee and half a stack cake. "I fret over Merit. She's wearing herself to bone waiting on Card to marry her. Cardwell," she said to Cecilia, "is Merit's bespoked, what they call fiancé. He's in the Army down in Georgia. He keeps saying he'll come back to marry her, but he ain't done it yet. Brother Port, I hope you won't vex me about them trees 'cause it ain't my place to say."

"I've made the case often enough," said Mr. Souch. "Your chestnuts will soon be dying like all the others. They should be harvested now while they're still useful timber."

"Airey says it'll give the park men the excuse they want to take the farm from us."

"It's not theirs yet. You can despoil your own as much as you please and still be within your rights. That chestnut down at your southwest corner is already touched with blight."

"Makes no sense to kill them before they're ready to go." Mrs. Grigg sighed. "That'll be a sad day. Those chestnuts have been standing here since before the first house was built." To Cecilia, "Not the very first house. That was burned to embers in the war. Fitches was for the Union. Southroners set fire to the whole place, and the Fitch folk hid up in caves nearly four years till they could start building the next first house. Our chestnuts was witness to all. When they die, I reckon it'll be God telling us to give in to the park."

"You haven't got that much time, Sister Bertha. I'll talk to Lorimer."

"Airey reckons we should lease."

Mr. Souch smiled tightly. "I know her views. Airey doesn't have a place in this discussion. Whatever Lorimer says to her, I'm sure he'll say something else to me, man to man. But let's not talk about it while you have a guest. I'll tell you what I came to, which is that I'm holding a singing in my meeting house this Saturday."

"I wouldn't miss it even if I was struck lame in both legs 'cause I could still be thrown over a mule," said Mrs. Grigg. "You know Lorimer ain't likely to come."

"His soul would fare better if he did." Mr. Souch

looked around. "Where's Jabez? He'll miss his ride."

"It was his grizzling that gave Merit her headache, so Airey brung him down with her to the Labhard place."

Mr. Souch took a carved bird from his pocket as he stood. "Give him this from me. I'm obliged for the coffee and cake."

"You going? Dinner's nearly ready. Lor shot a brace of rabbits yesterday, and I'm stewing them with greens. I ain't seeing you off with only that little bite inside you."

"You tempt me, but I mustn't stay." He took his hat. "It was a pleasure meeting you in person, Miss Howison."

Mrs. Grigg went out with him and returned bright-eyed as the truck rumbled away. "Ain't the pastor a fine gentleman?" She sat and packed a hefty pinch of snuff on the far side of her lower teeth. "I'm a woman pulled in two, Miss Howison, say it as maybe I shouldn't. Women like men, that's a plain fact, and I miss having one by me. You might tell me Port Souch only comes here for our trees. Well, it's true, he does come for them, seeing his job is to buy stumpage. He's a hardheaded, dealing man, and I admire him for it, but he comes here for more than trees, and I don't know what to do."

Cecilia smiled encouragingly.

"He'll never move up here." Mrs. Grigg took up her embroidery. "He's got a house and a big garden down in Galt's Crossing I'm itching to put to rights. Airey says we're duty-bound to lease the farm till Lorimer's old enough to take it over, and I know that's true and right, but Lor's a boy who's stepped up to a man's work, and Airey's doing a man's work, too, and it ain't justice to keep them striving here when Lor ain't—I mean to say—if Lor might not want the place when he's full grown or if the park's going to take it anyway. If it does, that'll near kill Airey. She's real proud that Fitches owned all this back to scratch."

"I know she is."

"Pastor Souch's made it plain that me and mine all have a home under his roof, but Lor won't never get along with him, and Airey ain't built to be chided nor bid."

Cecilia believed it.

"I'm troubled and asking the Lord to guide me." Mrs. Grigg leaned back to spit. "The pastor says the government can take our place without paying us a single penny if we don't sell to them soon. The Strickers got themselves a lease, but they can't hardly put a shovel in the ground before some park man tells them they're breaking the terms. Old Mrs. Stricker, she says they'll snip and snipe till her and her boys throw in the hat and leave. They aim to run us off, and I need to look after my chicks."

"Have you spoken to a lawyer?" Cecilia stopped. "No, of course not."

"We ain't got a nickel for coffee, let alone for lawyers," said Mrs. Grigg. "The one John Martin hired wangled him a real good price, but they all wanted to sell, and his boy helped with the writing. I got no one."

"You have me," said Cecilia before she thought.

Mrs. Grigg laughed kindly. "I ain't been school-taught like my chicks, but I know you ain't no lawyer, Miss Howison."

"One of my friends is." *What am I saying?* "With your permission, I could ask him how someone secures a park lease. I'm sure, given your circumstances, the park would negotiate."

"You'd do that for us?" Mrs. Grigg leaned forward, dawningly hopeful. "I ain't got words to say how obliged we'd be. My boy's birthright comes before all. I'd turn down the pastor and stay here, no matter the sacrifice, if that's what my chicks want. They come first with me."

"Let me speak to my friend. I'm sure he'll look into it for you. More than that, I can't promise."

"The Lord bless you, Miss Howison."

Lord help me.

"When they hear that it's Miss Howison's helping me, those park men will back away faster than fat dogs from a riled sow." Mrs. Grigg got to her feet. "I'd be pleased if you'd stay to dinner with us, specially since the pastor couldn't. I'm making spoon bread."

Cecilia wavered. "I'm very fond of spoon bread."

"You've come to the best place on the mountain for it," said Mrs. Grigg. "Everybody'll tell you so."

"In that case, how can I refuse? Thank you."

"Now, there ain't a thing for you to do," Mrs. Grigg replied as if Cecilia had offered. "It won't be a big sit-down, seeing that Airey and Polynegry are at the Labhards and Merit won't have no appetite, but me and Lorimer will welcome company." Mrs. Grigg disappeared for a few minutes and returned with a cloth-covered plate crusted with flies. She shooed them and chopped sausage meat into a frying pan, "We're short of this, losing a full litter like we did last spring," covered the pan, briefly opened the oven door, releasing the aroma of spoon bread, and began to sing. "*He sends His show'rs of blessing down, To cheer the plains below, He makes the grass the mountain's crown, And corn in valleys grow.* Ain't that true? Every day's full of blessings, except those times when the Lord tries your soul." She finished it and began another.

Cecilia sat back to enjoy the concert. The company of any woman was better than most things she could think of.

Merit emerged from the back rooms, pale and blotched. "Mam, you should have called—oh, Miss Howison, beg pardon, I didn't see you there. I reckoned you'd gone."

"She's staying for dinner," said her mother. "Airey'll roar like a staked bull when she hears she missed her. You look better, my poor gal."

"Thanks to those pills. Mam, I'll stir that."

"Do let me help," Cecilia said politely.

"Since you're set on it, you could fetch some milk from the springhouse," said Mrs. Grigg.

Cecilia quelled an unbecoming prick of indignation and went with a pitcher to the kitchen yard. Beyond the log cabin, a creek marked the edge of the farmyard. A rock-walled vegetable garden climbed the steep far slope. Who plows that? she wondered, looking at its neat rows, knowing it must be Airey.

The springhouse was a stone hut built into the creek. It was cool inside, having no floor but a raised stone and the creek. Skinny muslin-wrapped sides of pork hung from its rafters, shelves held jars of sausage, dark fruit, and honey. A lidded enamel milk pail stood to its waist in the water, its bail attached to a rope that ran up to and through a pulley fixed on a rafter, and down again to a miniature paddlewheel idling in the flow. A faster torrent would kick the wheel with enough force to raise the pail clear of danger. *Pioneer know-how.* Cecilia filled the pitcher with milk and backed out, turning and closing the door with her heel as she cradled the pitcher against her, to see Airey bursting around the corner of the old log house. She stopped, Airey's physical presence like a furnace blast.

Airey was dirty and angry. "Pastor Souch came by the Labhard place about the singing. Said you was here. What are you doing with this?" She jerked the pitcher from her arms.

"I asked to help," said Cecilia. "Your sister's not well."

"You're our guest."

"You ran all the way?" Cecilia trotted to keep pace, her lack of breath only partly due to Airey's longer legs.

"Somebody should have thought to tell me you was visiting," Airey snapped.

"I'm glad you're here now."

"You staying for dinner, or is Mam just making you work?"

"Your mother mentioned spoon bread."

Airey's scowl lightened. "Mam's spoon bread is sung in song across the mountains."

"She said as much."

"Mam don't hide knowing what she's best at."

"That runs in the family then."

"Saying otherwise is telling whoppers. Scripture's plain: *Lying lips are an abomination.*"

Cecilia moved her gaze from Airey's mouth. "I've brought a few more things I hope you'll find useful."

"You want me to play for you again?"

"These aren't a swap, they're gi—" *the pride of the old mountain stock*—"a loan. Of course I want to hear you again. I must pay this time."

"No. You like Mr. Brewken's music, and I ain't got no one else who'll listen to it, so I'll take the pleasure." Airey hung her hat above the washstand to sluice her arms and head. "I told Mrs. Labhard I'd be back tomorrow if you was still here. Poly stayed. She's faster than me anyhow."

"I'll step down." Merit, overhearing, came to the door. "Stitching all day tuckers me out. I'd be happy to pick bugs as a change."

"*If* you wear your bonnet," said Airey, brushing back her hair with her fingers. Cecilia fought an urge to smooth a stray wisp.

The house was filled with oniony aromas. Cecilia retreated to her chair, no longer needed, watching Airey moving around her mother and sister with the spare grace of a laborer. Airey smiled at her. "You look hungry."

"It smells delicious."

Sounds of splashing at the washstand, and Lorimer came in. "How d'y do, Miss Howison?"

Royal padded over to see if she smelled as interesting as her car. Lorimer went to loosen a length of twine from a nail in the wall. It freed a long fringe hung from a rod, which swung over the table. He looped the twine to a rocking foot paddle by his chair and pumped. The fringe swept the table's length like a fan. Seeing Cecilia's interest, he said, "I heard some folks up north of the Sankgallon Gap built a fly brush like this. They pull theirs by hand, but I reckoned I could chase off flies and eat at the same time."

"Ingenious," said Cecilia. "Did you invent the raising paddlewheel in the springhouse?"

He grinned shyly. "Yes, ma'am. Stops the milk

being washed away."

"Lor's going to be our Edison of Applesell Bald," said Airey. "One day, folks will travel here from far away to be taught by him. Those rocks on the shelf are his examples."

"Specimens," Lorimer said curtly, and Cecilia caught his muttered: "As if anybody'd come up *here.*"

The family gathered at the table. Merit said a short grace. Cecilia was offered the first helping of stew, the first spoonful of bread, the first glass of milk.

"Have as much as you want," said Airey expansively. "Fitch land has every best thing from here to heaven."

Yourself included. Cecilia glutted herself instead on the lightest, creamiest spoon bread she had ever eaten. Mrs. Grigg watched, gratified, and asked sociably, "You come from a big family, Miss Howison?"

"I'm the youngest of four, two boys and two girls."

"I suppose you folks got a sizeable place."

Cecilia thought of the rolling valley that was Old Waring. "Yes. We grow cotton and tobacco, as well as corn, barley, and some cane. My father breeds horses along with other businesses, so we don't depend on the crops alone."

"Must be a comfort in these hard times. If it wasn't for Airey's fiddle and those chestnuts, we might have starved last year."

"We hauled sacks and sacks of nuts off them," said Airey. "We fed like hogs."

Mrs. Grigg said, "The pastor don't understand what a living chestnut's worth. Airey, did Mrs. Labhard mention when the Jecks are leaving?"

"She didn't. She did say the Webbers will be out as soon as they clear their black gum and take the harvest."

"This cove's getting emptier than a miser's wallet."

At the end of the meal, Lorimer hooked the fly brush against the wall and went back to the fields, Royal at his side. Mrs. Grigg said, "Merit and me will clear the table, Airey. You take a look at those things Miss Howison brung you."

Airey brought the Pennicote and Drake parcel to the table and read Cecilia's message.

"The phonograph's in my car," said Cecilia. "You'll want it for those." Airey untied the parcel and looked at the albums.

"These are recordings," said Cecilia.

"I know. I ain't never seen so many together before." Airey opened the top album and flipped through the stiff sleeves, studying the label of each record. "Batch."

"That's a name you know: Bach," said Cecilia.

"Bach. This is Bach. And Bee-th-oven—must be Beethoven. First time I'm seeing them wrote down." Airey put aside the top album to open the one beneath. "Mozzart—that'll be Mozart. What are these other names?"

"The people playing the music. Here, a violin and a piano."

"I've heard a piano." Airey shut the album and picked up the sheet music hesitantly.

"I didn't know if you had many scores—" Cecilia looked at Airey hunched over the fanned-out pages. "Is there something, or have I—oh, golly. Do you know what these are?"

"It's...is it...wrote music?"

"Yes. This," Cecilia extracted the shop-soiled

Bach, blessing Marvin, "this is what you played me: and here's the *Preludio* on the first page."

"I see Bach." Airey put her finger reverently on the name. "He wrote this. I recall one time long past when Mr. Brewken showed me his paper music, but I never saw it again after that."

"That means-that means." Cecilia stopped, her mind jibbing. "That means you play everything—you play it all—from memory."

"Hornpipes and two-steps, they ain't hard to remember."

"I mean the rest, Bach—you remember it?"

"Mr. Brewken would have fits of saying goodbye to the world and burn his things. His paper music must have gone up the chimney early on. He told me all fiddlers learn by hearing and remembering, so that's what he made me do."

"Extraordinary." Cecilia put a hand to her reeling head. "It's a great gift, but you can't memorize all the music there is."

"I don't need to. I learn what I like."

"But to be a member of an orchestra—" Cecilia regrouped. "There's too much to memorize. If you can read music, you can learn anything without needing to hear it first."

Airey looked at the sheet music. "That'd be a help."

"Let's put these aside and listen to some records. Or if you'd like to play, I'd like to hear you."

"The folks on these records are known real well, ain't they?"

"Yes. They're famous throughout the world."

Airey laid her hand on the sheet music. "I can't read these. I ain't the kind of fiddler you're acquainted with."

"Miss Fitch, I've attended concerts by famous musicians since I was a little girl, I listen to records such as these every week, and still I'd like to hear you play."

"I got my pride, Miss Howison."

"Which goeth before destruction, Miss Fitch."

"That's true," said Mrs. Grigg, washing dishes behind them. "Airey, you get swelled up like a frog from time to time. There's plenty of fiddlers more grand and famous than you."

"She's got something to be swelled about," said Merit.

"Kicked down and raised up again." Airey shook her head. "Any pride I got is wearing a hunted look."

"Would it stop you hearing other violinists?" asked Cecilia.

Airey's face flickered. "Not to hear them, but I won't play to folks expecting me to fall short against them."

"Airey, my ears ain't believing themselves," said her mother. "You won't chance being judged? You're the same gal of mine who took Freed's dare and set off down the creek in the washtub?"

Airey smiled. "I was little."

"You got scrapes where I didn't think no one could *get* scraped."

"Your brothers ever gave you a dare?" Airey asked Cecilia.

"My brother Trenton did, to jump a fence. I came off my pony in spectacular fashion."

"Same for me, out of that tub. I washed up on some rocks and stuck fast. Freed had to cut a pole to pry me loose." She looked again at the albums. "I got to know where I stand. Reckon I can't flinch."

"All we need is my phonograph," said Cecilia bracingly.

"We'll go to the tobacco shed 'cause Mam don't like Mr. Brewken's music. There's some leaves still in there, but if you ain't bothered by them, we can be by ourselves."

How could I mind? "I won't mind."

Airey disappeared with several chairs, returned to bring the albums, her fiddle box, and Cecilia to the tobacco shed, collecting the Grafonola without effort on the way. The shed was a narrow annex built against the long side of the barn, as dim and richly scented as the library at Old Waring. Sunlight through its rough boards turned Airey into blades of gold.

"What would you like?" Airey set the Grafonola on a chair. "Me or these grand fiddlers?"

"You."

Airey rubbed powdered feldspar across her palms, scoured the fingertips of her right hand with a rigor that made Cecilia's own hands tingle, tightened and rosined her bow, tuned her violin and said, "I'll give you something different from Bach."

Her bow met the strings. Music lifted like slow silver lace. Cecilia heard Airey's elegant, meticulous playing and became increasingly aware, as the music branched and flowered through the shed, of a driving sensuousness. Airey's body was still, as if forgotten. She had merged into her violin, and Cecilia needed only to listen to share all she felt. The violin paused, sprang through a handful of charming short pieces, moved to a singing beauty, and finally, as if she could never be far from him, the certainty of Bach.

Cecilia realized that she herself must appear like

someone in a trance. "I could listen to you all day."

"I'd play all day if I could. Now some old-time music? Or..." Airey glanced at the albums. "No. I reckon it's my turn to listen."

"You needn't fear what these will tell you." Cecilia turned to the Grafonola and locked back its lid. "Have you used a phonograph before?" She showed her how to insert a needle. "Replace these before each record you play. The old ones go in this cup. My brother Tom used to commandeer them for his miniature ballista, to the cat's delight. The handle turns this way. Don't tighten the spring too much." She wound it and set the brake. "What would you like to listen to first?"

Airey leafed through the albums. Cecilia saw the sun glowing in her hair, watched it gild her temple and cheekbone, and felt like the phonograph's spring: tightly wound. She wanted to touch where the sun touched, but as strongly as this, she wanted to see how Airey would listen.

"Here's a lady's name."

"Maud Powell. She died about ten years ago. Would you like to hear her?"

"Not right yet." Airey worked back up the pile. "This one." She held the album to let Cecilia slip the first record from its sleeve. "He was Mr. Brewken's favorite."

"Mozart." Cecilia put it on the spindle, released the brake, and gently lowered the needle.

A flourish: the orchestra welcomed the violin, who entered with high-stepping notes. For one second, Airey's eyes blazed at Cecilia, the next, everything disappeared from her face. She leaned toward the Grafonola and did not move. Cecilia could look at her now as intently as she liked, for she had vanished from Airey's world. She studied her mouth, her eyes, brown, green and gold—the phonograph's tone arm began to loop, and she turned the record over as Airey sat back impatiently—her sharp hunched shoulders, knees like pine knots against her skirt, her whole lanky body locked in fierce attention.

The final notes faded. Cecilia collected herself in time to lift the tone arm and reached for the album. Airey said, "Play them again."

"The whole thing?"

"Yes."

Cecilia played it again. Airey listened with the same concentration, her fingers following the violin, her eyes kindling. Cecilia watched, unsettled, fascinated, bewitched by her.

The music ended. Cecilia parked the tone arm and set the brake. They sat in silence. Cecilia sifted her own feelings.

"Mr. Brewken played that," said Airey abruptly. "In a band like that."

"An orchestra."

"He was its main fiddle player, the leader of them."

"Concertmaster."

"He had all of this sounding in his head while he was teaching me. He had *this* in his head." Airey rammed her fists together. "Play it again."

"Will we play it all afternoon?"

"I got to. You tell me what I'm hearing. I know the fiddle, but I don't know the rest."

Cecilia explained the instruments as fast as she could through the movements, certain, if only she could lay the score before her, that Airey would knit music to notes before it ended.

When it did end, Cecilia let the turntable wind down to a clicking stop. Airey looked up, her eyes dark. "I don't know nothing about this." Her fingers jabbed at the Grafonola. "This. What did Mr. Brewken reckon he was teaching me for? I could have been playing *this*."

That's it? That's all it takes to persuade her? "Do you want to?" *Let everything be this easy.*

"My first music was this. It's what I fought to play. And now here's more—heaps more. Show it to me. Tell me."

"You need a proper teacher."

"I don't need teaching to play, I need to know more about Mr. Brewken's music."

"It's called European concert music, or serious music."

"All music's serious."

"According to their degree."

"No. Each is as serious as this. Jazz is different from radio dance and radio dance is different from old-time and old-time is different from this, but they're each serious 'cause they was built proper. It takes work to shape them right. I reckoned I'd got this concert music more than right. Turns out I'm like a fly thinking it knows a cow from sitting on one ear."

"Mr. Brewken taught you nothing more about concert music than individual pieces?"

"Not straight out. I saw bits of newspapers he kept with his name on them, and I heard him talking to himself when he forgot I was there, but when I asked, he said he'd never blight my soul by speaking of the fools and knaves who trample on music's holiness, so I never found out."

"He must have had a troubled past."

"His troubles was of his own making."

"I'm glad you were at least aware that there was more to know about this music and that you wanted to know. Simply to know? Or would you like to play it for money, as he did?"

"I'll play anything for money. But this music—Mr. Brewken played it in distant lands. I need work closer by."

"If you could play it, say, in Charleville?"

"Where I'd be seen as peculiar as a two-headed pig?"

"Their small-mindedness would stop you from going anywhere? Then how will you ever know where you stand against these other violinists? Or do you think you can judge for yourself against recordings in a barn?"

Airey shot to her feet. Her violin flew up. Music exploded through the shed, hot and spiky as a pine fire.

Cecilia was pinned to her chair. "What was that?"

"I can't remember the name of who made it. It's long, with two knees."

"Paganini? He's famously fiendish to play."

"He ain't water through a sieve."

"Why did you play it?" But Cecilia had heard. "Because you can. Because you can play this music. No one who plays the way you do is content to stay in a barn. You don't want to be measured. You want to be heard. You should be heard. You must be heard."

"The fiddlers on these records who get listened to round the world, they got proper teaching."

"How are you different? I don't know who your Mr. Brewken was, but he was master enough to have given you your craft. You should be playing to audiences right now. It's appalling that you aren't."

Airey gave her a half-smile, raised her violin, and filled the air with delicate pain, taking Cecilia away from the shed, away from the earth, piercing her again and again, as St. Catherine was pierced by the angel's arrow, until the last cooling note fell like a star through her heart.

She took a ragged breath, knowing Airey was completely focused on her. Airey said, "I want to make folks feel how you're feeling. Knowing they want me to give it to them, like you do—all of them knowing I can and needing me to show them how much."

"Then give it to us. By making yourself what they want to put on stage. Technically, you're ready now for the violin section of any orchestra in the country, but to be hired, you need to prove you know instrumentation, counterpoint, composition—everything that's part of a full musical education."

"How will I get them?"

"By attending a music school, called a conservatory, or by going to a tutor—a teacher—who will finish what Mr. Brewken started."

"I've saved up a jar of dimes and quarters to pay for getting myself to Atlanta and maybe a couple weeks room and board, but there ain't no extra for education—and no need of it."

"To play old-time? Play with whom? In a string band such as the Melodious Mountaineers, who wouldn't have you?"

"Mam told you about that? It was a blow. Then I remembered that the Carter Family is mostly their women folk, and last month down in Heresy, I heard a record of a string band that's all women, and they put the grit back into me."

"I don't believe the rules change between here and Atlanta. Every one of the women in those bands has a husband or father holding the musical door open for her."

"Then I'll play alone, like I do now."

"And how is that working out, given your audience is shrinking by the month?"

"Rockefeller ain't asked me to compare millions, so I'll admit not bountifully."

"An education in concert music would prove a better investment."

"Which man will open the door for me after I'm done?"

"If you needed a man for this music, I wouldn't have raised the subject. Women, unmarried women, are earning salaries playing it right now."

Airey's attention sharpened despite her skeptical look.

"I'll give you an example of someone I know. Miss Lieve D'Haese was taught by a man who had been taught by the greatest pianist who ever lived, an equal to Paganini. She had a career in Europe and, after the World War, in the Americas. When she retired, the Dardhardt Conservatory of Music in Charleville begged her to join. She's also a visiting teacher at some lucky local colleges, mine included. She did all this as an unmarried woman, one who would have been rejected by every band in Atlanta. She finally married, two years ago. Mr. Vernelle's a good clarinetist, but *she* carries the spark from a virtuoso—a master—a giant."

"She teaches the fiddle?"

"I wish she did. You need a teacher of her caliber.

You're everything that teacher will want. After two or three years, you'll be able to open your own doors."

"Three years! Before earning a cent! Where am I going to earn enough jars of money for that? Why are you telling me this when it'll never come to pass?"

"It could—"

"Ain't you looked round? Who plows and harrows? Who hoes and trims? Who reaps and takes to the mill? Who's striving for a lease from the park and for Lor's schooling?"

"It doesn't have to be you."

"Who else *is* there?"

"Your mother."

"Her new notion for help ain't no better than her last."

"You dislike Mr. Souch so much?"

Airey's smile was stiff. "You've spotted how that land lays. He's got no skew in his core, but I ain't seeing the little ones happy living with him as their steppap down in Galt's Crossing. If I get that lease, Mam will stay here at home, and so will they."

"Aren't you putting yourself where God never meant a daughter to be?"

"I ain't the man of the house, nor even a man, but I took on the thinking and deciding, as well as the working."

"You *should* want your family to be happy, but *you* can't decide for them what form it takes."

"Being thankful for the blessings we're given."

"A blessed life is merely receiving? King David danced before the Lord. I think we're created to be happy and are so when we accept the life we're meant to live. Your family's happiness isn't in your power to decide. Making *yourself* happy *is* in your power—or don't you think God wants you to have the happiness you want for them?" Cecilia studied her closed face. "*Thou wilt shew me the path of life: in thy presence is fullness of joy.*"

"You know your Scripture."

"Yea, verily, even an Episcopalian."

Airey smiled grudgingly. "You'll be saved yet."

"*Your* responsibility is to your God-given talent. Why do you think you have it?"

"What will God say if I choose myself over those depending on me?"

"*Well done, thou good and faithful servant.*" At Airey's scandalized look, "Because you'll be doing the work He's given you to do and leaving your family in His care. Unless you believe you do a better job."

"If He wanted me to have this music, He'd have given me the jars of money I need for it."

"Jars? When He can supply you with rich supporters, patrons, who will give you—"

"Fitches don't take nothing on bended knee."

"It wouldn't require that."

"Help from lowlanders always does."

"Would it be charity if *I* arranged it?"

"Especially we don't take nothing from Howisons."

Stung, Cecilia asked, "You wouldn't accept help from someone whose grandfather is a co-founder of the Dardhardt Conservatory? Whose father and a brother are on its board? Most musicians would pray for any Howison to be on their side, down to the youngest and least."

"Those that do the giving call the tune. Even you."

"You'd prefer not to play, except on your own

terms? That need to learn this music, to know where you stand against other violinists, that need to be heard, all that comes second to your pride?" Cecilia closed the album. "Then I won't waste my breath trying to convince you. I myself prefer a pride that accepts the cost for the sake of the prize. *Better is the end of a thing than the beginning thereof.*" At Airey's frown, "What do you want? What do you want above all else? What will you do to have it?"

Airey's gaze fell to her violin. "When Mr. Brewken was teaching me this, I took every minute I could get out of him. I practiced: between my chores, down at the Settlement school, after Mr. Brewken died, after Pap died and our troubles came on us. Oldtime, parlor, radio, this music. To play. To play every day. To play better every day. To make the music better every day. I didn't never stop." She touched the body of her violin with a caress so intimate that Cecilia felt she should look away. "I won't stop. I can't."

"Because you burn for it."

"To play anything. To play it all. If I can't get no place with old-time or dance or any other, then with this, my first music. But I ain't sure I'll want what Mr. Brewken ran away from."

"We both know you'll find ignorant and unfriendly attitudes in the lowlands. You'll be insulted and scorned, just as you are here, being a girl in a man's world. But if there's a chance of success—and it's more than a chance—why not follow the music wherever it takes you? Why not accept the help you need to have it?" She saw Airey's mouth tighten. "You've told me you won't take my help. Fine. I won't give you a thing. I'll swap." At Airey's wary look, "A real swap. My side will be to find you an education and the money to pay for it. When I do, your side will be to throw yourself into the fire—and burn." Airey's face became blank. "No? It's too much to ask? You won't dare? This, from the girl who went down the creek in a tub?"

Airey's hand locked on her wrist. "Don't never dare me. You think I'm afraid?"

"Yes. Of what?"

Airey's breath seemed to stop. "I'm afraid—of this. Of having this. Of living my life in music. I've hungered and prayed for it. Now it's before me, it could come to pass, and I'm risen in hope higher than I've been before. I want it, I've got to have it. What if I get it? My soul trembles and cries out."

Oh, golly. Cecilia's heart shrank, but Airey's hard grip on her wrist opened a layered awareness: of the depth of Airey's need, of her passion, that she had that need and passion, of her body, tense in her urgency. An answering need and passion flared through her. Her own certainty returned like a spear to her hand. *I can do this. I will give her this.* She said, "I'm a Howison. I swap only when I'm sure. Don't doubt you can trust me. Trust me. Dare all. I want you to dare—I demand that you dare."

"Why? Why such fierceness in you?"

"Because of music, this music. What music does to me. What the music *you* play does to me. How *you* play music. Don't you see? The power is yours. Take it. The bended knee is mine. Accept it." Cecilia leaned close enough to feel Airey's breath on her lips. "What revelation are you waiting for to tell you that your moment has come? That it's here before you? Take my swap."

"You ain't—"

"Take my swap. I dare you."

Airey's eyes darkened.

"A deal? Yes? Say deal."

Airey squared her jaw. "Deal."

"Thank you." Cecilia hid her shudder of triumph. "Unhand me, Miss Fitch."

Airey looked down, surprised, and let go without apology. Cecilia's arm tingled, not from pain. They assessed each other.

"Now what?" asked Airey.

"Now I set to work. I'm certain I can get you at least an audition with Mr. Potz, although I won't rest there."

"This Mr. Potz on records?"

"No, he's the music tutor at my college, the Collines Female Academy, although it's more of a finishing school than a college."

"It did a good job." At Cecilia's puzzlement, "Finishing you."

"I'm glad you think so."

"But he ain't the best there is? I want to be taught by those greats. That's how I got old-time, from fiddlers passing through Galt's Crossing, and parlor music, from bands on Mr. Huber's radio he runs off a car battery, and jazz from records they play down in Heresy—the greats of each, and each gave me a boost. That piano teacher of yours, she's acquainted with any concert fiddle greats?"

"Yes. I've met several. One day, you'll know their names and maybe even them."

"You're already in the place I'll be climbing to."

"I've never scaled its height and never will. There's a difference between *can* play and *must* play."

Airey grinned. "You don't burn for nothing?"

Oh, Miss Fitch. "Right now, I burn to get you to that life of music. I'll do whatever I must, I will not cease from endless fight, nor will my sword sleep in my hand, until you're in Jerusalem."

"If I get there..." Airey paused. "When I get there, what will I be playing?"

"What you just heard."

"The lone fiddle part?"

"In orchestras. Aren't you tired of playing by yourself?"

"I like being in a string band, and I like just me."

"If you like string bands, you'll find being in an orchestra very heaven."

"I ain't played with anyone behind me since Christmas. Sometimes Lorimer will thump a log. It ain't the same."

Cecilia laughed. "Hardly accompaniment. Are you the only musical one in your family?"

"My brother Freed had a voice like a meadow-lark's. Pap's was nearly as good."

"Your mother also sings."

"She reckons so."

"Harsh in your judgment, Miss Fitch."

"Mam's got something she does best. You et it today. Freed's best was knowing the woods: each flower's name, where cress grows thickest, places deer come in hard winters, such-like things."

"Your mother spoke of him as dead."

"He died four years past."

"I'm sorry."

"Freed and me got along real good." Airey put away her violin. "We'd go sit by the falls and eat ramps or we'd make a den in the old corn crib and talk the sun down." She smiled without grief. "You got a favorite brother or sister?"

"A brother, though both are dear."

"I don't know nothing about you more than what you told Mam at dinner. Will I meet your kin?"

"Why not?" asked Cecilia, wondering if it would ever be true. "You can visit any time you wish, although Auntie Nelma's spoon bread isn't as good as your mother's."

"Then I ain't stirring. But it means you've got to keep coming up here."

"How could anyone not want to come here?"

"No place is more blessed by God."

Cecilia heard her realize that she had just agreed to leave it. "Wherever you go, this will stay in you. I hear it in my mother's voice when she tells stories of where she grew up and in my sister-in-law's when she talks about Georgia. And I know how my own childhood feels to me."

"You got some grave notions in your head for a butterfly."

"Am I spoiling my little show?"

"Showing what you are."

Cecilia turned to the albums, wary of moving too quickly to places a little too deep. "Shall we talk or shall we listen to more music? Which do you prefer?"

"Talk *and* music, but music first. With me, it's music first every time."

"I expect nothing else. Now, Beethoven." Cecilia flipped through the albums. "Do you know his sonatas?"

Airey nodded. "Mr. Brewken taught me some parts. I play them quite occasional."

Of course you do. Your wonders never cease. "Beethoven wrote these for violin and piano. And no," as Cecilia saw her about to speak, "I wouldn't dream of playing with you. You outperform any violin student I accompanied at college, and they were far in advance of me."

"That would stop you?"

"I, too, have my pride."

They listened to the sonata, then again, Cecilia taking her through its structure. At the end, Airey said, "You're a good teacher. I can hear all the things you tell me."

"I wish I were better. You will have better. It's my business now to find one for you."

Airey's brows knit, but she said amiably, "Let's give this another play-through."

They listened to it once more, individual passages repeated, all of it again. The need to control her thoughts through the repetitions, to do nothing but describe structure and change records while Airey was seduced by the music, was a mocking torment. Cecilia shuffled to the first record of the set, marveling at her own fortitude.

Airey shook her head. "I reckon we've played it enough."

"You don't want to achieve four score and seven?"

"I'll be winding this machine plenty after you've gone. I've got time for that. I ain't got time enough with you."

Cecilia glanced at the angle of the sun. Unwise to be late again so soon. "I'm sorry we won't set a world's record today, but perhaps on my next visit. I must go."

"You ain't hardly got here."

"I've been here for hours."

"It don't feel more than a minute." Airey closed the Grafonola. "Seems I've driven you off."

"That isn't possible."

Airey smiled curiously at her. "Spoken like a bee." She gave her middle finger a delicate exploratory lick. "Reckon I'm as sweet as honeysuckle."

"I—" Cecilia found her breath. "I rather like honeysuckle."

Down the mountain, through the cove, barely aware of the road, Cecilia floated in a place where everything was Airey, where everything was scented with the rosin still lingering on her wrist. She stopped under a peawood tree—*I can't drive in this state*—until the world filtered back to her. Late afternoon sunlight slanted across the fields. All was still, as if untouched by time. Peaceful. Fundamental. She tapped the steering wheel. Was she doing the right thing? The best thing for Airey? To send her to the hothouse of a conservatory, into the dreary life of auditions and rehearsals, the petty jealousies of orchestras, the indignities of boarding houses and drugstore lunch counters, into the humiliations of being ill-educated in a world of culture—was this the reward for her talent? Shouldn't she be kept here in this paradise?

No. Nothing stayed the same. In Airey's case, it should change as soon as possible. That conviction—the way she poured herself into her violin—had to find its true home. Cecilia's hand paused on the gearshift. Tom's voice: *Do you think you can give her the choice between a barn dance and the Avender Concert Hall?* Yes, she could. She must. Cecilia turned back onto the road. Because Airey would die here if she weren't set free. Airey knew it, too.

Mother asked Cecilia to take a box of old clothes to St. Anne's Church the next morning. The factories north of Avender were blowing their smoke westward, leaving the sky crisp as hard candy. She imagined Airey living down here. Would she like these big, clogged towns? She remembered how Airey had lifted her chin, how she had said *can't flinch*. Airey wouldn't let herself be daunted by anything.

Cecilia handed the box to the women at the church and went to Patmore's office, to be told he was in a meeting. The client came hustling out a minute later, and Pat emerged to greet her.

"I couldn't believe my ears when Miss Billings phoned in." He took his hat from the stand. "Lunch? If we stay here, people might think you've come for legal advice."

"I have."

Patmore looked appalled. "I can't act for you, Cecy. Not without speaking to your father."

"It's not my own problem."

"A *friend's*?" he said with dour humor, ushering her to his car. "Not here. Let's talk over lunch."

He led her through the Biltmore Hotel's dining room to a table as far from the door as he could manage. She saw several wives lunching with their husbands—*this would be my portion if I married someone like Pat*—as he said, "good afternoon" and "how nice to see you" to each table they passed. Cecilia caught knowing smiles in their wake. After ordering for them both, he turned to her. "Now, Cecy, this friend of yours—is it you, really? There's nothing you could tell me that would make me think less well of you."

"I know that. I truly am here on someone else's behalf. A family, in fact. We Howisons once had business dealings with them, so I feel I can meddle, as Tom would say. I have permission from Mrs. Grigg, the mother, to speak with you. The name's from her second marriage. You might know Fitch."

"Fitch? Fitch." He scoured his memory. "The only Fitch sounding a bell is a mountain family. They sold half a mountain to Sankgallon Gap Timber a long time ago."

"Yes. Those are my Fitches."

"Mountaineers!" He groaned. "What's going on? They aren't the sort of people you should be talking to."

"Really? Why not? They're a hard-working Christian family."

"I don't care if they're the sole support of their parish and an example of clean living to shame us all." The waiter served their soup. "What are you doing consorting with them?"

"It's not your place to ask me those questions."

He reddened. "I wish it were. Does your father kn—but that's none of my business, either." His lips compressed. "I'd...no. You'd better ask me what you came to ask me."

"They live in the area that's been given to the national park. They don't know what to do."

"They need to start packing."

"They want a lease, but is it possible? Mrs. Grigg isn't sure of her legal standing. I don't know if her first husband willed the farm to his son, to all his children, or if he even left a will. Can she act for her son? Is he able to speak for himself, even though he's only about thirteen? I'm sure Mrs. Grigg wants to sell the farm, and I'm certain it's the wiser course, but I believe the older children, or some of them, want to keep it. How long before the park will simply declare their land—I don't know the term—before the government simply takes it over?"

"The state can condemn it any time it wishes," said Patmore. "It hasn't wanted to be seen coercing the local people, and I think it's been admirably restrained. Leases *have* been granted, but if it wants the whole area to revert to woodland, why allow farming at all? I don't speak as an expert, as I haven't involved myself with any of the cases, apart from a preemptive sale of mining rights for one longheaded old codger. If the mother's smart as he was, she'll follow his example and then negotiate as good a price per acre as she can while she can."

"The park's valuers might take advantage of her."

"She could find her own surveyors for an independent survey or hire a lawyer to investigate comparable properties in order to argue that—" He put down his spoon. "No."

"I know you wouldn't turn away from a widow and five children who truly need help."

"Working against the park won't help *me*. I'm not interested in looking like a country lawyer with only poor farmers for clients. It would be as bad as working for the unions."

"Who'd despise you? I know Daddy was against the park. He thought it should be a national forest."

"I'm not letting everyone think I'm gone in the

head and Red besides. These are hard times. I need clients who can pay their bills." He looked at her plaintively. "It's not that I don't feel for this family. I'm not by nature an ambitious man, but I have no choice."

Cecilia fought her spurt of anger. *You have to help. I've promised.*

"Please don't think less of me," he said.

"If you want to work for influential people, you can work for me. I might not be as important as Daddy—"

"No, Cecy. Never. I'd never take money from you, for this or anything else."

Cecilia looked around the room. Who could help her? Most here would be for the park, if only through loyalty to the party. She recognized one of her father's political cronies sitting with other men in suits too sharp to be from Avender. *They* would be for the park. Everyone was for the park except the people living there. "Can you recommend someone who'd be willing to represent a family fallen on hard times?"

Patmore reddened. "Please don't do this. You shouldn't be involved. Your father will tear the hide off me for not stopping you."

"He'll know you couldn't, and you can't. You *can* speak to a fellow lawyer for me. Tell him I intend to pay. You know I've a little money now and more when my trust starts in November."

"Let me think." Patmore finished his soup. "Is the family presentable? Are they honest? Can they read and write?"

Cecilia wondered about Mrs. Grigg. "Of course they can. They're not moonshiners, and they're not savages."

"Give me the widow's address." Patmore took a notebook from his breast pocket. "I'll talk to a friend or two."

"If he needs payment in advance—"

"Cecy, you mustn't say such things! As if anyone I know would take money from a girl, especially a Howison girl."

"I don't need chivalry, I need legal advice for my friends. If I don't pay him, he might decide he's excused from doing his best."

"He couldn't." Patmore was glum. "*Pro bono publico.*"

"I also don't want him to be out of pocket. There's no need when my trust is about to start."

Patmore blinked rapidly. "I'm not looking at what's in front of me. You're willing to spend your own money on a family that has none. You're really ready to do it. I think you're noble and...and..."

"It's a mystery to me why it's noble to ask for help and be able to pay for it."

He remained moist. "You're a true woman of the South."

"What does that mean? That if I choose to do more than be refined, wise, and good while sipping lime cup in the shade, I'm an earthly saint?" She looked at his uncertain face. "I'm sorry. It drives me mad to be praised for nothing. You're the one who's kind and good because you're helping me even though you don't want to."

"You never have to ask me for a boon," he said thickly. "I'm yours to command."

Cecilia wondered what she had been doing other than asking him and being rebuffed but feared his trembling look. She saw Daddy's political friend getting to his feet and smiled warmly across the room. He came over, a little surprised.

"Miss Howison." Mr. McClure took her outstretched hand as Patmore stripped the napkin from under his chin. "A pleasure to meet you again."

"I thought I recognized you, sir," said Cecilia. "I'm so glad I did." *You're rescuing me from a proposal.*

"You're very like your mother," said Mr. McClure. "She's always delightfully gracious." He introduced his companions, whose names Cecilia instantly discarded. She exchanged courtesies with him while Pat spoke to the others, until one lifted his hat and Mr. McClure took the hint.

Patmore sat as they left. "Eric Munns."

"*The* Eric Munns?"

"Don't joke. He's one of the most inner of the party's inner circle. Eric Munns, Don Higley, Frank McClure. I'll take on your mountaineer family myself if I have to drive to Fittes Cove to do it. Eric Munns!"

Cecilia looked at his happy, assessing face and liked him a little less. "Thank you, Pat. It means a great deal to me."

Cecilia drove back to Old Waring feeling edgy and restless. This was bringing her secret life too close to home—and now it had given her the delicate task of handling Pat. Was her life to be spent doling out judicious sops of honey and hyssop to nice men?

Her life. Would it ever start? If it did, what would it be? She thought of Airey. Where would *her* life take her? If justice reigned, to a symphony orchestra somewhere: Baltimore, Boston, St. Louis.

Remembering Miss Howison with gratitude for so many things? *They did a good job finishing you.* Airey was looking at her and liking what she saw. Cecilia recalled, twenty or thirty times, Airey's tongue touching her fingertip. Who in the future could be half as beguiling as Airey Fitch?

Chapter Three

Trenton came out of his office that afternoon and caught Cecilia as she headed for the stables. "May I join you? Rosamund won't be in the saddle again until the son and heir arrives. It would be nice to have a touch of our old times."

It was a rare request these days. "Yes, I'd like that."

Half an hour later, they were ambling along the post oaks, Trenton's mastiffs sniffing, circling, racing ahead, and cut across the meadow, where the horses were fetlock-high in new growth. Cecilia looked at the dark mountains along the horizon.

"What would happen if the foundation was presented with a candidate right now? Today?"

"Not a thing. Every penny's been awarded. Why?"

"You don't hold back anything for a late surprise?"

"When have we ever been surprised? It's a small world here. Dardhardt hears its destined pupils from the first shake of their rattles."

"Then any promising latecomer...?"

"Will have to wait until next year and hope that more banks don't fail. Unless you have an investment tip for us?"

"If you don't mind speculative capitalization."

"We do. Do you have a candidate?"

"Apparently not."

Cecilia crossed the Howison Foundation off her mental list with a touch of relief. *Far* too close. After all, she still had Mr. Potz and Mrs. Vernelle.

Cecilia let a week pass before disappearing for another full day. First to Avender, parking in front of Pennicote and Drake and emerging minutes later with a sheaf of sheet music under her arm. She glanced at the courthouse clock as she spun around the square. If she ignored the safety of everything on the road, including her nerves and suspension, she could be at the far end of Fittes Cove by midday.

The sun was overhead when she stopped at the Hinterhouse general store, her dust catching up with her and billowing across its porch. Inside, the man behind the counter, *D. Keller, Prop.*, touched a finger to the brim of his hat. "Nice of you to stop by. You're the young lady taking an interest in Airey Fitch, ain't you?"

"I am. I'd like ten cents' worth each of peppermint and silver bells."

"Folks hurry along when they know she's playing." He shook the candy into striped bags. "She's always throwing in little things to liven us up. Reckon they're from that old misery Brewken, but they fit good."

"I hope to help her make the most of her talent."

"On radio?"

"Eventually, I expect." *A radio symphony orchestra?*

"She ought to be heard far and wide. Pride of

the Cove."

"Soon, Pride of the County."

"Gets my vote." He gestured to the pile of mail beside him. "Lucius, he carries the mail and drops it off here. Folks need to come fetch it, but the Fitches don't get down too often. If you'd be so kind, there's a letter for Miss Merit you could take up to her." He handed over a battered envelope. They both looked at the return address: Fort Vickerson, Ga.

"Her fiancé?" Cecilia asked.

"Don't know who else but."

She took the candy and letter to the car. It was addressed in smudged pencil: *Miss Fitsh, Fistch Farm, Hinterhus, Fits Cove, Halden Conty*. Postmarked June 15, 1931—it had taken over two weeks to arrive. She put it in her pocket. No wonder Merit suffered sick headaches.

Two Fitches were waiting for Cecilia in the yard, two cropped redheads, two hideous variations of blue tartan dress, although Polynegry's was six years closer to the current fashion.

"I heard your car all the way down the lane," said Polynegry.

Cecilia noticed how the scooped neck of Airey's dress revealed the suntanned vee left by her work shirt. She said to them both as she got out, "It feels like months since I saw you last."

"I'd better cover your car," said Airey. "Rain's coming, and I got no partiality for bailing out Lake Monument."

"You're wearing pretty shoes," Polynegry said

to Cecilia as Airey tugged the roadster's roof to its front clips. "Everything you got on is pretty. You look like an actress. I got some *Photo Screen News*, that's a magazine with pictures, so I know. *Your* picture's in lots of newspapers. I've seen you on our walls."

"We was given a stack of *Charleville News-Heralds* to paper the rooms," Airey explained, buckling the car's side covers. "Polyfitchy here went round hunting you by name or photo."

"You helped," Polynegry said to her. To Cecilia, "There's heaps more of your mam and pap. Your pap's got nice horses."

"You must have the April editions, covering the Pendle Open."

"Polynegry, come along," Mrs. Grigg called from the door. "Let Airey and Miss Howison be."

"We can sit on the porch," said Airey, as Polynegry skipped away.

Cecilia saw chairs set out on the porch. One held a pile of sheet music pinned under the violin box. She wondered if they had been brought out every day in the hope of seeing her. "Before we do, I've something for your family, and you'll find a parcel for you on the front seat." She went inside.

"You're always bringing us treats," said Mrs. Grigg. "Look, Polynegry, your favorite. You have some, Miss Howison."

"They're for you. I was also given a letter for Miss Fitch."

Merit snatched it from her hand and ran out the kitchen door, leaving a half-hemmed handkerchief and needle to float to the floor like a parachute.

"She thanks you," said Airey from the porch.

"It'll be from Card," said Mrs. Grigg with relief.

"No, Jaby, that hanky ain't for you. I'll bring you gals out some buttermilk, then you can play fiddle much as you want to, Airey, 'cause I'm going to the barn to clean out those side cribs."

"How's your side of the swap going?" Airey held a chair for Cecilia as they returned to the porch.

Cecilia sat demurely, liking this. "I've written letters, and you've seen what I brought you today."

"You don't waste no time." Airey sat and riffled the pile of scores. "I ain't been idle neither. I've looked at these every day. I saw words Mr. Brewken taught me, *allegro*, those things."

"Do you know what it means?"

"Fast."

"*Allegro ma non troppo?*"

"Fast, but rein back a bit. Ain't no need for a catechism: I know them all."

"It's hard to teach when I don't know where to start." Cecilia gave her one of her new purchases. "We listened to this on my last visit."

Airey propped the score on the chair in front of her. "Here's Beethoven's name." She picked up her violin and played slowly. "Here," she touched a marking with a finger, "that's where Mr. Brewken said the notes had to be loud as thunder, and they're marked with two curly F's below. Here's where he said to hang on to this note a little bit, and there's a dot beside it."

"I might as well go home."

"Don't." Airey did not look up from the page. "Mr. Brewken was teaching me these just before he died. Now I'm seeing it all laid out like a railroad track. It feels like a different thing. A fixed thing."

"And because it's for two people, you need to

pay attention to what Beethoven writes. The more players there are, the stricter you must be. When you're in an orchestra, you'll have your music on a little metal stand in front of you. I'll get you one." At Airey's frown, "You need the right tools."

"I didn't know I needed a little metal stand."

"You do. As you learn what else you need, you'll ask your patron to get it, and he will. It's what a patron is for."

"That'll make my pride worse than a swelled-up frog. So far, I got these records and paper music and I know I need them, but I ain't got enough of the one bringing them."

"Am I failing you?"

"You're the one who preaches happiness."

Cecilia looked at her, but Airey again lifted her bow. "I was going to play you some other music, but I'll do this one instead by reading it." She started to play and stopped. "All these marks make it harder. It's easy in my head."

"It will soon become just as easy on the page."

"I've been listening to the way those fiddles play alongside each other in orchestrys, but the music Mr. Brewken taught me was for a fiddle by itself."

"You liked the Mozart concerto, and I'm sure you'll like symphonies. You'll be playing everything with someone else: chamber music, duets—that is, one other person—trios, quartets, which means with another violin, a viola, and a violoncello."

"Sounds like a fancy string band."

Cecilia smiled. "It is."

"If I'm working for an orchestry, when will I play those other ways?"

"In your own time, with fellow musicians,

simply for pleasure, or at hotels or private parties, to earn extra money."

"I'll need that money. Any quartets in the records you brung? I'll want them till I get the hang of this paper music."

"There are, but is it right for you to learn from recordings? I don't know. You have the greats here, but you need a teacher."

"The Lord gives us what's best for each season. Like you, here and now."

"Do you think I'm God-given?"

Airey looked up. "Ain't you, Miss Howison?"

Cecilia squirmed. "Only until I find my replacement. Shall we look at the violin part of the Mozart we listened to last time?"

"I've been playing those records six, seven times every day. Mam's pretty much settled me in the tobacco shed."

"Is that your practice room?"

"It's a good place when it ain't full of leaves. Other times, I sit in the corn crib or I go over by the bean field or down to an old cabin or sometimes, when it ain't going to rain, I walk up to a cliff ledge, where I got plenty of room."

Cecilia imagined her like a wild highland troubadour, playing to the hills and sky. "That must be wonderful."

"No bear's bit me yet." Airey looked at the scores Cecilia had brought. "How's that said?"

"Duh-vhorz-shak." Cecilia opened the score. "Here's your part—"

"At the back!"

"—as reference in my piano version. I know this Dvořák sonata almost by heart: it was one of the set pieces in my sophomore year at Collines."

Airey lifted her violin and worked through the notes, linking a succession into a melody, exploring it, Cecilia nodding at each adjustment as she watched the subtle shifts of Airey's fingers on the bow, the quick choices her fingers made on the strings.

"Mr. Brewken used to play my part first and make me hear and play till I got it learned by heart, then we'd play together, him taking the other part, which I see now was shaped from the piano half. I got enough of this in my head now. It'll keep till after you're gone." Airey put her violin and bow firmly into their box and leaned down for Cecilia's buttermilk. "Seems you don't like this much."

"Have it all."

"You must get mighty fine things at home if you can pass this up."

"The finest things are here," said Cecilia, and instantly rain fell as if a bucket had tipped over. She jumped. *I'm being told to stop talking.*

"You ain't been much in the mountains or else you wouldn't be surprised by rain. You wait, it'll stop as quick as it started."

"Does it catch you off-guard?" Cecilia watched the earth darken and water pour off the edge of the porch roof in ragged sheets, shredding the climbing roses into a fleet of cockleshells.

"Plenty often." Airey finished her own buttermilk. "You'd best be a salymander if you want to live this high up."

Merit appeared at the door with Jabez. "He heard you talking." She spat tobacco juice delicately into the rain. "Miss Howison, I thank you for bringing that letter."

Airey asked, "Card say anything?"

"Says he's fixing something for me and not to lose heart 'cause I'll know as soon as he's got it to tell me."

"He wrote more than that, seeing you're putting every flowering laurel to shame."

Merit blushed. "He says what he always says. Miss Howison, your glass's empty. I'll fetch you more."

"We're bountifully full of buttermilk for now, thanks." Airey took Jabez as Merit went inside and hammocked him in the length of her skirt. "We got the best rain up here. When spring comes, flowers bust out of the ground like they was called by Gabriel's trump. We got the biggest huckleberries and the sweetest chestnuts. And," she gave Jabez a tussle, "we got the prettiest boys that ever was."

"He's less redheaded than you are," said Cecilia.

"Jaby's my half-brother. His pap was Mr. Grigg." Airey helped Jabez off her lap onto the porch, where he investigated a puddle. "He was born a month before his pap died. You're a half-orphan like us, ain't you, Jaby Grigg? He won't remember his pap, though. Mr. Grigg said *he has my ears*, but that was Mam's fingers sticking them out at the back. Jaby favors him in most else, though, don't you, round boy?"

Jabez looked at her and went back to splashing his hand in the puddle.

"They say farming's hard on women," said Airey, "but it's been harder on Fitch men. Pap went before his time, right after my brother. I was fourteen. Freed had been hit across the head some years before, and it turned one eye mostly blind. He was hurt while helping the Labhards with their thresher, and the cut turned bad, and he died of poisoned blood. Pap had been poorly already, and Freed's dying pushed him down like an empty sack. He didn't have nothing left inside."

"It must have been difficult for you."

"The Labhard boys worked alongside us the next few springs. Those years was a testing time. Merit ain't up to heavy work, but she took in sewing for money, and I left off school. Then Mam married Mr. Grigg. That didn't help a whole heap. Mr. Grigg had been digging coal in Tunis, and he came up here with coal-sick in his lungs. That's when Mam met him. She tried to do right by us, but it reversed our fortunes."

"He wasn't a farmer?"

"No closer than a green bottle is. But me and Lor made sure we got plenty to eat. This land pays back good when you work it." Airey's hands flattened on her thighs. "The park don't care what happens to us as long as lowlanders get what they want."

"A lease would—"

"I don't want a lease. I want us to keep our own."

"You don't have that choice. No one here has."

"I can't understand folks who'd rather this land be overgrown by brush and brambles so thick you can't cut through them than having farms thriving with corn and squashes and beans. Why do they want nothing when they got something?"

"They want the nothing," said Cecilia. "They want wilderness."

"Wilderness is when nobody's in it. Before any of us came. Folks from the city go on walks all over here all the time. *They're* in it."

"The concern of the campaigners," Cecilia felt she should put the case, "was that logging was destroying a rare and beautiful place."

"Then stop the loggers. It ain't our fault."

"You sold to them. You sold to Sankgallon Gap Timber Company Limited."

"I know who we sold it to. My grandsire figured Sankgallon would take off timber like he did, hauling out the biggest trees one by one with horse and chain, not by bringing in rail tracks and rod engines and skidders everywhere." Airey scowled at the far mountain ridges. "Everybody can make themselves believe that what suits their own selves best suits them they're doing it to."

"Their reasons don't matter. What matters is that you can't stay here, not as owners. Not forever."

"What are we supposed to do? Get work down in the mills? Mam took up with Mr. Grigg to keep us out of them. Now she's looking to do the same again." Airey stopped. "She sorrows over what's laid on me and Lor, but everything's hard work. Lor's got land now, his own land. That's worth working for."

"Your land, too."

"I ain't a son of the family. This wasn't never for me."

Cecilia knew the same closed door. "Women give up their homes. They know from the start they will."

"That don't make it easier." Airey stood to rescue the pile of scores from Jabez's tugging hand and took them inside.

Cecilia intercepted his muddy fingers as they reached instead for her skirt. "I wonder, Mr. Grigg, if you'll remember any of this. Will you hear Beethoven and think it a memory of the Arcadia you came from? No—down, boy."

Airey laughed behind her. "Don't you start

climbing our guest, Jaby." She swung him high. "You want to be a bird on the wing?"

The rain swept away through the trees in a ripple of air. From nowhere, silent plumes of mist drifted up, moving on unseen currents through the forest, shrouding the trees.

"Told you it don't last long," said Airey. "If we're quick, I'll show you something." She flew her brother into the house and came out with a long, much worn, handmade leather coat. "It'll be wet in the woods. I'll get you some boots."

"I don't care about damp feet."

Airey led her down a path between the house and the creek, past the springhouse, where the sound of whirring paddles and a faint clanging witnessed to Lorimer's engineering, through a gap in an old stone wall and into the woods. Airey's sleeves grew sheer with the water thrown down by her hat brim and the boughs she held from Cecilia's way. Vapor was blooming as if from the wet earth, billowing past them and vanishing. The path turned sharply at a stand of buckeyes and stopped at the creek, where a young sycamore, still living, had fallen sideways from bank to bank. They used it as a handrail to cross the nearly submerged stepping stones. The forest grew denser, the path narrower, and all Airey's care in bending back the crowding branches of hornbeam and dogwood could not stop Cecilia's hat from wilting under sudden sprays.

"Unlike this former confection," she said to Airey's concerned glance, "I'm not made of straw and feathers."

They climbed until they were high above the creek. Rocks split the water into dozens of dark brown channels, each fraying again and again into finger-high white waterfalls. Insects darted and hovered.

"We're going there." Airey gestured below.

"You lead," said Cecilia, looking at the drop. "That way, you'll break my fall."

"If I do, I hope you *are* made of feathers."

Cecilia watched Airey scramble down and said goodbye to dignity and her manicure. Airey turned and offered an arm with a touch of consciousness, steadying her from one boulder to the other. Cecilia thought she could throw her full weight on Airey and not budge her but wanted to try, wanted to stumble full length against her, to feel what that lean body would do.

They reached the foot of a massive slab of rock that jutted at an acute angle over the creek. A beach of fine silty sand had collected under it. Airey bent almost double and walked to its widest point. Cecilia followed, glad of the leather coat as her back scraped the rock above.

They were surrounded by echoes of water. Sun sparkled across the creek. Airey sat and lay on her back, her head inches from the water's edge. Cecilia lay beside her, the sand harshly cold against her calves. She took off her hat and pushed it back into shape. Airey gestured.

She looked up. Sunlight, bouncing off the creek's many channels, was reflecting on the underside of the rock in rillets of light that crossed and recrossed the others in an endless weave, bright, pure, alive. Airey lay still, listening, and in the next instant, Cecilia heard what she heard: from within the sounds of the water came musical notes, a teasing sense of melody, a song hovering to be born. Cecilia forgot the chill of the sand, caught by wonder and delight. *How beautiful. How beautiful.*

She became aware of something else. Airey was watching her. She knew what lay behind her intensity: the need for another person to share what she was feeling, to understand it. Cecilia turned her head and looked at her.

Airey's slow smile made Cecilia shudder inside. Airey went back to the dancing light, and her whole body seemed to lift into the music-spangled air. Cecilia tore her gaze from her and looked up again, breathing hard. *I like you. I want you.* She let the thought go, only listened, only watched.

The sound and the light began to fade, a faint inexorable dimming loss. *No, stay.* The music broke into tones, notes, the lines of light becoming less complex, less bright, now glimmering touches against the face of the rock, abstract, the notes now clucks, pops, aimless small noise.

"The water's dropping," said Airey. "Lorimer says an underground cave fills up when there's a big rain and then pours into the creek, driving the water high and fast enough to make that music. If the sun's out, it makes the lights."

"A show worth coming for."

"You know what I come for."

Cecilia hoped she did. "*The voice of the Lord is upon the waters.*"

"Us sinners can take in only so much of God's handiwork. Places like this make us see and hear it a bit farther."

"Beauty dissolves the ordinary world to gossamer, and through it, we glimpse the divine. This must happen to you when you play."

"Not every time. Sometimes when I'm playing Bach or *Louisburg Blues* or *Stardust* or anything, and the shape's right and I'm inside the music like mist in a cloud, sometimes I get to where my next breath could be drawn at the foot of the Throne."

"Do you play here?"

"This place don't need nothing but itself." Airey pointed with her chin. "I pick strawberries sometimes along the path. I got pails of them a short while back. They was like jewels."

"When I was a little girl, my mother took me to visit my Great Aunt Ruth. It was a long drive, and we stopped for a picnic. I wandered off into the woods. Olney, our driver, came after me and found me in a patch of wild raspberries. We ate every one of them between us before he took me back to Mother. She was frightened and angry that he hadn't found me quickly enough, but we both felt our scoldings were worth that joy." Cecilia gave Airey a thoughtful smile. "I learned that the loveliest things are usually secret things. Things other people don't want you to know or do. Things you don't tell."

"I ain't never had no secret things."

"No wish you never shared?"

"I got it now. A soul who hears what I hear, who sees what I see. Who knows why."

"What I see dazzles me." Something she could not keep from her voice made Airey sharpen her gaze, puzzled and alert. "You know you do." Cecilia shifted to the random flickers of brilliance above them. "When you're playing in an orchestra and I'm in the audience, I'll point you out and boast that I know you."

"You'll be where I end up?"

"You might be only as far away as Philadelphia."

"You wouldn't come to Philadelphy."

"Why not? Where do you think I'll be?"

"I don't know. Lots of folks travel far away when they marry, like Merit's going to."

"I might be far away but never married."

"Not never?"

"I've been saved from that fate by a trust, an allowance left to me by my Great Aunt Ruth. It's not much, but I'll be able to live a small, independent life on it."

"You want a small life?"

"I want a free life."

"Free? For what? With no husband?"

"Do *you* want to marry?"

"It's what God made all Creation for. When we're doing our work beside the one He's given us, then we got claim to that happiness of yours."

"I didn't say I intended to be unhappy."

"Being by yourself will make you happy? That wouldn't suit me. I want what my mam and pap had and what Merit'll soon have with Card. I've seen lonesome. Mr. Brewken was by himself, and it was part of what killed him."

"Have you someone in mind?" Cecilia asked lightly.

"Back in school, I had some boys I called friends, but then Pap got sick and died and I took on the plowing and hauling, and nobody came round."

"You minded it?"

"Work was that hard, I didn't notice." Airey rolled onto her side. "I can't understand you. You're like a sorrel in bloom and you must be swarmed by beaus, but you're up here with me instead of down with them."

"They can swarm all they like. If one gets within cannon range, I repel him with doubleshot and shrapnel."

"I ain't known a girl who didn't want to marry so fierce she'd use ordnance."

"Now you do."

"You what they call a man hater?"

"I can't hate what doesn't matter to me." Cecilia tucked her hands behind her head, not closing the leather coat when it fell from around her. *A girl likes to feel she's using every persuasion.* "I want better than mere marriage."

"There's better? That would be worth seeing. You'll sing a new tune when the Lord sends along the man He means for you."

"Commendably trusting. Most girls feel duty-bound to assist the Lord by making themselves into what a man seeks to marry."

"You don't believe girls come by it natural?"

"If it came naturally, why are we drilled in its fine art from our cradles?"

Airey considered this. "It rubs my fur wrong when Merit fusses at me to prink before we go to box suppers or singings. I don't like simpering ways. It ain't proper for a redeemed soul. I ain't tempted to talk like a fool nor by ribbons or fancy hats and never was."

Cecilia raised herself on one elbow. "Have you ever had one frivolously feminine urge in your life?"

"If that means getting excited over sparkly pins and wanting boys to like me 'cause I'm wearing them, I ain't never."

"That's what I mean," said Cecilia. "I admire it."

"Why?"

"Because I like women who can stand on their own two feet. I like women who can make a fist. We're raised to live for and through men. *Refined, wise, holy, and good!* I like women who choose to live for themselves."

"That's why you're set against marrying?"

"I don't have to set myself. It's the way I've always been and want to be."

"I know when a thing don't fit me. It's like wearing my clothes wrong-side in. I can drive a plow and plant and haul. I like knowing I can. I never felt wrong-side when I did any of them." Airey nodded at herself. "I stand on my own feet. I reckon I'm one of those women you like."

Do I have a pulse? "That's why I'm here. My Great Aunt Ruth said a woman who couldn't tie her own shoes or butter her own parsnips wasn't fit to have a soul, let alone a mind."

"She was a standing woman, too, by the way you talk of her."

"She was her own best example." Cecilia remembered her great aunt's shrewd, powdercreased face. "My Great Uncle Nestor spent his entire inheritance before they'd been married a year. Great Aunt Ruth found a book that explained the stock market, invested what was left of her own money, and reaped the reward of her courage and intelligence. She became the major investor in her brother's—my grandfather's—businesses and ran them jointly with him, behind the screen, of course. I inherited her stock market book, as well as my trust. Her dullard son, my Uncle Wendell, became manager of all her trusts, and they'd be doing better if he took my advice."

"You want to buy and sell in stock, like your auntie?"

"I've made it clear to Uncle Wendell that if any of my own trust survives his care, I'll be using it to make my own investments. My brother Trenton calls me Ruthless because I'm a lesser Ruth, but I try to be as clear-headed as she was. She told me that timing was as important in money as it was in music. She taught me not to fool myself with hope, but to see plainly what was before me, plan accordingly, and remember that the heavens didn't need to fall in with my wishes—in fact, when I needed the heavens the most, they probably wouldn't."

"She sounds like a woman of sense."

"Hard-headed in everything but music. She lost herself there."

"You get that from her. I ain't seen nobody listen so clean through. I reckon music gets more inside you than it does in me."

"That can't be possible."

"Maybe you feel it closer 'cause you're outside the *must-play* of it."

"Would you change places?"

Airey smiled quickly. "No."

"Nor would I. I do my best not to want anything I must suffer for." *Although I'm failing here.*

"Then you won't never have nothing worth a cent."

"The price of being a butterfly."

"You keep saying you are. You say you want a free life with nobody in it. You're expecting me to believe both. Why?"

"Because I want to be taken for what I am."

"What's that?"

There's a time for everything. "I'll tell you what I'm not. I'm not made to be a wife and *châtelaine*, a society matron, a pillar of the church. I'm not prepared to embrace the placid and safe and dull. I want to choose every moment, to fill my life to the brim. I don't want the years to slip away while I'm arranging chrysanthemums or making smart conversation at dinner parties." She stopped herself. "What would be *your* perfect life?"

"To play music. To learn it. Hear it. Talk about it." Airey seemed surprised at her ready answer, continuing seriously, "To learn new things all the time. To love somebody and being loved back. To do in my given time what God built me for." Her slow smile dawned. "Seems I ain't wanting a small life neither."

"It sounds like a life lived to the brim."

"What'd fill you to *your* brim?"

Cecilia looked across the stream. *The life you're going to live.* To be part of a world where people could be their best—a world where the best would be expected and freely given. *A world that would amaze me every day.* "Never knowing what's around the corner."

"That would be life to the brim?"

"I'd rather be daunted than to see my days stretching pitilessly ahead of me like a barren plain."

"You're a Howison, you can do as you please."

"I have a trivial freedom. Not the sort I want."

"Get it then."

"You'll have a free life because you have something that gives purpose to your days. Great Aunt Ruth's seen to it that I needn't lift a finger, and I doubt I ever will."

"Don't you let your money hold you back. I

never did, and see where it's got me."

"Yours is a shining example, but what if you live for something not in your stars? I was born to expectations. Many are worth honoring, but they're surrounded by much I'm not able to accept—that I won't accept."

"When you don't?"

"I circumspectly rebel."

"How?" At Cecilia's hesitation, "like being here with me?"

"Do you think I'm here to cock a snook at society?"

"Are you?"

"I'm fighting everything to be here."

"Fighting everything ain't living life to the brim. Look at Mr. Brewken."

"I can't. He's dead."

"That's what I mean."

Cecilia laughed. "I'm living life to the brim when I'm here with you."

To her intense pleasure, Airey blushed. "I ain't never known a girl who reckoned friendship was the best thing life could give her."

"You see it now. Come one, come all."

"Ain't you wanting—"

Cecilia anticipated her. "Children? No. Do you?"

"One day. That's up to God."

"If you were meant to have a husband and children, shouldn't you have them by now?"

"Merit's older than me, and she ain't yet neither wed nor mother."

"I gather that's not by her wish."

"No, it's Card trying to get time to come up to be married. Once they do, she'll be with him and have her own little ones. Without them, her life will be doleful, like mine would be."

"That life of music and learning, that perfect life you described, the one filled to the brim, you'd call that doleful? Wouldn't you call it full of joy?"

Airey was quiet for a long time. Cecilia listened to the birds, the rush of the water, the patter of rainwater from high leaf to low. Airey said at last, "Music's what I got to have, but I can't see no joy in a life without nobody I can talk to from my soul."

"Isn't that what we're doing right now?"

Airey turned her head as if catching more meaning than the words. "God gives us what we need when we need them. Friends one time, husband and babies later. Or maybe not, if He builds us for something that needs to be done alone. But I don't reckon God's so cruel to have me raised in love if I ain't going to get it again in my grownup life."

"Then I hope you will." *But let me be something you need first.*

"You'll change your mind one day."

"I'm not against love."

"That's another thing we don't get to choose. Since it's you, I reckon you'll get snapped up faster than a bug in a hen yard." Airey glanced down. "You bring that man of yours along to hear me in Philadelphy. He'll like music, too, 'cause you won't pick nobody who don't. Your shoes are wet through. We'd better be getting back."

"You've been lying in a damp dress."

"That don't matter compared to being here."

"You're an odd millionairess, Miss Fitch."

"I keep my treasure in the right place." Airey sat up. "I'm glad you saw and heard this. I'm glad you liked it in the same way as me."

They returned silently through the shining wet woods. Cecilia hovered on the porch, knowing she must go, knowing Airey wanted her to stay, wanting to stay. Mrs. Grigg came to the door. "I didn't hear you two come back. Merit's picked us a load of corn. It's balm to my heart to hear her singing. She don't mind nothing after she's got a letter from Card. You come inside, Miss Howison, and dry your pretty shoes. You want more of that buttermilk?"

Cecilia made her excuses, ignoring Airey's smothered giggles. Airey came with her to fold down the car's roof. Water cascaded from it, soaking her skirt against her.

"What shall I bring you next time?" Cecilia asked. "More records? More sheet music? What would you like?"

"More of yourself."

"That comes with the rest."

"Then come earlier and stay longer."

Cecilia laughed as she shut the roadster's door. "If I stayed any longer, I'd be going home by moonlight." The side mirror gave her a glance at those long thighs in nearly transparent cotton. *Or never going home at all.*

Cecilia slipped into the winter sitting room that evening, wanting to think through the day. Could it be that defeat was not absolutely certain? She thought of Airey lying beside her at the creek in that ridiculous dress. How easy it would have been to have leaned over and—

"But it wasn't the time," she told a steel engraving of the original Waring. "The Buick and I have more trips to make. Patience in a monument."

Thoughts of Airey brought a need, an obligation, to consider what she had never considered before. Before, she had always chosen among girls who had made it clear they wanted what she wanted or were willing to learn a new pleasure. Airey was different. It would matter more to her and in more ways. Cecilia reminded herself that she would be opening for her a new and golden world, a world of warm, brave women friends and special happiness. What could be better than a life where you stood on your own feet?

Scenes of Airey at small, discreet after-concert parties or in out-of-the-way clubs, of Airey sharing summer cabins or driving vacations with a few pals, should have been more satisfying than they were. Cecilia shifted uncomfortably in the overstuffed chair. Would this be enough for Airey? *It would be enough for me.* It was a better life than either of them was living now.

Would they stay friends? In some way? It would be lovely to take her out to dinner in Philadelphia or Baltimore or Boston. Cecilia tried to imagine why she herself would be in Baltimore or Boston. *Traveling, perhaps, with my own pals?* Or traveling by herself? *I don't know what it's like.* She had never lived away from her family. Had never been alone.

As if to prove it, Mother looked round the door. "That's where you've tucked yourself! It's quite late, darling."

Cecilia took herself to bed, feeling twelve years old.

Pat came on Friday evening, as agreed, to take Cecilia to Charleville. "Do you know what Tom's arranged?" he asked as he parked in front of her sister's house.

"He and I usually work out the programs together, but he's not been home. It's rather nice having a surprise."

Her sister Phyllis gave her a hug, her brother-in-law Oliver a kiss on the cheek. He shook Pat's hand. "Patmore. Eric Munns mentioned meeting you in Avender."

Cecilia saw Pat expand and made no objection when Oliver steered him away. She ran into Phyllis again in the ballroom. "Phylly, have you bought all the chairs in the state?"

"Borrowed from the Trimble Hotel, and every single one's reserved. Ah," Phyllis looked across the room, "Herbert Boice."

"Heavens, Boice Soda here? What hath Tom wrought? Has Mr. Potz arrived? I'm hoping to speak with him."

"He hasn't come, but most of the Dardhardt Conservatory have, and I'd say nearly all the First Families."

Tom appeared at their side. "Cecy, you look enchanting. Don't you agree, Phyllis?"

"In a Vionnet gown? Who wouldn't?" she said, turning to leave—Phyllis was always turning to leave when Tom approached—and he smiled mockingly at her retreating back.

"Would that I believed the loan of her ballroom spoke of the enfolding embrace of a sister's love, but my mind isn't capable of such feats."

"There's a good crowd tonight."

"Mine own tiny coup. No mere board member could have secured a guest of Dr. Neihoff's luster. 'Twas a Howison and a Howison alone. *Invictus!*"

"Dr. Neihoff?" Cecilia felt dislodged. "But he's—"

"Did I not mention? When I heard he'd be visiting the Vernelles for a few days, I reduced him, by means of an artillery barrage of charming telegrams, into giving this concert, although Mrs. Vernelle closed the deal by agreeing to accompany." He lifted a hand. "I would have told you before, dear, but I feared you might, in an act of selfless and beautiful charity, bring your little mountain girl down to hear him."

"Tom!"

His smile was unapologetic. "Unfeeling of me? Quite the opposite. I put it to you that Phyllis's—that the entire room's—reaction to your undiscovered genius would have been everything you'd want to avoid. It certainly would have been what *I* want to avoid. And let us not dwell on brother-in-law Oliver's views! He already dislikes me for the company I keep, and I stay diplomatically south of the tracks. Oh—hello, Pat. It's manful of you to grapple with the Howison obsession at close quarters."

"You don't think I'll enjoy it?"

Tom clapped him on the shoulder. "That's the stuff that wins fair hand. I must go. Daddy wants to intrude upon the program. Vexing!"

Cecilia barely heard Pat's, "Cecy, you look in need

of a glass of punch," through her crackling anger. Dr. Neihoff! Such a violinist—here!—and Tom had said nothing. Nothing at all! How—how autocratic—how bigbrotherish! How *rotten. Although*, she admitted as she cooled, *he's not entirely wrong*. She would never bring Airey to a setting where Boice Soda, to name one, would make her unwelcome. But there had been other days and other hours to meet Dr. Neihoff, and Tom had said nothing.

All was not lost. She saw a violin resting on Phyllis's grand piano. Dr. Neihoff must already be in the room. She edged through the crowd toward it.

"Punch, Miss Cecy? A glass of lime cup?"

Cecilia looked at the maid offering the tray. "Kitty! I didn't expect to see you here. Aren't you working at the hospital?"

"Drusella's sick, so they phoned to ask if I'd help the family this evening."

"How lucky you could, with this crush. You look well."

"Thank you, Miss Cecy. It's nice to be remembered."

"We miss you at Old Waring. Are you coming to the fireworks party tomorrow night? Have you spoken to Tom?"

"I haven't been to the fireworks in years." Kitty moved away. "Perhaps I will."

Cecilia's progress to the violin was hindered by friend after friend. She caught Tom staring past her with pale constraint and wondered how big an intrusion Daddy had demanded.

"My dear Cecy." Mrs. Vernelle, by the piano, freed her from the crowd. "You look lovely—but you always do. I haven't had time to answer your letter, though I'm happy to say that now there's no need." She turned to the couple beside her. "Helen, Barukh, I'd like to introduce one of my former, and favorite, pupils: Cecilia Howison, Tom's sister. Cecilia, Dr. and Mrs. Neihoff."

Cecilia shook their hands triumphantly. Mrs. Neihoff was a plump older woman with black hair, black eyes, and the most stylish hat and dress Cecilia had seen on someone not the governor's wife. Dr. Neihoff was as round, as dark, his hair and beard salted with white. He said, "I am happy to greet another of this most musical family."

"It's an honor, sir. I hoped I might have a moment to—"

"Dr. Neihoff, Mrs. Vernelle, a word, if you will." Tom came to sweep them both away.

"Such an enthusiastic and well-informed young man," said Mrs. Neihoff, as Cecilia foamed with frustration. "My husband's been overwhelmed by his courtesies."

"We ourselves see Tom Howison in so many different settings," said Mr. Vernelle dryly, glancing at Cecilia and adding, "Dardhardt is, of course, tremendously grateful to the family during these straitened times."

"Mrs. Neihoff," said Cecilia, "I wanted to speak to your husb—" A gong summoned the audience to their seats. Pat came to take her to the chairs he had reserved. Cecilia sat with Spartan control.

Tom, stony-faced, returned to move Dr. Neihoff's music stand aside and let his father take the floor.

"Friends." Her father held up hands to subdue a murmur already dying. "I'm not one of tonight's performers, never fear! I did, however, think this an auspicious occasion, given we celebrate the Fourth tomorrow, on which to make my first formal announcement that I've agreed to accept my party's invitation to run for the Senate."

The guests clapped, and some cheered. He said a few words on his humble desire to serve, of his firm intention to do his duty to his state and his neighbors, and added that he hoped one or two here today would vote for him, provoking laughter across the room. Oliver, as the most senior party man present, gave the expected praise, after which her father suggested that their eminent musical guests should be kept waiting no longer, and the music stand was replaced.

Tom made the introductions: Mrs. Vernelle, a musician much respected, indeed, loved, and Dr. Neihoff, well known to all who esteemed great artistry, currently traveling in the United States before assuming a teaching position at the illustrious Kehr Institute of Music in Montreal. The recital would be in two parts, with an intermission for refreshments.

Cecilia was still pupil enough to listen closely to Mrs. Vernelle while Neihoff's violin transformed the night into soft onyx and opal. She barely noticed the shifting in the audience, the suppressed coughs, knowing that she was wrong: Airey should be here, should be hearing this.

At the end of the first half, she rose, concentrated on Dr. Neihoff.

"Cecy," Pat was saying, "would you mind? I was asked to join a few of your father's friends in the study...?"

"You don't need my blessing." She followed the Neihoffs out to the cool evening lawn, lost them, saw Mother surrounded by the female half of Charleville's leading citizens and backed away, only to be caught by Rosamund and Trenton.

"Cecy, Trent wants to join the men, but he won't leave unless Junior and I have a chaperone."

"I was hoping to—" Cecilia sighed. "Of course."

"Always a trouper." Trenton patted her arm and left.

Rosamund said, "It's good to remind people who'll be running the family businesses when Papa Howison's in Washington. I'm fine here alone or would be if Phyllis thought to provide some cushions."

Cecilia fetched three. "I'll be back as soon as I can." She sped from cluster to cluster until she found the one containing Dr. Neihoff. The guests, recognizing her, made an opening as she approached. *Howison invictus.*

Dr. Neihoff half-bowed. "Miss Howison, this time we may speak without interruption."

"I particularly wanted to, sir—"

"I am flattered."

"—because I'd like to tell you about a musician, a violinist, whose talent I hope to have judged by an expert."

He inclined his head guardedly.

"She lives in the mountains and plays with exceptional skill. She hopes for a life in music, an orchestral place—"

"Many hope."

Mrs. Neihoff was listening with interest. "You said in the mountains?"

"My wife is scholar of folk music, about which I confess to know nothing. I cannot help you."

"Of course not, sir. I'm speaking of a mountain musician who plays Beethoven and Bach." As his eyebrows rose in disbelief, "To hear her is to be convinced of her promise. No student of Mrs. Vernelle could be mistaken—I can't believe I'm mistaken. If you were able to find some time for her, I'd bring her down to you. She's eager for the opinion of another violinist. If she isn't good enough for an orchestra, she'll try other music because she *must* play, but if she *is* good enough, she should know."

Dr. Neihoff listened with his hands folded on his ample front. "The plea of a beautiful young lady cannot fall on uncaring ears. My own story is known: I myself began as poor boy without help, and I stand here today because of a teacher's kindness. I would say yes to meeting your friend for this reason alone, but regrettably, it's not possible. Tomorrow, my wife and I depart to resume our travels."

"You've no time at all?" Cecilia's heart fell to the ground.

"Our train leaves at an early morning hour. I am sorry. Have you not spoken with one of many teachers I meet here?"

"I will, sir, if it can't be you."

His wife said something to him in another language, German or Yiddish. To Cecilia, she said, "We must leave tomorrow without fail, but we pass through Charleville again on our way north. It might be possible to stop for a few hours."

"If you were able to—oh, for even just an hour—I'd be extremely grateful."

"Nothing I will promise, nothing," said Dr. Neihoff. "Commitments cannot be altered."

"If we find we can," said Mrs. Neihoff, "how should we reach you? Through your brother?"

No. What else might Tom guard her from?

"Perhaps you wouldn't mind telegraphing me directly? Old Waring, Avender. I entirely understand that your plans aren't likely to change, but I hope you won't forget me."

Dr. Neihoff smiled. "Forget such an eager petitioner?"

It had been worth trying. She stepped away. There was still the elusive Mr. Potz, and why not Mr. Feldstedt?

The guests were drifting toward the ballroom. She stopped at the doors, where Tom watched the maids picking up empty glasses. He was as stiff as paper, his hand clenched on his cane.

"Tom, are you ill?"

He connected to her in a series of movements: shoulders, head, eyes. "Sprightly as a flea. I saw you and Dr. Neihoff in lively chatter. May I surmise the subject of your *tête-à-tête*?"

"My uninvited guest."

"That still rankles. And...?"

"They're leaving tomorrow morning."

"Then I obstructed nothing." Tom raised his brows at her expression. "You truly thought your mountain rustic was worth his time?"

"I know she is."

"Faith hasn't moved a mountain yet. But let me make amends. If, through the blessing of a heaven I know not, you ever have your opinion confirmed, I promise to join your cause." At her look, "Oath of a Howison, Cecy. Obtain the imprimatur of an expert, and you will not find me backward."

"Said confidently, knowing you'll never be called upon for a penny."

"Naturally, but should the muse so decree, I'll

rejoice at the opportunity to raise myself a little closer to your level."

A fatherly cough brought them back to the ballroom. Tom surveyed the lawn again. Not even the maids were left. "Let music restore our harmony."

Cecilia slipped to her chair. Pat's time with the party men had given him a varnish of alcohol and a persistent urge to hold her hand, until Trenton leaned forward and caught his eye.

The room became quiet. Dr. Neihoff nodded to Mrs. Vernelle. They spoke again to each other in music as only old friends can, reflectively, deeply. A lively final piece lifted the mood, and the applause was hearty. The politically minded slid off to another room; the musically inclined crowded around the piano. Cecilia wanted to crowd, too, but Pat was holding out her wrap. She saved herself from being steered into the chairs. "Honestly, are you fit to drive?"

"Cecy, I'm hurt." He grinned. "All right, I'm a trifle smoked, but I won't put us into a ditch."

At the Nicolls, she avoided his claim to every dance by accepting a dozen other astonished and gratified invitations. As they left, he said, "You were the most entrancing girl there."

"When Bab Shuttleworth was holding court?"

"Bab was in the room?"

Cecilia prepared herself for a long ride home, but Pat said no more. The night was dense and warm outside the city. She was lulled by the motor's hum, the flash of insects in the headlights, into a dream of dancing with Airey.

Pat veered around a small animal, his Packard shearing a long curve until he straightened on the road. "Raccoon."

"Who's now fervently against the repeal of the Volstead Act."

"Your brother-in-law pours with a liberal hand. Frank McClure's going to call me next week about some work."

"Into the thick of politics you go."

"I want Frank as a client first. If your father wins—and of course he'll win—*you'll* be in the thickest part of Washington."

"I'd rather stay here."

"Your father won't leave you behind. He knows the prettiest girl in the state will be an asset in the Capitol."

"Pat, I'm shocked at you. What are you calling my daddy?"

"A shrewd man." Patmore laughed. Seriously, "I don't see how I'll support life if you go away." As if veering around this, too, "I've written the park's land surveyors about the Fitch farm. I'm meeting with one of them before I contact the widow."

"Thank you, Pat. I knew I could rely on you."

"I want to say something else." He pulled off the road and turned on the dome light. "I know you don't want praise, but I think you're an angel. Most girls spend their time on their looks and clothes—they'd never bother even thinking about a needy mountain family, let alone concerning themselves with them. I know you're doing much more than helping the Fitches with the park. No, you don't have to deny it, I'm not asking you to tell me. I think you're the most wonderful girl I've ever known." Before she could deflect him, he took her hand. "You know I love you, Cecy. I've been of that mind since we were fifteen. Won't you take my heart? Won't you marry me?"

"Oh, Pat!" She was furious and dismayed. "You haven't talked to Daddy, have you?"

"I will when I take you home. I mean it. I'm really asking you flat out." His hand was tight and hot over hers. She could see the veins in his temples. "Do you love me at all? I think I'd know if you did. Could you see yourself loving me?"

She looked at him in despair. It was too late to be kind. "Pat...I'm-I'm so fond of you. We've grown up together. You've always been in my life. It's why-why I can't feel about you in any way except as a—"

He groaned. "Don't say *brother*. Don't say *friend*. I can't endure being one of those. I love you the way a man loves a woman: heart and soul and body."

"I—girls are raised to-to think they should marry the man who loves them. To think of that love as their crown. Your love *will* be a crown for the right woman, and she should crown you with her love in return. I can't marry for fondness and esteem. Would you really want that?"

"I'd bless God if he gave you to my life."

"Would you want a marriage—could you marry—where love was one-sided? I can't see it being a blessing for either of us."

"You might come to love me."

"I'm sorry—oh, I'm so sorry, Pat—I know I never will. That's why I can't marry you. I can't do it."

He looked at her with such shining pain that she quailed. He finally took a gulping breath, wheezed, gulped again, released her hand with a faint "Pardon!" and dug for his handkerchief, mopping his eyes as if he could wipe away reality. He looked at it again. "Let's take you home."

"We can't leave it like this!"

"I guess we can."

The rest of the drive was silent. Pat looked as he would in old age. Cecilia wanted to shrink, to vanish, to turn time back through itself. At Old Waring, he helped her from the car and kept her hand for a second, not looking at her, before getting behind the wheel and driving away.

Chapter Four

The lights were on. Mother must have seen Pat's car disappear, for she was in the hall to intercept Cecilia.

"Pat's not coming in? I was hoping to—Cecy, what's happened?"

"Oh, Mama!"

Mother whisked her into the boot room. "Cecy."

"Pat asked me to marry him. I said no."

"Good God." Mother leaned against the sink. "What a foolish boy."

Cecilia smiled wanly. "Do you think he should have chosen a better time? It popped out of him before I could stop him."

"Did you say anything to—"

"I've done everything possible to make it clear that he had no reason to hope. I've tried hard to discourage any idea that I—Mama, he looked so awful."

"A man doesn't court a girl for the fun of it. You don't feel that you could love him? Is there someone else?"

"No."

"It's not about romance, my darling. Everyday love, real love, is built on other things. A life with a good man who respects you is beyond price."

"You love Daddy."

"I certainly do. We married for love, but we also

married to suit ourselves. We each knew the life we wanted to live and saw the other as the best partner for it. Pat loves you, and no one could think you were making a poor choice in marrying him. You're from the same background, and you share so many things."

"I don't-don't think Pat and I share enough. I like him, you know how much I do, but he's not the one I want to be with all my life. To grow old with."

"Old?" Mother's amusement was mixed. "Time enough for that. Cecy, you're twenty, almost twenty-one. Most of your friends are married. Many are mothers now. I know your father loves his baby girl and doesn't want her rushing into matrimony, but you have to start being in earnest about life."

"I like it as it is."

"I'm worried about you. I blame Aunt Ruth's bequest. You don't have to think about your future, and it's struck me that you don't want to. Darling, you can't stay in girlhood forever. Woman was made for marriage. It gives you a purpose. I don't like the thought of a spinster daughter—there's no pleasure in being alone. Do you want to wither away as an aunt, the one everybody forgets until she's of some use to them, the one visited out of duty, growing more peculiar as the years go by?"

"Of course not."

"I'd like you to think things over. If you feel you can't marry Patmore, there's no more to be said. I'm sorry for him. I'll call his mother tomorrow." Mother put her arm around her. "I know you're sad and troubled by this. I'm glad you are. It's a serious thing you've done."

"Mama, I know. I know!"

Mother held her, and Cecilia began to cry

because Mother expected her to cry, weeping tears of guilt and rage. Mother ran water on a towel and cooled her face. "You'll want to go to your room for a few minutes—"

"I want to go there for the rest of my life."

Mother kissed her. "This is your daddy's big day. Settle yourself, then come say good night to our guests. We won't tell anyone, not even Daddy, until tomorrow morning."

Cecilia navigated her moment in the sitting room with a control long perfected, but in her room, she brushed her hair with angry strokes. Why had Pat been such an idiot? If she hadn't been distracted by her thoughts, she could have—but she couldn't have steered him off forever. Not when he was determined to hear what she had never said.

Never said? asked a voice. *You said nothing—because he was part of the mask you showed the world.* It had fooled him, too. She protested: *He wanted to be fooled.* That made it no better. That made it worse. And now she would face kindness and pity for everything but her real loss of a friend.

It began in the morning. Daddy pulled a curl. "I'm sad to see my honey drooping. Patmore's—but your mother said you were feeling badly enough. I won't add to it. I'm sorry about the news."

Cecilia telephoned the Blassetts to excuse herself from their Fourth of July picnic, knowing they knew why, or would by lunchtime, and hid herself in the pantry for the rest of the day, helping Auntie Nelma wrap sticks of candy with red, white, and blue ribbons for the servants' party. She joined Grandfather on the south balcony at sunset. The farmworkers' decorated cars and wagons were congregating by the river, and fireworks were being set up. Where was Pat this evening? Her mind shied, fleeing to happier thoughts. How was Airey celebrating the Fourth? Singing at a Fittes Cove church? Playing for a dance? Making her family jig and reel outside the kitchen door? Fitch farm thoughts brought her to the lease, which brought her back to Pat. She knew women of her sort who married their kind men, out of gratitude or wearied by passion or fear. But how could they, when there were women like Airey in the world? She remembered Christabelle displaying her ring, her shrugged shoulder. *I'll never want safety that badly*—Cecilia flinched. No? She had wanted it badly enough to hide behind Pat. And now, with no one to hide behind, her faint panic shamed her.

"Your mother told me about young Patmore," Grandfather was saying. "I'm glad you had the sense to refuse a Reaveley. They're all very well here in the county, but Washington will give you better material to choose from."

"What do you recommend: captain of industry or Mayflower blue blood?"

He laughed. "They'll be lining up, lambie, every one. Pick the one that suits you best."

I'm trying to.

Pat's misery crowded Cecilia during the morning service. Would the party men drop him now? Had she ruined his political career? More reproach to her, given how much he wanted it. Would he still act for the Fitches, or did he now feel himself absolved from his promise? No, he was foursquare. Honorable. And Daddy was still going to be senator.

John George met her stiffly when she returned from church, opening the car door without a smile. She found Rosamund in the pantry refreshing a bowl of armeria.

"What's happened? John George wasn't his cheerful self."

"If you don't take care, you'll miss all the excitement." Rosamund inspected a wilting individual and decided it deserved another day. "Tom came home just after the fireworks party last night. He was as tight as a drum and decided that Kitty—you know, John George's sister—"

"Yes, I spoke with her at Phyllis's."

"—decided that she might welcome his, let's say, his romantic advances. John George heard them together in the store shed and rescued her."

"Oh, no. No."

"Oh, no, indeed. Your parents were still entertaining, so John George called Trenton."

"Did Trent break anything?"

"Not Tom's spirit, I'm sorry to say. He dragged him into the stone trough. When Tom was fished out, all he said for himself was many thanks for the cold bath, it had refreshed him for further jinks high and low, and he drove away just as he was."

"It's not like Trenton to take advantage of Tom."

"I suspect it's very like Tom to take advantage of a decent colored girl—and this time, one of our own people." The words hung in the air. Rosamund thumbed the round heads of the armeria. "I must say, I'd prefer it if Tom wasn't living here by the time Junior arrives."

Cecilia walked away, feeling the news settle on her like a heavy cape as she went upstairs to the old nursery, sitting inside it as she looked at Tom's rock specimens. She carried its weight that day and the next and the next and the next, as she rocked on the porch swing, as she half-played the piano, as she waited for him.

He appeared at the door of the summer room one morning as she was trying without interest to conquer a new piece of music. She looked up at him.

"You as well, Cecy? Thinking what everyone is thinking?"

"What should I think?"

"Having known me all your life, that I'm my mother's son and a gentleman? I hoped it of you, at least."

"Being a gentleman hasn't stopped sons before."

"I didn't *do* anything."

"John George found—"

"Found me with his sister, I admit, but found me soused as a herring, having fumblingly attempted a kiss and having been slapped for my effrontery. Down I fell, such was my state, and stayed down, and at that very moment, John George burst upon the sorry tableau."

"Which part do you expect me to excuse?"

"I'm not seeking to be excused. I would never have intended the little I actually did were I not filled with the clear blue light of gin. I'm less than proud of myself, but I'd never, not with-with one of the family's—you must know I'd never—"

"*She* couldn't know. How could she know,

when—oh, Tom, how could it be in you?"

"My bright, particular star, all men have feet of clay, but I promise you I would never have perpetrated—would have done nothing—that is to say, I was offering what I considered, could be construed as, a salute."

"A salute? Save all women from such an honor."

He flushed. "That I must blame drink is my humiliation. It makes beasts of men, and I was beastly. I truly never intended her harm. Truly none. Would have done none. Oath of a Howison."

Cecilia studied his face. He was Tom, brittle, nagged by pain, by his place in the world, his wickedness being weak when he should be strong. She slowly realized she believed him. The leaden cape lifted like a curtain, and her sudden lightness startled her. "You need to write her a letter."

"A letter? Overzealous, don't you think?"

"Zealous? This is Kitty, who nursed you through that awful year."

"We were children. It was a long time ago."

"You owe her an apology."

"Being bothered by foolish men is the colored girl's burden."

"Being bothered by *you* should never have been."

"Cecy, you don't understand. I'm happy you don't."

"Will you write her a letter?"

"In other circumstances, I'd say yes, simply to be worthy of you, but a far, far more final sentence has already been passed. Daddy summoned me before breakfast this morning for a bracing chat, despite my less than perky state, and explained that, given his party's platform of virtue and restraint, he preferred not to have to suppress rumors of unsavory behavior by his curly-headed lad, especially in the Negro press. I was given the choice between a tastefully run sanatorium or relocation to some distant corner of our fair land."

"I can't believe—"

"Now, now, Cecy, you mustn't rob me of my moment of glory. I've attained that noble distinction of black sheep of the family, a calling few are fit for and fewer still can follow."

"Be serious."

"I am serious. I'm not kicking against an Old Testament parent. I know I'm going to the devil, but I don't have to make Mama unhappy on my way down."

"She'll be unhappy one way or the other."

"But she won't be responsible. I'm better off over the horizon."

"Dardhardt, the board—"

"They'll manage without me. The Howison name will open other doors. I'm happy to go. My copybook here is blotted beyond repair. And financially I'm doing well out of the deal. Tom Howison, Remittance Man! Pride, what can humble you now? We both know Daddy's decision is right."

Cecilia was about to protest, thought of Kitty's fear in the dark shed, and was silent.

Tom tapped his cane against the welt of his shoe. "As an apology, I think you'll agree that exile shall serve far better than a letter."

No, it won't, but she knew no argument would convince him. "When do you leave?"

"Daddy wants me to fade slowly rather than appear rushed out on a rail. He also needs to settle the financial details with Uncle Wendell. Dividends, capital, quite above my head."

Her fingers struck minor chords across the keyboard. "Old Waring will be strange without you."

"Come visit me in California, if Mama will let you and if I haven't yet sunk into such complete depravity that a loving sister would turn her shamed and saddened eyes away."

She caught a note in his voice that made her frown. "Would you sink?"

"If my faith were not in *your* beacon, what could keep me up on a true course?"

"Your own honor?"

"Men's honor comes from the light women shine down upon them."

"Quite a responsibility." She slid a few inches along the bench. "Why don't you shine a light on this fiendish piece in return?"

"What is it?" He sat beside her and gave a strained laugh. "*Reminiscences of Don Juan*? No wonder it's beyond you."

She looked sideways at him and began to play.

He would not stay for the evening, though she wanted his company, fidgeting until he was gone. She went outside to watch the sunset fade from the mountains. In the darkness, she lifted her arms and shook off the world of men. It was not hers. She felt a moonlit path through the night, and it led to Airey.

As soon as Cecilia was on the early morning road, with her cargo of books, sheet music, and records from her own shelves rattling cheerfully beside her, her spirits rose with every lift in elevation. Today she needed, she must have, as much of Airey as it was possible for her to get. Let all the Fitches but one be off picking bugs at a neighbor's.

Through Hinterhouse, waving at Mr. Keller standing at his door, up the drovers' road, down the lane, swinging into the Fitches' yard, only to swerve and brake behind a Model A Ford sedan. The man and woman standing beside it turned in astonishment.

The woman stepped over, "Good morning," and looked at Cecilia with inquiring semi-recognition. "We never imagined we might be disturbing a social occasion."

"I'm unannounced." Cecilia slammed the car door.

The man raised his Homburg hat as he considered the roadster's cream leather. "You're known to the Fitches?"

"They're friends of mine."

"Remarkable!" His gaze moved from Cecilia's shantung dress to her Leghorn-straw hat. "Such tact is becoming, but if you will allow me, I surmise that one or more of the family holds a position of farm laborer or servant?"

Cecilia controlled a gasp. "My connection is through music."

"Ah," the woman nodded, "music, thanks to our encouragement and guidance, remains one of those traditional folkways preserved here in the living museum of the past."

Who would talk like this? "You must be from the Siffville Settlement?"

"Indeed we are," said the woman. "I'm Mrs. Welland, a teacher at our school. This is the Reverend Ousby, shepherd of our flock."

Cecilia shook their proffered hands. "The younger, more musical Miss Fitch would have been a welcome addition."

"One cannot deny her talent, but we found her—although we don't want to disparage a connection of yours—sadly obstinate. For her own scholastic benefit, we finally had to forbid her instrument."

"Did she accept the ruling?"

"It grieves us when children can't learn to subdue their willfulness. Her brother was the same."

The Reverend Ousby sighed. "He was a very backward boy."

Cecilia stared. Lorimer, backward? But he must mean Airey's older brother. "He died some years ago."

"Yes, we were sorry to hear that," said the Reverend Ousby. "Despite our efforts, the only things in his head were hunting and fishing. A rough boy, and not a rough diamond, I fear."

"Then he must have been strikingly different from the rest of the family."

"It would not become me to judge."

Cecilia saw Mrs. Grigg at a window and gladly excused herself.

"I ducked down low when they turned up," Mrs. Grigg whispered from within the door. "Then Polynegry heard your car down the lane, and we reckoned we could show our faces."

"They say they're expected."

"I never—"

The Reverend Ousby's heavy tread shook the porch. "Good morning, Mrs. Fitch. I'm sure you remember me."

"Yes, sir. I'm Mrs. Grigg now. None of my chicks have gone to your school for quite a spell."

"No, and it's to be regretted. If you don't educate children, they stumble through life ignorant of God's light."

"Amen," said Mrs. Grigg respectfully.

Cecilia looked down at Polynegry's worried face. "Isn't Airey here? I think you should ask her to come home."

Polynegry slid through the adults and ran down the yard. Cecilia stepped inside. Her eyes adjusted, and she saw Merit standing by the table, her embroidery clutched against her as the Reverend Ousby said, "How glad I am to see you still employing the skills of your foremothers!"

Mrs. Grigg answered, "A drummer from Ohio came round offering piecework a few years back. Me and Merit do it pretty steady. He pays twenty-five cents for hankies."

The Reverend Ousby seated himself. "And where is your other daughter in these labors?"

"Airey never took to sewing. Nor cooking. She's worse at cooking than sewing. She works alongside her brother."

"That's distressing news, for her sake. Now, Mrs. Fitch, you must be wondering why we've come and without Cardwell."

"I'm Mrs. Grigg these days. I did wonder. You'd all like some coffee and pie?"

He gestured for Mrs. Welland to join him. Cecilia, at Mrs. Grigg's beseeching glance, took a chair, an imploring glance of her own at fate. How soon would these people be gone? How soon would Airey be here instead?

"This coffee is purely coffee," said Mrs. Grigg, bringing cups to the table. "My gal played down in

Heresy for the Fourth, and we bought sugar and coffee on what she earned."

"I'm sorry she's persisted with that undesirable instrument," said Mrs. Welland.

"We like real coffee," said Mrs. Grigg.

Merit, still standing, spat her tobacco wad politely into the lard tin and asked, "Sir, you spoke of Cardwell? He wrote me he'd be coming up with you all when you came back from your church meeting. Come up for us to be married."

"And married you shall be, except now you're going down to him in Georgia. Mrs. Welland's been called to her sister's sick bed and saw that, by serving as chaperone, she could travel with me."

"Card said yes to that?"

"He assured me he was happy to accommodate my having extra time with a few select brethren after our convocation."

"He wrote to you, but he didn't to me?"

"I'm sure a letter's coming," said Mrs. Welland. "We sent him a postcard this morning to say you were on your way."

"On my way? Right now?" Merit looked around wildly. "This here minute?"

"Just as our souls must be ready every hour of our earthly lives," said Mrs. Welland.

The Reverend Ousby nodded. "The day cometh like a thief in the night, in the twinkling of an eye. And we're confident that Cardwell will have something arranged by the time we arrive at Fort Vickerson."

"But him and me was going to be married *here*—in Fittes Cove—with Mam and us all and his cousin that works at the mill and our friends!"

"If you stop to think for a moment," said Mrs.

Welland with a teacher's smile, "you'll see this way is far better. We're saving you a great deal of trouble and money. Naturally, the Reverend Ousby won't charge for the wedding service, and we plan to ask the convocation's photographer to attend at our own expense. Imagine that, Merit! You'll have a lovely photograph to send home."

Merit made a small noise.

"We seek no reward," said the Reverend Ousby, "only the pleasure of sharing the news of your happy event in our church circular."

"And perhaps with local newspapers in both states?" Cecilia asked.

"So we hope, so we hope. By letting the world see the Settlement's selfless service, these two young people can give back to the school, which has given them so much."

"Mam, what'll I do? You know I want to be with Card bad as fire, but I can't just pick up and leave!"

"You can," said Mrs. Grigg. "Card will be expecting you, once he gets their note. What's he going to think when you don't show? And if you don't go now, honey, when you're given the chance of a free ride all the way to him, when will you?"

"Oh, Mam!"

"We thought," said Mrs. Welland, "we expected, that you'd be delighted."

"It's just—"

The kitchen door darkened. "Sorry I'm late." Airey had not stopped to change out of her work clothes. She saw Cecilia, and her eyes warmed. Cecilia did more than warm. Airey glanced wider and stiffened. "How d'y do, Reverend Ousby, Mrs. Welland?"

"You've grown taller," said Mrs. Welland.

"What have you done to your hair, child?" asked the Reverend Ousby in horror. "I saw your little sister and thought *lice*, but surely not you, too? After all of Nurse Dunne's lessons on bodily cleanliness!"

Polynegry, slipping in, froze where she stood.

"Those two and my boy Lorimer was real sick with fever in early spring," said Mrs. Grigg. "I feared I'd lose them, they was that bad. I prayed like never before and opened the Book for strength. My eye lit on *the leper in whom the plague is, his clothes shall be rent, and his head bare*, so I stripped them and cut their hair close as could be, and they started getting better from that minute. Merit was spared, praise the Lord."

"Luckily for the newspaper photographs," Cecilia murmured.

Airey caught this and frowned. Mrs. Welland explained their purpose. Airey said to Merit, "If you want Card to come here and get wed proper, you say so. They can't boss you no more."

"Young lady," said Mrs. Welland, "that is both unbecoming and ungrateful. I'm forced to remind you that you were educated by us, housed by us, fed by us, and taught useful skills."

"You're in our home," said Airey, "so I ain't recalling to your faces what you taught us."

Cecilia saw Merit looking at the open front door as if she could already see herself walking through it. Airey had seen, too. "Do what *you* want, Merit."

"It ain't what I dreamed for, but I miss Card every day like I was split by a froe from head to heel, it hurts that much. If I could fly to him, I would." Merit said to her mother. "I reckon-I reckon I'll marry Card any way I can."

"It means going with them," said Airey.

"I'd go with Old Scratc—" Merit stopped. "It's real kind of Mrs. Welland and the Reverend to put themselves out for me, and it's my chance."

Airey turned to the Reverend Ousby. "How much time has she got?"

"We could stay for lunch," he said, eyeing Mrs. Grigg's interrupted preparations on the sideboard.

Cecilia groaned to herself.

"I ain't got much to pack," said Merit. "Oh, Mam! I didn't think I'd go off like this!"

"I'll help you," said Airey.

"No, I want Mam. It's more fitting."

Mrs. Grigg followed her to the back rooms. Airey took Jabez on her hip and went to the coffeepot with grim hospitality.

The Reverend Ousby planted his hands on his knees. "I'm sorry to see you're the same girl who left us—aside, that is, from looking like your own brother. And now I hear you've been playing fiddle at dances. Had you received our admonishments, you wouldn't now find yourself condemned to mannish toil and sordid display, which bring you neither reward on earth nor blessing in heaven."

"I earn the same money a night Merit does a week sewing flowers on those hankies."

"On whom shall God's favor fall: your sister and her dainty, womanly work or a young lady who exhibits herself to paying audiences?"

Cecilia saw Airey's eyes turn to ice and said, "May I ask about your journey to Fort Vickerson? It must be at least three or four days by car."

The Reverend Ousby, reluctantly deflected, replied, "Indeed it is. Like Saint Paul, we'll be staying with little communities of the faithful along our route."

"When we arrive," said Mrs. Welland, "I'll serve as Merit's matron of honor before joining my sister."

"I'll go, too, and be Merit's bridesmaid!" said Polynegry.

"How'd you get yourself back?" Airey asked her. "I'm the one to go."

Cecilia sat up in alarm.

Mrs. Welland beckoned Polynegry to her. "You never attended our school, did you, child? What's your name?"

"Polynegry Fitch, but I like Poly."

"Polynegry? Ah, Pola Negri!" The Reverend Ousby's upper lip lengthened. "After the motion picture actress."

Airey said in a flat voice, "Mam saw her in a movie when she was carrying Poly. She thought it was a real nice name. Polynegry, you go pick us some salad."

"We've known far worse, haven't we, Mrs. Welland?" said the Reverend Ousby. "That unfortunate lad whose father picked the first word his finger found in the family Bible."

"Whosoever Johnson," she supplied.

Airey said, "Better a word from Scripture than calling him *backward boy* or *dirty savage*. Or—" as Mrs. Welland bridled—"thrashing him across the head with a switch."

"We never want to be driven to such extremes, but you're perfectly aware that he needed all he received, and you were nearly as bad. *The rod and reproof give wisdom*."

Airey looked away without answering. Cecilia

could think of nothing inconsequential to say. Jabez squirmed to be down. Airey sat him firmly on her lap. Cecilia finally managed, "I'm afraid I don't know a great deal about the Siffville Settlement."

"I regret that's the case," said the Reverend Ousby. "We're one of the few Settlement organizations that teach the three R's, as well as Bible school and such traditional skills as needlework, rug making, basket weaving, and chair caning. All these offer our mountain folk a means of augmenting their income while leaving their unique culture undisturbed and, further, helping them to better themselves by removing aimlessness, sloth, and a coarse understanding of the ways of God."

Cecilia ground her teeth and asked, "Do you feel you're achieving your goals?"

"Here and there," said the Reverend Ousby. "Here and there. Our young Cardwell is one of whom we can be proud. He was a superb carver of figurines. We sold many of his pieces."

"Nobody wanted the trash we had to make," said Airey. "City folks bought it out of pity."

"Now, that's simply—"

"Airey," Mrs. Grigg appeared at the door from the back rooms, "fetch out the taters and put them greens to boil."

Airey left Jabez on her chair and stepped to the kitchen, banging spoons and bowls, thrusting kindling into the cook stove. Cecilia continued to turn the conversational grindstone until Polynegry came in with a basket of young lettuce, tomatoes, and cucumbers.

"If Nurse Dunne were here," Mrs. Welland asked brightly, "would she judge these comestibles safe to eat?"

Airey turned to answer, face like fury. Cecilia replied, "Mrs. Grigg is a superb cook. I'm afraid I shamelessly hope to be invited to a meal each time I visit."

"I'm intrigued by your connection with the Fitches," said the Reverend Ousby.

"How flattering."

Merit, in shoes for the first time Cecilia had seen her, emerged with a threadbare carpetbag and a basket tied with twine.

"We reckoned you wouldn't have much room left in your car," Mrs. Grigg said to the Reverend Ousby, "so we squeezed her worldly goods into these."

Airey said, "I got even less to pack."

Cecilia's concern flared into dismay. *She can't go.*

Lorimer and Royal poked their heads through the front door. "You stay outside, Roy." He looked at the carpetbag as he came in, "Who's leaving?"

"Merit's traveling south with these folks to marry Card," said his mother, dishing out in the kitchen. "Right after we get dinner into them."

"*Today*?"

"I got to," said Merit. "They're leaving today."

Lorimer shot a half-frightened look at the Reverend Ousby but said stoutly, "You want me to come with you?"

"It's real thoughtful of you, Lor—"

"I'm the one going." Airey slammed a plate of bread on the table.

This absolutely must not happen.

The Reverend Ousby chuckled as Lorimer unhitched the fly brush. "The old pioneer sufficiency isn't quite dead, Mrs. Welland."

"A screen door or two would work greater wonders."

The Reverend Ousby said grace. The Fitches ate slowly, each looking at Merit, who smiled tremblingly back. Mrs. Grigg lowered Jabez's feeding spoon with a long sigh, to his indignation. "First bride of the family! I reckon you'll look pretty as a flower."

"Oh, Mam! Don't start me off again!"

"I ain't trying to, but when I think of that dress you embroidered to get married in and recall *to see the bride, the glitt'ring bride*, I can't help bawling like an orphan calf."

"Oh, *Mam!*"

Airey said, "I'll make sure that photographer takes lots."

Inspired by desperation, Cecilia asked, "Mrs. Grigg, *would* you go? If you could?"

"Surely." Mrs. Grigg dabbed her eyes with the back of her hand. "I'm real fond of Card, and Merit's my firstborn gal. But I can't ask these folk to carry me along out of their own pocket."

"Will you accept the journey as my gift?" *The perfect solution.* "Your expenses down and your train ticket back? And the bus from Charleville?"

Mrs. Grigg gaped at her, but Merit was smiling like a pale sun. "Mam, I'd give anything for you to be standing beside me. Airey, it should be Mam. Miss Howison, you're—"

"Howison!" Mrs. Welland glanced significantly at the Reverend Ousby. "I *thought* you seemed familiar. Now I understand! You're acting as patroness to this worthy little clan! How wonderful that our First Families are taking an interest in the forgotten folk in their uplands backyard!"

"As a friend of the family," said Cecilia, "it's of course an honor to offer even so small—"

Airey's look stopped her like a steel blade. "Miss Howison, we thank you, but we ain't needing your help for this. Mam, Merit's right. Your place is beside her, and it's my jar of money that's going to pay for it. I'll stay and look after the little ones."

"I can look after myself," said Poly.

"But Airey—that's your Atlanta money," said Mrs. Grigg. "I won't take it."

"Merit ain't going by herself, and you ain't using no money but mine. Fitches live off their own." Airey left the room and returned with a pickle jar filled with coins.

"Will this suffice for two extra passengers?" the Reverend Ousby wondered aloud. "And we mustn't risk a discourtesy to Miss Howison by forgetting her wonderful gesture."

"That jar's what you got," said Airey.

"I find your—" he began.

Mrs. Grigg said quickly, "We won't be looking for more to eat than bread and sop, and what I'll be bringing ain't nearly as much as Merit."

Cecilia saw that her battle was nearly won. She turned a radiant face to the Reverend Ousby. "Sir, may I say how moved I am by the fact that, even at some trouble to yourself, you're ensuring the bride marries within those traditional folkways only a mother can provide?"

He gave a compliant smile. "And joyfully given, Miss Howison, joyfully given." He opened a wide, soft hand toward the jar. "I'll manage that for you, Mrs. Fitch."

"You keep hold of it, Mam," said Airey.

"Airey," Merit tried to speak through a fresh cascade of tears. "It means you giving up Atlanta."

"I'll earn that back and more come the harvest dances," Airey scoffed, going to the sideboard. "Mam, now it's you who's got to pack instead of me."

"I can't hardly swallow a crumb anyway." Mrs. Grigg hurried away.

Merit took up Jabez's spoon. "Airey, Pap would be blessing your heart right now, like I'm doing."

"I'd join your prayer, child," said the Reverend Ousby, filling his plate with Indian pudding, "if I thought she'd be replenishing her little hoard by some other, less sinful, means. Let us hope her sacrifice today will be imputed to her for righteousness."

Cecilia watched Airey's knuckles whiten on the cream jug and said to her, "Part of your sacrifice is staying behind."

"When Mam and Merit go to sit with sick neighbors, it ain't no trouble to look after the little ones."

"It'll mean," Lorimer bit his lip and glanced at Poly, "Airey's cooking."

Airey overheard him. "You ain't starved yet."

Lorimer passed the cathead biscuits to Poly. "Fill up good."

Mrs. Grigg returned in a fresh dress, ancient, polished shoes, and an embroidered hat. She carried a well-stuffed flour sack tied at the top to form a handle. "I got my best dress in here, but the hat nor shoes won't fit alongside Airey's jar."

The Reverend Ousby pushed himself from the table. "That was good mountain cooking. We must wend our way if we're to reach Gartnerville by this evening."

Merit rose to her feet like a soldier under orders. Poly stared at her, suddenly realizing to the bone what this meant. “Merit, you ever coming back?”

“I-I don’t know, Polywoggle.” Merit picked up her carpetbag and basket.

Cecilia glanced at the family’s faces and retreated to the backyard. She heard, over Poly’s desperate sobs, Mrs. Grigg’s final gabbled instructions, the Reverend Ousby’s heartiness, and Airey’s harsh replies. Their voices receded. A darting thought made her dash into the house to snatch up her bag, wrap her tiny bottle of Worth cologne in dollar bills and a handkerchief, and she reached the car as the Reverend Ousby was starting its engine. Airey, holding her sister’s hand through the sedan’s window, moved aside.

“Miss Fitch.” Cecilia thrust the small bundle into the gloom of the backseat. “Please, will you take this bridal gift from me? With my best wishes. May you always be happy.”

She stepped back. The Ford began to turn in the yard. Lorimer and Poly stopped it by scrambling onto the sidemount for final goodbyes. The Reverend Ousby roared the motor to clear them off, and the sedan lumbered down the lane. Cecilia watched the Fitches listen to its engine fading through the trees until no sound was left.

Airey said, “I ain’t never going to see her again.”

“It’s longer for me ’cause I ain’t old as you,” said Poly.

Jabez, on the edge of the porch, was not seeing his mother. His face began to knot.

“Come on, Jaby,” said Airey, going to him. “I’ll make you bread and syrup.”

“Merit says he shouldn’t never be given—” Poly

sat on the earth and buried her face in her hands. "I don't *like* marrying. It takes folks *away*."

Cecilia crouched beside her. "Your sister's going to a wonderful new life."

"Merit wants to be with *Card* more than with *us*."

"That's what grownups do. They go away from their families to be with the one they love."

"Melvin Labhard didn't. Him and Flora moved in with his folks. We could use Card right here on the farm. I don't *like* Merit being happier with Card. I wish she'd be *un*happy and *stay home*." She jumped to her feet and rushed into the house.

Cecilia stood. The books and music in the roadster were the last thing Airey would want, but they might as well be delivered. She took them in and saw Poly outside the kitchen door, sitting on Merit's sewing chair with her arms locked around her knees. Royal was snuffling his way uneasily along the edges of the room. Airey came from the back rooms with Lorimer. "I can't give him syrup every time he wants Mam. We'll run dry."

Lorimer picked up Merit's half-finished handkerchief from a chair. "What about her work?"

"Mam'll finish it when she gets back," said Airey.

"I'm going to the shed."

"You know Mam don't like you smoking."

"I'm going to." He gave Airey the handkerchief and went out, Royal at his side.

Airey sat and spread it in front of her, forearms resting on the table as if they had no strength. "This won't never get done. Mam's good, but not as good as Merit. Look at those stitches."

Cecilia sat opposite her. "I'm sorry those people

took such liberties with—"

"Liberties." Airey looked up, and her vision seemed to clear. "Plenty was taken today. I always expect the worst from Siffville, and I ain't never been disappointed. I didn't expect nothing like that from you."

Cecilia straightened sharply.

"I reckoned I knew you. Seems I was mistaken. Patroness. Is that how you see us? Is that what you've been doing? Is that what it'll be like for me if my work is Mr. Brewken's music? Is it the same? You told me his music was all I'd got left to choose, seeing old-time wasn't never going to take me. You're right. It won't now. My money's gone, and I told Merit a whopper 'cause there ain't enough places left round here where I can earn it back."

"You-you committed yourself to concert music."

"I promised to give my all. *You* promised to get me heard. Where's any of it? I learned early to hold some seed corn back no matter what my hopes, and that jar was it. Except now I'm holding nothing. I done it to myself, it was right I did, but now you—you're the only rope I got to hang on to. What's at *your* end? What's there?"

"I promised to help you. I will."

"You promised plenty. You told me to trust you. I did. Now I'm in a place I fought never to be. I got nothing and no hope of more. The Siffville folks made us work, they made us crawl, they whipped us, all the while telling us it was for our betterment, they took from us then and today, coming here knowing they could do whatever they pleased to us. And they did it. They did it." Airey smoothed the handkerchief with flat hands. "I didn't never want to bear this again.

Freed's gone. Pap's gone. Merit's gone. Siffville—they've torn us apart. I'm torn apart." She lowered her head to her hands, her hair falling like silk.

Cecilia reached to comfort her. Was jolted to her feet by a flash, too bright, too clear, of that first moment in the meadow to this moment. *Oh, God. God.* "I'm their kind—I'm exactly their kind. You're right. We come—we've all come—to get something from you and-and the consequences are never ours to face." She flew from the house, running as she heard Airey behind her, fingers on the roadster's door handle.

Airey's hand reached and covered them. "What's this you're saying? What's this?"

In one move, she could be in her arms. "It wasn't—I'm not—" Cecilia pressed against the car. "I must leave. I must *leave*."

Airey let go. "Miss Howison—"

Cecilia jerked open the roadster's door, got in without looking at her, spun the wheel, and drove too fast down the lane she did not see.

A frightening slew on the drovers' road made her brake and stop. She rested her forehead on the steering wheel. *Who do I think I am*? Pat's voice came like a whisper: *I think you're an angel.* She put the car back into gear with a groan of self-contempt. *Get away from here.*

She drove in and out of the valleys, trying to outrun her thoughts, finally finding herself home, dogged by them. The sound of the phonograph in the summer room made her detour around the house to the cluster of yellow poplars where the old rope swing hung. She sat and shoved herself into hard, flat arcs.

Airey was right. The Siffville generosity was an exercise in power, for power. Exactly as hers was. Hers, false gifts from a false friend. She was lying to Airey—to Airey, who spoke to her from her soul. *How have I not burned up in shame*?

She leaned against the swing's ropes, half-welcoming the burn on her bare arms. Airey was right. She was one of those who gave what they wanted to get what they wanted. She winced at the memory of the girls from the mills, from the roadhouses, eager and deferential. She thought of Airey's bowed head, her hands limp with grief.

She could not call back what she had done. But she could repent. She could stop. She would stop. She was stopping. It stopped now.

More than this. She must atone. How? By writing a letter? She shrank. Impossible. How could she write *Forgive me for trying to seduce you*? Only one thing was left to do, one thing she must do. Keep her promise about music. Any music, and not to rest until Airey had it. Keeping that promise needed no trips to the mountains. She would not see Airey again. Tom had been right. She did not know the roads. She was too accustomed to riding roughshod wherever she pleased.

She crept up to the nursery to play Brahms on the old upright. She played Brahms, she played Bach, played records, she slammed tennis balls against the side of the barn, she rode Swan from one corner of Old Waring to the other, she helped Henry polish the silver, drove for miles, arranged the flowers, did Trenton's bookkeeping, weakened once, alone in the office, looking up faded entries in old Sankgallon ledgers to feast on the words *Fittes Cove*, *Applesell Bald*, again to the piano, the tennis court, riding, driving through the arid valleys.

Mother surveyed her one afternoon. "You look a little frayed, darling."

"Heavens, I'm Sporting Girl personified. Varda is close to hitting me with a shoe to get me out of bed in the mornings."

"I think Patmore's too much on your mind. Are you finding you're missing him?"

How to be honest? "Of course I am. We've been friends all our lives."

"A trip might do you good. I'd go with you to Cousin Welsh's if your father and I weren't about to start traveling for his campaign. You could come with us as far as Cedar Falls. Your friend Christabelle is still there, isn't she?"

"Yes, but she's been ill for a while."

"Not the old lung trouble? Oh, that *is* a shame. She was always flushed, too. I wonder if you should see Dr. Benjamin."

"I'm blooming with health," said Cecilia in quiet panic. She was never going back to the mountains, but she did not want to be away from them, not yet. *At least I'm close to them, if never her.* "I wouldn't want people to think I was holding myself as more of an injured party than Patmore."

"That's nicely said, darling. Let's see how you are when your father and I get back."

Cecilia saw her glance at Tom's chair. When she and Daddy were back, Tom would be gone. "I could use some work."

Mother gave it to her: addressing stacks of envelopes for Daddy's postal campaign, sorting the linens in the attic for Washington, copying the same thank-you letter ten dozen times, ready for Mother's signature. None of them distracted her. Should she try moving to new pastures? Could she? No. The grass would always be greener on Applesell Bald, and she would always know it. Airey's eyes the color of a mountain stream. Airey's smile like slow honey. *Go away*, but Airey would not.

One of the secretaries at Collines Academy finally told Cecilia, with a superior smile, that Mr. Potz had gone to Maine for the summer. Mr. Feldstedt declined her invitation with a note. She looked up every music school in the country and wrote asking for their requirements and fees. She visited the bandmasters of the Biltmore and the Peakview hotels, to their awkward surprise; she went to the Trimble Hotel and its competitors in Charleville, to be told each time so sorry, Miss Howison, no openings, and never for a woman, married or unmarried. She wrote to WSM and WSL radio stations; they replied that they would only correspond with a *bona fide* agent or the lady's husband, no offense intended. Tom was away with friends. Mrs. Vernelle was out of town. Everybody was visiting, vacationing, not home, not here, not helping her.

Nothing helped. The memory of Airey's body almost touching hers at the car door made everything leap inside. Time was not making this easier to bear. It was making it harder. Would it drive her insane? She wondered half-seriously if she ought to take Tom's place in the sanatorium.

Rosamund joined Cecilia in the summer room one afternoon, knitting while Cecilia played restless scales.

"Why are you trying to wear yourself out?"

"This is hardly hot jazz."

"I mean everything you do. This can't be guilt over Pat. A maidenly depression of spirits is proper, heaven knows, but there's no sense prolonging it. Pat won't be comforted, and it's time to remind every other boy with the right pedigree that you're someone to be sought."

"The bid price, to open...?"

"You're the stocks expert."

"I'm torn: my market value or my actual value?"

"That's plain nonsense, and you know it. Try dropping your handkerchief and see how many come running."

"I prefer to keep it in my pocket."

"Surely Pat hasn't put you off men? Or was there more going on in those mountain trips than teaching some little girl music?" Rosamund turned the heel of the bootie. "I hope you weren't speaking with a country boy. You aren't used to the type. They say just what they think, and that makes them hard to resist."

Cecilia wondered how she knew. *The sweetest mountain boy can't hold a candle to a mountain girl.* "No handkerchief dropped there or picked up."

"I'm glad to hear it. Since you're fancy-free, why not direct a few smiles at young men whose daddies could be useful to your father's campaign?"

"You're turning into quite a Howison."

"I always was the right material. Why do you think I married Trent?" Rosamund held up the bootie. "What do you think for trim? Little roses or little forgetmenots?"

"Little Venus fly traps," said Cecilia.

Rosamund laughed.

Cecilia played for her and considered smiling at young men for Daddy's sake. When would she smile again at someone for her own sake? Where? In Washington? When? *What do I want*? The vague shape of an elegant, cultured woman living a wittily adventurous life in some distant cosmopolitan setting swam before her eyes. Where could she be? At Cousin Welsh's? In California? What would a liaison with such a woman be like? After they parted, wouldn't she find herself ruined for other girls? Was that a price she wanted to pay? *Will I ever find out*?

Henry intercepted Cecilia one afternoon with a telegram as she came in from the stables. Were music schools this eager to reject her advances? She took it upstairs and stood in boots and jodhpurs to read.

"*Arriving Charleville evening Monday. Must leave Wednesday. Tuesday for your friend. Her home preferred. Vernelles will drive. Neihoff.*"

Cecilia read it twice. *Golly*. She could keep her promise to Airey at last. At last. And not just an hour with Dr. Neihoff, but an entire day. Promise kept with compound interest.

She scribbled a reply on the telegram form and wrote a letter to Mrs. Vernelle. "I assume the Neihoffs prefer to visit Miss Fitch at her home because of Mrs.

Neihoff's studies in folk song. The setting is all she could wish for, and the Fitch farm is not difficult to reach." But as she began to draw a map of the route, she paused. This would not do. She had to take them. She had to make the introductions. How peculiar, how awkward, if she wasn't there.

She put down her pen. Not be there? Not witness the moment when Airey might be handed the keys to her kingdom? *I have to be there.* This one last time, coming with company and leaving with them. *I have to see her.* Just once more. What danger could there be with Mrs. Vernelle and Mrs. Neihoff as chaperones?

She discarded the map and wrote suggesting a rendezvous at the Peakview Hotel.

To Airey, a telegram: *Famous violinist Dr. Neihoff coming with wife, two other musicians, to hear you Tuesday 4 August. Expect to arrive late morning.*

Letter and telegrams went on the tray in the hall. She could frighten herself with the power one person, one Howison, had for ill and now, perhaps, for good. As for the power Airey had over her, that would eventually die from the withdrawal of oxygen. *Except for this last blast of mountain air.*

Chapter Five

Cecilia sat on the terrace of the Peakview Hotel under a hot sun, wishing she had finished the map and had left the Neihoffs to find the Fitch farm for themselves. There was still time. The bag of limes in her car could be donated to the hotel. She wished she could donate everything down from her hat brim to an icehouse.

A familiar Ford Model T touring car turned into the forecourt, Mr. Vernelle at the wheel. Cecilia rose to meet it. Dr. Neihoff opened his window, dabbing his face with a large handkerchief. "How pleasant once again to meet you, Miss Howison. I hope I will not expire with this heat before I hear your prodigy."

"It's terribly warm, isn't it? We'll be cooler in the mountains. My friend wouldn't, I think, be called a prodigy, although she clearly was when she was a girl."

"She is not child?"

"She's about my age."

"*Ach*. I was expecting a different thing." Dr. Neihoff glanced at Mrs. Vernelle. "Quite different thing. Well, we have come this far."

Cecilia, conscious of the dust of the foothills road and the heat in Fittes Cove, was glad to see clouds drifting in the higher hollows. At Hinterhouse, Mr. Vernelle jibbed at the drovers' road. Cecilia revved her engine commandingly and led the way. They crept up into cloud, above it. Mist was rising from the forest as they turned into the lane, making the birches pale sketches of themselves. The air was filled with the scent of leaf, fern, damp earth. Cecilia thought she had never smelled anything so alive.

They parked side by side in the farmyard. Dr. Neihoff stood silently as Mr. Vernelle unloaded his wife's traveling keyboard. Mrs. Neihoff surveyed the house with disappointment. Cecilia hurried up the slope. Airey met her on the porch. She was wearing shoes and her blue tartan dress. Her wetted hair was plastered to her skull. Cecilia thought she looked like a scarecrow, a yokel, like the laird of a highland castle, a goddess, the most ravishing woman she had ever seen. "Miss Fitch, I'm sorry I couldn't give you more notice."

The bones of Airey's face were as sharp as a gazelle's. Her eyes were reserved. "I thank you for your telegram. Mr. Keller brung it up special. Polynegry's taken Jaby off for the day. Lor's gone hunting. Mam's still down with Merit and Card. I got chestnut coffee and buttermilk for you all." Her voice was slow and soft, a duelist awaiting her opponent. Cecilia saw her gaze rest on Dr. Neihoff's violin case.

"I'm sure either will be welcomed. It was very hot in the cove." Cecilia turned to make the introductions. Mrs. Vernelle's smile was stiff. Dr. Neihoff looked up, looked down, his beard fluffing over his cheeks.

"Your house is modern," said Mrs. Neihoff as if it were a fault.

Airey hesitated, and Cecilia knew she had not understood her. Cecilia repeated it, translating quickly in reverse when Airey replied, "This part is. You can walk round the back for something older. Come in and set."

Her violin and bow sat on a chair facing others arranged in a half-circle. Mrs. Neihoff, when she could see, swept the room with an assessing eye. "How old is that sideboard?" As Cecilia translated, "it looks far older than the house. Your clock's also old, isn't it? A lovely piece."

"My dear," said Dr. Neihoff, "we come to hear this young lady play fiddle."

"Forgive me, Miss Fitch," said Mrs. Neihoff. "I'm interested in what survives from one culture and time to another: stories, songs, poetry, and the objects that accompany them."

"I play my pap's songs," Airey said directly to her, beginning not to need Cecilia. "He taught us some in the old tongue."

"Gaelic?" asked Mrs. Neihoff.

Her husband said, "We should get to business. Young lady, you have prepared some pieces to play?"

"Yes, sir." Airey took up her violin and infinitesimally retuned her E string as they settled themselves. She leapt into a refreshing fall of notes. Cecilia recognized it: Bach, a different sonata than before, though as well played. Half a minute later, Cecilia saw Mrs. Vernelle shift and Dr. Neihoff straighten.

When it ended, Airey said, "I got another tune I've been playing since Miss Howison brung it on a record. I'll give you a piece from the middle. Where I ain't got nothing to play, I'll pick out the orchestry part, but I reckon you can all fill in from your heads."

She started the slow movement from Tchaikovsky's violin concerto, playing it exactly as it was performed on the record. Cecilia knew it well; it was from her own collection. *What are you doing, Airey*?

She sat in despair as Dr. Neihoff's chin sank again into his beard. Why, after the freshness of her Bach, did she think this imitation would impress him?

Airey finished. Her bow stayed high. She began the movement again. This time, it was a pulse faster, a touch cooler, the underlying gypsy sob controlled, the music turning to loss seen through time, eloquent and weary, building heart-piercingly, making a last desolate lift—the music stopped. Airey lowered her bow and violin, her face blank. Cecilia knew that she was at complete attention.

Dr. Neihoff leaned forward. "Tell me, Miss Fitch, why you choose these pieces to play to me."

"'Cause they're different from each other. Bach I learned a long time past, but the second just a few weeks ago. I wanted to show you what I know real good, how fast I learn new things, and what I do with them."

"Yes, I hear you play Kreisler's way and then not. You think Kreisler plays wrongly?"

"No, sir. Except when I heard him on the record, I reckoned it'd be better another way. He sops his notes good. I like my bread a little drier. He's a great, but that ain't how I'd play it. You heard how."

Dr. Neihoff pursed his lips. "Mr. Vernelle, will you set up your wife's clavichord?"

"I got more tunes," Airey protested.

"I shall hear them," said Dr. Neihoff, "but now you hear and learn something from me."

Mr. Vernelle removed a long wooden box from its case. Airey frowned, her bow tip impatiently tapping the air.

"While we wait, Miss Fitch," said Dr. Neihoff, "you know the rest of Bach's sonata? Yes? Please play first piece while the keyboard of Mrs. Vernelle is put together."

Airey hesitated, looking at Mr. Vernelle on his knees vigorously screwing the four legs of the clavichord into the underside of the keyboard case, turned, and played Bach's *Adagio* as if contemplating a life of loss, as if alone.

Dr. Neihoff heard her courteously. He opened his own violin case. Airey involuntarily stepped toward it.

"This is Italian," he said, holding up his violin. "And yours? Is not American."

"It's my teacher's. I took it after he died, seeing nobody else wanted it." She gave it to him.

He peered inside. "Too dark to read label, but French, I think. Good tone, very sweet. Maybe too light for you, but good. Gut strings. You have not tried steel? You have? I, too, prefer gut, though snap, snap, snap all the time." He gave back the violin, looked at her bow and said, "French, also. Acceptable, not more. Rehair soon, please." He tuned his own violin. "On this measure, Miss Fitch, you made two downbows." He played them. "Why?"

"That ain't how?"

"*This* usually how." He drove through the notes. "Yes?"

Airey hung for a moment. "That works, but I reckon the push is the same here as before and then I'm on the right path for this upbow." She played both measures.

"I do not say is wrong to play in ways not usual. I want to know if you have thought the why. Now here," he played an arc of notes, "these should come together from this—" he played a chord—"to this, as final gather-in, a *sweep* of feeling before conclusion, not as long exhale."

"Show me again." He did. She repeated it and said, "That's how it was built."

"Yes. What Bach makes, we do. How long have you played?"

"Since I was rising five. That's when Mr. Brewken came here and taught me."

"Brewken? Brewken?" Dr. Neihoff looked at Mrs. Vernelle. "This—it must be—Broeggen? Kees Broeggen?"

"How extraordinary. Christophe," Mrs. Vernelle asked her husband, "do you remember Kees Broeggen? Concertmaster of the Melita Symphony?"

"Never met him," Mr. Vernelle grunted, getting to his feet and turning the clavichord right side up. "Heard of him. He vanished during the war. Rumor said he went back to Europe."

"But not," said Dr. Neihoff. "He came here, to teach her. Now many things make sense to me. You do not get nothing from nothing."

"I'm speechless," said Mrs. Vernelle. "Kees Broeggen, so close to us." She turned. "You've a very good ear, Cecilia."

Airey sent Cecilia a glancing smile and asked Dr. Neihoff, "You knew him?"

"I meet him five, six times on first trip I make to America. He was anxious that I know he trained with the greatest teachers: German, French, Polish. German I hear in him, and Polish not in him, but in you. You have French style of holding your bow."

"People reckoned he was good?" asked Airey.

"He was esteemed. After short solo career, he was, like me, a concertmaster. He also led quartet for many years, though a little trouble stopped it. Do you know what concertmaster is?"

"You're the best of the orchestry."

"Yes, is true." He ignored Mr. Vernelle's *moue*. "I also lead it. I organize. I shape. To conductors, I give perfect instrument. If conductor is deficient, and that is very many times, I carry. Maestro Broeggen was good fiddler, good concertmaster. Now you have his violin."

"He died eight years back."

"Of the drinking?"

"Yes, sir," said Airey with restraint.

"That being his little trouble. Such waste." Dr. Neihoff turned to Mrs. Vernelle. "Dear friend, do you need note?"

"Please." She had her husband move her chair and said to Airey as she began to tune, "This is a clavichord, which will fill the part of a piano to a tolerable degree."

"Can you play that?" Airey asked Cecilia.

"Not very well."

"Tell me, Miss Fitch," said Dr. Neihoff, "why you keep playing this music after Maestro Broeggen dies."

"I like it."

"As you like the folk music Miss Howison tells me you also play?"

"I ain't met a music I don't like. This kind here needs plenty of thinking over."

Dr. Neihoff nodded. "You are right, and returns endless reward for that thought, I say as one who likes it most of all."

"Barukh," said Mrs. Vernelle, "I'm ready."

"Thank you. Now, Miss Fitch, I teach you short piece. You know it?" He played the opening measures.

Airey shook her head.

"It is a work composed for piano and violin, but we will have clavichord. Lieve—Mrs. Vernelle—and I now will play it for you."

Mrs. Vernelle's clavichord gave the first pouncing chords. Dr. Neihoff's rich-voiced violin almost obliterated its chimes with a fire of tense, sweet, wild notes. At the end, he turned to Airey. "So."

"It goes a lick. You play good."

"Yes. And yes, is fast, because driven. *Appassionato*! All feeling, all burning, all tenderness. Now you learn this from me." He lifted his violin. "Opening as follows."

They proceeded a few measures at a time, Mrs. Vernelle patient on the keyboard. Dr. Neihoff stopped Airey again and again. "No scrambling. Quickly, yes, but precisely. Repeat."

Airey repeated badly, repeated well, improving each time. Dr. Neihoff let her decide her own fingering, stopped her to show another, saying, "You can do this because you have long fingers. Yes? You like it?"

"It puts me in a better place for what's coming." Airey played as he had shown.

They continued, Dr. Neihoff making her revise two measures, three measures, until he nodded. Cecilia was on edge, not knowing whether it was a good sign or bad. *He wouldn't be spending all this time if she was hopeless.* Airey's technical skill was undeniable, given the Bach and Tchaikovsky, and she was learning as quickly as she had wanted to prove, but was it good enough? Was it good enough for him to be kind to her?

Cecilia saw Mr. Vernelle lift his nose toward the cookstove. Finally, Mrs. Vernelle suggested, "Shall we pause here?"

"I am busy! I...*ach*, apology." Dr. Neihoff shook his scowl from his face. Airey remained scowling. "Miss Fitch, we work too long without rest. We begin again after eating."

Airey put down her violin with stiff reluctance. "Yes, sir. I'll get dinner."

"Let me help," said Cecilia, as the guests went outside. "I'll-I can set the table."

Airey smiled distantly as she put on her mother's apron. Cecilia wondered if she had heard or even noticed her. Cecilia located what she needed for the table and finished with a basket of biscuits, covered with an old flour bag against flies, feeling tugged at every moment to explain herself, her abrupt departure, every moment knowing this was not the time, that there would never be a time. She joined the others on the porch.

"—just because she wants it," Mr. Vernelle was saying.

"Musical sense," said Dr. Neihoff.

"No one doubts that," said Mrs. Vernelle, "but you can hear she hasn't had proper grounding."

"Age of four to twelve or thirteen?" Dr. Neihoff stroked his beard.

Mrs. Vernelle smiled. "You always see possibility."

Cecilia clenched her fists. *See it here. It's here.*

Lunch started with the diversion of the fly brush, which Cecilia operated at the foot of the table. Dr. Neihoff set aside an unyielding biscuit and began a barrage of questions, finishing, "Maestro Broeggen never taught you to read notation? *Tschah*, disgrace. Very bad for you. You must learn much and much.

Come, fetch the music."

"Not at the dinner table, Barukh," said his wife, and he laughed. "Always I do this. Many little gravies on scores."

Cecilia watched Airey discussing music with them, eager and bright. *She's having a taste of her full life right now.* Talented. Self-sufficient. Someone who didn't need Cecilia Howison's attention. And I won't need hers, she thought stoutly. *Quite soon.*

A minute later, Airey looked up, smiled at her, and turned back to Mrs. Neihoff. *That's all she has to do.* Cecilia concentrated on slowing her heart rate and the fly brush.

Dr. Neihoff was saying, stunned, "You know *all* of Kreutzer from heart? This is very, very good. And, I ask, Rode?"

"Mr. Brew—Broog'h—" Airey tried to say the word as Dr Neihoff had said it.

He supplied, "Broo, then a little throat-clearing, then close."

"Mr. Broeggen told me I got to learn Kreutzer and Rode and Paganini and some others like they was the blood in my hands. I know their tunes are for practice, but Kreutzer's takes more from inside me to play."

"Now I have full understanding," said Dr. Neihoff. "Kreutzer, most specially, to know, to study, to play always, is education for violin in itself. Your teacher thinks. He knows he will not be with you forever, so he gives you what will keep teaching you."

The meal ended, and Cecilia helped Airey clear the table. Airey covered the dirty dishes with a towel. "I'm glad you telegraphed me. Not just about these folks coming. I was lonesome, missing Merit and

Mam. The words *famous violinist* had me pretty near running round the house. Jaby reckoned I'd gone jay crazy. You surely keep your side of a swap." She turned her head as Mrs. Vernelle's clavichord sang a sweet chime. "I'm starting again."

"You're good," said Cecilia. "You're showing them."

"I know it," said Airey. "I'm doing my best. I like learning this new tune. Dr. Neihoff's got what Mr. Broeggen got. It's what I've been needing all these years." She went to him, and Cecilia slipped back to her seat.

"We begin from here." Dr. Neihoff showed Airey the score, and the lesson continued. Dr. Neihoff made Airey play from the page. "You must learn to read until scores speak in your fingers."

"Those notes on paper ain't telling me everything."

"True. You must know about the composer, how he thinks in his composition, what gives shape to his music, from whom he learned what he knows, then you and he meet together on page as one, fiddle and bow. You do this for every composer: Brahms, Beethoven, Mozart, all. Their music, need not say, is theirs, they compose, but it is not born—is not *music*—until you make it with them when you play." He looked up at her. "This scares you, Miss Fitch?"

Airey lifted her chin. "I got reason to be?"

"Good, for learning this music is greatest blessing anyone can have. To live each day with these great minds, yes, is blessing."

They played section by section. Finally, Dr. Neihoff said, "Now, both together play from start to end, bringing technique, intonation, complete understanding of your partner—" he bowed to Mrs. Vernelle—"and composer, all as one."

Airey watched Mrs. Vernelle play the opening notes and joined her, two rapids merging. Cecilia saw Dr. Neihoff's intense gaze shift back and forth from Airey's bow to her left hand. The notes raced to their high finish. He breathed out noisily, his chin sinking into his beard.

Airey asked, "You want us to play it again?"

"I think not. Lieve, my thanks. You have served graciously, but I now put Miss Fitch through scales."

Airey looked daunted but said, "I'll boil you folks some coffee first."

To rescue them, Cecilia said, "I brought limes to make lime cup—it's like lemonade."

"It's my house," said Airey, "I should be making it."

"You're the student."

Cecilia crushed limes in a pitcher while the Vernelles and Mrs. Neihoff stepped out to enjoy the breeze. Airey and Dr. Neihoff were picking up their violins as she carried tin cups to the porch. The first scales began.

"How beautiful it is here," said Mrs. Vernelle. "So cool. The scent of these climbing roses! And bird song—we've lost so much in our cities. Do you know the family well?"

"I wouldn't presume to say so. It's difficult to be a regular visitor at this distance."

Mrs. Neihoff asked, "How did you happen to hear her play?"

"It's impossible to know Miss Fitch and *not* hear her play. We met by chance. She invited me to a solo recital, and by the end of it, I knew I had to bring her to someone's attention."

"I'm glad you did," said Mrs. Vernelle. "How pitiful that she's been unheard."

"Outside her own people," Mrs. Neihoff corrected.

Mr. Vernelle said, "I like her stillness. Doesn't distract the listener by throwing herself about like a stormy willow."

That's the old-time fiddler in her. Cecilia hoped his praise included more than Airey's stance.

The scales went on. They went on. Mrs. Neihoff and the Vernelles exchanged music gossip. Cecilia watched the clouds shift along the shoulders of the mountains, knowing that this day, her very last day, was slipping away, was nearly over. The scales changed to short exercises. Dr. Neihoff's voice and violin constantly interrupted Airey's fiddle. He played passages, had Airey repeat them, had her expand on them. Once Airey answered him sharply, a furious cascade of notes following. His sedate violin answered. Finally, he appeared at the door. "I think now is time for lime drinking for me and Miss Fitch also." He took Cecilia's chair as she went inside.

Airey was leaning against the table, her head bowed, her arms loosely crossed.

"Are you all right?"

"Better than anything." Airey did not move. "I don't know nothing. I got ten mountains to learn before I'm fit to play."

"Dr. Neihoff wouldn't be spending all day here if he thought you knew nothing."

"His touch is like a hawk fetching notes from the sky. I wish I'd got it."

"You have your own touch."

"Don't mean it's a good one. Mrs. Vernelle plays that clavichord nice. It sounds like frozen leaves. I never heard a thing like that before." She watched Cecilia smash limes. "I didn't learn close to enough from Mr. Broeggen. I'm trying hard as I can, but I know what Dr. Neihoff's hearing."

"Are you nearly finished?"

"No!" Airey's eyes blazed. "I don't never want it to stop. He says he'll hear some other of the tunes I practiced."

"Are you going to manage them?"

"This ain't as long as I played at Jim Acklin's wedding. Zachary Dettwiler, who came to help me out with guitar, he took a nip too many and I did the rest of the set by myself. And even that ain't as long as I played at the Stocklys." But she took her glass of lime cup with an effort.

Cecilia brought the pitcher out to the porch. Dr. Neihoff drank in two gulps and returned to the house with the Vernelles. Cecilia wanted to follow them, wanted to end the day watching Airey, but could not leave Mrs. Neihoff sitting alone.

Mrs. Neihoff sighed deeply. "What music must be here, waiting to be discovered! I don't think researchers have visited this valley. Fittes Cove is formidably remote."

"It's higher and farther into the mountains than the others," Cecilia agreed.

"Magnificently so."

"But emptying just as quickly. The national park."

"*Think* of what is being lost." Mrs. Neihoff glanced across to the far peaks. "And yet..."

They fell silent, listening to Paganini flare from Airey's violin. *She's good.* Cecilia felt the day lift from her. *Whatever happens, she's good.*

The sun slipped behind the flank of Applesell Bald. The house's shadow crept across the two parked cars. Chickens flew awkwardly to roost in the branches of maple trees at the edge of the yard. A lumpy shape approached from the lane: Poly, carrying a muddy, tearstained Jabez.

Cecilia hurried to meet her.

"Jaby et a bug, and he's been sick."

"We'll take him to the kitchen door." Cecilia scrubbed him with the corner of the washstand towel. Jabez seemed comforted by her firm hold. "He doesn't look as if he'll be ill again."

"I'll go get his other clothes," Poly whispered hoarsely.

Airey was playing a romantic caprice when Poly returned with a faded baby dress. "When are they going home?"

"Soon, or we'll have trouble getting down the drovers' road." As Cecilia spoke, the music ended, and Dr. Neihoff's voice said, "Yes? You hear? But do not always avoid *portamento*. Is effective at a right moment."

"If you say it," Airey replied.

"I say, and maybe you believe." He laughed. "I am right quite often, Miss Fitch."

"I'd better go in," Cecilia said to Poly. "Take Jabez to his bed and be very quiet." She went inside. Mr. Vernelle was slackening the wires of the clavichord, Dr. Neihoff was opening his violin case.

"—reckon it's best," Airey was saying.

"I do. Brahms is one of greatest composers. His violin concerto you will learn in time."

"For why?"

He looked surprised. "We speak of this all day."

"No." Airey took a step back. Her face seemed to turn to bone. "You taught me a duet, and now you're telling me about this concerto, but all day long, you've been talking to me about playing in orchestrys. About me being in one. That ain't what I want. Mr. Broeggen taught me the lone fiddler's part. That's what I want. I ain't playing behind nobody. If I can't be boss, I don't want none of it."

Cecilia felt the day and her hopes shatter around her.

"Being part of orchestra is noblest calling," Dr. Neihoff replied with considerable starch. "Playing together and lifting souls to paradise is most sublime way of serving music."

"One way. A good way. That way ain't for me."

Airey, stop.

Dr. Neihoff frowned. "This ambition so many have, yet so few attain. More than skill is needed, more than—"

"What ain't you been hearing?"

He gave her an acute look.

Mrs. Vernelle began reprovingly, "My dear Miss Fitch—!"

Airey seemed to make herself the tallest in the room. She lifted her violin. Music took the place of air, contemplative and savage, inward and absolute. Dr. Neihoff had played this beautifully in Phyllis's ballroom, but now Cecilia heard it for what it was: passionate striving, holy rage, a spear pinning them where they stood, quivering in them after Airey's bow lifted and came to rest.

Dr. Neihoff's gaze did not leave her. Mrs. Vernelle was grave. Cecilia saw Airey's tense magisterial hands, her stern mouth. *Who is this*?

Dr. Neihoff blew out a breath. "I hear this morning your excellence as a musician. I was amazed at what you had made of yourself in your isolation. You immersed yourself in what Maestro Broeggen taught you, while deep union with music you taught yourself. But I say to you," his voice became flint, "the eminent place you desire requires more than this, more even than those other skills you have, which are consistency, scrupulous quality, resolution. Do you have that rare gift which most is needed? I speak of the mental strength to open your soul every night to strangers, dedicating yourself to bringing them to that place of union you have forged. You have this? How will you give it to us? What will your *soul* give to us? No," he raised a hand as Airey began to speak, "it is not for you to say what you cannot know, and I will not presume. Now I ask you. Miss Fitch, is this your choice? Do you have the certainty to choose? This or nothing?"

"This or nothing."

"Very well. The attempt, I support. To the possibility of your success, I say not yes, not no. It is you who must make it yes."

Cecilia's mind clamored. *What is he saying*? *He's saying—*

"You must work, very hard, but power and control you have, truth of intonation you have, beautiful, clean phrasing you have and, above all, intensity and fire. So. Let us see."

Mrs. Vernelle stirred. "I don't disagree with your assessment, Barukh, but I'm afraid I'm more cautious. Although there's no question of your skill, Miss Fitch, it's an extraordinary leap to become a—"

"Concert soloist." Cecilia choked as her throat

closed. "Because you-because you're a—" she exhaled the word, "virtuoso. No—virtuosa."

"Exactly, Miss Howison." Dr. Neihoff gave her a little bow. "The skill we hear. A solo career, perhaps one day we will see."

Cecilia hardly heard him, the word fizzing through her, *virtuosa, virtuosa, virtuosa*, "One of the greats—a master."

Dr. Neihoff said to Airey, "The pieces you play for me all violinists learn, but they do not all make them their own, make them new, as the virtuosi do. As you do. Miss Howison speaks truly: a master of music. Being what you know you are."

Airey's smile dawned slowly, lighting her from within until she shone. Her eyes were amazed, looking at him, through him, looking over them all to a peak they could not see.

Finally, she said, "I thank you, sir."

"My supreme pleasure, Miss Fitch. I leave you these scores. Practice, I need not say. I will think hard what we must do for your future and will very soon write letter to you."

Cecilia saw that Airey was still airborne, while her own voice gabbled inside, *I didn't see it, I didn't have the ears—I'm such a fool—virtuosa, virtuosa, virtuosa*.

"Now we must go," said Dr. Neihoff, buckling his violin case. "It is getting dark for safely driving that donkey's track. Imperative we not miss tomorrow's train. Christophe, unfix quickly."

"It's hard to see down here," Mr. Vernelle grumbled, unscrewing the clavichord's legs.

Airey did not stir. Cecilia lit the lantern that hung over the table. Dr. Neihoff spoke to Airey in a low voice while the Vernelles wrestled the clavichord into its case.

Mr. Vernelle got up, dusting his palms, and shook Airey's hand. "Honor to meet you, Miss Fitch."

Cecilia pulled herself back to the ground, back to the room. Now she was going to say goodbye to Airey and leave. This was the moment, her last moment, *but what a summit to leap from*. She said, "I have to lead them down, so I mustn't linger. Thank you for-for everything. I'm happy I was able—"

"Come back."

"I'm afraid I—"

"Take them as far down as the cove and come back."

Cecilia's body seemed to surge forward, although she did not move. *Would another hour be so wrong*? *As a last service*? Cecilia knew it was the sirens' call, but cruel to leave Airey on her own this night of all nights. "I really shouldn't, I—"

"Come back."

"I...of course, but I won't be able to stay long."

Cecilia led the others down to Hinterhouse as fast as caution allowed, stopped, and walked back to the Ford. Dr. Neihoff reached out both hands to take hers. "My inestimable Miss Howison. You have done wondrous thing."

"I can't tell you how grateful I am that you—"

"*Tschah*, it is not for *you* to thank *me* for being given such a day."

"You should feel proud," said Mrs. Vernelle.

"I've nothing to be proud of, only to be glad

about."

"I'm pleased that Miss Fitch asked you to return," said Mrs. Vernelle, "and naturally you must go to share your friend's joy. Will you be safe coming down that terrible road later?"

"I'm familiar with it," said Cecilia, and reminded Mr. Vernelle of the turns to take them back to Charleville.

She was in the Buick and spinning round before the Ford had disappeared beyond the curve, bouncing up the drovers' road so fast she parted company with the seat. She thought of nothing, told herself nothing, until her headlights thrust eagerly down the lane and found the house. She swirled to a stop in the yard. The trees and the house were a single mass of darkness against the hidden sun's fading light. Like a soldier going over the top, Cecilia ran to the porch. Airey met her at the door.

"Oh—" Cecilia looked at her in her glory, not knowing what to say.

"I dared my all," said Airey.

Cecilia laughed a little hysterically. "You certainly did. If I'd known—if I'd had ears! And now. *Now!*"

Airey braced her raised forearms on the doorjambs. "There's no higher thing. I need to learn heaps, and I know folks won't be quick to welcome a girl they ain't never heard of, but this ain't the Melodious Mountaineers. If I mean to have it, I can. Nobody will stop me. Dr. Neihoff said women have always played fiddle. He gave me some ladies' names, all of them soloists, like I'm going to be. Not too many. Enough."

"Soloist." Cecilia rolled the word on her tongue. "The well-known soloist, Miss Fitch. Miss Fitch, the eminent soloist. Miss Fitch, the virtuosa soloist. Miss Fitch, the world famous virtuosa."

Airey laughed. "You like the sound of those."

"I do. Dr. Neihoff might speak cautiously, but why not admit the fact? A fact you never doubted."

"No reason to."

"None. And now for the world. You'll have the world. You shouldn't hope for renown in, say, Timbuktu, but you'll have it in every important city on every continent. You'll see them all, you'll play in them all: New York, Boston, Chicago—Paris, Berlin, Rome, Moscow—Montevideo, Buenos Aires, Tokyo."

"How, when I couldn't go on the road with the Melodious Moun—"

"*Don't* mention them again," said Cecilia.

"The Mel—they're a good band. Nearly the best."

"I wish them every success. Since these other women soloists manage to travel, so can you."

"That's a worry set aside."

"You're worrying about travel?"

"No." Airey smiled her slow smile. "I'm thinking *thou blessest, O Lord, and it shall be blessed forever.* He created me for this. I know it like I know my soul is His. He blessed me with it, and it's mine. It's mine."

Cecilia felt Airey leave her, rise to a far high place, and her face looked young in a way Cecilia had never seen before. Airey's gaze gradually came back to her. "You did this."

"The little I've done grants me no claim. You are who you are."

"You strove for me."

"Don't you understand?" Cecilia asked fiercely. "My part is nothing. You're astoundingly gifted. You're going to play with the greatest orchestras in the world, play to hundreds of thousands of people, you're going to record music for the ages, be sought by every newspaper, by radio, be presented to presidents and kings—"

"Records *and* radio. Mam will bust."

Cecilia caught her breath and laughed. "Prepare for a life of superlatives, Miss Fitch."

"That means good things?"

"All the reward and honor the world can heap on you."

"Reward—money?"

"Yes, far more than playing in an orchestra. A great deal more." *With prudence and good management, accepting only the best engagements and making sensible investments—* "There's no reason you won't be rich."

"You reckon I could earn maybe..." Airey leapt with wild surmise, "twenty dollars a show?"

Cecilia smiled at her tenderly. "I should think two hundred."

"A *show*?"

"Not at the beginning. Your first fees will be modest, but I understand that some of the virtuosi—I should say, the *other* virtuosi playing today—make a thousand or more a night."

Airey pushed her fingers through her hair. "Thousand dollars. That might just cover a pair of church-going shoes for Polynegry, a bag of candy, and still see some change."

"You'll have expenses. Trains, hotels, a manager, a secretary, your impresario's percentages, both here and in Europe, your evening gowns, your accompanist—"

"Maybe a good idea to throw out that bag of

candy."

"Dr. Neihoff will make sure you learn about all this."

"I ain't sure I can bear the waiting for him to write. I'm like a bubble ready to pop."

That's both of us. "Concentrating on your work will help."

"It will. It's real work now. Proper work."

Cecilia saw her glow at the prospect. *She understands work—it's why she'll be one of the greats.* Did the spark of genius drive them, or did genius catch fire only in those who did not fear being driven?

Poly called, "I hear Lor coming home."

They went inside. Airey said, "We swapped you from a family of bats, Polyfitchy. If we go walk in the woods tonight, we'll see a human child hanging upside down by her toes."

"I ain't a bat! Where's my wings?"

"We trimmed them. They're your arms, that's why they're so skinny. And Mam cut off your fur when she clipped your hair."

Cecilia now heard the slow thud of hooves approaching the house. She knew so little about the Fitch farm, but that buttermilk had to come from somewhere.

"...most foolish thing," Poly was saying. "I don't squeak, and I don't eat bugs. That's Jaby."

Jabez, asleep in a quilt-padded box beside her, woke at his name. Airey tickled his stomach. "Jaby, my little piglet, if it's got six legs and they're all still moving, it don't go inside of you. Yes? We got an understanding here between us? I reckon you'll like better some pone in milk."

"I'd like that, too," said Poly.

"Go to the barn, then, and wait for the cream milk." Airey lit a candle lantern for her. When Poly was gone, she said to Cecilia, "Stay to supper with us."

"I don't think I can." *I can't.* "I'm already very late."

"I ain't sending you off with nothing in your stomach. It ain't safe for you to drive famished."

"I don't want to make more work for you."

"How could you be work?" Airey broke dry pone into a bowl. "I'd like you to stay."

No. Absolutely not. "Yes. Thank you. But I must leave directly afterward."

Airey scrambled eggs in another bowl. "I ain't a good cook like Mam, but I can bake a chicken and make stir-eggs. If you're pleased to eat plain, I ain't bad."

"I'm not the one who'll have a life tossing down caviar."

"What's that?"

"Salted fish eggs."

"Folks eat them on purpose?"

"It's a delicacy."

"Maybe I ought to find out more about this soloist work. I ain't yet understood the risk to life." Airey laughed at more than this, laughed with astonishment. "I can't hardly think. I was making pone this morning, tight as a string and wondering what would happen today. Now it's happened. My brain's blowing round like a feather in a storm. This ain't like nothing I've ever known. This ain't the same as going to Atlanta. Folks like the Vernelles, they're new to me. It's all as new as sunrise on the first day."

"The Vernelles think you're wonderful."

"When I heard Dr. Neihoff play, I didn't reckon

I had a fly's chance in a bucket of syrup, but he said a few kind words. He said I got finesse on my *spiccato*. That means I do it good."

"You did everything perfectly."

"Perfect enough." Airey put down the bowl and snatched up her violin for a long-legged jig around the kitchen. "I didn't never think I'd be so full of joy."

"I'm-I'm so pleased and delighted for you. I can't tell you how much."

"You look like you've come on the pearl of great price."

Cecilia jumped at the words. "I've always thought it."

"You're the friend I never hoped to have."

If that were true. Cecilia looked at the music Dr. Neihoff had left. "You have another friend. See what he's given you. Some of these are old." She picked up one in Gothic type, its pages brittle.

"That ain't the same as what you did. Him and me, we're both fiddlers. We share work." Airey covered the bowls with cloths. "I got to step out and help Lor."

Alone with the dozing Jabez, Cecilia took off her hat. Airey's violin was on the table. She touched the curve of its belly. Today was supposed to be the last time she would see her, but now she would be seeing her for the rest of her life: on concert posters, in reviews, in photographs beside interviews. *Your thoughts on our fair city, Miss Fitch*? or *Miss Fitch, some words for the aspiring musician of today*? or *Could you describe for us, Miss Fitch, the high points of your recent world tour*? Cecilia smiled to herself. This was what Howison power was for. To make this possible. To do this.

Airey and Poly came into the house with their pitchers. At the sight of Airey, tall, happy, still made of light, Cecilia felt everything inside burst into flame. *What am I doing*? Even visiting Tom in California would not be far enough away. She needed to head past him to Siberia.

Lorimer arrived with an armload of wood. "Evening, Miss Howison. Airey says you're staying for supper."

"Only right she does," said Airey, adding cream to the pone.

"How was the lesson, Airey?"

"About what I hoped. Here, you set the plates. I ought to have fetched some side meat, but it's too late now. I stirred eggs."

"That's fine by me," said Lorimer.

"Airey always burns meat," Poly said to Cecilia.

"Not every time," said Airey defensively. "You two want to hear about today?"

"Not till you get done cooking that," said Lorimer, unhitching the fly brush, but it was too late. Airey scraped the eggs onto a platter and sat to say the blessing. Poly nudged her. "Get on."

"I'm going. Miss Howison is my witness. That doctor who came is a doctor of music, as well as a fiddler. His wife was purely elegant. Miss Howison's own teacher and her husband came along to help. I played, and the doctor taught me a good new tune. We talked about me playing Mr. Broeggen's music—*Broeggen* is how it's said—for my paying work, and he reckons I can."

"Folks will pay to hear that?" asked Poly.

"Miss Howison says for better money than weddings and dances."

Poly and Lorimer looked at Cecilia.

"Your sister's going to be very well off—and famous. She's what people call a virtuosa."

"That's a good thing to be?" asked Poly.

Lorimer broke loose some egg with his fork. "What's it mean?"

"You know I'm the best fiddler hereabout," said Airey.

"Everybody knows."

"I'm still going to be that, only all over."

"The mountains?" asked Poly. "Down south?"

"The world."

Poly looked at her in awe. "You're going to be like those Hollywood stars and sail on big ocean boats?"

Airey hesitated, and they all looked at Cecilia, who nodded.

"When are you going to start this traveling job?" asked Lorimer.

"I got to wait for Dr. Neihoff to write me about that."

"It'll mean big changes." Lorimer's eyes were alert.

"It won't be no different from me going to Atlanta. I'll be sending money for hired men, just like I always planned."

Cecilia saw Lorimer's face darken as he turned away.

Royal trotted into the room, a fleck of rabbit fur on his muzzle, sniffed the chairs used by the Vernelles and Neihoffs, and came to Cecilia.

"Royal, don't go bothering Miss Howison," Lorimer commanded.

"He's a gentleman," said Cecilia. She idly scratched

his ruff while the Fitches talked, all of them oblivious to her heroic refusal to look at Airey as often as she wanted to. Although I'm not fooling you, sir, she thought, moving aside Royal's questing nose.

Lorimer and Royal went for a last check of the animals. Airey took Jabez to bed and came back to help a yawning Poly with the dishes. Cecilia glanced at her hat by the door. *You've indulged your imbecility—now go home. Go.*

"If I'm a bat, I can stay up all night," Poly was saying.

"Do bats yawn? Any more and I'll know they swapped you back." Airey set out a washbasin and flour sack towels.

Cecilia retreated to the porch. *I can't say goodbye in the midst of their baths.*

Airey followed, alarmed. "You ain't going?"

"I wouldn't leave without a word."

"You'd better stay. I don't want you driving so far at night. Fittes Cove is nearly empty—what happens if that monument of yours breaks down again? You take a bed here."

Why not try me in the fire? "I'm afraid I can't."

"Maybe it ain't like what you got at home."

"I don't mean that. I just…can't."

"You'll be by yourself in Mam's room. Her bed's clean and ready for her 'cause we expected her back by now."

"I really don't think I should." *Think*?

"Yes, you should," said Airey. "It's too far away for you to go home now. Stay, and I'll give you a breakfast that'll set you up for the drive. Your folks would rightly blame me if I let you leave so late at night."

"My parents aren't home," said Cecilia's treacherous lips.

"Then more reason to stay."

To refuse would be discourteous. To agree would be insane. "Thank you. I will." *I'm an idiot.* "Because it's so late." *I'm a fool.*

"That's grand." Airey's smile did its work again. She went inside to finish her chores, and Cecilia stepped to the edge of the porch to breathe steadying cool air.

Stars appeared in swathes above the dark bulk of the mountains. Beetles and frogs sang under the porch and along the creek. The only light came from the house. Moths flew in past her, helplessly lured, and Cecilia knew how they felt.

She could hear Airey talking to Lorimer. The light changed. Lorimer or Poly must be taking a candle through to the back rooms. Their footsteps faded. Airey was crossing to the kitchen. Cecilia heard the cookstove's reservoir being refilled. She readied herself for the next ordeal.

"Nice cool night." Airey joined her on the porch. "It'll be hotter tomorrow."

Cecilia said nothing. Airey was a vertical line of crescents where lamp light from the house touched the edges of hip, arm, breast, cheek. Perfume from the climbing roses seemed to wrap around them.

"What are you thinking?" Airey asked after a pause. It was an unusually direct question from someone mountain-bred.

"I'm thinking how dark it is here."

"I got a blaze inside me. I must be lighting up everything from here to Chiny."

"You will, in time."

"People knowing me all the way to Chiny. *In*

Chiny, too. That raises every hair on my head. What will world-famous be like? I ain't never seen a virtuosy in *Photo Screen News*."

"You'll be famous in another sphere, one with its own magazines. There you'll be fêted, sought after, wanted—" Cecilia stopped herself, heart hammering.

"That's as far away as one of those stars."

"This night will become as distant as any of them."

"Never forgot."

"I-I hope you won't forget me," said Cecilia, ashamed that she needed an answer.

"There won't be nothing to forget 'cause there won't be a time when we ain't friends."

"That's lovely of you to say."

"You're looking at me like you was saying good-bye."

"It's not what I was thinking."

"I don't know much about you yet. We ain't spent a lot of time together."

"Does it take time?"

"Seems not. But even when I'm old as Miss Stricker, I still won't have got to the deeps of you."

Cecilia leaned against the house, her hands behind her. "Do you want to?"

"More each time you come. You've taken a hold on my mind. It ain't like no friendship I've known. Lor and his friend Davie, who came up when his folks still lived here, they just fooled around like big old puppies."

Sounds like heaven. "When you get into the world and meet more people—"

"I'm in the world right now. The Settlement folks call us remnants of the past like we're something different, something apart, but we ain't. We just live higher up. We buy store-bought clothes and cars and radios when we can pay for them. Not having no money nor opportunity don't mean we ain't as much in the world as anyone else. We live by old ways 'cause we got to."

"There are some things you don't know about."

"Lots more than some." Airey turned, and Cecilia heard her catch a breath. "You look like one of those statues."

"Caryatids?" Cecilia asked, feeling as if she were holding up the house.

"I ain't knowing what those are. I mean when movie actresses pose in magazines as Liberty, Truth, and Beauty. The light's on you like that. What's the thing you didn't want to tell me?"

Cecilia did not pretend to misunderstand. "I shouldn't have spoken to you so wildly."

"You said you was their kind. That things have consequences. They do. I spoke hard words to you and meant them. You never answered me."

"They brought me face-to-face with something."

"Something that made you run. Appears it's still got you in its jaws, even here with you rejoicing for me."

If she could see that, she saw too much for safety. "I—" Cecilia stopped. "I have...a weakness. It often makes me foolish or cruel."

"Is it a sickness?"

"Some people call it that. I don't, but I'm sorry—not often enough—for the things I do in its name."

"Was it making you do some things you did up here?"

Cecilia looked at the light touching Airey's lips,

looked down. "I can't tell you."

"We ain't just friends for the easy road. I'll take the hard road, too."

"You don't need to know this."

"Tell me. I need to know as much about you as I can get." Airey took a step toward her and stopped as if against a wall, saying half-incredulously, "You ain't going to. You're going to match me in stubborn."

Cecilia crushed her hands to pain to stop the catastrophic urge to give in, to tell her. "I—it's not right or kind—"

"It ain't right at all. I'm full of exaltedness, and I can't even help you."

"The best help you can give is to let me finish my swap."

"You done every last thing you promised. What's left?"

Let me go. "Give me a little time."

"You already took that. I didn't like it."

"I need to…understand my best course."

"Hurry on that. And I claim a right to be told, once you do."

Cecilia was silent. Airey shifted and said, "I ain't going to vex you. You tell me if you ever want to." She nodded toward the kitchen. "There's washing water warm in the stove and a towel laid for you. Privy's across the yard. When you come back, go through the side door and turn left for Mam's bedroom. I ain't got a spare nightshift, but you can have a clean shirt of Mr. Grigg's."

"I don't need a nightgown." *I need armor.* "I'll be fine. Good night." Cecilia fled inside, quickly scrubbed her face, did her teeth with the toothbrush kit in her purse, tucked away since Ethel, and was in

Mrs. Grigg's room, shutting the door as if tigers were about to crash against the other side. She stood in the darkness to assess her situation. Could it be worse? *How?* No permission to stay out. No word sent to Grandfather or Trenton. Worst by far: being here. *Do I have a backbone at all*?

She groped her way to Mrs. Grigg's bed. Its mattress was filled with husks and slung on ropes that creaked as she got in. She lay still, clamping her arms across her ribs to control her breathing, to sound asleep, in case Airey should pause outside her door.

A minute later, Airey's step came past, hesitated, moved on. The creak of another roped bed. Airey was close. *So close.* Airey answered a sleepy query from Poly. She could have been murmuring in Cecilia's ear. *I'm naked, and she's four feet away.* Another creak and the house was still. Cecilia grimaced in the darkness. *If this doesn't prove the Howison mettle, nothing can.* She lay for a long time wishing she had not put it to the test.

Chapter Six

Cecilia woke in a confused tangle, wondering why she was wearing nothing and ached in so many places. In a strange bed. She was—she was in Airey's house. It was not safe to be in a bed in Airey's house. What madness had seized her? How fast could she get away?

She glanced at the small, high window. Late. Voices from the main room of the house. They were all up. She saw with horror a basin and a pitcher of hot water on the side table. Who had brought them? She knew. Airey had. She was glad the cool night had kept her snuggled under the quilt. *And that I'm not a light sleeper*. She washed, looking at a small sideways photograph of her father and sister in the wallpaper, put on yesterday's clothes with a little shudder, tidied her hair with her pocket comb, and went to join the family.

"We saved you some Johnny cake," Poly said when she saw her. "What Airey *calls* Johnny cake."

"Where is she?"

"Out back fetching water," said Lorimer, sharpening the blade of a hoe by the kitchen door.

"You want some berries?" Poly lifted a heaped bowl. "Airey woke up early and picked them specially for you."

"There's enough for everyone," said Cecilia.

Airey, in shirt and overalls, arrived with buckets

for the water barrel. She smiled at Cecilia, and Cecilia gripped the edge of the table. "Morning, Miss Howison. Hope you slept comfortable. Polynegry, I told you not to touch those berries—"

"She said to share," said Poly, and to Cecilia, "You're always doing nice things. Bringing candy and them yesterday to hear Airey. I bet folks always oblige you."

"Because I'm willing to ask."

"It's like you're a queen. I'd like to be one and do nice things."

"Queens have to be as good as they are beautiful."

"I'm not very beautiful. Can I be half good?"

"No, you have to be good through and through."

"I'd rather be bad than good. Good's hard."

"Sometimes being good is hardest of all," said Cecilia with feeling.

Poly considered this. "You're real pretty. Is that 'cause you're good or the other way round?"

"In my case, looks are deceiving."

"Polynegry, don't you listen to her," said Airey. To Cecilia, "I'll make you breakfast."

"There's no need. I'll buy a doughnut on the road."

"Even Airey's Johnny cake is better than a old doughnut," said Poly.

"Thank you, Miss P. Fitch," said Airey. "At least I don't feed folks bugs."

"He et it himself!" Poly looked mutinously at Jabez. "I got to take him again today, don't I?"

"Just this morning, so I can feed Miss Howison and make biscuits for dinner and practice." Airey popped a berry in Jabez's mouth. "I'll set some biscuits by in case I kill me and Miss Howison with breakfast."

"Don't let her make bread," Poly warned Cecilia as she carried Jabez away.

Lorimer said, "See you again soon, Miss Howison," and left.

Cecilia was abruptly aware of being too alone with Airey too aware of last night's conversation. "I must go," she said quickly. "I don't want to delay your practicing. You have a virtuosity to polish."

Airey frowned reproachfully. "No Fitch sees off a guest without feeding them. I don't want you to go."

"I can't—"

"You got to eat. Stay today. You can leave later and still get home before supper."

Don't even contemplate it. "I'm afraid it wouldn't be wise to stay, Miss Fitch. Oh," she felt a stab of longing, "may I call you Airey?" To have the word on her lips, if only once.

"I'd like that, Cecil-i-y. Cec'ly. Why ain't it wise for you to stay?"

"Because-because I can't just stay and stay."

"Why not? Your folks'll come fetch you when they want you."

Cecilia thought of Daddy arriving like his own *posse comitatus*. "They expect me not to worry them."

"There ain't nothing for them to worry over, you staying at a friend's."

"I-I could stay until midday." *I can resist her for that long.*

"I was happy last night, thinking about you being on the other side of the wall from me."

"I was thinking the same thing." *Though we weren't feeling the same thing.*

"I wish you lived closer." Airey set a frying pan on a burner. "I wish you was just a step away, so I could see you any time I needed to."

I can never come back. "But you'll be leaving at some point to become a soloist."

Airey laid slices of bacon in the pan. "I'll make sure to swing by pretty regular to play with your Charleville orchestry. I'll call you on a telephone, and you'll come to hear me play."

Cecilia laughed. "You *are* a lord of the manor, aren't you? A prince of high command."

"That means you will." Airey gave the bacon a hopeful push.

"Of course I would. And it's why you're a great—a master. You know what you want, and you expect to get it."

"I will now." Airey laid cutlery for her. "What will Dr. Neihoff be planning for me?"

"He'll already be thinking about which tutor or college place you should have and how to fund it. If he can't find any money, or not quickly enough, you mustn't worry, as I've been given a promise of support for you."

Airey went to the cookstove. "I ain't discouraging nobody's help, not now I'm driving my own plow." She brought over sorghum syrup and the pan of Johnny cake, saying apologetically, "Keeping it warm don't make it no lighter." She fetched two cups of coffee. "While he's thinking, I got time to get our lease settled. I expect you've done some reckoning on that."

"I have," said Cecilia.

Airey grinned, started to answer—and leapt, dismayed, to the cook stove. "It always gets out from under me." She rattled the bacon onto a plate. "You can cut off the edges."

Cecilia laughed. "Housewifery is safer with you

as a violinist."

"I ain't never pretended to be level with Mam," Airey said loftily. "How long before Dr. Neihoff will write?"

"He'll need to speak to the Kehr Institute in Montreal first, and he's on his way there now."

Airey took the bacon away from Cecilia's struggles. "You don't got to eat that."

"It's delicious."

"You tell some whoppers for someone as good as she is beautiful." Airey tidied the kitchen while Cecilia ate johnny cake softened in coffee. "We could go to the lookout and pick some greens on the way back, or we could play a record and you can teach me about it and afterward I'll give you a little show—"

"Records and show," said Cecilia. *I'll bow out to music.*

Airey carried the Grafonola to the table. "Let's play all three parts of that Tchaikovsky I played yesterday. You tell me what I'm hearing."

"I'll teach you the placement of the orchestra, as well." Cecilia stood to keep her distance. "I'm the conductor, who marks time for everyone. The first violins are here, second violins there." She pointed to the places of the other strings, woodwinds, brass, and percussion, finishing, "The conductor stands on a box, called a podium, to be seen by them all."

"Where do I sit?"

"You stand at the conductor's left, in front of the orchestra. You'll already have rehearsed the work—you'll have practiced together—so everyone knows what to do. Put on the first record, and I'll show who's playing."

Airey wound the phonograph and set the needle.

Cecilia took her through it, beating time with one hand while indicating the different players with the other—"flute, and there's the brass giving it a touch of valor. Now the strings come in as if to overpower the soloist, but he's the king, he answers, and they must fall silent before his transcendence—and now I bring in the woodwinds—" realizing again how much fun conductors must have. She was swept into the mighty triumph of the last movement and brought her hands down sharply on its final chord. "That ends it. No more to be said."

"When it's good, you don't need more." Airey put away the last record and offered another album.

"No. Play for me."

Airey was unexpectedly hesitant. "Now I've been called a virtuosy, you'll be expecting something mighty fine."

"Don't you think I always expected something fine?"

Airey smiled at her, a strange, unknowing smile, and went to her violin, saying nothing as she sanded her hands, prepared her bow, tuned her strings. She lifted her violin to her collarbone and looked down its length. The first time she's played since she's known, thought Cecilia, and corrected herself: the first time since the world's known. Airey's bow came up. Bach: a sonata Cecilia did not name until Airey began the long *Ciaconna.*

Cecilia watched her, able for these minutes, while Airey was in her own world, to fill her eyes with her for a final time. The music took her to a place where only the profound existed, where only Airey existed. She drank in Airey's fingers on the strings, the grace of her line, the radiance of her tone, the breathtaking tense power of her body. She did not know how completely she had entered her own world of Airey until silence broke in.

They looked at each other. Cecilia's heart crowded into her throat. She tried to control her breathing, to let nothing show. Airey said, "Don't tell me you was thinking of that transcendence."

Cecilia thrust herself to her feet, a voice screaming *run*, was at the kitchen door before she could rein in her terror, pressing her arms over her ribs. "I was—I-I shouldn't look at you like that." She stared across the yard. "You don't know how beautiful you are."

She heard Airey put down her violin, walk to her, felt her stand so closely behind her that her overalls brushed her skirt. Terror was overswept with longing, a vibrating string that shook her, liquefied her. *Run! Run and never come back.*

Airey put a quiet hand on her shoulder. Cecilia shuddered and leaned back helplessly. Airey's arms circled her, hands closing below hers. She could feel Airey's palm on her stomach, the hard thinness of her fingers. She tipped her head back against Airey's shoulder. This felt right. It was right. She covered Airey's hands with hers, holding her embrace. She felt Airey's lips against her hair.

The sound of the Grafonola's spring clicking off made Airey stiffen. "This is what you weren't going to tell me." She was out the door, running as fast as Cecilia had wanted to run, across the yard and into the woods.

Cecilia stood with her hands still folded at her waist. She had no idea what to do. Her mind was a flashing blankness that rushed through her like noise from a flock of birds. She was in its whirlwind.

She followed in Airey's wake across the yard, through the old stone wall, along the creek path into the cool of the trees. Every scent, every rustle of leaves, every fluting call of a bird, the hum of insects, the lap of the creek, her feet on the earth, was a separate and clear sensation, as if she could only see, hear, smell, as if she were nothing but the physical world.

Airey was by the creek, one shoulder hard against a buckeye, as if she had run full tilt against it. At Cecilia's footsteps, she straightened and turned, gripping the tree trunk behind her. Cecilia could see every muscle taut for flight, but Airey stood her ground, looking as wild as a cornered wolf. Cecilia held her gaze as she closed the distance, put her hands on her shoulders, rose on her toes, and kissed her.

For a heartbeat, two heartbeats, Airey's mouth was shocked, ignorant. In the next, she seemed to shimmer, and her lips moved on Cecilia's. Cecilia had never tasted such sweetness. She brushed Airey's upper lip with a feather edge of her own, and Airey leapt inside her own skin. Every nerve in Cecilia's body answered, but she stayed softly against her, kisses gentle. Airey was kissing her, Airey's arms were coming around her. Nothing else mattered.

Over a long time, the voice of the creek returned, the singing of insects, the birds. Cecilia linked her hands behind Airey's head and leaned back in her embrace. Airey's eyes were astonished, her mouth half-smiling, half-alarmed. "What's this?"

"*This* is what I wouldn't tell you. Couldn't tell you. I wanted to kiss you the first moment I saw you. I've wanted to kiss you every minute since."

"I ain't felt such a thing as this." Airey lowered

her head, and they kissed again. Sweet, endlessly sweet. Cecilia's mind soared in it. They broke off, searched each other's faces, kissed. Airey finally pulled away with an unsteady breath. "Back at the house, back last night on the porch, when I saw you in the light, I felt—I just wanted...and before that, when I looked at you or thought about you and I'd feel, but I didn't know—"

Cecilia kissed her, felt every muscle in Airey's body tense and pressed harder against her, kissing her hungrily, losing control, wanting her, wanting her now, until again Airey pulled back.

"Airey!" Cecilia choked and governed herself.

"What's this?" Airey asked more slowly.

"You know what it is."

"Is it—fornication?"

"Does it feel like it is?"

"I don't know. I'm—"

"What does it feel like?"

"Like-like pitchwood—fiery, all sparks."

Cecilia kissed her lightly, kissed under her jaw, along her throat, kissed the sheltered skin just inside her collar, Airey giving a small jump, a small snorting breath, with each kiss, telling Cecilia they were burning through her. Cecilia was stopped by her overalls, reached for the clasps, and Airey retreated against the buckeye. "This...it's strange. It's—"

"It's wondrous strange." Cecilia held on to the straps.

"It means—" Airey looked at her, at her lips, and Cecilia saw a change in her eyes. "It means something I didn't know could be or that God built in us."

"I want you to be sure."

Airey touched Cecilia's mouth with a delicate

fingertip. Cecilia did not hide her reaction. Airey's eyes darkened. "I'm sure as I can be of what I don't know nothing about."

"I'll show you."

"How do you know?"

Cecilia tightened, angry with herself. Airey's breath caught. She answered for her. "'Cause you done this before. With a—girl."

"That's why I know." Cecilia felt Airey's arms fall away from her. "That's why I knew, the first time I saw you."

Airey twisted out of her grasp. Cecilia thought she would escape across the creek, but she stopped and braced herself on the fallen sycamore. Cecilia forced herself to stay silent, not to explain, to explain away. Airey looked down at the water sparkling by her feet. She asked without turning her head, "This—it's your weakness, ain't it? This—"

"Women."

Airey flinched.

"Women," said Cecilia. "It's what's in me. It's what calls me."

Airey's hands rasped the bark. "I—it's new in my head. All I feel is for you."

"That's how I feel. For you."

"But I ain't the—it's like I'm down in a hollow with the sun coming up over the ridge saying for lo the winter is past, but you're high on the mountain where it's been up for a long while and this don't-don't mean, for you, it ain't—I'm just-just another, I'm just..."

"Do you believe you're just another girl, Airey?"

Airey lifted her arm to shield her face and doubled over the sycamore in pain. Cecilia stood defenselessly, every possible word she could say a weapon against herself. Airey finally pushed herself wearily upright, as if she had prayed for a burden to be lifted, and it had not been lifted. She said, "I got to get squared on this. I got to think."

"Why?"

Airey looked at her at last.

Cecilia said, "You can't think it through. You can't reason it away. You know what you feel. You might not like it, you might despise me," she ignored Airey's dismissive gesture, "but you haven't stopped wanting to kiss me."

"Nor never will, Jesus save my soul."

"It's in you. It won't leave."

Airey looked faintly terrified.

"Don't tell yourself you aren't going to touch me. You know you can't stop yourself. Be glad one of us knows what she's doing."

Airey pushed her fingers through her hair with a shaky laugh. "You're the most downright—"

"Come back to me."

Airey walked slowly from the creek, stopping when she was a breath away. Cecilia waited for her to understand that she would make no move. Airey leaned down and cautiously kissed her.

Cecilia kissed her back. Kept kissing her. Airey moved closer, making small sounds of wonder as she reacted to each new way to kiss, until they stood full length against each other. Airey's arms came round her. *Don't rush. Don't rush her.* Airey's strength slowly melted, she was leaning on her, lost in their kisses, until Cecilia had to say, "Airey, I can't hold you up."

Airey laughed breathlessly. "I can't...can't hardly stand up."

"We could…lie down."

Airey's brows snapped together.

"What do you want?" Cecilia asked.

"There ain't no going back from this."

"You don't know what this is yet."

"Yes, I do." Airey dropped to her knees in the deep pool of leaves beside the path and raised her hands for her. Cecilia was washed with a bodiless flame. She threw her weight on her, was caught, they tumbled onto the quilt of leaves, they were in each other's arms, they were kissing. Cecilia heard herself saying, "Airey, Airey," and saying it intoxicated her. At some point, her hand moved, she knew it was moving, although she felt no command over it, under the overalls' straps, under Airey's shirttail, fingertips brushing Airey's naked back. Airey exhaled sharply. Cecilia drifted her hand up, found that Airey wore nothing under her shirt, and stopped.

"I like your hand on me," said Airey.

Cecilia traced the muscles of her back, slid around to the promise of that first day, the curve of her breast, small, beautifully shaped, and Airey jolted as her hand moved to possess it. Cecilia was light-headed. "Airey," she managed. "I need your clothes off."

Airey's fingers went instantly to the clasps of her overalls. In one movement, Cecilia was on her knees, stripping off her own clothes, freeing Airey's from hers with practiced skill, brain smoking at the beauty of her body, and she flung herself on her as if into the sea.

Airey became completely still, her lungs filling with deep breaths. Cecilia rose on them like a bird on a wave. She boxed in Airey's head with her elbows and kissed her with flickering kisses. Airey began to shift, a shoulder, one hip, a leg, exploring Cecilia's weight on her. Cecilia laced her fingers through Airey's short hair and brought her back to kisses. The urge for more than these light touches flowed and ebbed, ebbed and built. At last, Cecilia could not resist trailing her lips to Airey's throat, to her breastbone, tasting the fine textures of her skin, tanned and pale. Pale as milk and sweet as honey. She put her lips to her breast. Airey gasped as if burned. Cecilia stayed, enjoying Airey's stuttering breath, her stuttering body, her sweet hard beauty, moving up again to her mouth. Airey wrapped her in a bear hug, kisses now rough with hunger, kissing her face, her throat, the hollow of her throat.

"Airey, if you keep doing that, I won't be fit for—no," she took Airey's hands as they began to slide down, "no, learn first" and pressed them into the leaves. She moved her lips to her breasts, to the quivering drumhead of her stomach, Airey yipping and trembling, moved lower, to her belly, to the dip where belly met hipbone, Airey soft with an animal resilience that went to Cecilia's head, nuzzled against her, kissed her, traced her with her tongue, moved lower still, exhaling lightly on her. Every muscle in Airey's body became steel cord. Cecilia ran a hand up to her ribs. "Do you know where you're going?"

"I-I reckon so."

Airey's thundering heart under Cecilia's palm told her she knew exactly. "I'll show you something better." She turned her head to kiss the hollow of each thigh, took those long thighs in her arms, breathed in her sweetness, looked up at her, looked down, her heart pounding with desire and joy, and put her mouth on her.

Airey yelped. Cecilia savored her, moving softly. One touch with her tongue made Airey almost jerk from her arms. Cecilia waited. Airey eased toward her, pulled back, forward again, breathing hard, to meet her. Cecilia went like a slow incoming tide from the mild and vague to the particular and definite, hearing Airey's rapid breaths deepen, hearing them start to tear from her, but they held no fear, her striving body held no fear, and Cecilia was overcome that such a woman had put herself in her hands. She submerged herself in her, wanting this to last forever, wanting this to be perfect. Airey's awareness lifted away from her, she shook like a rope at its limit, was for a second sharply rigid and, with an explosive grunt, completely limp.

Cecilia put a cheek against her. All the glories of a woman's body were here. All were here. She saw Airey's hands still dug into the leaves, as if she had been holding on to the earth. Cecilia brushed leaf crumble from her own forearms and breasts and slid up, resting one hand on Airey's hip, propping her head with the other, to look at her.

Calmly, remotely, Airey looked back. After a silence, she said, "My head's filled with dew."

"Airey. My beautiful one." Cecilia did not stir, although her need for Airey's touch ran like lava under her skin. They lay together without speaking. Cecilia was aware of the cool earth under her side, brushed away a woodlouse trying to scale Mount Airey, listened to the creek's singing, to the buckeyes' shuffling leaves, watched the pulse at the base of Airey's throat. Airey let out a long happy breath and lifted her hands to run them down her own body.

"You feel wonderful," said Cecilia.

Airey laughed. "I do. I could leap on mountains."

Cecilia smiled. *And you've read your Canticles.* "Let me see thy countenance."

Airey turned to face her. Cecilia smoothed back her hair. Airey's kisses were tender and slow. Her fingers touched Cecilia's side, and Cecilia gasped at their strangeness: like tips of claws. Airey turned and now the fingertips of both hands, hard and soft, were skating across her back, feathering and icing. Cecilia squirmed in delicious torment, laughter trapped in her throat, finally rescuing herself by pulling Airey on top of her. Airey said, "Thou fairest among women," kissed her face, her shoulders, her breasts, sliding away as if overwhelmed, down to her belly, back to her breasts as if unable to resist, and Cecilia moaned under her lips. After a moment, Airey seemed to fear she was indulging herself and should move on. Cecilia put a hand on her head. "Take your time, Miss Fitch."

Airey grinned, face sharp with desire. "You're an interesting surprise," and at Cecilia's startled look, "You don't remember? You said you wanted to be one, that very first time we met."

"I couldn't take my eyes off you. I would have said anything to keep you there."

"You called me something new."

"And did not lie."

"I'm more than that." Airey put her hands on Cecilia's breasts and buried her face between them, kissing them, kissing down her body, fingers gliding ahead of her kisses, exploring, learning her. Cecilia wriggled and squeaked under the electrical storms of Airey's touch. Airey's hand went lower, paused. "You're slick wet."

Cecilia's heart drew in a little; this was often

an unhappy moment. Airey raised her hand and put her fingers in her mouth, looking surprised and thoughtful.

"Airey—"

"That's you." Airey put clean, wet fingers on Cecilia's flanks and brushed her belly with her lips. "This is you. I like this." She spread one hand over Cecilia's breast. "I like all of this." Her fingers widened across Cecilia's body in slow swoops, over and down every hollow and curve, drawing burning lines. Her lips took up the pattern, slowly, thoroughly, brushing over her like a cobweb until Cecilia began to go up in flame, began to think that she would have to come at once or kill her. Airey was at her hips, at her thighs. Cecilia felt her hesitation and shifted her legs to welcome her. Airey dipped her head; Cecilia closed her eyes, fire spearing through her at the first touch of her mouth.

Airey was unsure, seeking, although she was alert and beginning to find her way. Cecilia neither hoped nor expected to go anywhere today—even the strongest flame could not survive the damp of a first attempt, and hers was failing fast—intent now only on making Airey happy, on making her confident, rewarding each success with a warm "hmm," everything else with a polite "um," until Airey began to giggle.

She stifled exasperation. "What?"

"You sound like Merit teaching Jaby how to eat from a spoon."

"Did he?"

"He was that hungry, he'd have taught himself." Airey altered her position and began again more certainly. Flame rose through Cecilia as if it had never faded, rose and expanded, her gasps and hope more pointed, more urgent, and with a shock of delight her body became saturated with heat. She was dashing toward her threshold, bubbling with laughter—*so easy*—and now she was in that tip of flame, let herself be wafted up, and she came like the snap of silk in a whirlwind.

She floated down, opened her eyes, and saw Airey hovering uncertainly on all fours. She reached out her hand.

Airey's answering smile was a little shy, a little drunk on power. "Seems I can please you."

"*Please* me. Yes. Yes, you can. You do. You're—you amaze me. You amaze me, Airey Fitch." She folded her into her arms. Of course Airey would be different. Of course she would be.

"I didn't know nothing could be like this," Airey said, muffled against her skin. "I did know nothing could be like you. Jaby's skin is soft, but yours is soft in a way that busts me into bits. Looking at you puts a knot inside me. I felt it time and again and didn't know I was aching for you."

Cecilia kissed the fine hair at her temple. "*Thy lips drop as the honeycomb*. I ache, I burn for you. I want to do that to you again."

Airey's breath was faster in an instant. "I'd like you to."

Cecilia moved her hands. Airey's body turned for them, and Cecilia's desire leapt at once, untamed, unslaked. She had her on her back, kissed her, put her mouth on her breasts, on the long female strength of her belly. Airey's panting roughened.

Another panting, not Airey. Cecilia jerked away to look up at Royal's grinning face.

Airey saw him at the same moment and started to laugh. "Go home, Roy," and, more loudly, "Lorimer?"

"I've been hunting for you," his voice answered from farther down the path.

"Don't come no closer. I'm raw as a jaybird by the creek."

"Sorry! Pastor Souch has come calling."

Airey's face was a study of laughter and dismay. "I—oh, jiminy—I'll be back to the house soon as I've washed. You gave him coffee?"

"I'll give him more." Lorimer whistled Royal home.

Cecilia sat back on her heels, trying to appreciate Airey's giggles.

"The pastor surely picked his time," said Airey. "We got to get dressed."

Cecilia looked down at her clothes, crushed into the bed of leaves, looked at Airey, risen on one arm, and wanted to tear down the forest like a thwarted god. She rose, walked deliberately to the creek, stepped in with set teeth and sat abruptly, expecting to hear the quench of red-hot metal.

"Does that help?" asked Airey from the bank.

"Your being less jaybird raw would help more."

Airey waded into the water a few paces down and squatted to scoop water on her face and back. "You're looking like you could murder the pastor, and you look beautiful. I've never seen a mortal thing so beautiful."

"How long is he going to be here?"

Airey glanced at the sun in the trees. "If he thought Mam was back and aimed for dinner, he's going off hungry 'cause I ain't made biscuit or nothing."

"I'll stay out here until he's gone. Lorimer thinks you were bathing—"

"I am."

"—but I can't be bathing, too."

"Why not?"

"Airey! Think. You can't say a word about this to anybody."

"Not to Lorimer. This is for grownups." Airey's voice held a diffident swagger. "He'll think we both had a wash."

"*He* will: he's a child. Mr. Souch is a different matter."

"Ain't none of his business."

"It's nobody's business. Only ours."

"A secret?" Airey frowned, straightened, and waded to her. Cecilia took her hand and was lifted to her feet.

"Yes, it has to be. We're in paradise, jaybird naked and unashamed, but look around you."

"You're saying we ain't Adam and Eve."

"On the evidence."

"This ain't a sin."

"I know."

"Because I'm acquainted with sin. I'm a sinner redeemed. This ain't it."

"Who else would agree?" Cecilia did not want to brutalize the moment, but it had already changed. "*For this cause God gave them up unto vile affections: for even the women did change the natural use into that which is against nature.*"

Airey recoiled. "That's…that ain't this. I never knew what that meant. It don't get preached much."

"Preachers don't want to put ideas into people's heads."

"People? Men too? What the apostle says right after, about lust and *working that which is unseemly*, it's men?"

"That's none of *our* business," said Cecilia. "But Saint Paul's talking about us, Airey Fitch. Us."

Airey stood dripping in the sunlight. "That ain't this," she said finally. "I know what this is. Whatever those ladies was doing back then I can't say, but I know as I know my Lord Jesus everlasting that I ain't got no vile affections for you. There's nothing vile about it. It's all gladness and joy."

Cecilia took her hands. "O wise young virgin. Which is what you are. We are, and God knows us, but Saint Paul's condemned us in the eyes of the world."

She watched Airey understand it, relieved that she did, sorry she did, sorry to have lodged this hard thing in her heart, but Airey's eyes became imperious.

"I've been called heaps of things. Acorn-cracker. Hill hoojy. Brush ape. No-account. Ignorant. Gravy-sucker. Trash. Poor white. But us up here, we work hard and help our neighbors and fear God. We don't hit back at those who smite us. This new thing's just the same: folks scorning and condemning us from their own darkness, while we stand tall in God's light of truth."

Cecilia raised her hands and kissed them.

Airey said, "Kiss me on my mouth." After a long moment, unwillingly, "We'd best get back." She helped her from the water and shook out Cecilia's clothes, going over every inch to pick off flakes of leaf. Cecilia leaned back against the fallen sycamore, warm in the sun. At this stage in the proceedings, she usually felt both luscious and a little flat. She did not feel like that now. The sycamore's bark was rough under her hands and buttocks. The birds sang as if no day could be brighter. She thought, surprised, I feel serene.

Airey turned and stopped, looking at her. She held out Cecilia's clothes. Cecilia stepped into them. Her dress had survived better than she expected.

"Wait," she said before Airey stooped for her own clothes, putting her arms around her naked body. "Kiss me."

Only minutes had passed since the last kiss, yet it shot through her like a fuse. She managed to pull away before banked fires reignited. "When will I see you again?"

Airey looked slapped. "You ain't going?"

"I was planning to leave at midday. Mr. Souch's arrival tells me it's time."

"You can't." Airey paused, confounded. "I've got a thing to consider. I ain't waiting a day or two days or a week till you come back. I won't live through it."

"I can't stay. One night might be explained, not two."

"You got to stay."

"I can't." Cecilia considered. "Unless you invite me."

"I just did."

"If I tell Grandfather I've had an invitation, he wouldn't permit me to offend a well-respected mountain family, especially one we've had dealings with."

"We'd be offended."

"Then let me lose my mind and pretend that I'll get away with this. If you'd had your clothes on, I'd never have had such a deranged thought."

Airey grabbed her overalls and held them over

the creek. "They're going."

"I'll stay, I'll stay. Today. Tonight." *I am certifiably insane.* "I'll drive down to," no, if she telephoned, she would only be told to come home, "I'll send a telegram."

"You won't slip away from me?"

Cecilia looked at her seriously. "I'll never run away again. I'll never leave you wondering where I am or when I'll return."

"Thank you. It was hard after Mam had gone and you'd gone and me hoping and needing to see you every day and you never showed."

"I longed to see you." She could not explain, not with Mr. Souch waiting. "I invented so many reasons for my visits, and I had to space them out."

"You tell your folks whoppers?"

"I try hard not to."

Airey frowned at her fistful of clothes. "This ain't so joyful in a couple of places."

"It's like cradling a candle through a storm. Sometimes you have no choice but to burn your hands."

"Doing wrong shouldn't be put to the same yoke with doing right."

"No, but it is."

"I ain't easy on it."

"Neither am I, but I keep making my peace with it."

"If you can, I reckon I can, too." Airey found Cecilia's shoes and knelt to help her into them. Cecilia looked down at her bent head. *And who will glove my hand?* "I didn't want to leave yesterday. I didn't want to leave this morning. I don't want to leave now." Airey looked up at her with an expression Cecilia had never seen before. "I do want us to meet Mr. Souch dressed."

Airey reached for her shirt. "You tore off a button."

"I'm surprised I didn't rip it to shreds."

Airey got to her feet and into her clothes. "I want to keep kissing you, but if I do, we'll never make it home."

"How could I object?"

Airey's laugh was less than resolute. "Don't tempt me. I'm lady of the house while Mam's gone."

They walked back, had passed the old stone wall before Cecilia realized that she was holding her hand. It had been as natural as breathing. *A dangerous breach of habit.* She let go with a pang. Airey looked down, displeased. A moment later, Poly shouted from the yard, "What took you so long?"

"You gave him coffee?" asked Airey.

"He can't stand another drop. You said you'd make biscuit for dinner."

"I-I got to other things."

Cecilia stopped at the corner of the house. "You go in first." She turned to face the view she had faced this morning the moment before Airey had touched her and packed the last hours into her mind's vault, untouchable, unreachable. She slipped through the side door into the back rooms and stood in the darkness until her eyes accustomed themselves. This was Airey's, Poly's, and Merit's room: three beds in a row, one old clothes press, one small speckled mirror on the wall. Airey had been less than a yard away last night. Cecilia went into her room and brought her hair to order, telling her reflection, *I meant to resist her.* She looked at her kiss-swollen lips. *There isn't enough armor in the world.*

She came into the main room by way of the yard and kitchen door. Mr. Souch rose briefly. "I noted your car, Miss Howison. A pleasure to see you again. You're a regular visitor now."

"I like to think so." Cecilia leaned down to take Royal's greeting. "I can't get away to the mountains too often."

"It's pretty hot in the valleys," he agreed.

"And so enchanting here."

Airey said from the kitchen, "I've been asking the pastor's pardon that we ain't got dinner cooked."

"I didn't come for a meal, Airey," said Mr. Souch. "I know your mother's still away and wanted to see how you were doing."

"What are we going to eat?" Poly asked.

Airey looked blankly around the kitchen. Cecilia knew she could not make herself think. "Now, Miss Fitch," she said gaily, aware of Mr. Souch's gaze, "I see a basket of tomatoes, and I know we have flour and eggs. I don't claim to be a cook, but my great-aunt once told me that no girl should be without the art of the chafing dish, and I didn't escape."

Airey watched her with a small smile. "We ain't got a chafing dish."

"You have frying pans—skillets. And cheese?"

"Heaps of it," said Poly. "We got to use up the spare milk with Mam and Merit gone."

"If you'll mix up a slightly runny pancake batter," Cecilia said to Airey, "I'll see about lunch."

She lifted her arms to let Airey put an apron around her. Airey stood too close as she tied it at the back, her touch like a brand through Cecilia's clothing.

"I wouldn't have thought Colonel Howison's

daughter ever saw the inside of a kitchen," Mr. Souch jested.

"I don't," said Cecilia, "but I dislike being totally helpless."

"Except when a man's in the vicinity," he said.

"Oh, we're never allowed to be helpless domestically." Cecilia looked around as he chuckled. "Where can I find a wooden spoon?"

Airey handed her one, and their fingers met; Cecilia suppressed the memory of what those fingers could do and saw Airey not trying to. Airey reached for something she didn't need, to press against her. Cecilia gave her a quelling look. "Could you get me onions? And bitter greens, if you have them?" *Could you give me a minute to collect myself, you with your fox's grin?*

She chopped and stirred, hoping she remembered the right amounts in the right order, checked anxiously as she melted bacon fat on the cookstove, tore the youngest of the hardy dandelion leaves Airey brought and began cooking and stacking crêpes, appalled at how easily they burned, consigning half a dozen to the chicken pail until she got used to the heat. Her respect for Great Aunt Ruth rocketed.

"That smells good," said Mr. Souch from the table, where he was taking Lorimer through the issues of *Modern Mechanix* he had brought for him.

"*Crêpes avec fromage à la madrilène*, with mixed salad," said Cecilia. "More or less."

"We're dining at the Ritz," said Mr. Souch, and gave the blessing.

Cecilia saw Lorimer pushing a fork dubiously around his plate. "Don't eat it if you don't like it."

They all looked at her as if she had blasphemed.

"What the gracious Lord sends, we receive," said Mr. Souch. "Airey, you've had word yet from your mother?"

"Not since her card saying she'd decided to stay on a spell to help Merit settle in."

"Merit's husband will want to send his mother-in-law home at some point," said Mr. Souch.

"I reckon he will," said Airey with an edge of knowingness that made Cecilia look at her, worried that she was too obviously the citizen of a new country. A minute later, she realized that she was still looking at her, for the pleasure of looking.

"Cardwell's easy-going. He'll want to please his new wife," said Mr. Souch. "Now, Airey, I don't think it's *my* company that's lit you like a paper lantern."

"We're always pleased to see you, Pastor."

"You're not witnessing to the whole truth." He smiled. "I know it's your friend here." Cecilia summoned her blandest expression as he turned to her. "Miss Howison, I've been hearing about your kindness to the family. I'm glad you're teaching these young ones that the children of Mammon hear the same call to loving service as God's own poor."

"You give me undeserved praise," said Cecilia, not daring to look in Airey's direction.

"Poly-girl also tells me that you brought a music teacher to visit." His tone was less warm.

"I thought her talent required expert attention."

"Your impulse was a generous one," said Mr. Souch, "though it's not my belief that girls should play the fiddle or anything else. Not that I'm condemning you, Miss Howison."

"Airey plays at *weddings*," said Poly.

"No, she doesn't," he replied, firmly affable.

"There's no music at weddings. A wedding is God's holy union of soul to soul in the presence of public witness. The music comes after, when the dancing and drinking commence." He cut into his second misshapen crêpe. "Airey, you know my views. You're close on twenty, and no young man is courting you. You're at the age where you say *if I grow old*, but I don't want to think of you at twenty-five or thirty and still toiling for your brother."

"I won't be toiling here much longer," said Airey. "That doctor fiddler Miss Howison brung up is looking for something down yonder that'll lead to paying work."

Mr. Souch's fork and assurance paused. He looked at Lorimer. "If so, the fate of the farm's decided. You won't be able to carry on, not even with the help of neighbors."

"I'm ready to—" Lorimer began.

"Nothing's decided." Airey's tone was like the scrape of a sword from a scabbard. Mr. Souch's attention remained on Lorimer. "Son, I'd hold off building that big waterwheel."

"I'd like to see if it'll work."

"I'm sure it will. There's nothing wrong with your engineering. It's your science that falls into error."

"Lorimer don't talk about that," said Airey to the pastor.

"He doesn't talk of it with me because he knows, deep in his soul, that it's the devil's work."

"No, sir." Lorimer, flushed, his chin coming up. "I don't seek to cross you, but I know that little piece of phyllite I found last week is millions of years old. It's proved."

"There's no proof, only sinners leading other sinners into traps for the unguided mind."

"You believe in the exact truth of the Scriptures," said Cecilia, red cape to the bull.

"I do," he said, his tone telling her that he knew what she was doing. "I've never understood how you can pick and choose to please yourself among God's Word. Some people excuse their sins with *wisdom is better than rubies*, forgetting that our Savior told us not to seek to be learned."

"Yet the Apostle says, *I would have you wise unto that which is good*."

He nodded. "He does. Some creeds calling themselves Christian believe that bread turns into God."

Am I so obviously Episcopalian? "Some creeds, not far from here, believe their faith delivers weekly Pentecosts." She wondered why she had ever thought the Fitch children—Lorimer Fitch—could live with him.

"If we counted every kind of foolheadedness in the world," he said calmly, "we'd never come to the end of it. It's for each of us to work out our salvation in fear and trembling."

"In the light God gives us," said Airey.

"Who can be sure what he believes is His light isn't the temptation of the devil?"

It's you who heard a call. "I've been taught that you can tell true faith by its fruits."

"You're a fair way to being right, Miss Howison. Real faith has no truck with sin."

"Miss Fitch was saying much the same to me earlier."

"She's been washed in the Blood of the Lamb, when she remembers."

Lorimer slid out of his seat. “Thanks for the fancy meal, Miss Howison. Sorry I got to get going, Pastor. I’m moving the mules.” He clicked his tongue to Royal and escaped.

“That young man troubles me,” said Mr. Souch. “He’s good timber grown from good stock, but he’s running toward hellfire with his evolution and the earth unfolding contrary to sense and the Bible.”

“Lor latched onto science about the same age as me to the fiddle,” said Airey.

He laughed. “You’re spoiling for another fight, young lady. We’ll have it a hundred times because I’m holding to the promise, and I won’t let you go, but not today with Miss Howison here. I come each time with you all in my heart, and I’m sorry I haven’t yet found a way to be peaceable with you. Only Jabez here and I get along.” He stood. “Thank you, Miss Howison, for your hospitality.” Reaching into a pocket, “Polygirl, I nearly forgot the Bible cards Sister Furniss promised you. Airey, if you hear from your mother before I do, tell her I’ll pick her up from any train or bus she takes.”

“I will.” Airey went with him to the porch.

Poly leaned to Cecilia and said, “Lorimer’s never going to give in. That means he’s going to the bad place.”

“Why?”

“That’s what happens when you believe things that ain’t in the Bible.”

“People believe things in the Bible that aren’t there.”

“What?” asked Poly.

“For one, that God wants us to be miserable and afraid.”

Airey came in briskly. "The pastor can't help making even goodbye into a sermon. Polynegry, I got to turn the hay I didn't do yesterday, and I ain't practiced yet. You'll have to bug-pick the tobacco by yourself."

Poly groaned. "That means I got to take Jaby *again*. I had him all yesterday and all this morning! Reckon you'll owe me a whole month of Jaby days by the time Mam gets home."

"You ain't wrong," said Airey guiltily, and to Cecilia, "I got to wash the dishes, as well. You don't mind waiting?"

"For you? I haven't yet."

Airey grinned. "You could go down and telegraph while I'm doing chores."

Cecilia smiled back. "What a good idea. Why don't I?"

"In a minute." Airey turned to the dishes. As soon as Poly and Jabez had gone, Cecilia was where she expected to be: whisked to her feet, locked in Airey's arms, and kissed as fiercely as she had hoped any woman would. Airey said, "I-I'll be faster than a rabbit with a fox on its tail."

Cecilia stared at her.

"Practicing," said Airey to her disbelief.

"Are you seriously saying—"

"I got to, before we do a minute more of this 'cause otherwise I won't get it done."

Cecilia nearly squalled with frustration. "Are you made of stone?"

"A mountain of rock would melt close by you." Airey smiled painfully. "That's why I got to practice first off, before—" Her hold tightened. "Maybe-maybe I could later."

"No." Cecilia pushed her to arm's length. *This is why you're a virtuosa. You fiend.* "I said I can wait, and I can. Somehow. Do your practicing now."

"I—Cec'ly, I can't be this far away from you." Airey leaned against her restraining palm.

"You can and you will."

"You're stronger than me."

"When I'm with you," Cecilia felt Airey's heartbeat under her hand and nearly surrendered, "when I'm with you, I want to be my better self. Why don't I try now?" She went to her car, regretting this new fortitude with every step.

Mr. Keller was behind his counter. "Telegram? My, we're burning up the wires here." He called to the man eating peanuts on the porch, "Lucius, don't you get too settled," and took out a pencil and form book.

"To Thomas Howison Senior, Old Waring," Cecilia dictated. "The message is: Grandfather. Am still with Fitches. Invited to stay further day. Prefer not to refuse. Helping while their mother awaited from Georgia. Trust your blessing given." *Let's hope this is enough to save my skin.* "Love Cecilia."

He totted up the words. "Anything else, Miss Howison?"

Cecilia glanced around the store, knowing Mother's views on supporting local businesses in these difficult times. "Yes, I'll take a box of matches and, ah, a tin of soda crackers."

He brought them to her car. "It's kind of you to stay. The Fitches are pretty lonesome. Ain't many folks left round here."

"You are, sir."

"But I got a United States mail carrier coming by regular and him a three-ring circus." His gaze swept the empty crossroads.

Cecilia drove back in dappled sunlight. Airey's violin was singing through the trees. As she neared the house, she saw Airey on the porch facing a piece of music tied to one of the posts. Her bow lifted and hung in the air as she walked up.

"When will you be finished?" Cecilia stayed beyond reach.

"My scales are done. I'm teaching myself this Brahms tune Dr. Neihoff gave me."

Cecilia dared not pass her, taking her purchases in through the kitchen door. She moved a chair to a window for a covert view. Airey was entirely focused on her music, her bow up as she read, down to play. Stopping. Starting again, through an hour. Cecilia followed the quick, quiet control of those hands—*this is not helping my willpower*—until Brahms began again without pause, notes flying like skeins of gold.

The music ended. In the next instant, Airey was inside, violin under one arm, Cecilia in the other, swept into a kiss.

"We have the whole house to ourselves," said Cecilia, once she could.

"Polynegry or Lor is bound to come back unexpected. We'll go to the barn."

Once inside the big doors, the smell made Cecilia hang back, but Airey said, "Not this part," and took her through the stables, across a breezeway, where tools hung from pegs, into the back section.

It was brighter here, the shrunken wall planks letting in flat sweeps of light. A narrow central aisle ran between waist-high partitions, each big bin either empty, awaiting the harvest, or filled with corn. A heaped bunker of hay took up the entire back wall, filling the air with a slightly sour, flowery smell. Some of this must be the grass Airey had been mowing the day she had first heard her play.

Their kisses were hurried by what would come. They pulled away at the same moment, Airey shrugging out of her overalls, shirt, and drawers, finishing Cecilia's undressing for her, taking her in her arms and lifting her over the retaining wall into the hay. Cecilia lay, limp with desire, as Airey vaulted in. She wrapped herself around her.

"I was interrupted this morning. I claim my right."

"Time's gone by," Airey protested, capturing one leg between her own. Cecilia moved against her and showed her what a hand and thigh could do. Airey uncurled like a long piece of tin, her breath ragged. Cecilia bent to put her lips on her breasts. Airey reached up and came with a hard jut that Cecilia took against her whole body.

In the next moment, she was neatly turned onto her back, was gasping beneath those unearthly fingertips. Airey sketched sparks across her breasts, along her flanks and hips, her lips joining as they went down. *Once she learns it,* Cecilia fleetingly acknowledged, *it's learned.* She flailed, moaned, tried to find anchor for her heels in the yielding hay, began to sink, and Airey's hands slid under her like a raft. Their faint cantilever was the final impetus—she flicked into a quick dart of release and lay on Airey's palms, smiling into the spangled air. She started to move off and was instantly buried in a banked wall of hay.

Airey dug her out and would have started again, but Cecilia said, "If we don't deal with this, one of us is going to drown." They jumped and rolled across the hay, compacting it into a springy mass until they were laughing and rolling in each other's arms. Airey scattered kisses along Cecilia's body, she bowed her head, and Cecilia skipped a breath at the bliss of her mouth. A fiery ripple spread through her, another, another, each stronger, each surging her closer toward her usual landfall—and she swept past it with a faint farewell, was rushing toward a higher leaping point, was there, and she leapt.

A moment later, she bobbed back to the surface of herself, exhilarated. Airey was half-crouched, head turned away, jaw working. Cecilia said, "Spit."

Airey put a finger in her mouth and hawked gently. "You're curly everywhere." She came to lie next to her.

Cecilia turned to kiss her hairline, her forehead, the ridge of her nose, wanting to know every part of her: the hard arch of her hipbone, the corded scars on her knees, the pale down of her calves, her callused feet, the lean muscles of her thighs and back, her hard-knuckled hands, those rosin-scented fingers that released Mozart and Bach from gut and wood. Cecilia turned again, turned lower.

This time, she sensed that Airey wanted to pace what her body was doing. Cecilia contentedly repeated the same sequence over and over until she felt her seeking more and gave her more. Airey began jittering like a pond under steep rain. Cecilia gave her as much as she seemed to handle, heard her small knotted groans and reveled in her, in her concentration, in her determination to go where Cecilia led, in her sheer stamina, felt her whole body clench, and Airey slammed back and lay still.

Cecilia stretched out on her. Airey's heart was as fast as a hummingbird's, and Cecilia could feel her body uncoiling the last of its energy. Airey exhaled luxuriously. "I ain't never known having something and wanting it both at the same time. It ain't never finished, and it's always starting. My hands crave to be on you."

The next moment, they were, and Cecilia fell again into the flame, they fell together, mouths demanding, legs tangled, fingers obsessed, slithering on each other's sweat, plunging and peaking through the hours. Gradually, they could not raise a hand, could not manage even slack kisses, lay wordlessly against each other, Cecilia drifting to sleep in Airey's arms, knowing it was dangerous—*anyone could find us*—but feeling sheltered, safe, feeling a tranquility that seemed to sing in the air.

Chapter Seven

A sound woke Cecilia, a clang she did not hear again. She was uncomfortable. Her arm was under Airey's thigh. She kissed it and eased herself free. They were in a deep hay hollow, Airey strewn with it. Cecilia began to be aware of itches and tiny bites. She scratched her hip. The sunlight was low through the wall. How long had they slept? She heard a faint wailing.

"Airey, get up." She clambered through the hay and over the partition, scraping a shin—"Airey, wake up"—fumbled into her clothes, a centipede making acquaintance with flight, and found her shoes. "Airey." Airey stirred. One hand flexed and fell.

"Jabez's crying. It's late."

"N'sh."

"I'm going to the house."

Royal lifted a reproving head as she came in. Lorimer was at the kitchen table lashing together parts of a half-built model, his squirrel rifle close to hand. Poly was trying to distract Jabez with a spoonful of sorghum syrup. From the smears on his face, he was crying from surfeit.

"Poly, Lorimer, I'm sorry. Airey will be here in a minute. We should have told you we'd be late. Have you eaten?"

"I fried some corn," said Poly crossly.

"Thank you for being sensible."

"Where was you?"

"We lost track of time." Cecilia took Jabez in her arms. He was hot as a brick. "This child needs a bath. Poly, can you show me what you use?"

She bathed Jabez in a milk pan, toweled him dry, and had Poly lead the way to the back rooms. Across the open passage from the girls' room was another that held a single bed, a high shelf holding battered, mended science books, and a lower one crammed with models: a derrick with hoists, a swing bridge, cranes, conveyors. Cecilia sat on a stool beside an old carved rocking cradle. Jabez's head slowly lolled against her breast. You could hold a sleepy child in the classic maternal way and know *not for me*, Cecilia reflected without a pang, still moved by it and by Poly holding the lantern like a little shepherdess at the manger. She laid Jabez in his cradle. Poly lit their return to the main house. Airey had not come in.

Lorimer was using two Grafonola needles to pin a miniature mill wheel to his model. "Airey says things have got shook up since you come."

"When did she say that?"

"Early on this morning when you was asleep."

She didn't know then how much. "In a way she didn't like?"

"She was still shining to shame the sun, so I reckon she liked it. She's worked hard to be good. It's only fair she gets to go where folks will hear her."

"You work hard, too. And you'll get to go where you want to go."

He nodded, his attention on his work.

Poly settled beside her chair. "You smell of hay. You got some in your hair."

"That's Airey's fault."

"I can make necklaces from grass and flowers. They need special knots. I'll make you a real pretty one."

Royal came to his feet. Airey stepped into the kitchen, wet with sweat and plastered with hay.

"Why are you turning the hay at night?" Poly asked her.

"That's when I remembered I needed to." Airey's glance at Cecilia was like the touch of her fingers. "You two et? Lorimer, the mules pegged down?"

"It's my job, and I done it."

Airey nodded and went out to wash.

"Polynegry," said Cecilia, "your sister calls me by my first name, and I'd like you both to do the same. Cecilia."

"Cec-il-iy—it's hard. I'll try," said Poly.

Airey returned, her hair slicked back, and fried more corn. Cecilia took her share of raw and black. Airey ate slumped over, a hand shading her eyes. Poly peered under it. "What was you doing all day that's tuckered you out?"

"Learning."

"Lor ain't tired when *he* learns."

"Lor's smarter than me."

Lorimer grinned as he sat back, surveying his model. "Airey, the cornfield beans in little west acre need seeing to."

"We'll go after breakfast."

He fetched wood and went outside to wash. Poly followed him and came back to kiss Airey good night, hesitantly crossed to kiss Cecilia's cheek. "It's nice you're staying here," she said, "but we ain't seen much of you. I guess Airey has."

"Yes, indeed," said Cecilia. "Good night."

They were alone. Airey came to crouch beside her chair. "I reckon I shifted a ton of hay in ten minutes, I was that riled over not looking after the little ones. But pretty soon, I couldn't think of anything but you."

Cecilia wanted to say, *it's your first time; it sweeps you away like that.* "I was happy to settle Jabez." She leaned toward her. Was it only this morning they had kissed for the first time? She felt a little swept away herself.

Airey said, "I never kissed you before today, and now I don't never want to stop."

"Don't stop," said Cecilia.

Airey kissed her carefully, as if her mouth was bruised. Cecilia's felt the same. There must be a physical limit to the hours you could kiss. Mere pain did not stop the hunger for them. She felt Airey's breath catch, and now they were kissing as if parted for a year. Cecilia managed, "Where...can we...go?"

"Outside." Airey stood, bent for a kiss, finally broke away, and went to the back rooms. She returned with quilts, Royal emerging with her, interested.

This could not mean the barn. "Are we camping under the stars?"

"We'd be supper for bugs." Airey took the kitchen lantern from its hook. "We'll use the old corn crib."

"The children won't know where we are."

"When me and Freed used to sit in it, they'd see our light from the house but couldn't see us inside. That's why we went in there."

They walked down the yard, Royal trotting beside them. Airey knelt under the crib's deep eaves to hang the lantern on a rusted spike. "I'll go in first and lay these." Royal poked a nose after her. "Roy, you ain't needed in our doings." He yawned and trotted back to the house. Cecilia, swatting away feathery night insects, saw his dark shape settling on the porch and was touched. *He's guarding us.*

"Ready," called Airey.

Cecilia ducked through. The small floor was padded from edge to edge. Airey was pulling off her clothes, the lantern light through the logs turning her into ivory tiger stripes. Airey's hands were on her at once, stripping her, running across her with a precision that told Cecilia she had been thinking about this, and each riff and back drift struck fire. Cecilia grabbed one of her hands and thrust it down. Fingers able to sustain a vibrato on high E had no trouble sending her to the edge and keeping her there, on and on for as long as she wanted, and she wanted it for eternity. Just as she wondered perhaps not eternity, Airey's hand changed its approach, and her mouth joined it. *Heaven help me.* Cecilia slapped her palms to the quilt, twisting and panting for release, and it came, as bright and hot as platinum.

She opened her eyes to see Airey lounging like a cat, grinning at her. She tried to shuffle herself into a less wanton position.

"Cec'ly Howison, you're a wondrous thing." Airey's sticky fingers laced with hers and pulled her close.

"I'm played by the best." Cecilia overwhelmed her with a descending blizzard of small kisses and bites. How subtle could she be and still bring Airey to full blaze? *Let's find out.* She gave up on air and played through variations on the opening theme while Airey turned link by link into an iron chain, for an instant into an iron bar, and then collapsed, lank, across the quilts.

Cecilia kissed up to her lips. Airey's replying kiss was abstract, exhausted. Cecilia put a hand on her. "I'm not done."

"You got a mean streak of selfishness in you. I've remarked on it before."

"I've always been a bully," Cecilia agreed, moving her hand. Airey inhaled sharply. Cecilia expanded her fingers on her breasts, ran her tongue down her breastbone, felt Airey's long belly muscles tighten and lost her head, working roughly over her body, almost sick with wanting her. Airey's hands dug through the quilts to survive Cecilia's onslaught, up to the moment she snapped like taffy, sweet and clean.

Cecilia shook her hair from her face and looked down at Airey lying prostrate in the lantern's light. *This has to stop before I believe in female perfection.*

Airey blinked, stretched one long arm, hooked a wrist over Cecilia's shoulder, and pulled her down. At the first brush of Airey's lips, heat shot over Cecilia's skin like flames across a ceiling. *How is it possible*? It was possible, it was happening, and Airey was on her, circling intently down, around, up with equal intentness, and Cecilia gave a startled laugh. Airey stopped. "You don't like it?"

"Of course I like it."

She continued to like it. An electric current was vaporizing her, an expanding heat harder and harder to contain, until everything in her flared like a gas jet and engulfed her.

Golly. She blinked into the quilts. Airey's hands were gliding up her. She moaned faintly under their enticement. Airey rose over her like a wave, and they began again, and again, while insects buzzed and burned themselves against the lantern's weakening light.

At last, they lay spent in each other's arms. Cecilia was aware of their heartbeats, of Airey's abdomen faintly touching her with each breath, of each breath feathering her hair.

Airey said, "I can't understand how folks get chores done once they commence on this."

"It doesn't turn the hay," Cecilia agreed.

"I got to that."

"And got to me, as well."

"Got you?" Airey was still. "What have I got?"

"What do you want?"

"Wanting and getting are two different things."

"What you have is me, here, now." Cecilia rose lazily and straddled her. "Have what you want."

"You, here, now." Airey tasted the words. "That's the start of what I want."

Cecilia leaned down to kiss her. Airey returned them lightly, as if assessing each one. "About those other girls."

"They're not important."

"They are."

"Why are you asking? What do you want to know? How many?"

"There's many?"

"How many could there be in Avender?"

"How would I know? Maybe one, maybe a hundred."

"What do you take me for?" Cecilia sat up.

"What are you?" Airey's voice was delicate as a new leaf. "I'm in a strange place. Round here, when you get in the wagon with someone, you ride with them all your days. Women going with a lot of men, we call them—"

"Jezebels? Trollops? Is that what you think I am?"

"You say *how many* as if it's something to ask, but how can I know what to measure?"

"Women of my sort have our own measures."

"Your sort?"

"My sort. The sort of women who do this. Who live for this. Who want what this means. Who want it enough to obey the commandments it comes with. You already know the first and most important one. Silence."

"Secrets," said Airey without warmth. "What are the others?"

"To understand that time isn't ours to have. To accept that we mustn't waste the time we're given."

"Why not?"

"Because we're not meant to have any. We count ourselves lucky to get a day with each other, a week, rarely longer. More than that isn't possible. Isn't safe. Speaking for myself, it's better so." She felt Airey shift in protest. "I think it's ungrateful to cling to the first rose that blooms. We're so various, lovely in so many ways, that it's foolish to complain when we have to discard the flower in hand and choose afresh."

"But don't they ever—ain't you never—liked one so much you wanted to stick with her?"

"I've liked them all."

"Nothing no stronger than that?"

"Do you want to know about them? Do you really want to know?" Cecilia started to move off her, but Airey's palms on her thighs held her in place. Cecilia took no encouragement from it. "It began when I was sixteen. Our minister's eldest daughter saw the female half of the congregation as her own flower garden and one day decided that I was ripe for the plucking."

"She—a pastor's girl?"

"She soon sought new blossoms, but I knew I didn't want this heaven to end. I came across a few like-minded girls in our church's sorority—hardly surprising—and expanded my knowledge. Collines Female Academy gave me three happy years. After graduation, I joined a weekly women's club that meets in a hotel in town, all First Families and proper, yet with some knowledgeable spinsters and restless wives. I also discovered certain roadhouses where women from the mills and factories meet and dance. I seek with hope and sometimes I find."

"It seems Avender's got-got more than a good hundred."

"Perhaps it does. I'm cautious. It's hard to know what's attracting them when your name is Howison. I've been used badly a few times, and that's not easy to remember. I've done stupid things in dangerous places. But more times than these, I've been glad. I like women. I like the way they look, the way they think, the way they feel. I've had to lie and sneak, and I've hurt and been hurt, but it's worth carrying the candle for them. It's always worth it."

"And now with me."

"And now with you."

Airey's silence stretched until Cecilia was chilled by more than the night air. *So this time, too.* Then, drearily, *oh, God.* Airey's hands found hers. Cecilia said, "I'm not seeking your forbearance."

"On the day Merit went to be with Card, you tried to tell me that all those things you'd been doing for me—for us—was to get this. That this was in your head while you done those kind things."

"Yes." Cecilia looked down at her. "I was doing wrong and knew it—not for wanting this, I'd have been insane not to want you—wrong because it was my method of getting you. That I even had a method. On the day the Settlement people came for Merit, I kept you here through false generosity, holding myself better than my kind as I did it. For my selfishness, for my arrogance, for my dishonesty, I need your forgiveness. Will you give it to me?"

"You could have got here plenty of other ways. You chose the one best for me and hardest for you. And you asked. Each time, you asked. I don't never forget that. Then you ran away."

"How could I stay? How could I call myself your friend? I knew I didn't deserve the word. Didn't deserve to see you again. And I didn't. Wouldn't. Then Dr. Neihoff's telegram arrived—"

"You wasn't never going to come back?"

"I was wild with wanting to. The telegram gave me my excuse. I promised myself I'd simply come one last time—and then leave for good."

"You gave me up?"

"I refused to be with you because of how I tried to have you."

"You done that for any of the others?"

"No."

"Then why with me?"

"Because you're different. You must see that."

"Because I'm a poor girl on a hill farm? Reckon you ain't been with many of them. 'Cause I'm good on the fiddle?" Airey's voice held no edge.

"I haven't known anyone like you in either of those ways. Not anyone like you, Airey Fitch." Cecilia gripped her hands. "Not anyone like you at all."

"At the door this morning, when you was leaning against me and you moved to show you wanted me to hold you, I knew what I was feeling wasn't called friendship, and you knew it, too. At the ford, when you told me that—that I wasn't first—nothing changed inside me, but it was plain I was mistaken about what was inside you. I couldn't see how I—then you called me, and I had to come. I got to get accustomed to this new world I ain't finding too comfortable for my soul. But seeing you're here in it, I'm here, too."

"It's your world, Airey. I'm merely your first flower."

Airey sat up and bound her in her arms. Cecilia did not know if she were being embraced or silenced. Airey's lips were fire at the hollow of her throat, her hands burned down her back. It was as if their words were mist, spoken, risen, and gone.

Airey slowly eased Cecilia to the quilt, her lips and hands slowly met on her. Cecilia went up like a torch. Within a few choked breaths, she was grinding into her, wanting only this, demanding this, her hands on Airey's head, and she came on a punch of flame, hard and fast.

She turned and without a word had Airey outstretched and shuddering, unbreakable, until she did break, with a noise like cracking hickory. As if timed, the lantern went out. Cecilia settled into Airey's arms in the darkness and slowly slid toward sleep.

"Cec'ly." Airey kissed her ear. "We got to get to our beds."

Cecilia mewed in protest. She wanted to stay exactly where she was. She woke sulkily, pulled on her dress, and crawled after Airey into the night. Above their heads, constellations blazed through the flying clouds.

"Ketchy weather's coming," said Airey.

Royal passed them, heading for Lorimer's room, as they went into the house. Airey checked the stove's reservoir. "You wash first. I'll finish the kitchen after."

Cecilia used the hot water to scrub her underclothes, as well as herself, wishing she could float for hours in a scented bath. With Airey for hours in a scented bath. Airey was mixing milk and flour. *How domestic we are.* Cecilia smiled as they moved around each other at their tasks. Airey slid the dough into the warming oven and walked with her to the back rooms, dropping a kiss on her lips before moving on.

Cecilia closed the door, hand mutinous on the latch. She wanted to fling it open and drag Airey inside. Instead, she took two groping steps to the hooks for her clothes and lay down, her naked skin still fizzing for Airey's touch. She wanted to hear Airey getting into bed, wanted them both to be lying in the dark thinking of each other, and prepared for a sleepless night.

Her next thought was that it was daytime. That she was not alone. She opened her eyes. Sun filled the room, and Airey was setting a jug of steaming water and its basin on the dresser. Cecilia held out her arms.

Airey shook her head. "Little ones."

Cecilia threw back the quilt. Airey bent with a reproachful look and kissed her, hands tucked behind her back. Cecilia kept her own arms flat on the bed even as she ignited at the touch of her lips. *I see your virtue and raise it.*

Airey squatted to whisper, "When folks say some man's lost his head over a woman, I never understood. Now I do. It's real easy."

"I need to go home today."

"No."

"Airey, I must."

"I can't have you gone. It ain't right. You telegraph your folks again and tell them you're staying longer."

"They won't like it."

"Somebody's going to be riled. Ain't going to be me."

Cecilia sat up and hooked her legs around Airey's waist. "Then I'll have to see what I can do." Airey raised her hands, not to Cecilia's breasts, as Cecilia expected and warmly welcomed, but to her face. "Your eyes are as blue as the sky where the sun's just set."

"If you intend nothing more than to pay me compliments and kiss me like a maiden aunt, go do your chores and stop tempting me."

"No auntie ever held me like this." Airey kissed her again swiftly, stood, and was gone.

Cecilia pushed her fists into the bed. This was where virtue got you: naked and alone on a bed while the woman you burned for headed to the little west acre. She rose, bathed, and dressed in the faintly damp underclothes and frock she was going to tear into rags when she finally got home.

Home. A telegram would not be enough this time. She had to telephone. If Mother were back, what story could she give her? Perhaps the novelty of truth. Part of the truth. They invited me. I couldn't refuse.

And I can't. Not yet.

Poly, washing dishes, said, "Airey baked a salt-rising loaf for breakfast. That's it under the cloth. I'll get you something to eat." She cooked eggs in cream. "Airey didn't make spoon bread 'cause she said it would have us pining for Mam to be home. That's true, but not how she meant. I wish Mam would come."

"I'm sure she'll be on her way soon. No, let me set my own place."

"My heart feels bit through when I think about Merit."

"Think of how happy Merit is, and that will make you happy, too." Cecilia poured coffee. "Did Airey say how long she'd be?"

"Her and Lor took their tools and bags with them."

"Then they'll be harvesting all day." *I'm risking a family eruption for her evening.* "I need to make a phone call."

"Mr. Jecks, he lives down in the cove, he ain't got his telephone no more."

"Then I'll drive to Heresy." Cecilia looked at Poly and Jabez. "You two will come with me."

Poly skipped in excitement. "Lor'll be sicker than a dog that's swallowed a snail when he hears me and Jaby got a ride!"

The Heresy road took them around the foot of Applesell Bald. Its northern face revealed itself abruptly, new growth barely masking the scars from Sankgallon's runoffs and sluices, track beds and slicks. Cecilia shivered, reminding herself that no forest need be a wasting asset. Time—the park—would heal this.

Heresy stood where the loggers' railroad had once met the river. The railroad was gone, but rumbling trucks were still delivering long, bright-ended logs to the mill, and the mill was still throwing knotted clouds into the sky. Beside it, the river was as slow and thick as putty.

She parked the roadster in front of a McKinley-era hotel. "Luncheon first."

"We didn't bring no—" Poly lit up. "A pay-for dinner!"

They were directed to the small alcove reserved for ladies, Cecilia glad of it, as every other person in the hotel, apart from two elderly women sipping soup, was male and in suspended animation, staring at her as she crossed the dining room. She made desultory conversation with the two women throughout the meal to ask, at the end of it, if they would watch the children for a few minutes. They were pleased—delighted—to assist Miss Howison. "It *is* Miss Howison, isn't it? We thought so right off. The pleasure is certainly ours!"

Cecilia went to the bank of telephone booths in the lobby.

"Your mother and father are still traveling, Miss Cecy," said Henry. "Should I put you through to your grandfather?"

That would not do. Better to gamble. "Is Tom at home?"

"I'll see if he can be disturbed."

Cecilia heard a distant receiver being lifted.

"If it isn't the long-lost daughter of the house," said Tom. "Where are you?"

"Still at the Fitches. Didn't Grandfather get my telegram?"

"He did. He keeps repeating *that fine old mountain family* to convince himself all's well. You'd better come home."

"Soon. In a day or two."

"Cecy."

"I'm their guest. Their mother is down in Georgia. I want to stay until she gets back."

"Helping them out, I believe your telegram said. You're helping yourself to some deep trouble. You can't play Lady Bountiful with that sort of people. It isn't wise."

"I don't think anyone would call what I'm doing helping out. I'd like to stay, a friend with friends."

"Yes, if those friends are the Shuttleworths or the Blassetts. Not when they're mountain farmers. Not when they're Fitches. They aren't the type *you* make friends with."

"Can't I be part of Daddy's electoral reach *bas,* as well as *haut*?"

"The only *haut* you'll be in is water. I'm worried about you. You seem to have lost your sense of propriety. And to tell the truth, your sense."

"Should I draw back where Dr. Neihoff was happy to tread?"

"*What*?" An odd sound followed, as if Tom were staring at the receiver. "Dr. Neihoff? Dr. Neihoff was *there*?"

"He came with his wife and the Vernelles and spent the day. He believes Miss Fitch might well become a soloist."

"*Neihoff* said that?"

Cecilia laughed. "The Vernelles are my witnesses."

She heard an indrawn breath. "And to think,

those few months ago, I scorned the idea of a great artist flourishing in the wilderness. How are the mighty fallen!"

"You said genius had to be taught and that it didn't remain hidden for long. Both turn out to be true."

"My unsuspected power of prophecy. *You* must feel exalted."

"On air, actually. Of course, she needs a formal music education. Dr. Neihoff made that clear. He's promised to write her once he has something arranged. I'm hoping for a college place, though it's late in the day. She's going to need every bit of help I can find. Do you still stand by what you said at Phyllis's?"

"Can the oath of a Howison ever be forsworn?" He seemed to listen to her words again. "A college place? For example, at Dardhardt or a sister conservatory? Would that be appropriate?"

"Of course. They'd be lucky to have her. You see now why I want to stay."

"I'm hoping I do." He was silent. "It's not up to me either to permit or deny, given that Grandfather's *in loco parentis*. How can I reach you?"

"By telegram to the Fitches, care of the Hinterhouse General Store."

"General store!" He stopped himself. "I know—I trust—you'll never forget who you are." He rang off.

She returned, buoyant, to the two women, who purred under her thanks and left in a bustle of consequence. Poly and Jabez were quiet on the way home, dazed with ice cream. At Hinterhouse, Lucius was in his place on the general store's porch, whittling a long splinter of wood. Cecilia said to Poly, "I believe Jabez is safely left under this gentleman's eye," and Lucius nodded shyly.

Poly said to Mr. Keller, "We bought green-colored lemons and canned fish and clothes in Heresy, but Miss Howi—Cec'ly—says we'll get the rest from you, seeing you're a neighbor."

"I wouldn't have these diamonds in my ears without Fitch custom," he replied, pulling chairs forward for them. "What can I get for you young ladies?"

He began piling Cecilia's purchases on the counter as her mental eye roved through the Fitch kitchen, finishing with a toy truck for Jabez, an ancient amateur radio set for Lorimer, and a book of paper dolls Poly had fixed on and said nothing about. Cecilia looked around the store. Where was a bow of burning gold, the arrows of desire?

"I got something I been keeping a while," he said, knowing for whom she searched. "That Mr. Brewken traded it for liquo—*hem*, goods—a long time back. I put it by, figuring Airey might need it one day. Reckoned it would be when she joined up with a band like the Melodious Mountaineers, but when that didn't work out, I hung on for a better time." He came back from his storeroom with a folded music stand and opened it to let her see the delicate Art Nouveau brass filigree across the support.

"What a beautiful thing! Thank you, Mr. Keller. That couldn't be more precisely what I was looking for."

Rain had come and gone on this side of the mountain. The birches along the Fitches' lane shimmered with rainwater beads. Cecilia drove slowly to let Poly and Jabez catch drops on their tongues. At the house, Cecilia and Poly shelved the groceries and arranged the gifts on the table.

"Lorimer's bringing something heavy." Poly put down her paper doll and went out to meet him.

A swollen sack appeared around the corner of the house a few minutes later, Lorimer almost double under it. Cecilia made a jug of lime cup and took a mug to him. Poly and Lorimer were emptying beans into baskets. Cecilia was aware of a cat watching them from the rafters and very aware of the hay bin at the far end of the aisle.

Lorimer finished his mug in two gulps. "I could drink a bucket of this. We cleared pretty much the whole acre 'cause Airey said she had fidgets to work off. Reckon she worked off both our shares."

"Let me get you more." Cecilia went back to the house and found Airey surveying the boxes on the table, straight-browed. Cecilia said, "I want to contribute."

"You've done it lavish." Airey picked up Poly's paper doll. "This ain't food for sharing."

"I hope the toys will make Poly and Lor happy."

"Why?"

"Because I want to make them happy, to make you happy."

"Even though you never stay with no girl." Airey delicately straightened the doll's dress and put it aside.

"It's something I can give you here and now."

"I know what you can give me. Reckon I'll ask for it when we're better acquainted with the other."

Cecilia looked through her. Airey's destiny had been so much her goal that she had not considered the obvious consequence. Now it stared her in the eye. There would be no learning Airey Fitch, no getting to know her, because Airey Fitch was going away. The outcome of bringing Dr. Neihoff here, but now she fully grasped it. Airey was going away forever. *I'm a fool hoist with my own petard.* Oh, golly. *Oh, golly.*

Airey was frowning. "You ain't wanting us to be better acquainted?"

"I'm pondering the pitfalls of a butterfly's life."

Airey laughed. "You was never one of those."

Rather than answer, Cecilia pushed forward her gift. "And something for you."

"What's this?" Airey took off the brown paper.

"It's to hold your sheet music."

"It's a little metal stand." Airey opened it. "It's-it's Mr. Broeggen's! I clean forgot about it." She turned it in wondering hands. "I recall looking up at it. I didn't know where it had gone. I figured he'd sold it for shine."

"He did, to Mr. Keller."

"And Mr. Keller kept hold of it this whole time?" Airey's fingertips followed the filigree.

"He thought you might need it one day."

Airey was silent. "Folks here always knew about me. Like you did."

"If I'd known, really known, you'd already be somewhere else. No, no closer." Cecilia backed away as Airey reached for her. "It isn't fair when there's a thirsty boy waiting."

Airey went with her to the barn. Poly asked, "Airey, did you see all those things me and Cec'ly bought? I got a paper doll with clothes from Hollywood. Lor, you'll bust over yours!"

Airey asked Cecilia, "You didn't get nothing for

yourself?"

"She bought some dresses in Heresy," Poly answered, "but none with pretty ruffles, and some other clothes I ain't mentioning in front of Lor."

"You're a polywoggle." Lorimer left.

"New dresses?" Airey's grin would have lit a well shaft. "Means you're staying."

"I telephoned home to say so."

"Then everybody's got something and me what I wanted most of all." Airey hung up the last of the baskets of beans. "Polynegry, you get grating and steeping the corn I brung up. I got to practice after I'm done here."

"Fried mush?" asked Poly.

"I was thinking dumplings," said Airey.

Poly left with a faint whimper.

Cecilia pushed Airey into the shadow behind the small door. Airey was hot and damp, she smelled of earth and crushed leaves. Cecilia pressed her face against her.

"Cec'ly." Airey nuzzled her hair. "I got to practice."

Cecilia sighed and dropped her arms. "May I come with you?"

"Every place you want to." Airey fetched her violin. In the tobacco shed, she bent for a brief kiss. It lingered.

"You do that, villain, then abandon me for that devil's box?" Cecilia took an old horse blanket from a cross brace and lay down, hands behind her head, happy to torture her.

Airey was sanding her hands with feldspar, tautening her bow, tuning. She looked around as she lifted her violin. "You can't lay there like that."

"I can."

"I want to take every stitch off you and cover you up with me."

"Resist. Close your eyes."

To her equal admiration and outrage, Airey did, playing her warmup exercises by touch. Eventually, she opened them, but by then, she was seeing nothing but her hands, her bow, her inner world.

Cecilia concentrated on the music to distract herself from Airey's outer world. Airey's scales were attentive and thorough, her fingers silent and even on the strings, shifting from scales to exercises, each more than mere study, each a striving for something greater, to be one with the music. The violin was Airey, the passionate yearning was Airey, and Cecilia knew it to be the essence of her virtuosity, her touch, and that all those who heard it would seek it again and again.

So many would be listening. So many women. Airey in so many cities, eminent, glittering, enticingly regal. Women making themselves known to her in the hope of *droit du seigneur*. Women seeking to make her happy. A stab of loss made Cecilia set her jaw. *They'll never do for her as much as I have*. The thought was no comfort. Neither was the certainty that no friendship would long survive Airey's departure. Airey was not the letter-writing sort. *Although I might get that telephoned command from Charleville or Philadelphia.*

The music halted. Cecilia turned her gaze from the future to Airey.

"This tune's making you sad."

"Don't stop for that. You mustn't stop, even when your whole audience is in tears—or in rapture or on their feet in wild acclaim."

"What's acclaim?"

"When they cheer, call for encores, throw posies, when you find your dressing room crowded with bouquets and devotees after your performance."

"Every time?"

"When you're famous, yes. They'll ask for autographs, they'll want you to dine with them or attend their parties, they'll give you flowers and jewels, some wrapped in letters of devotion, some even in marriage proposals."

Airey laughed and played an *allegro* by Beethoven. "I ain't got to pay any mind to those proposals, do I? I'll never in no way want them."

"If a millionaire or grand duke signs his name, you'll have your secretary reply that you're honored, humbled, and gratified, but you fully understand his salute is to your muse."

"If he ain't one of those?"

"Less formal. You'll thank him for the gift and say that he must understand that you're married to your muse."

"What's a muse?"

"In your case, the goddess of music. The ancient Greeks gave each art a goddess to explain its wellspring of inspiration."

"Wellspring. They got that right, in spite of being idolaters. It springs from our souls, where even angels can't see. If you don't know the Lord God, muses ain't so bad a notion."

"Your suitors will understand that music is the only thing you can truly love and obey."

"Those grand dukes?"

"They'll have no choice." Cecilia was harsher than she intended, thinking of all those women who would have no choice.

Airey looked as if she would ask more, raised her bow instead, and continued Beethoven's sonata. She seemed to have no more questions, for she moved to the Brahms she had worked on yesterday. The future faded for Cecilia, her wistfulness faded, as the music drew her toward the sublime, drew her into Airey.

Airey lowered her violin at last. Cecilia saw her right arm quivering. "Do you always practice to exhaustion?"

"I mostly play before hoeing, not after."

A knock on the door. "You coming in," Poly called, "or are we feeding ourselves again?"

"Leave us a minute," said Airey. "I got a word to say to Cec'ly. You stir that corn a couple more times."

"If you ain't done by the time Lor's back, it'll be soup."

"What word?" asked Cecilia as Poly's footsteps faded.

"It can't be said by talking." Airey put her hands on the crossbeam above Cecilia's head and lowered herself full length to kiss her. Cecilia put her arms around her neck and tried to pull her down. Airey stayed suspended from the crossbeam, holding herself inches above Cecilia's body.

"You're showing off," said Cecilia.

"I want you steaming for me like that monument of yours did for water. I've been reasoning and seeking my path. What do you want? I can chop a tree, I can plow, I can dig and churn butter and sow and reap. Soon I'll be earning good money playing fiddle. I can look after you."

"Do you think I need looking after?"

"Not like I look after Polynegry and Jaby. Sort of that way."

"I've been taking care of myself for a while. I think I have it mastered."

"You should have someone who pays attention to nothing but you."

"That won't be you, will it? You think of nothing but music."

Airey laughed. "I reckon I can do both."

Cecilia moved to make Airey move. "You need to think about your future."

"I'm doing that." Airey lifted her to her feet.

"Your future career. Consider how you use your hands. Everything you do here could end your playing."

"I can't wear tin pails over them."

Cecilia turned them palm down, palm up. "I want to wrap them in lamb's wool."

"How would I hold a spoon? You'd need to feed me."

Cecilia thought about it. "I'd like to."

"What else would you like?" Airey's hands stayed holding hers.

Cecilia kept her expression light. "I'd like you out of harm's way. The sooner you're off this farm, far from sickles and scythes, the sooner I can draw an easy breath."

"Strikes me that virtuosys are too precious to live."

"Yes, an ordinary life. They're on higher ground. And how do you find being God's gift?"

Airey's spluttered. "You! Ain't there nothing you wouldn't say?"

"Not a thing, if it's true. You know you are. You can't say it in public—you must preserve a charming professional modesty there—but say it to me."

Airey's grin was fierce. "I'm the best. I've always been. When folks hear me, they'll know it, too. I'm the best fiddle player on earth."

Yes. "Yes." Cecilia almost climbed her. "Yes."

Airey clasped her off the ground. "You like it."

"I do." Cecilia started to work her out of her clothes. *I'm an utter Howison.* "Yes, I do."

A friendly bark made Airey lower Cecilia to her feet. "There's Lor coming in with Susy-lassie."

"That cursed hound takes pleasure in interrupting us." Cecilia straightened Airey's shirt.

"Seeing I'm best, and it's what you like, why don't—"

It was like trying to submerge a rubber ball. "If you want to take care of someone, cook for your poor family."

Airey gave Cecilia a kiss that said she was not deflected and opened the door.

After supper, Lorimer glanced up from the diagram from his radio set at the same time as Airey, their faces assessing. "Wind's shifting. Rain's on its way."

Airey said to Poly, "You settle Jabez to bed. Lor, me and Cec'ly got to close up her car. You damper the stove."

The wind was freshening. Airey wrestled down the Buick's roof and fastened its side curtains. She took the lantern from Cecilia and put a finger to her cheek to turn her face to its dancing light, said, "Your mouth's the most beautifulest there could ever be," and kissed her. Some time later, her lips moved to the rim of Cecilia's ear as her right hand unbuttoned Cecilia's dress with a casual skill that Cecilia would have admired were it not for the voltage coming from Airey's fingertips.

"Airey!"

"Hmm?"

"I'm not standing in the open with you doing that to me."

They were in the corn crib a minute later. Airey finished undressing her. Their kisses were glancing as they writhed around and over each other like animals in a den. Airey's hands raked her like a falcon, she swung a leg over her and turned to bury her head. Cecilia pressed against her, wanting her to feel what she was doing to her, wanting to be surrounded by her, to be drenched in her. Airey's shoulders were against her hips, inciting her to pitch and buck. Cecilia planted her fists against the wall to give herself thrust, hissing through her teeth as she rode the fire Airey was driving into her, holding on, not quite holding on, letting go, shooting through layers of golden heat into a high point of radiance.

She drifted languorously back to the darkness. *She's ruining me for other women.* A murmur: Airey's happiness. Cecilia smiled. "Are you going to stay down there all night?"

Airey came to nestle her head against Cecilia's breasts. Cecilia inhaled the scent of soap, wood smoke, Airey, herself. She did not plan to start again, but found she had, as if to touch her was to burn, and now it was Airey who doggedly endured, muscle locking into muscle, who pulled feral noises from her lungs, who detonated from within with a guttural sound and turned over like seaweed limp on a tide.

Cecilia sat back on her heels, one hand on Airey's fine silky hair, lingering on what the light revealed of thigh, ribs, shoulder. Airey's heaving lungs slowed. She put both her hands over Cecilia's. After a minute, she asked, "What are you doing?"

"Looking at you."

"What for?"

The lantern outside was flung sideways in a whip of wind, tossing shadows around the corn crib.

"Because you're Airey Fitch."

Airey's thumbs traced the back of her hand. "You said earlier I'd be having a impresario and a secretary. You said I'd have dressing rooms. You said I'd be places like New York and Rome. You said it like you didn't see you with me."

Cecilia did not move. "I was imagining five or ten years ahead."

"That's what I mean."

"Five years from now...why would I be there?"

"Why wouldn't you be?"

"You can't know what you'll want in five years."

"But you already know what you don't want."

There was no deflecting this. "Whatever you feel now is now. This is new for you. We're in an idyll here, your mother gone and having freedom, but it's no more than luck."

"That ain't the reason it's different."

Cecilia tried to withdraw her hand, vehemently not wanting to do this, but Airey rose and leaned forward, refusing to let go. Cecilia said, "I've told you not to want what isn't possible. I know more about this than you do. Time has a price. The cost of days is some clever evasions. The price of a week is outright falsehoods. The price of a month? A year? I can't imagine the lies they would need. No liaison, no matter how lovely, could endure those years. Or survive it. Or be worth it. Who could face the dishonesty those years would demand? Who would want to?"

"You couldn't carry the candle so long?" Airey's voice was soft. "I reckon I could."

"How do you know? Why would you want to try?"

"I ain't got a clear idea of how lowlanders do things, but they can't be so different from us: they find themselves someone and marry them and that's their life. You say your sort of woman goes from one to the next as they please and you say that's best, but it ain't so. We been created to cleave soul to soul. I didn't never know a woman could cleave to a woman, but now I know it's true."

"Airey, this isn't something that leads to marriage."

"Why ain't it?"

"Because—clearly it isn't, and I don't care how many mules you can drive. Even Boston marriages aren't necessarily Sapphist."

"What's that word?"

"Sapphist. Lesbian. Women who desire women. There are other words, ones you'll hear from everyone but us. Invert. Abnormal. Degenerate. It's why we live in silence, behind lies, by changing ground, by moving on—because when they name us, they brand us, and once they brand, they can trap and destroy." Cecilia put her other hand over Airey's. "We risk all of that, we pay that price, for this. This, being with each other. If only for a day, a few hours. For even an hour."

"But if you can't stay with a girl no longer than that, what happens to your hearts?"

"Broken with tedious regularity or hardened."

"Which is yours?"

"I've told you I'm a butterfly. I prefer living flowers to ones under cellophane."

"You reckon that's what I should be?"

"Your life will be safer—and richer. Throughout your career, you'll meet so many fascinating, talented women, ones who'll know your world better than I ever can. Why wouldn't you be with them? Be with them all?"

"Is that what I should want?"

"Women who understand and appreciate what you are and what you live for? What could be better?"

"Ain't you that kind of woman?"

"How could I ever be part of your world? I'm not a musician of any caliber. I'm going to be Senator Howison's daughter adorning the Washington scene, and you're going to be immortal. This," she made herself say it, "is a lovely episode. I hope you'll always be glad we met. I want you to be glad we met."

Airey made a strange sound, a gasping choke. After a moment, she said, "Now I know how preachers feel when they see folks stumbling in darkness."

"I'm not saying this is sinful—"

"I ain't saying it neither. I'm saying I aim to do what preachers do: save a soul from the foolishness of her ways."

"Airey, I'm serious."

"I know you are. You reckon you've told me the rock-hard truth. Those words cost you to say and you had the grit to say them, but they don't mean nothing to me."

"You don't know enough yet to believe me."

"I ain't never going to believe you."

"You're in what's called a crush. It's wonderful—I know, I am, too. I'm your first—"

"You asked me how you could ever be in my world. That's a peculiar question when you don't believe in staying with nobody."

"Don't hear what you want to hear. I won't stay even for the time we have if I'm encouraging a dream—one that will make our ending harder for you."

"So if I was to tell you *go home in the morning*?"

Cecilia warded off the words before she knew what she was doing but said, "You can't shock me into seeing a truth that isn't there. I've been through this before—not exactly this—and I know it will end. It has to end. The hurt then will be less if we accept the fact now." The swinging lantern's light gave her glimpses of Airey's face. "I don't say I won't be sorry."

"You don't want to leave."

"Of course not." Cecilia pulled her hands free. "Though if I had any wisdom or self-control, I would."

"You keep trying to," Airey agreed, rolling her into the quilts.

Cecilia knew her kisses were meant to overwhelm her. Airey was implacable, unyielding. Cecilia fought her, fought to prove that passion alone was enough, was more than even Airey could master, both of them wilder than the wind outside, the quilts driven from under them as the light swooped across their warring bodies.

The lantern's mad swinging abruptly stopped. A moment later, they fell beside each other on the cold floor in exhausted deadlock. The wind seemed to hold its breath. Rain pattered across the planks of the crib's roof and fell softly, enveloping them. Cecilia put her arms around Airey and pulled herself against her. *How long do I have*? Airey's mouth found hers, and they kissed searchingly as the rain drove harder against the roof and into the ground.

Thunder cannonaded across the night. Cecilia barely heard it, spellbound by Airey. It wheeled closer, and high lightning lifted their darkness. Cecilia saw Airey shining in it, a goddess of white jade.

The rain hesitated, crashed all at once as if poured from a black barrel, streaming down the roof, drowning the lantern. Thunder broke almost overhead. Cecilia's eyes were scorched by lightning. Airey rose to her knees. "Poly's afraid of thunder."

Lightning split again, making Cecilia cover her face. The air crackled. "Don't go—you'll be struck."

"I'll run. You stay here."

"No." Cecilia found her way into her clothes and followed her. They reached the porch as lightning hit something nearby with a crack and stench of carbon. Thunder filled the deep bowl of the mountains. Poly's frenzied cries pierced the darkness. Airey pulled Cecilia into the house. "I'll bring her here to the stove."

Cecilia shook the wet cling from her dress and added wood to the firebox, leaving it open for the comfort and heat of the flames. She felt scratched by a thousand thorns. The end began when they started thinking they could change the world. Reality always defeated them. Airey was stubborn; she would struggle for longer. Cecilia sat watching the fire. It would be sensible, it would be kind, to leave now. *I can't be kind. Not even to myself.*

Airey returned with Poly swaddled in a quilt in her arms. She settled close to the stove, cradling her. "Poly honey, you know it's just Old Man Donney and the Blazing Dog setting to."

Poly's head butted hard against Airey's ribs. Thunder curled through the house. Cecilia's ears were filled. Airey hugged the quilt around Poly. "Old Man Donney's sure hammering hard."

"I don't like him," Poly sobbed.

"He don't like you nor nobody, but it takes more than a mean old man banging on an anvil to frighten a Fitch."

Poly and Cecilia cringed as lightning bleached the darkness at the windows. Thunder shocked and rebounded.

The next minute, dressed in a nightshirt old and long enough to have been his father's, Lorimer came in bearing a quietly crying Jabez. Royal followed with the air of an old trooper inured to artillery barrage. Jabez struggled to be free, settling into the bend of Cecilia's hip. Lorimer and Royal joined them on the floor.

"My clothes are damp, Jaby," said Cecilia, but he stayed pressed against her, tears rolling to his baby dress, jumping each time thunder slammed and Poly squirmed in her cocoon.

Cecilia tucked an arm around him. His tears slowed as he watched Airey and Lorimer calmly cocking their heads and saying, "That one's less loud than the one before," "the count's getting longer—it's moving away."

The lightning was far off now, a line across the sky. The thunder seemed to bank against other mountains. Through the steady fall of rain, Cecilia heard the swash of the treetops. She felt her dress drying and saw that she and Airey were wreathed in steam, ghosts among the children.

Royal's ears came up. The sound of the rain

changed again, lighter, softer, healthy rain from a good sky. Airey raised her head, noting it, and smiled at Cecilia before bending again to Poly. Cecilia did not shift. *I'm in love with her.* A perfect stillness unfolded. *I love her.* Airey lifted her head again, sensing Cecilia's gaze, and Cecilia looked at the fire to hide her eyes. *I can't be.* Airey was going away. *She's going away.* It changed nothing. It meant nothing. Peace was here, certainty and peace. *I love her.*

The fire burned low. Lorimer was leaning against Airey's shoulder, nearly asleep, Royal beside him. Jabez sagged against Cecilia, toes splayed toward the stove. Cecilia wanted time to stop, wanted to stay here forever, but Airey stirred, woke Lorimer, got him to his feet, put Jabez in his arms, and let Royal steer them to bed. She followed with Poly. Cecilia looked at Jabez's head on Lorimer's shoulder, at Poly's bare dangling legs, all of them precious, all of them part of Airey. *So this is what it feels like. This is what it is.*

She went to the kitchen for a wash basin. Every act, soaping her hands, taking the towel set out for her, had a clear edge. Going into the darkness of the back rooms, she met Airey coming out, felt her smile, felt her fingers touching her hand as she brushed past her. Her contentment furled around her like wings. She closed the bedroom door and leaned against it. She knew where Airey was. In the kitchen, doing chores, and here with her. She undressed and got into bed, lying with her hands at her breast. A dynamo spun inside her, a gyroscope, aligning her on her new bearing. *I'm in love with her.* When had this happened? Before tonight, but she had not known, had not seen. *Am I that dull-witted*? Or did the creek rise so slowly that you only realized you'd been lifted high into the air when you found yourself looking down? *It must have, for here I am.*

She lay awake long into the night. The rain diminished and stopped. Everything was quiet. She was wrapped in a bodiless flame as soft as a breath. In the darkness, a faint, cold dissonance grew louder: *Airey's going away. She's going away forever.* Cecilia turned her head from it. It hissed, *How will you live? The candle is your heart.*

Because the candle is my heart. Those callow words she had spoken: *I don't want what isn't possible*—what nonsense. All things were possible. She had the power to make them possible. The only thing not possible was to live without Airey. She would do whatever she had to do, dodge, deflect, deceive, for as long as she had to, forever. Peace and certainty came again, came and stayed. *I love her*. She slept.

The sun was high when Cecilia woke. A pitcher of hot water waited for her on the dressing table. She looked at it, her heart full. If she stayed ten thousand days, she knew it would be there ten thousand mornings. She heard the trees rustling, the creek rippling, axes chopping. Behind all these was another sound, the music of the spheres, and hers turning within them.

Ten thousand days. She saw them like a sunlit river sparkling into the distance and rose like an army of dominion. *I'll make them happen. I'm not a Howison for nothing*. She smiled at the happy woman in the mirror as she took her standing bath, imagining traveling on her trust money and always happening to be in the same places as Airey's tours or renting apartments in new cities for her to return to. No reason they would not always be lucky, be blessed. She wanted to sing as she put on one of her new dresses. Avender traffic would come to a halt if she wore it there. She wasn't in Avender, she was in Airey's world. She went out by the side door, saw Airey and Lorimer in the yard working a cross saw through a birch log, and stopped to look at her, the only thing she would always want to see.

A splashing noise made her glance down. Poly was scrubbing Jabez's baby dress in a basin while he played naked beside her. She kissed them, went in to find biscuits like shoe rubber warming on the stove, poured herself coffee, and stood above Poly in the doorway, settling in to adore this woman who moved with ravishing strength.

"I like cut wood." Poly hung Jabez's baby dress on two nails. "It's got a pretty smell."

"I'm sorry the storm bothered you last night."

Poly hunched a shoulder. "I'm too grown up to be frightened."

"When you're young, you hear things more clearly and feel things more sharply. They'll become easier to bear with time."

"You and Airey know lots," said Poly. "I don't know why she's going to fiddle school. What she got left to learn? I want her to come back on lots of visits. Mam's been gone for *ever.*"

"Your mother's away only for as long as Merit needs her." *And if that's ten thousand days, so much the better.*

"Mam went to Charleville once. She learned about trains then, so she knows how to get on one now."

"She might be back today," said Cecilia.

As if she had wished it, the growl of a car engine grew over the rasp of the saw. Royal loped around the house.

"That ain't the pastor's truck," said Poly.

"I think I know who it is." Cecilia hurried through the house, reaching Royal's side as a navy blue Pierce-Arrow swept past them and swung to a stop. She went to the driver's door. "Tom."

Chapter Eight

Tom stepped out, languid and trim in a dark cream suit, leaning lightly on his ebony cane as he surveyed Cecilia against her setting. She knew what he saw: the weather-worn house, the crooked palings, herself in a machined dress, the Fitches in their patched work clothes mustering on the porch like a row of wary fox cubs. She took his kiss on her cheek. "Such a surprise! Whatever brought you here?"

"I was galvanized by your telephone call. It's not often that one has the chance to gaze upon one whom even Dr. Neihoff hails as gifted. In addition, Mama and Daddy came home, days sooner than expected, and found you not. Their fears being entirely unallayed by Grandfather, I stepped into the breach and declared I'd seek you out." He contemplated each of the Fitches as he spoke, pausing at Poly and moving to Airey. "A gentleman at the crossroads directed me hither, and thus my valiant steed and I arrive." His gaze stayed on Airey.

"I'm glad you came," said Cecilia, deciding it was true. "You need to meet her—"

"There's no question of that."

"—and the family."

"It appears unavoidable."

"Tom, don't be horrid." She felt her hackles rise, ready to defend the Fitches as she had so often defended him.

He turned away from the house. "Cecy, Dr. Neihoff has come and gone."

"Bringing him here turns out to be merely my first task."

"And logically your last. What holds you in residence, looking like one of the family? Speaking of *en famille*, the gentleman below asked me to bear these upward."

Cecilia stuffed the mail in her dress pocket. "Come and meet them." On the porch, she held out her arms for Jabez. "This is Jabez Grigg, their half-brother, Pola Negri, Lorimer, and Lorimer's dog, Royal." Lorimer, man of the house, shook Tom's hand. Cecilia continued, "Airey, my brother Tom."

"How do you do, Miss Fitch?" Tom surveyed her from overalls to short hair.

"A pleasure to meet you," Airey said formally. "Come along inside. I'll heat some coffee."

Tom paused to understand her, paused again inside the house to adjust his eyes, and surveyed the shabby settle, the rag rug, the chairs. Airey offered him a seat with a touch of regret.

"I fear I've interrupted your work," he said to her as she stoked the fire under the coffee pot. "But isn't that always the way when one visits a farm?"

"Doesn't mean we can't be sociable, specially for Cec'ly's brother."

"You're not what I expected, Miss Fitch."

"What was you expecting?"

"My sister told me of Dr. Neihoff's visit. She proclaims you a nonpareil."

Airey smiled at Cecilia, who felt every molecule of her body smile back. "That word's new to me, but I reckon if Cec'ly says it, can't be no bad thing."

"Allow me to rephrase. You have so marked an aptitude for serious music that Dr. Neihoff believes you capable of a solo performing career."

"He reckons maybe. I reckon for sure."

"I'm certainly eager to hear you."

"She doesn't play for free," Cecilia began hotly.

"Seeing you're Cec'ly's brother, I will," said Airey. "I ain't met none of her folks, but I'd have known you. You and her are like twin blackbirds."

"I'm not as comely as my sister."

"Nobody could be. I'm guessing you've come to take her home. That means you and I will have a ruction."

"Tom hasn't come to take me home," said Cecilia.

"Cecy, I might not be here to throw you over my saddle-bow and return pell-mell, but I place before you the wisdom of laying a swift course to the ancestral hearth. Troubled hearts await the cheer of your presence."

Time for troubled hearts later. "Do they think I'm misguided? In danger?"

"Daddy worried, in a jocular way, that you must be wearing out your welcome."

"Ain't so," said Airey. "We're real glad she stayed."

"I know that my sister is the most delightful of houseguests, and apparently earning her keep in the bargain, but our mother isn't entirely clear why she's prolonging her stay in your charming home."

"Your mam don't like Cec'ly visiting neighbors?"

"She measures those geographically and politically."

"Lor," said Airey, "you and Polynegry best leave

us on our own for a spell."

Cecilia handed Jabez apologetically to Lorimer as they retreated from the house. Airey set down three cups. "I'd have figured a Howison could visit anybody she pleased for long as she pleased."

"You imagine a freedom my sister doesn't have. The eyes of society are upon her."

"We got pictures of her and you and your family all round the place," Airey agreed.

Tom's mouth twitched as he glanced at the wallpaper. "Everyone knows her, as everyone knows me. Like sparrows, our each fall is remarked. My sister understands it too well, and it's as constraining to her as foot binding."

"It would be a mark against her good name that she's here? She don't act like she was better than us."

"Would any of us dare, given Fitches once were, and remain, extensive landowners?"

"You mean we still got the best part of the mountain? You folks ain't done real well with your half, seeing it's all mud and stump now."

"That's the Howison way, I fear. We suck forth the sweetness and then carelessly or, in this case, lucratively, discard the fragile flower."

Airey looked at him for a moment before pouring coffee.

"Despite our comparatively recent ancestry, we at home are concerned over what Daddy's principal constituents would think of a Howison so, shall we say, determinedly out of place."

"As long as I'm not shocking the party grandees with my choice of friends, as long as I keep myself out of the public eye, what does it matter what I do?" Cecilia asked impatiently.

"As you're always in the public eye, it does matter, and more acutely in an election year. It matters because you're a Howison."

"Grant me strength!" Cecilia pushed back from the table. "What's a Howison to the greatest talent of the century? We should be putting our hands on the floor so she can walk without harm, not insulting her by suggesting my staying a day or two will kill every one of the First Families."

"Cec'ly—" Airey began.

"No." Cecilia brushed her away. "I won't have it said that I'm of too fine a clay to be in your home when I'm not worthy to unloose your shoe's latchet." She controlled herself with an effort. "Tom, I know you enjoy rules that aren't extended to me. Boys will be boys. But it's ridiculous to think that I'm causing a storm in anything bigger than a teacup by staying here. What can Mother or Daddy do to me? Make my life miserable with their disapproval? In four months, I can snap my fingers at the lot of you."

Tom put a hand over his heart. "Zounds, the spirit of the girl! You're quite right. These aren't the dear dead antebellum days. You must forgive me. I foolishly assumed that, since you've never been anything but winsomely biddable before, you'd be no different now. Clearly," he turned to Airey, "things have changed. Should I congratulate you? My sister goes from being the blossom of fragrant damselhood to lip-curling scofflaw in the twinkling of an eye, apparently under the soul-stirring luminescence of your—bow."

"I don't rightly," Airey began.

Tom had turned back to Cecilia. "Or shall I conclude that you truly are your mother's daughter, pledged to raise the sacred banner of all that is refined and wise even here?"

"I've lost all patience with the sacred banner. I've more important things to think about."

"Your rebellion knows no bounds." Tom's cane tapped the floor. "Miss Fitch, your muse must be as compelling as Dr. Neihoff has judged and my sister believes."

"There's that muse again," said Airey. "She comes around plenty. I'll play so you can tell your folks to stop their fussing." She brought over her fiddle box and prepared briskly. "You got something you'd like to hear?"

"As you choose."

Airey raised her violin and lit the dark room with a miniature palace of crystal filigree.

"That-that has a keyboard accompaniment," said Tom, "which I didn't miss. A local violinist I know, Gustav Feldstedt, plays it a little slower and rather less well than you."

"Dr. Neihoff said Mr. Heifetz does it faster than me."

Tom smiled faintly. "You see yourself as somewhere between the two?"

"I can't say how good your Mr. Feldstedt is. I've heard Mr. Heifetz on Cec'ly's records. He's better than me at some things, at least right now. I'm better at others. We're different. This is the way I play it."

"I hope one day you'll illuminate them both. You can't have had many opportunities to hear this music performed."

"Not one. I got taught by a man who knew, and I've been learning more from paper music and those records."

"On our childhood phonograph." Tom nodded to it.

"Yours, too? I'm obliged to you." Airey lifted her bow and played him a showy burst of fireworks. "I learned that off a record. It sounds like a bee."

"That's exactly what the composer called it. *L'Abeille*."

"You know about music as much as Cec'ly."

"More," said Cecilia.

Tom raised a protesting hand. "I'm an educated listener who putters on a keyboard. Cecy truly plays."

Airey gave them a lively Spanish piece, a sleepy nocturne, and finally Bach. Cecilia watched Tom's face become unguarded and wondering as the music lowered step by step to stillness.

"Forgive my presumption," he said, "in requesting a private concert from one such as you. I should tell you that I promised my sister I would support any musician endorsed by an expert. Unquestionably, I have it before me." He rubbed his hand over his face as Airey put away her fiddle. The strain he had shown since he had arrived was gone. "Cecy, I'm a little at *plus-non-point*. What's a feller to say? You must be used to it by now."

"I'm never used to it."

"She plays for you every day?"

"Yes."

"Practicing," said Airey.

He said to Cecilia, "I am racked by pitiful envy. Imagine uncovering a Shakespeare or a Michelangelo."

"That's more or less what I said at the time."

Tom took a sip of coffee, mastered himself, and said, "How fortunate that I failed to dissuade you! We need to speak about this rather urgently, given I'm imminently to depart westward."

"Yes, today. Now."

Poly and Lorimer were standing shyly at the door, the music their signal that hostilities were over. Tom said to them, "You've a very talented sister."

"We know it, sir," said Lorimer. "She won a cup at a competition."

Tom smiled at Poly. "You have a lovely name. I know a friend of Miss Negri. I'm staying with him soon."

"You're going to Hollywood?" Poly came to him. "I read as many *Photo Screen News* as I can get. I know all the stars. You're going to Hollywood to visit them?"

"I'm going to feed on the elixir of freedom."

Poly went to pile a plate with biscuits. "We ain't got a pie 'cause we asked Airey not to. Lucky Cec'ly does cooking. She made us dinner when the pastor came."

"This," Tom said after a microscopic pause, "from a girl born to be served?"

"Rubbish," said Cecilia.

"We all should serve each other," said Airey. "Like our Redeemer showed us how."

Tom's eye glinted. "You must find the Howisons thoroughly unsanctified."

"You ride yourself too hard, Mr. Howison."

"Nicely put."

"Cec'ly is the best person I know, but this ain't no surprise to you, seeing you grew up with her."

"We're in perfect accord on that, Miss Fitch." He smiled at Cecilia, who busily stirred her coffee. "Such homage from so great a talent must put you on your mettle."

"I'm afraid Airey flatters me. I've undergone no transfiguration." *Except the one I have.*

"She's a chip off her mother's block," Tom said to Airey, "and that's entirely igneous, forged in a heavenly fire. The other stratum in our family, represented by my humble self, is porous sandstone, easily eroded. Still, I believe a little friction keeps everyone on their toes."

"Just like now," said Airey.

"I'm finding you are, Miss Fitch, and I speak with a full heart, not what I first took you to be, but—what shall I say?—an impressive andradite."

"Those are rocks, sir," Lorimer ventured.

"Correct, old man. You know something of them?"

"I got a collection. I could show it to you, if you wanted."

"Capital," said Tom, to Cecilia's surprise.

Airey smiled at him as Lorimer sped across the room. "Now I'm seeing your sister in you. Lorimer's a lonesome scientist up here."

"A condition you've shared."

"I was always a soloist, though Dr. Neihoff told me that in years to come I might want a quartet on the side. Maybe I'll set one up. *Melodious Mozarteers.*"

Cecilia's heart danced. "Tom, we really must speak today."

Lorimer brought chairs into the sunlight by the kitchen door and spread his collection across them.

"This house has an abundance of chairs," said Tom.

"That's 'cause Mr. Grigg took up caning them for money," said Lorimer. "He paid up front for the frames and splits, but he liked giving each its own style instead of sticking with the pattern. The agent wouldn't pay him a cent for them and left them all here. Mr. Grigg said he wouldn't never cane another chair long as he lived."

"We wasn't sorry," said Airey.

Lorimer hesitated over his collection and offered Tom a lump of gray rock.

"A fine piece of gneiss." Tom took another. "Metamorphosed conglomerate. Both are from this mountain, but this," he accepted a third, "this is dolomite. You found it somewhere else."

"Down in Lovat Cove." Lorimer nodded.

"How do you explain these three types?"

"The mountains are all folded-up rock. This one, gneiss—" Lorimer pronounced it as Tom had, and Cecilia guessed that he had never spoken the word before—"was deep-down sea dirt that was lifted up in a folding."

Tom reached for another sample. "And this silt-stone proves it. If you arranged your specimens in order of geological time, you could tell our mountain range's entire story."

"That's why I'm collecting," said Lorimer. "I keep my eye sharp every time I go hunting."

"I was myself an ardent collector in my young days. A friend and I must have hammered off half the state."

"You found all the rock types?"

"That goal remained unachieved. I was struck by polio when I was about your age."

"I'm real sorry, sir. We knew a boy who got it. His muscles quit, and he gave up the ghost."

"I was left merely weak in one hip, which ended my boyish scrambles. My friend Kitty," Tom paused, "my maid, who sat beside me through the tedious year I took to get better, told me many times that the Lord had spared me for a reason. What that reason was she never said, and I'm unable to discern."

To be Airey's patron.

"No doubt revelation will come. Now, Mr. Fitch, this is...?"

Lorimer brightened as he selected a rock as round and flat as a coin. "My best discovery, Mr. Howison!"

Tom tipped it to the light. "An immaculately fossilized bryozoa."

"It's a prehistoric sea critter that got stuck in the rock," Lorimer explained to the audience.

"How did it get up here?" Poly looked at the slope behind the house. "Was it the Flood?"

"The Flood didn't happen how the Bible says," said Lorimer dismissively.

Poly stared at him. "The pastor'd say Old Coaly spoke through you right then."

"You know better than that, Polynegry," said Airey. "Just 'cause you don't like what he says don't allow you to be false witness."

"Let's cast Satan far away." Tom's cane pointed westward.

"To Hollywood?" asked Poly.

"I'm sure he'd find it congenial." Tom smiled blandly at Cecilia's warning look. "Carry on, Mr. Fitch."

He and Lorimer settled into discussion. Poly took Jabez out to the yard, where he picked up his own rocks. Airey traced a line on Cecilia's back with one finger. It burned through to her heart, burned down. She knew she should shift out of reach but stayed exactly where she was, her face composed while she looked at Tom, seeing him through Fitch eyes: a dapper, gray-faced young man, an idle man. *Not for long.* She looked at Lorimer and thought of another thing Tom could do.

After the final specimen, Lorimer said, "I got some models I could show you. I want to be an engineer, and they're how I'm learning."

"Bring them forth."

Cecilia put a hand on his arm. "Not until I've spoken with you."

"We must mind our manners, Mr. Fitch," Tom told Lorimer. "A lady's wish is paramount."

"I'll have them waiting for you!" Lorimer and Royal dashed to the back rooms.

"Let's speak outside." Cecilia led him to the front porch. Airey followed with two chairs, saying, "Mr. Howison, you stay for dinner. After seeing Lor's models, you'll need to get back your strength."

"How kind, but I wasn't planning to linger."

Airey frowned. Cecilia, knowing she was about to be more forcibly hospitable, said, "Tom's not as persuadable as I am."

"You are? That's news. Gives me hope I'll win your soul yet."

Cecilia heard the scratch of Tom's cane on the porch planks and realized that Airey was standing too close to her, that Airey's smile hid nothing. "I'm sure Tom would be delighted to stay."

"I'll get some side meat in the oven."

Tom lowered himself to his chair as Airey left. Cecilia sat beside him. They watched mist rise from the hollows like vapors from a cold sea. He said, "A magnificent view. One understands how the

Olympians must feel looking down from above the clouds of the world."

She was aware that he was as rigid as glass. "It rained heavily last night."

"So prosaic! Are you inured to the poetry of the place?"

"I think it beautiful beyond words." She turned to him. "You know better than I, far better than I, what Miss Fitch needs. Recommendations, letters of introduction, but above all, money. Trenton's told me there's none in the foundation, and I've little hope that Dr. Neihoff will be able to locate a bursary at this late date, which means the only money she'll have is what you can raise—alongside your own and, of course, mine, once I have it."

"I'd prefer we delay this chat until after you've heard from Dr. Neihoff."

Cecilia paused, surprised. "But you wanted to speak now. We already know the financial demands her education will make."

"Nevertheless."

"I don't—" She could not insist. "Then I want to speak to you about something else."

He watched the floating mists. "What else does the redoubtable Miss Fitch require?"

"It's not for her. It's for Lorimer."

"Lorimer? I hadn't noticed he plays an instrument, unless he has a Sousaphone tucked up the chimney."

"He needs to be in a school where they teach science well, before his mother marries Mr. Souch. Mr. Souch is a preacher who believes that evolution and geology are works of the devil."

"Ah," said Tom. "That dread being must bask in

the attention he receives from this righteous place. Do you hold all the Fitches dear?"

"I ask primarily for Miss Fitch's sake. I fear she'll be tempted to stay here to shelter Lorimer from his new father."

"Do you really think she'd give up her ambition for her brother?"

"She'd delay it. If she doesn't, if she leaves, she'll be distracted by worry and guilt. I want nothing disturbing her, nothing from home, nothing at all, once she's in the place Dr. Neihoff puts her."

"But when the Fitch lad comes tripping home from that school spouting Permian and Ordovician, won't this new preacher-papa forbid him from returning thither?"

"It's why I want you to have him admitted into Ruyerford Prep."

"Ruyerford?" Tom laughed in sardonic admiration. "Your mind's been busy as a bee, hasn't it? I'll wager the entirety of my new allowance you hadn't a particle of this notion before I arrived, and now you have Lorimer's future planned. Ruyerford!"

"It solves everything."

"Lorimer's a nice boy, but I don't care a feather for him. Not enough to go cap in hand to Gerrish."

"Lorimer must remind you of when you and Gerrish used to hunt for rocks. You both had the certainty of an education. Lorimer has none."

"Even if I coax Gerrish into admitting a last-minute boarder, how will Lorimer pay for...Ah, wait—wait! Dim eyes, awake and behold! You intend my humble self to serve as *his* benefactor, as well. You take *noblesse oblige* too far."

"I didn't know it had limits."

"This is well outside mine."

"It would cost you a little of your pride and a little money, and I suspect only for a few months. There were charity boys at Ruyerford while you were there. Didn't they earn money by cleaning the laboratories and doing yard work? Lorimer would do that. He'd be hard-working and frugal. Heaven knows he's expert in both. They both are."

"Cecy—"

"Please, Tom. If it could wait until my trust starts, I'd also pay for him, but it can't."

"Gerrish wouldn't accept a penny from you in any case."

"That grand old Southern chivalry, obliging me at every turn. If you won't help Lorimer for his own sake, help him for Miss Fitch's. Could you enjoy yourself in California knowing you'd had the power to liberate such a talent—and did nothing?" When he remained silent, "I'm not asking so very much, not even for her. Your direct support needn't continue once the First Families start donating, as they will as soon as you ask them. So much good from such little effort hardly seems fair, does it? Two lives made better because of you and one of them destined to be great beyond all telling."

Tom watched the mist drift and dissolve into the air. He seemed to gather himself up, and his hand tightened on his cane. He looked directly at her for the first time. "If getting Lorimer into Ruyerford will catapult Miss Fitch out of your life, I'll crawl to Gerrish across burning sand."

Cecilia did not speak. She held his gaze. She finally asked, "How long have you known?"

"I've only *known* today. I've only *known* since

this minute, when you understood what I said and didn't slap my face. I thought, on first seeing her, that you were staying here because of—but then I found myself mistaken. You were staying here for her music, and my relief was vast. I grasped that straw because I shrank from having to grasp the nettle of my suspicions."

"You had suspicions? Before today?"

"Before—before. In the speakeasies and houses of pleasure south of the tracks, I hear whispers: of pious parsons who buy the backsides of boys, of *grande dames* who come for strap-and-whip at the hands of Cuban bucks, of nice young women who play mossy-face with other young women not quite so nice, and I've ignored the last because none of those could ever be *my* sister. I refused to be inflamed by insinuations even as they recurred. I laughed to scorn the impossible. Inconceivable to me that you, my shining star, *sans peur et sans reproche*, were or could be anything but faultless. I never saw in you—but what did I know to seek?"

"Do I look different to you now?"

He shrugged as if burrs were next to his skin. "That proves nothing. I'm a romantic. I wanted you to be what my faith thought you were, so I took you for what you seemed. When you spoke to me yesterday of Miss Fitch taking up a college place, I knew your discovery wasn't a little girl. She must be older. How much older? Even then I wouldn't believe—but I feared, feared just enough—and so I came. If only I could go back to that ignorance! For here you are, not repudiating something any other girl would recoil from in horror."

"I don't deny it to you, although I don't agree

with your—shall we call it a description? I don't—I won't—admit anything to anyone else, no matter how plain the evidence."

"If you say nothing, there's nothing to deny? Old Thomas More's defense, and look what happened to *him*." He scrubbed his face with his hand. "I don't suppose the Fitches are secret moonshiners, are they? I could use a stiffener."

"Not a drop."

"My cursed luck. Cecy, I don't hurt anyone but myself. The dissolute younger son is a traditional rôle in life. When I'm discovered facedown in the gutter, everyone knows who I am—what I am—and they dismiss me. You're as well known as I, so the dimensions of the lie you're living fall beyond my comprehension. You're so close to the edge of the pit that you daren't speak or even breathe because of the danger, yet you come here and entangle a whole family in your affairs. Your affair." He ground his palm against his cane. "Unless...unless I'm wrong? Unless you didn't? Was it she who—*she* did this to you. You were swept away by her violin playing into a foolish, girlish crush. This has to be true."

"It isn't true."

He turned away, not before she saw the sickness in his eyes. "Then you—*you*—came for, and chose to, and-and these people couldn't know the rules you played by."

"You don't know them, either."

"How did you justify your—no, I can't ask. I don't want to know how long you've been—it's clearly been long enough for you to have the arts to-to beguile an innocent."

"You're indulging in dramatics. I don't press my

attentions on unwilling women."

A shudder ruined his self-command. "Cecy! My God! *Attentions*! A Howison—my own sister—one of *them*! Oh, God, I need a drink."

"*Them*? What nastiness is in your head?" She smiled without amusement. "A flint-faced harridan with a monocle and Russian cigarette? Can you know me and still consider me a monster?"

"What a curious conscience you have, my dear! I don't know you at all. You *are* a monster because you don't believe what you're doing is wrong."

"No, I don't. I think *your* life is empty and self-indulgent. You aren't happy."

"You are?"

"Yes."

"Damning you all the more. I'm not a stranger to the forbidden—far from it—but I, even such as I, stop at the brink, while you plunge into the pit as if it were Elysium."

"For pity's sake! Stop talking like a fool. You say you're an outcast, yet here you are upholding convention as earnestly as Gerrish, revered rector of Ruyerford."

"We're not talking of man's laws, but higher ones—natural ones—that make us instinctively draw away from an unclean thing. I abuse only my own life. I don't, save in one drunken moment, surrender to my peccant desire. *You* actually and deliberately spread your—contagion."

"I hurt no one."

"Yes, you do. You're hurting Airey Fitch."

"She wouldn't agree."

"That's because she doesn't understand. How can you do it? How can you risk her life? That talent—

she's a miracle, you know she is—and yet you *still* did this to her, knowingly, not caring how it will warp her, how it will ruin her, ruin her music. Are you that selfish? That voracious? That debauched?"

"I might almost fancy you're suggesting I've depraved her."

"What else can I call it?" He made a repulsing gesture. "I don't care about Airey Fitch, even if she were the greatest violinist living, though she might have been, were it not for you. I do care, though God knows why, I care about what she's doing to you. You *have* depraved her, but what have you done to yourself? Gone from playing with your own kind to meddling with—living with, for Christ's sake—decent, good people. Those children! How could you?"

"Do you fear I'll taint them all? That I'll destroy them, in some unspecified way, because I can't contain my unbridled lust? I've more control than that."

He looked ill. "The worst is that you have that control."

"I have it because I live at the edge of a pit others have dug for me."

"And now you're exposing this entire family, as well as your protégée—may I call her your protégée?—to that abyss. Do you hope the Howison prestige will silence the tongues that will inevitably wag? Tongues may hesitate for a Howison, but they won't for that poor girl you have in your clutches, not when they understand what she is to you." His mouth contorted. "And this is the—for *this*—you expected me to write letters of introduction? To recommend? Do you think I'd spend a cent on that pitiful trull? Not while I breathe. The only help I'll extend is to the boy, and quickly, to get him out of this pest hole."

Cecilia fought for voice. "You promised me."

"No promise exists when it's obtained by misrepresentation."

"You don't care about what you just heard? You don't think it's important? Her genius isn't important?" His fingers flicked dismissively. Cecilia felt steel rise in her, rise to her hand. "I do, because it's the only important thing. I won't rest until she enters her life of music, with your help or not. It's what I must and will have. I will have it."

"I'm certain neither of you will have anything."

"Do you plan to stop me? To stop her?"

"I don't need to stop her. You've done that yourself. As for me, I assure you, should you persist, that a shrugged shoulder here, a deprecating murmur there, will guarantee that you'll meet a brick wall as high as heaven. Since Dr. Neihoff, for all his reputation, will never find funds at such short notice—though now there's no need—I can safely say that both your little ships are dead in the water."

Cecilia felt the earth fracture under her. "Are you going to tell him?"

"Write him a tattling letter? Do you think I'd soil myself? I shan't have to, shall I?"

"You can't stop me from spending my own money."

His smile was as thin as a hair. "Uncle Wendell isn't bright. I'll need very little effort to persuade him of the wisdom of diverting your income back to replenish lost capital. For your future benefit, naturally."

"You—seem to have thought of everything."

"Interesting how inspirational one's revulsion can be."

"I'm not without choices."

"Don't misunderstand me. I'm sure you have none."

"I don't misunderstand you."

Tom wrenched himself to his feet and stepped to the edge of the porch. "The one good I will do—the only good I *can* do—is to speak to Gerrish about a place for the boy. If Gerrish agrees, I'll pay a stipend toward Lorimer's expenses."

"Thank you."

"I don't want your thanks. I don't want to talk about this ever again. Or to you."

"Our single point of agreement."

"You aren't happy, you know." He turned to her, and his eyes were wet. "You never will be."

"We're only unhappy when we refuse to live the lives we're given."

"No." Tom's cane stabbed the porch. "*No.* You don't live a life. You live a disease. You *are* a disease." He wiped his face with his cuff. "I can't bear it. I can't. You sound just like the Cecy I've known all my life. I look at you and-and I'll always see her, in spite of what I know, what I wish I didn't know, what I wish I'd never learned. I wish I'd never come here. I wish I were blind drunk." He began to step off the porch, realized it was too far from the ground, and tried to pass her to the stair. Cecilia stood and barred him.

"I have to go now," he said in a nasty small voice. "I can't stay."

"Is it a promise about Lorimer?"

"Oath of a Howison," he said before he thought and sneered at himself.

"What of me?"

"I couldn't do that to Mama, to the family. And I

trust you'll be…sensible." He sought something in her eyes and did not find it. Contrition? she wondered. He said, "Don't rush home to see me off."

"I wouldn't dream of it."

"Seraphically kind." He dropped his gaze and pushed past her to his car.

The engine's growl brought Royal bounding into view, Lorimer at his heels. The Pierce-Arrow slithered in the rain-softened earth, straightened into the lane, and was gone.

Lorimer stood, rigid in abandonment. "Why did he go?"

"He was taken ill." Cecilia sensed Airey at the door and locked all she felt in her heart's deepest vault.

"He could have laid down on my bed," said Lorimer. "He shouldn't drive if he's sick."

Airey said calmly, "He wouldn't have gone without seeing your models no otherwise."

"Aw." Lorimer kicked up a splinter. "That's just—" He stomped into the house. "I'm putting them all back."

Airey came to Cecilia. "What did he say to you that's made you look like this?"

"I have to…to sit with it before I can speak to you."

"Tell me."

"Not now."

"Tell me. It's bad, I can see."

Cecilia turned her face away. "Let me stay out here a moment."

"You don't have to sit with it by yourself. You ain't alone no more."

I'm more alone than I've ever been. "Airey."

"It's best you tell me."

"I think a pan's on fire."

"Cec'ly! You too?" Airey hovered until Poly shouted, "Smoke!" and she rushed inside.

Cecilia's legs lost their strength. She sat and waited for her lungs to pump her through the minutes that would transform this into the past. *Airey, this is what people think.* Tom's sick eyes. *This is what people do.* His words like saw through bone. Howisons were both sparrow and sparrow hawk, the city on the hill and the wolf on the fold. Better to push the shaft of that clean through. Cecilia looked plainly at what was before her. She wished as fiercely as Tom had that he had never come.

She sat watching the mist build and build to become nothing. She felt part of herself sliced away, felt its raw, wet edge. Tom was gone from her. She had a moment to grasp it before it overwhelmed her. He was gone. He had said—what had he said? *Even I.* Did he mean in those brothels and dens? No. No, he meant Kitty. *Of course.* She felt a distant pity. He had been given the choice between his heart and the world, and he had chosen the world. Safer, easier, to stand with it than to stand against it.

Safer to hate what it hated, but not easier. Each act of loyalty had corroded him, had turned him into what, today, could finally pick up the whip. She despised him for it. She would never mourn him, not even his memory. She refused to mourn him. She would learn how to. She looked down at her hands, wringing themselves in her lap.

"Cec'ly?" Poly whispered from the door.

"Yes, honey?"

"Airey says to call you for dinner."

Cecilia drove down her thoughts and thrust

home the bolt. She stood with an effort. The fly brush was swinging aggressively. Poly handed her a platter of blackened pork. "At least there's plenty of taters. We reckoned your brother would, but I ain't supposed—"

"It's all right, Poly." Airey looked at Cecilia, and Cecilia realized that her attempt at happy guest-hood had not convinced them. She threw an extra chain around the vault.

"Don't see no reason to be nice about folks who don't do what they say they'll do," Lorimer muttered, one shoulder hitched.

"I'm sorry Tom didn't stay to see your models."

"You don't need to beg pardon for your brother," Airey said to her. "Lor, you recall that one time Mr. Broeggen came up for dinner? How was he?"

"Fine, till just before the pie."

"Then what?"

"He got itching for a drink, and…oh."

"You saw that," said Cecilia in a smothered voice.

"There's a wasting can't help but show," said Airey.

"He was never right after his attack." But the damage was not from being crippled or being crippled by polio. Cecilia thought of Mother's wish: *I hope your first love will be your last*. She knew why now. So did Tom.

"He could come back," said Lorimer. "He'd be real interested in my models."

"I know he would," said Cecilia.

"We're making Cec'ly feel bad," said Airey, and to her, "Those taters will go down easier if you heap on the gravy."

Cecilia ate to bring a hopeful look to her face. *I*

would eat glass for you. Although these will do.

At the end of the meal, Airey said to Lorimer, "Cec'ly and me got to talk something over. That birch log will keep another day."

"Please don't change your plans," said Cecilia quickly, not wanting to talk, not wanting to think, not wanting to feel anything more than she was feeling this minute.

Airey's glance took it in. "A shame 'cause now Lorimer and me don't got an excuse. We're stuck, Lor, but I reckon it's my turn to fetch Susy-lassie tonight. Cec'ly, you'll walk down with me?"

"I'd like that," said Cecilia. The evening might be bearable. It had to be more bearable than now.

She helped Poly clear the table, sat on the kitchen step, and pretended to mind Jabez, inert with grief. Tom's barbed arrow sat in her heart, jagging and drawing blood every time she breathed.

Airey and Lorimer reduced the log to sections, sections to lengths, through the afternoon, Lorimer adding them to the stack climbing the barn's wall while Airey rested her crossed hands on the maul's handle and sent a look to Cecilia that told her she was not fooled by her casual pose.

The mist cleared as the hours passed. Lorimer and Airey finished their work in sunshine. Airey came to the washstand. Cecilia did not have the strength to hide what Airey saw in her face. Airey glanced up. "Polynegry, where'd you get to?"

"I was on the porch making these." Poly stepped down from the kitchen to give Cecilia a necklace of braided loosestrife. "This one's for you."

"How pretty." Cecilia put it on.

"No flower could have a finer setting," said

Airey. "Poly, you get harvesting some salad while me and Cec'ly bring in Susy-lassie. Supper will be that fancy canned fish she bought us."

Cecilia said, "It doesn't need cooking."

Poly made a gesture of salvation that Airey, toweling her hair, pretended not to see. Cecilia's heart turned over. *I like you. I want you. I love you.* Airey hung the towel on its nail. "Coming?"

Cecilia went with her down the front yard, over the lane, and into the fields. Beyond this, she had never ventured. The low sun cast a golden shimmer across the slope. Her hand was in Airey's. They swung at a good pace along the path that followed the creek, the tawny wheat swaying in the gold-washed breeze. What could Tom's world offer her as lovely as this?

Where the fields ended, a strip of meadow went with the creek as it dropped to the forest. Susy-lassie was standing by a sassafras tree looking at them, her roan flanks coppery in the sun. She seemed in no hurry to come home, dipping her head to the grass. Airey stopped at an old stone gatepost. "What came between you and your brother?"

"You can't guess? The fact of us."

"He knew?"

"He came with suspicions. It only needed a slip, the smallest of slips, to make him sure."

"And he had plenty to say about it."

"He did." As Airey waited, "He was sorry for you. For being duped. Ruined."

"I'm happy to tell him what I think of *him*." A whirr, and a basswood sapling across the meadow shuddered.

"Airey—"

Airey took another rock from the gatepost and

threw. The sapling jerked again.

"Don't make that poor tree Tom's whipping boy."

Airey weighed a third. "I'll save this one for his head."

Cecilia took it from her. "He isn't coming back."

"Good news for his head. He ain't welcome no more."

"You can't say that—"

"Just did."

"—because he's promised to see what he can do about Lorimer's education."

Airey looked scornful. "That wasn't never *his* idea. You put it there. You reckon he'll stick by his word, seeing he ain't going to keep his promise to me?"

"How do you know?"

"He won't waste his money on a ruin." Airey frowned. "Why is he helping Lor? What's he swapped for it?"

Cecilia smiled bleakly. "Do you think I bargained with him?" She stopped Airey's hand reclaiming the rock. "No." Her gaze swept the cove, golden and green below them. "He's finished with me."

"I'm finished with him before that. Grown man talking like a book." Airey tapped the rock. "I'd better watch out or I'll be damning my soul with murder of those who speak malice to you."

"I'd prefer you not to do that. It would be you against everyone who thinks as Tom thinks, and that's everyone."

"I don't care."

"You're as ornery as a mule."

Airey gave her a compressed smile. "Being a lowlander, you don't value a mule. There ain't nothing like one for digging in its hoofs and setting itself to a job."

"It can't pull up the whole forest."

"It'd bust itself trying." Airey looked as stubborn as two mules and a hickory log. Cecilia's heart melted. *You'd try to pull the world off its orbit for me.* "I'd rather you busted yourself for your career."

"It don't got to be one or the other. It can't be, not when you're hurt by unkindness."

Cecilia moved without will or thought and was in her arms. If any fortress could be strong enough, it was this one. She pressed against her, knowing Tom's words were waiting to flay her but here unable to be harmed. Airey's kisses were gentle on her brow. Cecilia asked against her collar, "Aren't we bringing Susy-lassie home?"

"She's in no hurry."

Cecilia was in no hurry, either. "When will Lorimer and Poly start wondering what's become of us?"

"Not for a while."

Cecilia slid her hands inside Airey's shirt, needing the comfort of her skin. "I don't want to keep talking about Tom."

"I'm more than done with him."

They waded hip-deep into the meadow grass. Cecilia took off her clothes, knelt, and lay on her back, looking up at the sky. Here within the Fitches' pocket of land, everything was being folded toward evening, although the sky above her was as blue as noon. Airey undressed. Cecilia felt invincible in her own nakedness. To be held in someone's regard, in her steady regard, was more powerful than anything she had known.

Airey lowered herself beside her. Cecilia turned to meet her lips. At the hot strike of desire, all of Tom's words burned away, all sorrow and fear. She lifted to Airey's hands, ravished by her touch, needing her, dissolving into her, dissolving into a blazing depth that built into a swift river, a tide, she was racing on its crest, was lofted into an ocean of fire, they were flying through it, open, perfect to each other, and Cecilia came as if hurled into light, and Airey was the light.

Brightness ebbed from between them like a ripple of sun back to the ocean. Airey moved over her, looked at her. Cecilia knew she saw what must be plain even to the constellations behind the blue sky, and her face became the one Cecilia had seen by the creek when she had knelt at her feet. *A face she's hidden from me.* She put her arms around her and drew her down.

The breeze across the meadow gradually brought them back to their separate selves. They shifted, nestled. Airey trailed an arm and leg across her, cheek against her shoulder.

Time circled and slowed. Airey grew still. After a few minutes, Cecilia realized that she had fallen asleep.

She laughed to herself, feeling sharp and alert. To have this. To know what it was. *Nothing can take it from me.* How early had Airey woken this morning to do her chores? Cecilia feathered a wisp of pale hair. Soon Airey would be hard at work on Beethoven, on Schubert and Mozart, on harmony and analysis and form. Would be hard at work somewhere else. The thought gave her no pain. While Airey slept, she could rejoice over what she had brought to pass.

She felt the shadow of the mountain creep along

them, felt the earth under her, felt Airey's forearm lying warm against her own skin. She thought of this same arm tensed, driving the bow across the strings with fastidious power. An answering quiver ran through her, and she turned her to look at her, to drink her in.

Airey stirred. Her lips parted. Cecilia kissed her as she woke, kissed her, wrapped her in fire, blade after blade of opening flame whirling around them, bright beyond bearing, faster, higher, until its incandescent core was sweeping them up, they became its brilliance, and Airey's release was fierce and triumphant.

They clung together, aware of the deep waters they floated on, kissing fearfully, sustaining each other, until Airey's lips slowed and her embrace fell away.

"You *can't* be going to sleep again."

"I'm tuckered out."

"It's not my fault you spent the day splitting wood."

Airey smiled, but her eyes were intent. "That brother of yours is still there scouring your soul."

"You can't march a brother off the plank with one push." Cecilia looked up at the trees. "I find facing facts helps to clear the decks."

"Is that so?"

"When the wind changes to a new quarter, you can let it blow you over or you can set a new course." Cecilia doodled in the scatter of goldenrod pollen across Airey's breasts. "Wishes, regrets: there's no point to them, not when new worlds are waiting for you."

"I ain't never seen a sailing ship." Airey's hand stopped Cecilia's finger. "I'd rather have that little monument of yours and go where I want."

"It's why I have it. And look: it brought me to you." Cecilia blew the pollen away in a cloud. "That day in the meadow—why were you there?"

"You reckon I'm always sleeping in flowers? I'd been playing fiddle at the Stocklys' house down in the cove. They'd packed their wagon ready to leave and threw the grandest so-long party anybody ever seen. They danced the whole night long, me playing till sunrise, then I got maybe two, three hours sleep on the floor. I was helping them pack their last things when their baby girl was sick over my dress and shoes. Millie said she'd wash them and send them back by a neighbor. I'd walked down to their place with my overalls over my good clothes, so overalls was the only thing I'd got to wear home. I took the railbed road 'cause there's nobody on it. By the time I got to the creek, I was that tired and hot, I stopped to wet my head and look over my fiddle. I didn't know I'd fallen asleep till you woke me."

My enchanted prince. Vast pitiless gears of fate had turned like watch cogs to bring them together.

Airey answered her thought. "Everything's got its reason. We got ours. To be happy and know why."

Cecilia sat up and reached for her clothes. "If Susy-lassie gets any closer, you can milk her horizontally."

Airey squinted over her shoulder to where Susy-lassie had ambled hintfully to the gate. "You reckon you'll ever tell me what you're feeling without me having to ask?"

Will I ever need to? "Did my telling you about Tom whet your appetite?" Cecilia shook out her dress. They had been lying on it, and its starch was thoroughly crushed. Poly's loosestrife necklace was flattened. Cecilia put it in a pocket and felt something else. "There are things better not known." The mail Tom had brought from the general store.

Airey stood to pull on her clothes. "There ain't nothing about you I don't want to know."

Cecilia glanced quickly at the letters. One had Mrs. Vernelle's return address, presumably her bread-and-butter letter to Airey. The second made her jump: Patmore's handwriting, addressed to Mrs. Grigg. *Good as his word.* The last was postmarked Fort Vickerson. She pressed it under her palm. Airey had not seen it. She could slip it back in her pocket. Could give it to her in the morning. In ten thousand days. Her lips were saying, "Airey, I'm so sorry. Tom brought up some letters, and I forgot them. This one must be from your mother."

Airey turned, her hand half-extended. They looked at each other. "Got to be done." Airey hitched the overalls' straps over her shoulders, took it, and read. Her face closed. "Mam's home on Friday. She's coming by way of Galt's Crossing."

"Friday." Tomorrow. *Tomorrow.* "I'll go home right away."

"No."

"Airey, I have to. I can't be here when she arrives."

"Stay at least till she gets home. Stay tonight. I need every minute I can get hold of. What if she don't come until real late?"

"She won't want to arrive to find a guest. I'll leave as soon as we bring in Susy-lassie. You know I'll be back as quickly as I can. We'll go—we'll take a trip. I have a friend in Cedar Falls who understands—"

Airey wasn't listening. "No. You stay tonight."

Cecilia offered her Mrs. Vernelle's letter instead of an argument. "This is also for you."

Airey gave it scant attention. "It's from Mrs. Vernelle, thanking me for having them here. That's mighty kind, seeing she played nearly the whole day. She says-says I'll find…" Airey fished in the envelope and pulled out a narrow, much-folded note. "It's from Dr. Neihoff." She opened it as if it were gold leaf and began to read. Stopped almost at once. "It-it ain't good news."

"Impossible." Cecilia tugged it from her rigid fingers. The writing was tightly packed and clearly done in haste.

"Dear Miss Fitch," Dr. Neihoff had written, "I am addressing you through Mrs. Vernelle, who has already put a stamp on her envelope. I telephoned the director of the Kehr Institute the moment we returned. He informed me that no student places remain and that all stipends have been awarded. I did not request either of him, as I believe you have neither the education nor the musical background to make a suitable entry into an academic class. You also are too old by several years, and I feel you would find a position in any classroom an uncomfortable one."

What was this? How could this be? Cecilia glanced up at Airey, who was as stiff as a crow in a storm. The letter was not finished. Someone had to read it.

"Your attainments clearly need to be addressed by different means. Your natural talents are so manifestly superior, your skill of so high an order, that you merely require tutelage in the areas of essential knowledge you lack."

Cecilia drew in a breath. "Airey."

Airey turned her head an inch.

"Listen." Cecilia read his words aloud and continued: "If you continue to desire a solo career once you have completed this education, and demonstrate the qualities needed for it, I will arrange for you to proceed to a preeminent master, whose privilege it will be to give you your final gifts."

Airey was no less pale, but her eyes had kindled. Cecilia read on.

"I have spoken with my wife concerning your studies this very evening after our most pleasurable day with you. Indeed, we speak of nothing else. Having received the director's permission, I am able to extend my wife's and my invitation to you to accept our house as your home while I award myself the felicity of teaching you, as a private pupil, those necessary things which I hope and expect will fit you for study with one of these masters."

Cecilia felt Airey expand.

"I do this, my dear Miss Fitch, because I feel, and Mr. and Mrs. Vernelle kindly concur, that I have the requisite skills to bring you to the full realm of concert music. That I shall have the honor of being your second teacher, after Maestro Broeggen, I contemplate with satisfaction." Cecilia turned the page. "My wife expresses herself happy to guide you in areas of dress and deportment suitable for the circles you seek to join, and may I say myself that you could have no finer teacher."

Airey gave a breathless laugh.

"I turn now to matters of a financial nature. These, as we know, are difficult times, and my wife and I have agreed upon certain economies to allow me to teach you in our home. I do not tell you this to bring attention to our small acts, which we do gladly, but to clarify the constraints within which I offer my services. You and I are both acquainted with the adversity of poverty, I in my youth and you today. I do not soften my words: while your housing will be free of charge, you will need to provide yourself with funds for all your musical expenses, travel, clothing, and the like. How fortunate that you have a kind and generous friend in Miss Howison and, through her, a similarly generous family! I am certain the necessary money will be made available to you. If not, a circumstance that would very much astonish me, I believe you will neither be discouraged nor stopped from making your way to me in time."

Cecilia looked up. The setting sun had placed Airey against a sky of crimson banners. *You can't have a clearer sign than that.* She felt something rise under her. It was her own road, and now she was about to walk it. She said, "Airey, the money is absolutely certain," and returned to the letter.

"My wife and I arrive in Montreal on Thursday and will have your room ready by the end of the week. We urge you to come immediately, as there is no time to be lost. I would be grateful if you would send me your decision via telegram, perhaps through the good offices of your friend. Again, Miss Fitch, it would be my honor and great pleasure to guide your next steps toward that glorious career which you believe, and I trust, is your destiny. I remain your faithful servant, Barukh Neihoff."

Airey lifted her head and looked farther than the sun. Her face was reverent. "God don't waste much time."

Sadly, no.

"But the money—"

"Tom isn't the only one with money. You'll have all you need very soon. Next week."

"That means-means we got a lot to, no, first we need—" Airey stopped, bewildered by the open way before her. "We got to wait till Mam gets home."

"The Neihoffs are in Montreal by now."

"I can't leave this soon. How will Lor get the corn in?"

"Are you going to delay for a field of corn?"

"I can't go before the park's settled. We still—"

Cecilia was conscious of Pat's letter in her pocket. "Are you trying to postpone this?"

"No." Airey looked at her. "No. There ain't no pushing this off, nor wanting to." She took back Dr. Neihoff's letter. "I got to write him."

"We'll drive to Mr. Keller's now and telegraph."

Airey shook her head. "There's Susy-lassie to bring in. She's looking at us wondering what's going on in our heads."

"Airey!"

Airey grinned. "Mr. Keller needs to ride old Molly down to Lovat Cove to get it sent, and Molly don't budge after dark, except for a birth or dying. This'll keep for a night."

"Your mother's back tomorrow."

"She can't get from Galt's Crossing to here before dinner, seeing the bus sets out from Charleville. You and I need time to talk through what we're going to do."

Cecilia's heart gave a little shiver. It was a conversation she would shed blood not to have. "When are you going to tell Lorimer and Poly?"

"Today. I got to."

"Poly won't take it well."

"I ain't looking forward to telling them." Airey pushed her fingers through her hair. "Maybe knowing Mam's back tomorrow will make it easier."

Tomorrow. Mrs. Grigg would already be on her way home. Now there were only hours left until it was time to leave. And after that? A day in Charleville with Airey to buy her clothes, have lunch, put her on the train. And then. And then. Cecilia did not know what would happen then. It was something new.

"Let's get Susy-lassie back before the little ones start hunting us."

The crimson sky had darkened to the rim of evening. Cecilia finished getting dressed. She felt suspended in the air, knowing she was falling, but the ground not getting any closer. They let Susy-lassie lead the way home, walking apart, wrapped in their separate thoughts, moving closer together, holding hands. Royal came to the edge of the yard to meet them, and their fingers separated. Cecilia took no satisfaction from knowing that Airey had finally understood.

Chapter Nine

"You've been gone for ages," said Poly, meeting them in the yard.

"We got to talking," said Airey, and gestured to Poly to go with her to the barn.

Cecilia stopped on the porch to think. Going in, she asked Lorimer, "Shall we start supper without Airey?"

"Best to open those fish cans before she does," he agreed from the table, where he was carefully winding radio wire around a patent medicine bottle. "Otherwise, something bad will happen."

Airey and Poly came in with jugs of milk as Cecilia finished setting the table. Airey gave a vague grace. After a moment, Poly said, "Airey, you ain't taken a bite of nothing."

Airey brought herself to attention with a set of her shoulders. Her face became austere. "I got two big things to tell you all, and I can't eat till I've delivered. First thing is, Mam's home tomorrow."

Lorimer whooped, and Poly danced round her chair. "Jaby, I *told* you. How'd you find out, Airey?"

"That brother of Cec'ly's brung some letters up with him. Cec'ly remembered them when we was getting Susy-lassie."

Lorimer snatched the crumpled letter from her. "Merit wrote this. Look, she says right at the bottom: *Give Lor and Poly and Jaby big kisses from me.*"

"You need to hunt a bag of squirrel first thing in the morning!" Poly told him excitedly, and to Cecilia, "Mam likes stewed squirrel better than anything. Airey can't do much to that. We'll pick beans, and I'll make flower chains and hang them all over the house!" She kissed Jabez. "That's from Merit!"

Lorimer's head turned warily. "What's the other thing you got to tell us, Airey?"

"I got another letter, from that music doctor. He wants me to go up to Canady, that's where he lives, so he can teach me what else I need to know."

"Can't be much left to teach." He paused. "Canady! How are you getting all that way?"

Cecilia said, "I'm responsible for the money."

"Then it'll happen. When?"

"Pretty much as soon as Mam gets home," said Airey.

"No!" Poly crashed her chair to the floor. "Nobody's going away again never *ever*!" She dodged Airey's arm and flung herself on the settle, head in her arms to muffle her despairing howls. Cecilia put a settling hand on Jabez.

Airey looked at Lorimer. "I'm sorry, Lor. I'd hoped to stay here and help a bit longer. Cec'ly's money will pay for hired men."

"I don't want it."

"I know we don't take charity, but with the corn and all, we'll need men—"

Lorimer slammed his hands on the table. "I don't want them. I don't want *none* of it."

"You can't do it by yourself."

"Airey, I don't *want* it. I don't want no help. I don't want this *place*. You been striving to save it for me, but you never once asked if I *wanted* you to. Why would I want a place like this that's costing us our whole lives?"

"This—'cause it's our place."

"You got bats in your head," Lorimer exploded, jumping in his chair. "You're so proud of Fitch land that we don't dare speak a word against it for fear of sounding like traitors, but Merit left and Mam wants to just as bad. We're going to be hustled off by the park sooner or later, and that's the best that *could* happen. I don't give a straw for this old farm, not if I got to carry it on my back till I'm on my knees under it."

Airey looked as if he had punched her. "It's our home. It's always been our home. Fitches been here from the start."

"That don't matter. *We* don't matter. Nobody *cares* about us Fitches, except you. What about me? You say I'm a scientist, as if I could ever be one up here at the back of beyond—or an engineer or anything! If Mam sells up, we can find work in the mills, or she can marry the pastor and at least we'll be down where I got a *chance* of something!"

Airey sat carved from stone. Her voice, when she finally spoke, came like grit. "It don't matter to you? Fitches fought to stay here all through war and hard times, and it don't matter?"

"Is that what Fitches are all about? Too stupid except to work themselves to death for nothing? Those first Fitches you're almighty proud of got on their hind legs and came here to escape their misfortune. Ain't we got their sense? We've been getting poorer ever since Grandsire sold half the mountain, and now we're at bottom. You're proud of us ending here?"

"Fitches put their blood into this place," said

Airey.

"So does every farmer. You talk fine talk, but it looks like Fitch dirt ain't good enough for *you* 'cause *you* ain't staying."

"I'll be earning money and sending it home."

"Why? What good will that do us? No school, no neighbors, no friends—how are we going to live? How are we going to fetch a doctor? Buy coal oil and coffee? You're going to send money to pay for hired men till I'm old and near my grave? Wake up, Airey! There ain't hardly nobody left here. The Strickers will be going soon, and the Labhards are talking of selling by Christmas. It's *over.* This farm, everything's *over.*"

Brother and sister held each other's stare until Lorimer, flushing, looked down.

Cecilia took a frightened Jabez onto her lap. "You need to know your lawyer's advice."

"We ain't got a lawyer," said Lorimer.

"One of my friends is acting for your mother." Cecilia handed Patmore's letter to Airey. "You need to read this."

Poly crept back to the table, her face blotched with tears.

"It's not wrote to me," Airey said in the same grit.

"You're going to be reading it out to her anyway when she's back," said Lorimer. "Why not now?"

Airey opened it slowly, read it slowly. "He says he can represent Mam once she agrees. He wants to come up and see her. He says he's handled a similar case, and—*and leases are not awarded save to the very elderly, to allow them to live out their days,* and that they ain't for *a young man hoping for an inheritance no longer his under the law. Given this, I will recommend to you certain steps before you sell—*" Airey looked around with unseeing eyes. "Him too. They're ending it. Our place. Our home."

"Where you grew up," said Cecilia. "It doesn't mean you have to die here or should want to. Lorimer's right. Is he to be sacrificed, are they all to be sacrificed, to furnish you with fond thoughts of what you've left behind? Must they suffer for what you alone hold dear?"

"It's no sacrifice. Fitches have pride in—"

"What greater distinction does the Fitch name need than that which you'll give it?"

Airey looked gaunt in the lantern's light.

"You've chosen your life," said Cecilia. "Let Lorimer choose his."

Lorimer said, "I'm sorry, Airey."

Airey shoved back from the table, grabbed the kitchen lantern and her violin box, and was out the door.

They stayed unmoving in the dim light of the stove. Royal put his head in Lorimer's lap. Cecilia finally said to Poly, "Let's find another lantern."

Lorimer twisted in guilty relief. "*That's* why I never spoke before."

"It had to be said. Mr. Reaveley will work for your best interests. Is Airey likely to be angry for long?"

"When she storms up, she's worse than Old Man Donney and the Blazing Dog. Most times, it don't last."

"This time?"

"It'll last."

"That's a pity. You've always known the family couldn't stay here."

"I knew it when Freed died."

"I don't want to go *no* place!" Poly kicked the table leg. "The park did this. I hate the park!"

"What would Pastor Souch say on that?" Lorimer asked her.

"He'd say it's God's will 'cause he always does, but God don't *want* us gone from here!"

"Where's that wrote? I don't recall Lord Jesus asking us to keep what we like. He says *take up your cross.*"

Cecilia looked at him with respect.

Poly digested this. "We got to offer it up to Him?"

"Put your mind on it," said Lorimer.

"I wish I could make God make Airey stay."

"I wish she'd stay," said Cecilia, "but I know she can't." To Jabez, "I see that hand reaching for the bowl, sir."

"Jaby don't mind where he lives, as long as he eats."

Cecilia fed Jabez her supper, bathed him, and settled him to sleep in his bedroom. Poly and Lorimer were preparing their standup baths when she returned. She stepped out to the porch. Clouds were speeding silently across the stars like frigates into battle. Airey had gone without a look. Their last night here together, and she had gone. Poly detoured on her way to bed to give Cecilia a kiss. Lorimer came out a moment later and stood beside her.

"Will Airey come back?" she asked.

"She's never stayed away all night, not even

when she was fired up like a rocket." He cocked his head. "She ain't in the shed, but she's got her fiddle, so she'll be practicing."

"Do you know where she might be?"

"Reckon so. You leaving us tomorrow?"

"You won't want me here when your mother's back."

"We'll miss you. It's been nice you being here."

"Thank you. I've enjoyed it more than I can say. But I must speak with Airey tonight, and I don't care if she's erupting like the Fourth of July."

He grinned. "If she is, don't forget it was you who decided to find her." He looked around. "Royal can take you."

"He'll know the way?"

"Royal knows the whole mountain. I'll get you a light." He came back with a small candle lantern. "Royal, find Airey. Find Airey."

Cecilia bent to pat Royal's compact shoulder. "Good night, Lorimer."

He was looking into the darkness. "Airey's going." Again, meditatively, "she's going."

Cecilia left him on the porch. Royal led her down the same path she had taken with Airey, through the meadow and into the forest. Overhead, the wind was rushing the treetops, immense and purposeful. She stumbled along the path, the little mica-sided lantern more hindrance than light. She kept it aloft for comfort. Royal padded ahead, checking over his shoulder every few yards. Trees appeared in the circle of lamplight and vanished, branches snagged and held her until she pulled free, something barked on the night slope, and Royal stopped, head up, before moving on.

The woods were thicker now, as if she were moving away from human life instead of toward it. The way became steeper. Cecilia put out a hand to block her descent. How far had she come? The trees above her seemed as high as a cathedral, the wind higher still, and above them all, she felt the cold Olympian stars.

Smell of wood smoke. Two more steps, the sound of a violin. She pushed aside a long jointed arm of rhododendron and thought she saw a dab of light in the darkness. It stayed. Her lantern picked out shaggy horizontal lines of logs, a small cabin so overgrown it could have been a pile of moss. Royal barked once and led her around to its sagging door.

Airey was playing in front of a small fire. She looked up as Cecilia came in, not pausing until the exercise was finished.

"How much longer do you need?"

"I got six of these to go. You staying?"

"Of course. Royal knows that." He was judging whether the corner by the fireplace was suitable; it seemed to be, for he settled and lay his head on his paws, an adjutant awaiting further orders. Airey moved to let her take one of the two armchairs standing by the fire. Cecilia looked around the fire-lit room. These two chairs, a collapsed bedframe, three curling newspaper articles pinned on nails, two tin cups on the oak mantelpiece. Airey started the next piece. Even now, even tonight, after all that had happened, the violin came first. It would always come first.

Airey finally lowered her bow. "Coffee?" She filled a sooty, dented kettle from a bucket near the door and stood it on the fire iron.

"Where are we?" Cecilia asked. "I wondered if

Royal was leading me to Hinterhouse."

"Not that far. This is Mr. Broeggen's place."

"This? I didn't realize he was a hermit."

"Most of his things was taken after he died. This is his chair." Airey took it. "You're in mine. Him and me sat here most days till I got sent to the Siffville School, and then I came on Saturdays and Sundays. See that wagon jack brace over there, all turned to rust? Mr. Broeggen would heat it in the fire and stick it into a cup of liquor. He called it a toddy. When I was cold, it smelled good."

"Did he give you any?" Cecilia indulged her, grateful for this peace before what she knew would come.

"He said I could sip if I wanted to, but I'd taken the pledge with Pap. I dipped Mr. Broeggen's snuff till I swallowed it once and was sick worse than a dog and that was me done. I brung him tobacco leaves, and he'd cut and roll them and call them cigars. He'd have his cigar and toddy while he listened to me, and then he'd teach me and we'd play." Airey gestured to one of the clippings on the wall. "That's the *Melita Morning Sentinel*. They gave his name when they wrote about a concert. *Consummate bowmanship*."

Cecilia, watching her face, had a hint of what Airey must have been like when she was six or eight. "How did he come to live here?"

"How did he end up in this forsaken place, you mean to say."

"I do mean to say it."

Airey grinned. "He was lodging at Mrs. Sifferd's boarding house for timber crews down in Heresy, playing for a bed. I don't know how he got there. End of the rail, I guess. Mr. Sifferd works for Sankgallon and was given orders to make his boarders pay by company chit, which Mr. Broeggen couldn't do, so Mr. Sifferd spoke to Pap, and Pap said Sankgallon had done to Mr. Broeggen like it did to everybody and let him use this place, our old grand-uncle's place. Mr. Broeggen didn't have nothing else, so he took it." She leaned to check the kettle. "Some days, I'd come and find him wallowing in his bed like a hog. Some days, he couldn't lift his fiddle, his hands was shaking that bad. Some days, he'd yell and cuss in his other tongue or call on the Lord to strike him dead. I never did see him clear-wrung sober. He was all right when he wasn't too lit." She looked around the room. "This is the last time I'm here."

Cecilia followed her gaze. When she had been riding her pony and setting out dolls' tea tables on the lawn, Airey had been in this cave, learning sorcery. "How did he support himself?"

"By his fiddle, same as in Heresy. He'd go out enough for that. He played new dances, at least I reckoned so till I learned he'd just taken tunes from Mozart and the rest."

"It's an old trick."

"When Mam brung him a pie to say welcome, I tagged along. He played his fiddle for us. I couldn't get over it. I came and came and no stopping me, not that he tried too hard. Pap was ready to take a stick to him when he found I stayed here most of every day till Mam said she'd known from the start and no harm in it. Pap wrote to Siffville after he heard Mr. Broeggen swearing in front of me. I still slid down here every chance I got. At long last, Pap said even a fool like himself could see I'd been brung to fiddling by God." Airey pulled the kettle from the flames with the jack brace and dropped in a lump of ground coffee. "That needs steeping. After Mr. Broeggen died and Pap got sick, I went down the cove to Mr. Huber and swapped chores for getting taught as much old-time music as he could cram in me 'cause folks paid to hear that."

"You need never reproach yourself that you didn't do everything you could for your family."

"We each of us done the most we was able." Airey drew up her knees to set her heels on the edge of the seat. "Mr. Broeggen, too."

"He should have kept himself alive for your sake. He knew what you were."

"He was killing himself long before he laid eyes on me." Airey reached to pour the coffee. "Maybe it would have broken him to see me stepping up in the world."

Cecilia nestled her cup against her breastbone. "Jealous of a child?"

"Of the chances a child's still got." Airey looked at the clippings. "After he died, Pap didn't need this place, so I took it for practicing. Then Freed and Pap went home to our Savior, and I couldn't get here regular, but sometimes, when I wanted to be by myself or I got riled, like tonight, I'd come here for a spell."

"Are you still riled?"

"I raged like Satan while I was doing my scales. It went when you stepped in."

"You didn't suspect that Lorimer wouldn't want the farm?"

"He never let on." Airey's mouth tightened. "I can't hardly believe he said that. What have we all been working for—" She stopped with an effort. "I won't plow that field again. He's right: I'm leaving. I can't make him do what I ain't doing. But I reckoned he'd *want—*" Her hands clenched, and she was silent.

"You're both true Fitches. You want better than you have."

Airey looked at the fire. "When I came here to-night, I swore I'd lay down my fiddle and take on the park to spite everybody, but I heard your voice saying *setting your will against God's?* so I gave up that idea and done my scales."

"I'm glad you listen to me even when I'm not here."

Airey's smile flickered and faded. "If Freed hadn't died—but grown men can't stop the park. Nobody can. I know it, but I can't let it be. Why did we get this far, only to have it taken?"

"Why does anything happen? Why should you be spared the rod that's struck you so often before?"

"That's doubting God." Airey hunched into silence. "I won't never believe the park's anything but the devil doing his work through men."

It's never the devil. "I'm glad you won't be trying to fight for the farm from Montreal."

"Seems things have worked out real fine." Airey's voice was flat. "I got all I want and now no worries behind me. All except one."

Here it is. Cecilia put down her cup.

"I've been turning it over and over in my mind. I'm ready to go. I want to go. I know you can't come up, not for three, maybe four months, seeing as your folks don't like you visiting here and will like even less you being in Canady. You've got to wait for your auntie's trust money. I ain't liking one bit of that, but if Merit could stand it, I can, too." Airey knotted a little in her chair. "Three, four months! How am I going to live through them when I can't bear three hours?"

Time enough to find out.

"But then you'll come up to visit and can look around to see what we might do. A place—a little house maybe? Is Canady like here?"

"I've never been. It's colder. I can't come."

"Not right yet—"

"I can't come. Not to Canada. Not to anywhere."

"What's this?" Airey sat forward, her brows snapping to a black line. "This is your brother, ain't it? I knew he'd swapped for something."

"He threatened to inform the Kehr Institute about you."

"Inform?" Airey backed up. "About us? He'd do that? Why?"

"Because he wants me to take the curb and bit. For the honor of the family. For my own good. He'll destroy you if I don't."

"That's his swap?"

"It's not a swap. It's blackmail. It's very effective."

"You're going to bend your knee to him?"

"If I go to Montreal, if I stay in contact with you in any way, he'll expose you."

"He won't do nothing. You'll see. He ain't got the guts of a waxworm."

"It doesn't take much courage to write a letter, even to the governing board of Kehr."

"They'd waste their time on false witness?"

"It wouldn't be false, would it? No school could ignore such a letter, not even from an anonymous source, and Tom's beginning to be known in the music world. Dr. Neihoff, for one, knows him."

"Him that holds his family's honor so high, he'd snitch?"

"He'd prefer not to, but he would. I know he would. Although he's confident he won't have to—and he's right."

"You reckon I'll walk away from what's between us on account of him?"

"I want you to."

"And you?"

"I have to."

"If I take a rock and kill him?"

"Don't be absurd. Do you think killing him would end it? As if he's the only one who'll ever do this? The whole world is Tom. Has nothing I've said these past days made a dent? Even if we could edge past him, we'd meet someone like him again and again, and he would do this again. It's come rather early for us, that's all."

"He ain't walking us off a plank."

"He already has."

"We're not ended."

"Airey, we are. I'll admit to a foolish moment when I thought I was blessed, that I no longer had to face facts, but Tom's brought me back squarely before them."

"*His* facts."

"Facts. What I imagined isn't possible. Traveling with you on your tours? Insanity. Living with you? Delusion. None of that could ever or will ever happen."

"Girls travel together all the time. Minnie Lutz and Beryl Martin, they went up to Cincinnati and shared a boarding house room for a whole year and nobody said one word."

"Where are they now?"

Airey hesitated. "Both married."

"Making my point. You know it wouldn't be the

same for us." Before Airey could speak, "Facts. Let's say there was no Tom." She ignored Airey's savage nod. "Let's say I go with you on your tours. Will people accept us as they accepted Minnie and Beryl? Of course not. What will they take me to be? Not your chaperone, and not—no, I don't have the talent to be—your accompanist. I'd plainly be, I'd obviously be, your...intimate friend. Is there an impresario on earth who'd sign you on if I were part of your entourage? Does a program committee exist that would book you into their concert hall once they saw me with you? They don't present known perversion to their audiences."

"Seeing you would vex them? Then we'll make sure they won't. I'll travel by myself, like men do who go downriver for winter work, and in between, I'll come home to you."

"It's not a question of staying out of sight. Even if Tom isn't keeping watch, do you imagine nobody else will? That no one else will question why the newly famous Miss Fitch, why the world-renowned Miss Fitch, constantly refuses hospitality from nobility and millionaires to go back to some girl, to the same girl, year after year? You think that won't be noticed?"

"Who's going to care what I'm doing or where I am when I ain't on stage, aside from the crawling bug that's your brother?"

"Who'd care? You ask that, with *Photo Screen News* in the house? You haven't grasped the public's greed for the secrets of famous people? Hollywood studios work hard to put false faces on their stars, but the Yellow Press works harder to sniff out scandals. How long do you think it will take before one of their number bribes a cello player or a clerk in your manager's office to confirm the gossip it's hearing? How many seconds do you think your career will last after the headline MORAL TURPITUDE EXPOSED? It won't just be shocked captions under compromising photographs, it will be the police, the courts. Immoral conduct, gross obscenity—crimes that put us in jail. I've known it to happen. My family might save me, might hide me away in a private hospital, but you'd be destroyed in full view. And where do you think it will come from, the gossip that puts them on the trail? It will come from Tom. Or someone like Tom. Or from a moral crusader or a paid sneak or a rival. Anyone will do."

"Those movie stars, all of them wear false faces?"

"Yes, one way or another."

"Seems mostly they work out fine. I'll make one for me."

"Oh, Airey, you can't. You can't. Of all women on earth, especially not you. Do you really think you could hide yourself—hide us both—behind a false face? That you could lie that well for that long? Lie at all? You, who plays from her soul?"

"I'd put on a hundred faces to hide you from folks like Tom."

"He already knows, so why bother with the rest? You don't understand how difficult it is to wear even one. I thought I had the art perfected, yet Tom discovered us almost at once. I constantly check over my shoulder, watch my words, deny what I am. Why would I want that for you?"

"What about those Boston ladies? You told me folks know all about them, but they don't seem to come to hurt."

"Boston marriages? If they're more than simply

two close friends sharing a roof, they'd be hounded from existence. In our case, Tom already knows there's more. Anyone looking at us would know."

Airey's eyes warmed at this, but Cecilia pressed on. "I don't say that two girls somewhere haven't somehow managed it. They must have begun as obscure nobodies and stayed that way, and that's neither of us, is it? Even without Tom making this argument pointless, it's neither of us. You don't want obscurity, and thank goodness, because you'll never have it. You're already famous here and soon will be again in Montreal. Hundreds of eyes will be on you the moment your train arrives, eager to see Dr. Neihoff's mysterious virtuosa. By the time you start your career, there will be thousands, a few years later, tens of thousands, millions. The consequence of genius is the spotlight of fame. It's a light that never wavers, never blinks. Once it's on you, it will only grow stronger. Impossible to wear a false face in such a light, impossible to keep a secret because it leaves no shadow where anything—anyone—can hide."

"I saw a pole of electric light bulbs once, down in Heresy. When it came on, folks couldn't see nothing else, they was so purely blinded by it. That's what I want, a light brighter than any on earth. I want it so bright on me that nobody sees one speck of you."

"Speck? I said *neither of us*. They're seeing all of me right now. They've always seen me, they've always been looking at me. Because I'm Colonel Howison's daughter, a Howison of Old Waring, first of the First Families. As Tom says, I'm always noticed, always recognized, always known. I'm all over your walls. Not a day passes without the society columns reporting where I was or whom I was with. Tom told me that whispers are already including my name. How long before *Miss Howison, seen here with her young protégée* becomes *Miss Howison, arrested with her fancy-girl*? It doesn't need Tom to endanger you. I do that all by myself."

"I ain't never seen so many hard facts piled up in one place. I'd be purely discouraged—except for one that makes the whole lot of them dust under our feet." When Cecilia did not speak, "It being that the two of us have been brung together by God. You can't deny it. You know it's true. The candles in our hands are lit by the Spirit. We know it's true. There's no fact bigger than that."

"If God were for us, we wouldn't need candles. We'd be pillars of fire."

"You ain't seeing God's will in this? Even with what He's set alight in your soul?" Cecilia saw her realize that she had never heard her say it. "You know it's true."

"Yes, I do see God's will working through us. Everything that's happened has happened for a reason. It was to bring you to a life in music. And now you're here."

"But why this way? Why? It's for more than music. Why did He draw us together? Why did He bless us? Why did He bind us? So we'd go forth together in His light. To be testament of the light He put in us. I reckon the Lord God of Hosts is stronger even than Tom Howison."

"What the Lord giveth, the Lord taketh away. And has."

"You're real set on knuckling under, ain't you? Maybe, being a Howison, you've never had to fight back, but I surely wasn't born to take your brother's foot on my neck. You think I'll suffer something I know ain't right? What part of lamb you reckon I got in me? Your brother can't stop us. Nothing can. When God wants us to do something, it means we can do it. We can do this. I'll never believe no otherwise."

Cecilia made an abrupt gesture. "Believe what you want, but this is over. I'm not joining a doomed defiance, even one based on a fiery faith, not when it will prevent the one thing I desire above all else. I'm a businesswoman at heart. I've invested everything I have in you, and I won't throw it away in the hope that God is our secret backer."

"What one thing? My playing? That's what matters to you?"

"It's all that matters to me. It's *all* that matters. Because you *are* your music. You *are* your genius. You were born to stride the earth like a colossus. You're only yourself when you play. I want you completely and utterly Airey Fitch, all-conquering and glorious."

"How'll that happen, when doing this will break me like rock on glass?"

"You'll survive. What you do never needed me. It doesn't now."

"You don't know spit from frog grease."

"I've kept my side of the swap. Now keep yours. The world of music is waiting for you. Go to it. The fire is there for you. Throw yourself in. Accept the life God is giving you with open arms and live it to the brim. Burn in your own light."

"Don't go from me."

I don't need to. Cecilia gathered every atom of strength she possessed. "I told you the money for Canada was certain. It was to have been from Tom, but of course, that's vanished. Dr. Neihoff has said he can provide nothing. My trust doesn't begin until November, and when it does, Tom's promised to block me from using any of it for your support. I have no money to give you."

Airey's face was ashen. "You knew—knew this—you knew this back in the meadow. You knew it then. Why did you tell me I'd got money when there wasn't none?"

"Because there's quite a lot. It will come from the sale of your farm to Sankgallon Gap Timber Company."

Airey shot back as if Cecilia had stabbed her with the jack brace.

"Your lawyer has made it clear you must sell, but why sell to the park? It can't offer anything close to what Sankgallon can. My reading of the old ledgers tells me you possess about eight hundred acres across the southern slopes, mostly on the higher reaches and presumably as far down as this cabin. Red oak is your main cash crop, but there's also hickory, maple, white oak, locust, buckeye, and chestnut. Add in the land, add in a consideration for the final sale of the logged-out assets to the park, and my estimate is that you'll net twice the acreage total from Sankgallon than you'd get from the government."

Airey sat without moving.

"My brother Trenton is manager of Sankgallon. He's racing the park's clock and is keen to buy. Why do you think Mr. Souch has been scouting up here? Once Trenton hears you're willing to sell, he'll have a contract in your mother's hands as fast as it can be typed. Next week. And Sankgallon is in a position to pay a considerable cash advance to ensure speedy transfer."

Airey's lips had snarled back. "We won't take it."

"You have to. You have to accept somebody's money, so why not the best deal available?" Airey's teeth stayed bared. "You needn't fear Sankgallon will take advantage. Patmore Reaveley's already your representative, and I've every reason to think he'll extract the last penny he can from us. I suggest you also name him as your family's trustee. That will strip some weight from Mr. Souch's authority." Airey was silent. "You might prefer the park's money. In that case, Mr. Reaveley will do his best by you, but not only will you receive a smaller amount, it will take longer, delaying your journey north and Lorimer's going to school. That might be your choice. I don't think it would be Lorimer's. It wouldn't be mine."

"Sankgallon wrecked us."

"Lack of commercial enterprise wrecked you. You talk of charity—you were never in need of it. If you Fitches had seen your property as tangible assets instead of a landed estate, you'd have your own timber company and sawmills by now, your own shareholders and state contracts. Not that I'm sorry because the way things actually happened brought you to a violin."

"Howisons—now there's enterprise."

"I agree. We'll profit from this, even Tom, although it will torture him to know I've done it, and he's unable to object. I'm not sorry for that, either. But Howison profit isn't the point. *Your* profit is. To make it easier, let's say twenty-five dollars an acre for eight hundred acres. Divide by five children and one parent: that's over three thousand dollars each."

Airey jerked to her feet.

"If you won't listen to me, listen to your brother.

Wake up! Will pride finish what lack of business sense began?" Cecilia looked up at her with weary impatience. "I can't make you agree to sell to us. By all means, go down with your ship. Do the least possible good to your family and the most harm to yourself. *This* is why pride is a sin."

Airey turned away, caught at the mantelpiece and gripped it, the muscles in her arms standing like bone. "Wringing the most you can from what you've got—that's pride? Grandsire tried it, and we all learned why the love of money's a sin. Pride means knowing what the best of something is, then doing your best by it. Even when it's you. Deciding what's worth fighting for and doing the fighting. Knowing you got a right to a place on earth and claiming it. Your place on earth. Fitches of Applesell Bald. This is my place. It's my place. My home. My mountain."

"Your mountain is wherever you stand."

Airey stood looking down at the fire until its flames sank to blue guttering ribbons. "This farm. It's over. I know it. But Fitches take pride in living off our own. We'll do it this one last time. We'll take your deal." She rested her forehead on the sharp edge of the mantelpiece. "You hoped I'd hate you for bringing this on me. To make me glad you was giving me up. To make me want to give *you* up."

"Do you?"

Airey tipped her head. "You think one whipping knocks me flat? I got pity for you."

"Not enough to make this less hard on me."

"I want it hard on you. I want it so hard you'll sweat blood, like I'm doing inside. Maybe it'll bring you to your senses. I ain't got nothing else to use." She straightened, her hands flat on the mantelpiece, and finally pushed herself away.

Cecilia rose stiffly as Airey stooped to light the lanterns. Cecilia took the smaller one and went with Royal to the door. Airey doused the fire with coffee from the cups and kettle and put them on the hearth. The light from the lamps divided and stretched their shadows across the low roof. Airey glanced around the cabin and closed the door behind them. For a moment, they stood together in the wind and night, lanterns low, their faces in darkness. Airey stepped closer, stepped past her, and followed Royal into the woods.

Out of the cabin's shelter, Cecilia felt the chill of the night. A faint rain made the ground slick. She saw Airey's lantern ahead. The forest was a thick vertical noise. Her foot caught on roots. She refused to stumble, fearing help less than fearing that no help would come. At some point, the air changed, was filled with the susurration of wheat, and she knew she was in the open. Airey's lantern made a blur on the rising path. The high tops of the chestnuts sounded like waves as she climbed the last steep slope, and the house appeared, lit from within like a ship on the ocean of sky.

Royal shook himself on the porch and went through to the back rooms. Cecilia wiped rain from her hair with both hands. The next step seemed possible now that she was inside. She said, "You don't have to wait for the sale of the farm, and you mustn't. My pocket money is mine to spend. I'm given it on Tuesdays. It will cover your train fare and a little more. I'll take you to the station in Charleville any day after Tuesday."

Airey poured water into the cook stove's reservoir.

"I'll bring along a few things to start you off in Canada."

Airey fed wood into the stove.

"Let's say Wednesday. I'll tell the Neihoffs that you're setting out on Wednesday."

Airey dusted wood chaff from her hands. "I ain't taking your help no more."

"You need to. Who else will buy your train ticket? Who—"

"Not you."

"I want to finish what I started."

"What you started ain't finished till we're in our graves." Airey left to check the animals.

Cecilia waited, tidied the kitchen, and finally bathed. Airey did not come back. She went to her room and stripped off her damp clothes. She got into bed. This was the same bed on the same day that she had woken to the music of the spheres. *Let me never have another day like this.* She pushed the pillow from her face. *Unless I can die in the morning.*

She tried to be asleep before she began listening for Airey to pass her door, before what was waiting for her in the dark rose to look her in the face. She pressed her palms against her breastbone, but the vault of her heart would not close, it gorged up faces, words, Tom, noises, pain, harsh noise, a noise that would not stop, and she found that she had been asleep and that the noise was real, and it was the coffee grinder.

She blinked sandy eyes and saw the pitcher of water on the dressing table, steaming and innocent.

She washed and put on her other set of new clothes. Now that today was today, she felt composed. Fear of amputation was always worse than amputation. *I'm not crippled yet. I'll have Wednesday.*

She went into the main room. It smelled of wet wood, soap, blackstone, and stewing meat. She helped herself to coffee. Poly was on the porch, plaiting honeysuckle vines. Cecilia watched Royal rousting hidden hens as Lorimer inched along the flower beds straightening and hammering down the palings.

"I'm glad you're up," said Poly. "Mam's room is the last one to clean. Airey went to look in on you and said you was sleeping as peaceful as an angel."

I had three minutes like that? Cecilia thought of Airey watching her sleep. "I wish she'd woken me. I could have helped you clean the house."

"Her and Polynegry and me did it," said Lorimer, emerging from behind the climbing roses. "Then she went up the mountain."

"The farm's going to be sold."

"I know. That lawyer of yours wrote to Mam about it."

"No, next week. To Sankgallon Gap Timber."

He whistled.

Poly's voice caught. "You come here, and everything changed."

"Poly!" said Lorimer.

"I seem to have done that, didn't I?"

"Where will we go?"

Lorimer's gaze moved from Poly to the forested slope. "School."

"I want to stay *here*! Airey does, too. I know. She looked like a cold wet string this morning. She's *sorry* we're going."

"I'll miss this place bad," said Lorimer, "but I ain't sorry. Neither will you be, once you've got friends and dresses and Bible picnics and such."

Poly gathered Jabez and her flower chains with

dignity. "I'm going to decorate."

Lorimer smiled and worked his way around the corner of the house.

Cecilia was left on the porch. She looked down at the wind winnowing the golden fields, at the clouds tumbling and climbing, at the blue mountains rolling peak after peak away from her, everything making ready, everything on the march. Only she was still.

Poly was draping flowers over the mirror in her mother's room when Cecilia finally went inside. Poly helped roll her laundry into a bundle and went with her to the Buick, saying, "Tell Airey I need her back to help to hang flowers over the doors."

"Didn't Lorimer say she was up on the mountain?"

Poly looked surprised. "Didn't you hear her? She ran past here while you was folding your clothes. She's gone down the lane."

"No, I didn't hear." Cecilia was agonizingly casual. "Are you sure?"

"My ears are."

Cecilia was now feverish to go. "Then I'll meet her in a minute and you and Lorimer again next week." She waved to them both as she rolled out of the yard. Once out of sight, she concentrated on the lane ahead. Airey was nowhere to be seen. She slowed. Impossible to have missed her. How had she missed her? Was she staying out of sight? The drovers' road was coming closer. She slowed again. The lane was empty.

Airey stepped from the high bank almost onto the roadster's sidemount. She braced against the car for a moment, panting from her run, wrenched open the door, and flung herself in, knocking Cecilia flat, binding her in her arms. They grappled, mouths gaping in shapeless kisses of animal need. Cecilia felt Airey's muscles straining, her lungs working, her heart ramming against her ribs, her body more real than anything on earth.

The car lurched. Airey reached back to turn off the engine. She pushed herself to one elbow. "I got my place on earth. I know what it is."

"Airey—"

"I can't stop you. You're stronger than me. You've set this cup to my mouth and yours. There's no turning aside from the drinking of it. But something's stronger even than you. Looks like you don't know what it is. Maybe you won't never. I watched you step out of the house and look round like you was done here. Darkness came down on me. I know I'm never going to hear those words you ain't never said to me. For all my life, I'll look up and you won't be there."

She slid backward out of the car before Cecilia could speak, was up the bank, turned to look at her, and was gone.

Cecilia sat up, knowing Airey would not come back. This was not the last time she would see her. The next time would be the last time, when she collected her for the drive to Charleville to put her on the train—*don't think about that*. Not here. Not yet. She turned the key.

Rain had washed the drovers' road into a series of pools. She let it take her attention. Airey would be walking home through the forest. The leaves would be catching in her hair.

Lucius raised his whittling knife in farewell as she left Hinterhouse. She left the cove, where corn stood like armies. Left the foothills road, left the ridge, joined the turnpike.

The lowlands were airless. Tired trees hung at the edges of pallid fields. She stopped at the Peakview Hotel to send a telegram to the Neihoffs, care of the Kehr Institute. Paused at a gas station to have the attendant lower the car's roof. On the road again, the wind tearing past her head with a satisfying scream.

She turned into Old Waring's long drive. The mountains were dim in the side mirror. Mrs. Grigg might already be home. Airey would be delivering her own news, and Mrs. Grigg would be wondering what she had done to bring Miss Howison upon her to scatter her family like chaff into the world. The white fence beside the roadster stretched for miles, oaks flashing by at decorous intervals. She pulled into the old stableyard and stopped.

John George stepped from one of the garages. "Miss Cecy!" His eyebrows rose at the mud-caked Buick.

"I've been roughing it in the bush. Who's here?"

He hesitated. "Mr. Trent's out in the fields till lunch. Mrs. Trent's lying down. Your mama and papa went to Charleville after breakfast to see Mr. Tom off to California." He paused. "Your mama will be doubly glad to have you home."

"I expect she will." Cecilia went inside, and the house closed around her.

Varda met her at her bedroom door. "Miss Cecy, you should have told me you'd be away for so long. I'd have packed you a proper case. What's…this…you're wearing?"

"Never let me see it again. And the rest. Take them away, all of them." *Don't let me start keeping things.*

Varda clucked as she helped Cecilia out of her clothes. "You are *covered* in scratches and bruises. Did you roll down out of those mountains?"

"It feels that way."

Cecilia lay for an hour in her bath, concentrating on being inert, on floating. Remembered Airey's lips on her wrist and sat forward, a jolt of pain making her grip the edge of the tub. She wrestled the memory into her vault. *Think of next week*. Think of Charleville next week. Think of Wednesday. She sank a grappling iron into Wednesday and held tight.

Varda arrived with towels. "You've heard that Mr. Tom has gone?"

"Yes. He came to say goodbye to me yesterday. Do you know if he saw his friend Gerrish before he left?"

"I don't, but he did drive out for the evening. He's asked Olney to box up his rock collection and send it to Ruyerford."

Tom's geological collection gone. All cords cut.

"Are you all right, Miss Cecy?"

"As well as can be expected."

She sat, wrapped in a towel, trying to salvage her nails, glancing through her mail, looking at the floor, out the window, seeing nothing. The gong for lunch roused her to dress.

Trenton, alone at the table, did a theatrical double-take. "We need to install a revolving door for our prodigals. Tom tells me you've been a missionary for the muses. Is his report anywhere near true?"

She gave him a version of Dr. Neihoff's visit.

"If Kehr has no scholarships, haven't your efforts gone for nothing? How will she pay for it?"

Cecilia told him. He listened, his biscuit suspended in midair. When she finished, he sat back and laughed. "Miss Ruthless! You're worth your weight in gold. The Applesell Bald tract! I'll call Port Souch right after lunch. He'll be up there next week with a contract and a sack of greenbacks or my name's not Howison." He saluted her with his glass of iced tea. "My thanks for a good turn, and a very good turn it is. Now?"

"I'm driving Miss Fitch to the train on Wednesday."

"I'm sorry I won't have the opportunity to meet her—"

Cecilia went icy at the thought.

"—but I meant: what next, now that your missionary work is done? Daddy's campaign could use you."

"Yes, I'd like that." *Anything. Keep me busy.*

She survived the evening with her parents by personifying sunny good humor, but not the night. Her bedroom felt roofless in the dark. She lay exposed. *Airey.* Was Airey lying awake, too? Could she sense Cecilia through the night sky? *Let her sleep. Give her rest.* Cecilia turned on her side to face the barren hours.

On Saturday, Cecilia was in and out of Avender's hot and crowded shops, assembling enough for Airey's first weeks in Montreal. Each choice, a valise, a hairbrush, a box of stockings, was like a small drug.

Airey would be holding this and this, and these would be next to her skin.

She packed the new valise that evening and went downstairs to listen to Schubert. Rosamund slipped into the room and settled. At the end of the symphony, she lifted her feet for the footstool Cecilia shunted under them. "Is whatever was happening up there over?"

"Yes."

"Is that what you want?"

"Does it matter? Yes. It's the best thing."

"Tom told us he'd gone to bid you a fond farewell, but it struck me that something up there had knocked him off his perch. He said the sister was all you'd claimed for her. I assume—let's be frank—there was a brother."

"What bothered Tom was that I was there at all."

"Master Tom has a skewed sense of niceties. As for this young man, you've done the right thing. I'm sorry for you."

"Does it show?" Cecilia realized that she needed someone to acknowledge it.

"I can't shake the feeling I'm in the room with a pulled wire. Should I worry you'll snap?"

"Howisons are made of sterner stuff."

"Papa Howison's campaign will help you take your mind off it. You could give stirring speeches for the Women's Civics Society or to the Young Leaders of the Future."

Cecilia knew Rosamund hoped a Young Leader would distract her. "So much to be inspired by."

"And think of those congressmen you'll be meeting in Washington."

Think of them, think of anything, think of letters,

phone calls, dresses, weather, music associations, luncheons, flowers in vases, think of nothing, keep your thoughts from her, but it did not work, not in the hectic day, not in the night as she lay awake with one hand on the new valise, her longing for Airey like a shimmer of flame around her.

John George took the valise down to the car at first light on Wednesday. Cecilia went to the kitchen. Her father was drinking coffee and talking to Henry. "Off to town, Cecy?"

"I'm going to the mountains."

"Yes, the Howison taxi service." He looked down at her. "You've had a hard summer, Cecy."

She met his eyes, startled.

"That business with Patmore and now Tom leaving—let's say I'm proud that you've kept on top of yourself." He reached into his pocket. "A little more allowance. Buy something frivolous."

"Daddy, give me a hug." She breathed in tobacco and leather as his big arms came around her.

"You're my sweet sugar, but a young lady can always use a new hat."

The roadster growled at the first press of the accelerator. Along the turnpike, climbing the foothills road, Cecilia felt the minutes detach and fall away. Now each thing she did was for the last time. Here was Fittes Cove. A moment later, Hinterhouse. Up the drovers' road. Minutes were fluttering behind her like torn paper. Would Airey be angry? Resigned? Which would be worse? She turned at the blackened pine. Her pulse ticked. The last time along the lane to see her. Don't think. Don't think.

She parked in the yard. Her tires stood beside their previous marks. Nothing had changed. The house was the same. Why would anything have changed? Mrs. Grigg came to the porch, drying her hands on her apron, her face slack with surprise. "You here, Miss Howison? Airey didn't say nothing about you coming."

"No?" Cecilia felt a pause inside, the way one hears a slap and waits for the cry. "We agreed I'd come today."

"That's so? Best you step in."

Cecilia took the chair Mrs. Grigg offered. She accepted the coffee Mrs. Grigg offered. She waited.

"Polynegry will be sorry she didn't see you. She's picking berries by the falls. Lor's away hunting hogs, and you know they never mean to be found," Mrs. Grigg picked a speck of nothing from the oilcloth.

"Airey...?"

Mrs. Grigg looked at her with shamed dignity. "She's gone, Miss Howison. I don't got words to say about this. *Your friendship's like a drawing band, yet we must take the parting hand*—she should have taken a proper leave-taking, instead of skedaddling like I see now she's done."

"When did she go?"

"She asked Pastor Souch to pick her up yesterday morning and take her to the first White Star bus from Galt's Crossing and was all packed to go, but he didn't come. She spent the whole day out on the porch walking up and down, up and down. He came last night, real sorry for being called away on business, and said he'd come today, which he did. Lord abiding, she was like a wild thing from the day I come home till she got into the truck this morning. I reckon she nearly sawed her fiddle in half with practicing. It sounded more like she was strangling a cat than music. I asked why she was going if it cut her up so bad. She just looked at me like a panther that's been shot through but ain't ready to die. I ain't never seen that in her, not since Freed and her pap passed to their Maker. She feels about this place deeper than any of us."

"She has no money."

"I gave her what Port lent me, seeing we'll be man and wife as soon as this place is sold." Mrs. Grigg hesitated and cleared her throat. "I got to say it, Miss Howison. She's been ungrateful toward you. Why did she decide to go with Port yesterday when she knew you was coming today?"

Cecilia stood, knowing why. Knowing what desolation was. "I must go."

"You could have driven her as easy as anything in that fancy car. Her bus will barely be leaving Galt's Crossing, and by now, you could have had her all the way to Charleville."

"What?" Cecilia did not recognize her own voice. "When does her train leave?"

"Mr. Keller says it goes half past one. The bus gets there just before. Those Neihoffs are kind people, I know it surely, but my heart aches on my honey gal being taken care of by strangers."

Cecilia had stopped listening. "I might even have passed her bus on my way here." She turned unseeing to the door. "I might catch it. I might catch her at the station."

"Looks like she don't want to be caught."

"That's too bad. I'll come again, Mrs. Grigg. Give my love to Lor and Polynegry."

"You visit us any time, here or down in Galt's Crossing."

Cecilia was already out the door. The roadster spun in a fountain of dirt and flew down the lane. How many stops did the bus make before Charleville? Airey might still be miles from the city. Might still be on the turnpike. Let her be on the turnpike.

Down through the cove, over the ridge. In the lowlands, she went as fast as she dared, skimming past startled cars and trucks, came to the Charleville turnpike and stopped, staring in both directions as if the bus would be there. Nothing. Cars. She paused for gas, waved off the attendant's polishing cloth, and left the forecourt like a bolt from a ballista.

The turnpike was busy. Everything was bright and sharp. Cecilia ignored outraged horns as she passed car after car, weaving steadily through them, keeping the Buick at fifty-eight. She let nothing slow her, not the swaying farm truck, not the old Model T, passing it by inches, not the flatbed truck trying to tease her, sliding ahead on the hard shoulder, not the sedan, slipping between it and oncoming traffic and leaving it behind, its indignant honk faint in the roadster's roar.

She swept through the towns, hand on her horn to clear the traffic in her path. No bus appeared ahead of her, no bus to be seen. She glanced at each roadhouse she passed in case it had pulled off. Nothing. She checked her watch. One o'clock.

The hotel marking Charleville's limits flashed by. The minutes were draining through her like water.

Now she had to slow for city traffic, now she had to control herself, not scream at the boys on bicycles, at pedestrians, at the delivery trucks, the red lights, the horse carts, not choke with rage, and here she was at the turn for the city center, so close, five blocks, three blocks, two, and she could see the station entrance. She turned again and forced a space to appear in the parking strip along its front. She took Airey's valise from the footwell and ran as fast as she could, hearing nothing but the whistles and rumbles of locomotives. A group of talking men scattered for her, forcing her to dodge them one by one. A rolling cart of luggage made her swerve aside. She flew down the stairs, seeking the departures board, the valise banging her leg, not caring that her hat was half off her head, that she looked half off her head.

"Train north?" she snapped at the first porter she saw.

"Cincinnati train?" He pointed to the far track. "Just went, miss."

For a wild second, she turned to run to her car, to race the train north and stop it at a crossing. *No.* Her feet stumbled. No. Not even a roadster could catch a train. Airey had slipped her grasp. Airey had left her.

The porter was saying, "I'm sorry, miss, we'll get you on the next one." Cecilia turned herself to marble to be able to speak. "Thank you, no, I don't need to get on a train." She moved slowly up the stairs, welcoming the bruises the valise had hammered into her shin. *How can I be angry*? Airey had done what she wanted her to do. *Why shouldn't I be glad*?

The world was crashing over her in a dense wave, harshly bright. She was going up the stairs. She was walking through the station, where the shrieking of the trains was suddenly a thing apart, and everything fell silent, although people were rushing past her, people were talking.

She heard the sound of her own breath. She felt her blood pounding through her body. Her legs were moving on their own. She was walking along the line of parked cars. She was falling. She reached her car. She was falling. The valise dropped from her hand. The weight of every day of every year she would live from this moment rushed up like the earth and she slammed into it, huddled on the sidemount of the Buick, head on her knees. *God help me. God, help me.*

Chapter Ten

Water fell in a dozen small cascades. Birds skimmed across the creek, mayflies hovered in clouds. Every leaf sparkled with the diamonds left by this morning's rain. Cecilia turned away, taking the path away from the overhanging rock, crossing the creek over the wide plank bridge past the stumps of the buckeyes, following the steam shovel tracks back to her car.

An hour ago, she had been jarred by the sight of the new part of the house gone, despite knowing Mr. Souch had dismantled it before Thanksgiving, and by the stumps of the maples at the edge of the yard, though she had just driven past the close-sawn bases of the chestnuts. A hollow in the house's foundations was filled with leaves and water. The old log house, lacking an end, was already collapsing. The barn's door and sidings were gone. The corn crib stood roofless, rings of grease and oil on its floor marking where coils of chain had been housed.

She got into the roadster. Above her, she could see sluiceways and stanchions across the shaved mountainside. Looking below, the view remained almost untouched, with only a new road cut across the fields to join the old railroad bed road now again serving Sankgallon.

The letter in her handbag, which had been buzzing all morning like an insect trapped in a jar, could be delayed no longer. She took it out. A Ruyerford crest. The silence Tom had imposed on Lorimer had been almost total; Cecilia had received a thank-you note in September, a card at Christmas, and then nothing. Until this, which she had made her excuse for a trip to the mountains. She opened it.

Inside, a piece of blank paper. This was taking self-censorship too far. She unfolded it, turned it over, saw a drawing of a violin, and closed it.

She listened to the distant whine of skidder cables. Lorimer was an obedient boy, but this was something he thought she should see. She opened the small poster again.

Farewell Concert.

Marus Jurevič.

Marus Jurevič. She knew who he was. One of the greats. He had been in Washington for two concerts she had missed in early May. *Farewell concert on the eve of his return to Europe.* Some of Jurevič's recordings were in her library. *His Majesty's Theatre, Guy Street. Friday, 24 June. Accompanied by the Montreal Philharmonic Orchestra.*

This was not what Lorimer wanted her to read. Smaller type below. *On Thursday, Maestro Jurevič will be conducting in the McPhail Auditorium, Kehr Institute of Music, and not in the Aeolian Hall as previously announced, where he will introduce his pupil in a full programme.* In the margin, Lorimer's handwriting: *first one.*

Cecilia looked at the mist rising behind the trees. To have had no news at all, to have heard nothing at all, for almost a year, and now this impulse of Lorimer's that she might want to know.

She laid the poster on her lap. *Well done, Miss*

Fitch. Airey must have made blistering progress with Dr. Neihoff to be with Jurevič now and to be playing a full concert on Thursday.

Thursday, June 23.

Today was Monday.

June 20.

She sat looking at nothing. Parched curiosity sifted like dust from a vault. Would it be nice to see Miss Fitch play? Perhaps. Yes. It would be nice. After all, what had last year been about? Extravagant to go all the way to Canada for a single concert, but—why not? Tom was traveling in Mexico, far from family news, she had money and time and nothing urgent to do, and it would put a period to the end of this particular sentence.

She drove down to the turnpike and stopped at the Peakview Hotel to telephone her father's office in Washington. Elliott took the call. After pleasantries, she told him what she needed. She heard timetables being flicked. He said in the muffled voice of someone holding the receiver between shoulder and ear, "It will mean two changes. You'll take the L and N from Charleville," *of course*, "and a night express from Cincinnati to Detroit. Change at Detroit and the CNR gets you into Montreal at 2:30 on Thursday. A room? I understand the Windsor Hotel is very good. Yes, I'll book for—one night?" She heard his surprise. "Returning on Friday? You'll have to stay overnight in Detroit, I'm afraid. Avender by Saturday evening. And back here in Washington soon, may we hope? No trouble at all, Miss Howison. A pleasure as always. The tickets will be held for you."

She telegraphed the concierge of the Windsor Hotel to ask him to reserve a single concert ticket.

She returned to her car, feeling settled and unsettled. Strange to have plans that included any interest in doing them.

Rosamund was on the veranda, Eddy in her lap. "You're back late. Trent was all for calling out the troops."

"Did he expect to have to drag the river?"

"I've stopped worrying about that. No, Eddy, you mustn't strangle your auntie with her own beads."

Cecilia disentangled his fingers. "I'm going away for a few days. Leaving Wednesday and returning on the weekend."

"You'll miss your meeting with Wendell." Rosamund glanced at her. "You're doing something you know I won't approve of."

"Daddy's administrative assistant has already booked my tickets." At Rosamund's searching look, she added, "I'm not canceling the meeting, just postponing it. Uncle Wendell doesn't escape that easily. Oh, and I'm taking Varda with me."

Rosamund relaxed. "As long as you're doing something that will make you happy."

"I don't know if it will. In a way. Yes, I suppose so."

Rosamund leaned to brush Cecilia's cheek with a finger. "You could use a little."

Varda was more stern. "Miss Cecy, you can't go. Your passport's in Washington."

Cecilia felt a plunge of disappointment, a stab of relief. The next minute, "No, you've forgotten. You put it and yours in my writing case when we got back from Cuba."

Varda checked the desk. "So I did. But you don't have enough clothes here."

"It's too late to send for them. I won't need much. We're only staying one night. Two suits for the train and an evening gown."

"Evening gown?"

"I'm going to a concert."

"All that way for a—" Varda closed her lips.

Cecilia sat alone at the piano that evening. *Is this wise?* She risked opening scars. But it would be the closing ceremony for her last, lingering dread: that one day she would meet Airey around a corner, in a doorway, on the street, in Charleville, in Washington, anywhere. After the concert, Airey must surely be sailing to Europe with Jurevič beyond any possible encounter. Would finally and completely be gone.

She ignored Trenton's protests that young ladies did not jaunt to foreign countries, not feeling particularly young. She wrote apologies to the Orchestra Committee in Washington for missing the next meeting, regrets to friends about this tea dance, that luncheon, their bridge party. And then it was Wednesday morning, and John George was driving her to the train station in Charleville, Varda beside him with a hat box on her knees. Cecilia led them to the far platform.

"Right first time, Miss Cecy," he said.

"I've been here before." No pain; it took more harrowing thoughts than this to cut her now. A porter helped John George stow the luggage in her compartment. A few minutes later, the train whistled and lurched forward. Charleville began to move, faster and faster, until she was flying between the buildings like an arrow.

Varda watched her so closely that Cecilia finally asked, "Did Rosie tell you to keep an eye on me?"

"You know this is a mistake, Miss Cecy."

"I'd rather be making a mistake than bored."

She wondered idly what she might feel on Thursday evening. Perhaps nothing at all. Perhaps the filleting knife. She glanced into the high school French grammar book she had packed at the last minute, tried the first pages of the novels she had brought, cast them aside impatiently, and sifted through the letters she had taken up as she was leaving. She considered one engraved card for many minutes. *Mr. and Mrs. Eric Munns request the honor of Miss Cecilia Howison's presence at the marriage of their daughter Erica Mildred to Patmore Clayne Dillan Reaveley.* The memory of Pat's eyes, on the last time they had met, told her it would be kind to refuse this. She wanted to write to him now what she had wanted to say to him then: that she understood, that she was sorry, that she had learned, as he had, that life went on. How life went on. She wrote a formal short regret. Varda posted it in Cincinnati as they changed trains. They pulled out into the long summer evening.

Cecilia watched telegraph poles go by. Train travel, as she had discovered going back and forth from Washington, was a wonderful escape from time. You needed only to rock in the train's embrace. When the porter came by, she had him make up the beds. In the darkness, she indulged in something she had not done for months. She thought about Airey.

Not running through it all again—that book was tattered beyond reading—but piecing together Airey's trajectory. Airey must have joined Jurevič recently, for he had been on tour in the States through late spring. Or had she been with him on it? If so, there must be a Mrs. Jurevič. Unless Airey was—with him? Cecilia smiled wearily. While she had been imagining Airey's life in Montreal in obsessive detail, Airey might have been turning into someone else. *I had not thought of that.*

Cecilia and Varda crossed into Canada in the morning. She sat drinking coffee in the dining car to give herself something to do. At last, the conductor sang, "Montreal, Montreal." She put on her gloves. *Now I really could meet her around any corner.*

The Windsor Hotel's concierge raised his eyebrows at her youth and her lack of male escort, but all was understood when she collected her concert ticket. "Ah, Monsieur Jurevič, he is supreme. *Merci, mademoiselle.*"

In their room, Varda unpacked Cecilia's evening gown and hung out tomorrow's suit. Cecilia stood looking at the streets below, at the green humpback of Mount Royal. *I'm in the same city as Airey.* Something stirred under her skin. She noted it and noted that nothing else followed. Who would have thought the day would come when those words had no power?

Varda asked, "Will you be going down to dinner, or shall I order you a meal here?"

"I'm not hungry."

"I won't let you get away without eating, not again. I'll have them send up soup and a roll."

Cecilia prowled the room, stood again at the window, wanting this to be over. Then it was time to bathe and have Varda dress her hair. Varda insisted on a touch of color to her lips and face. "You don't want to look like a ghost. I've put two handkerchiefs in your bag in case you need to blot."

Cecilia tucked them beside her ticket. It was time to go.

"Enjoy your concert," said Varda.

The taxi ride took minutes, passing a baronial building emblazoned with *KEHR INSTITUTE OF MUSIC* and pulling up to what was, despite its grand balconies and bas-reliefs, a modern school auditorium. She went up the shallow steps. Inside, the lobby was crowded with students, parents, and a more distinct segment in formal dress who must have been drawn by Jurevič's name. She went through into the vast hall, where the seats were already filling. She found hers halfway back. On stage, the musicians, looking like a mix of teachers and older students, were coming to their stations.

The hall grew dense with sound as the last seats were taken. A student began selling programs. She reached for her handbag, saw a familiar figure, Mrs. Neihoff, magnificent in black lace, heading for the roped-off seats at the front, and ducked down, straightening only when the orchestra began tuning in trills and fragments of scales. It swelled, fell to silence. Cecilia's mouth dried. *Here we go.*

The concertmaster, Dr. Neihoff, in white tie and tails, came on to warm applause. The lights went out in the room, leaving the stage lit from above and along its front edge. At any other time, Cecilia knew she would be thrilled when a tall man with a world-famous head of wild, curling dark hair, Jurevič, entered from the wing door. He bowed to the hall and to Dr. Neihoff, and led the orchestra through a delightful suite. Cecilia watched the violinists behind Dr. Neihoff. To think that she had once imagined Airey among them. After short applause, Jurevič turned to look at the wing door. Cecilia's fingers tightened. Airey came out to polite clapping.

Cecilia's breath faded. Airey's hair was still short, a harsh, elegant crop. She was in white: a curt jacket with white frogging over a narrow floor-length gown. She looked like a naval ensign, a hussar carved from ice, her only color her dark eyes and brows, the pale flame of her hair. A different person. A different creature.

Airey made her way through the orchestra, responding to the applause with a lift of her chin. Cecilia began to smile. *I remember that.*

Pain as intense as a blade drove into her, a javelin stabbed through her, its razor edges slashed her open, exposing each nerve, splitting her until she gutted blood, every drop shrieking like a frozen thing burned, and she knew, she understood, she understood completely: the body chooses, it chooses its own, it knows its own, must have its own. And here was its own. It had chosen Airey.

She was hooked from herself, hurled into the naked air, flying on a chariot of fire, her eyes forced open and fixed, burning high above the earth as she learned this truth to its last shred of agony. *O clouds unfold.* She rushed above its scorched and empty plain.

Then she was plummeting through the flaming air back into her body, into this ocean of fiery pitch.

She gasped, found that she had leaned forward a few inches, that the woman on her right was barely glancing at her, that nothing visible had happened. Her flesh was burning, her flesh cried out. *Airey. God, please. Please no.* She had thought herself healed. She would never be healed. Her fingers dug into her thighs. *I can't bear this. I can't live knowing this.*

Her eyes stung as if from fire. She stared at the fire. Airey, who was still coming through the orchestra. Only three or four seconds had passed. Cecilia felt Airey's steps, felt the turn of her hips, felt the hanging weight of the violin in her fingers, felt her nods to Jurevič and Dr. Neihoff, not shifting an inch from her, although Airey was burning her to death, sat and looked at her as if looking would bring this wasteland to life. Airey was remote, aloof, as she took her place. The entire hall, audience and orchestra, became quiet.

Cecilia noted without attention Jurevič's baton marking a beat. Meditative falling chords filled the hall. Airey raised her violin. It was new, red as an autumn leaf. Cecilia felt it touch her collarbone. Airey's bow came up. The first note sliced through her skin.

The music could not help her, as it had helped her so often before, to endure what had to be endured. *This*, this dead weight of pain, this corpse, this revelation lashed to her to be dragged until it killed her. Nothing, not even music, could help her with this.

And yet. The music gradually became cool water to her arid throat. She felt herself slowly respond, slowly sharing the audience's surrender to the violin's pensive beauty. She felt every shift of Airey's hands with elevated, sedate anguish. This was Airey, immaculate, imperial, completely now what she had always been. Cecilia knew that she herself heard most, felt most, because Airey was hers. She impaled herself on it, hating it, hating its pain. From the corner of her eye, she saw others turn wondering faces to one another and knew that they, too, heard in their own ways what Airey was: a lord and commander. *This Airey I will never know.*

Applause. Cecilia's hands came together once. Airey bowed slightly—*of course a bow, not a curtsy.* Cecilia glanced toward her neighbor's program to see the next piece, but it had fallen to the floor and Jurevič was turning again to the orchestra.

The audience hushed. Mozart's fairytale world embraced them. Airey's playing was ravishingly pure. Cecilia could hear this new violin giving her the depth of response she had sought in vain from Mr. Broeggen's. The final notes were as delicate as mother of pearl. Cecilia did not pretend to join the vigorous applause. She was no spectator. Airey bowed and left the stage, Jurevič behind her. Cecilia noted absently that someone—Mrs. Neihoff?—had taught her to walk beautifully in a gown. The hall's tension eased, as when royalty leaves the room.

Without Airey, the light from the chandeliers seemed pale. Cecilia crushed her bag in her hands. *You know how to bear this.* But she didn't. Not this.

The audience was rising, crowding toward the lobby. Cecilia stooped, pretending to search for something in case Mrs. Neihoff came back up the aisle. She did find something: her neighbor's abandoned program. She took it with her to the auditorium doors and stayed just inside them to read.

Aside from the opening Handel, Airey was playing throughout. It really was a full concert. After the intermission came a selection of short works to display a broad talent but none of the fireworks she would have expected at a debut. No Bach? No Bach. The concert would conclude with Goldmark's violin concerto. A lesser work, as she knew from her voracious reading last autumn. Airey's entrance into the world seemed muted, modest. Not like her. Had Jurevič chosen these pieces? Dr. Neihoff?

Cecilia realized that she had missed something, had somehow not seen, and looked back to the top of the page. The Kehr Institute Orchestra. Concertmaster: Dr. Barukh Neihoff. Conductor for this performance: Marus Jurevič. Soloist: Ara Fitsch.

Ara Fitsch.

Ara. Fitsch.

What was this? Cecilia felt sick. The Airey she knew would never have given up her name. *Has she changed so much*? No Bach on the program.

She became aware of a handbell ringing in the lobby. In the next minute, the crowd swept her back to her seat. The orchestra took their places. Dr. Neihoff and Jurevič came on stage.

Airey emerged to applause. Cecilia felt the desert inside her bloom with jagged flame. Pain did not matter. To watch her was to have a form of life. Airey came to her position, taking in the audience as its applause continued. Jurevič smiled and raised his baton.

Beethoven. Airey's violin was gallantly tender, although her face showed nothing. No reason to think Airey shared a single feeling with her. *Why would she*? Cecilia sat stonily through the applause. *No reason at all.* Schubert followed, his kind heart gradually reminding her that joy could exist. *But how*? *How for me*?

Airey was bright against the dark orchestra, her head half-turned to listen as the piece came to its end. Cecilia knew she had no thought beyond the music, but when the voices of the strings rose afresh through the hall with a mysterious shimmer and the violin began its grave and insistent waltz, she could not help searching her distant face. What did this unwearied sweetness mean, this longing? Cecilia pressed her palms together. *Stop.* It simply meant that Airey or Neihoff or Jurevič had considered this a suitable piece for tonight's program. Nothing more.

Airey bowed once, twice, to the prolonged applause and straightened, her face austere. The orchestra began with military swagger. Airey's violin captured it, charmed and tamed it, began its own tense, brooding, wistful journey. Cecilia felt the music speaking to her, although she knew she heard only her own longing. The violin sang, aloft and lyrical, rose to a beauty that took orchestra, listeners, the air itself, into a yearning passion, and then seemed to turn, to flay its heart, its song breaking as it tumbled across the sky, writhing, furious, harsh, exhausted.

A breath of silence, a rise of hushed strings. The violin entered like someone coming to a winter night's window to look at what could only be looked at alone. The music was exquisite loss. Cecilia heard grief, beautifully gentle, welling again and again, knowing no hope, despair descending, dropping to its depths, until it rose helplessly—but the violin stopped short, turned to face, to face again, solitude.

The brass called briskly. The violin leapt through increasingly brilliant, strident displays, until it hesitated, faltered, and failed. The orchestra rang like a church organ. As if recalled to its soul, the violin lifted in calm clarity, circled upward like an eagle in a dazzling ascent, master of itself, master of the horizon, falling back for a last leap, flying into the sun, topping the orchestra's final mighty chords, and Airey's bow sprang off the violin and slashed to her side like a saber.

Applause, cheers engulfed the stage. Airey's face was empty. Cecilia wondered if she heard it; she stood motionless. The surging applause, the calls from the audience, at last brought Airey to herself, and she bowed, saluted Dr. Neihoff, the orchestra, turned to bow again to the still-clapping audience, again, again, now understanding, now accepting, now alight in their acclaim. Jurevič stretched down his hand to her, and she took it, meeting his look. Before the audience was ready to let her go, she walked off the stage through the applauding orchestra.

Cecilia looked at the place where she had been. People were sighing as they clapped, nodding and murmuring, some pausing to mop their faces in the summer's heat Cecilia only now noticed. Airey came out again. The applause overflowed. She was presented with a bouquet of pink roses. Who chose them? Cecilia thought with automatic contempt. *Pink, with that hair*. Others followed: orchids, jasmine, gladioli, student ushers waiting on the stairs to fill Airey's arms. Unable to bow over the bouquets, she simply faced each section of the applauding audience, her slow smile dawning. The audience smiled back. Cecilia felt fierce. *Take it. Take it all.* Airey looked as she had looked on the night of the Neihoffs' visit: shining, rejoicing, somewhere above them, in a place only Jurevič knew.

She left the stage again. The audience was still

electric. *This can't be the end.* Cecilia's fingers knotted together. *I can't have this be the end.* No: Jurevič came out with Airey and mounted the podium. The applause faded to a greedy hush.

Airey's violin followed the woodwinds as if within a reverie. The last note of Tchaikovsky had barely ended before single flowers from boutonnières and corsages began to rain onto the stage, the audience calling for more, leaving their seats to crowd at the foot of the platform, not just students, who must know her, but the women in silk gowns, the men with diamond tie pins. Airey cocked her head at Jurevič and raised her violin; blazing notes tore through the room, famous showstoppers exploding one after each other, the audience shouting, more of them coming down to the stage, the members of the orchestra clearly feeling the heat and the hour but exhilarated. *It's not often they're part of history.*

Airey raised her bow as if to end the revels—and it hung as she stood, straight-browed. Jurevič dropped his hands. The orchestra rested their instruments. Her bow came to the strings. Bach's *Preludio* sprang into the dark auditorium. This was Airey on the kitchen step playing for her, playing for them all, playing joy and courage from a fountain that never failed.

The audience was silent after it ended, comprehending what it had heard. Airey took her violin in both hands and looked down at it with shadowed eyes. At some point, someone clapped, everyone was clapping, applause was sweeping the room, bursting like wildfire from different sections. Airey swept into a deep cavalier's bow, rose for a final nod to the orchestra, a final clasp of Dr. Neihoff's hand, and she left the stage for the last time, pacing Jurevič and glancing at him, and it was over.

Cecilia stayed in her seat as people around her shuffled toward the doors. The members of the orchestra left the stage one by one. The stage lights were turned off. Her heart was quiet. She was glad she had come. She had given her life for Airey, and it had been right.

Someone was standing at the end of the row.

"Miss Howison," Mrs. Neihoff was saying a third time.

"I'm so sorry."

"My dear, I recognized you as I came in after the intermission. I couldn't believe it. I've been waiting in the lobby, but when you didn't appear, I wondered if perhaps you were ill."

"How kind."

Mrs. Neihoff looked troubled. "It's entirely right that you're here but entirely wrong that you're alone. I'm joining my husband at the little victory soirée. I'd like you to come."

"Oh, no. I can't."

"Please, as my guest. I'm sure you'll be welcomed." She raised a hand as Cecilia began to protest. "If you don't mind my saying, I wondered why two such good friends had fallen out. It bothered me then, and tonight, it bothers me exceedingly."

"You know how girls can be. Our quarrel seemed important at the time." Cecilia managed a smile. "But after so long, I don't feel I should intrude."

"Intrude!" Mrs. Neihoff's bosom rose grandly. "Preposterous. You, of all people, made this night happen."

"I know that was through your husband's and your generosity."

"We've all had a part, which is why we should celebrate together. I'm sure you'll want to tell her how delighted you are for her, as you must be, having witnessed that."

"She's splendid, isn't she?" Cecilia said painfully.

"You won't have another chance for many years."

"She's leaving for Europe?"

"Yes, to work with Jurevič." Mrs. Neihoff held out a hand.

"I really shouldn't." But Cecilia sensed Airey in the building the way a bee knows water. *Go straight to her*. She took Mrs. Neihoff's hand and rose, faint with dread.

Mrs. Neihoff led her behind the stage, up a worn set of stairs and along a hallway, passing large and small student practice rooms until they arrived at one thronged with silk gowns and diamond tie pins, all here to be presented to Jurevič—and now Airey.

"Such a crowd!" said Mrs. Neihoff, unsurprised.

Dr. Neihoff saw his wife at the door and came to ease her in, stepping back when he saw Cecilia. "Miss Howison! Indeed, Miss Howison! How good this is!" His wife said something briefly to him in Yiddish, and his smile grew warmer. "My wife's invitation is mine. The year you have given us—such a year! What to say? Playing beside her tonight, so close, so distant! All eyes on her! I do not forget that Goldmark *Andante* as long as I live."

Airey was near, was within reach. Cecilia forced her lips to move. "She's certainly distinguished. Mrs.

Neihoff, I detect your touch?"

"It was a pleasure to dress her." Mrs. Neihoff smiled modestly. "The gown was our gift. Her hair—I told her shingling was out of fashion, but she insisted, and I think she's right, don't you? She should set her own look."

"Easier than fighting her," said Cecilia, and Dr. Neihoff laughed.

"Yes, wars all the time. I should have medal."

"May I say, you match her," said Mrs. Neihoff. "A lovely gown, but—heliotrope. I fear...?"

"Yes, I'm in mourning." Cecilia thought of Grandfather. Of herself.

"Why we do not hear from you." Dr. Neihoff pressed her hand. "But come, tonight is for being thankful. You must meet everyone."

They joined the edge of a dense cluster eagerly waiting to be introduced to their hosts. Cecilia slid behind the Neihoffs. She could see Jurevič towering over the crowd. His face was scored with deep lines, but his eyes were light and alive and his smile attractive as he shook hands left and right, saying, "Good evening, Monsieur Trouville" and "Sir Robert, allow me to remember you to the Princess Dražnaliska," another hand taken, another guest passed along, another step forward. Cecilia fought not to bolt.

The princess, majestic in emeralds and pewter-colored silk, looked at her over Dr. Neihoff's shoulder and laughed. "*Barukh, noch ein verlorenes Lamm?*" moving aside so that Airey could bend to embrace him. Cecilia's heart stopped. Airey straightened, saw her, and everything disappeared from her face.

Cecilia heard Mrs. Neihoff saying, "the girl who discovered" and Jurevič's "How extraordinary," as she took his hand, reached for Airey's, but it was not there; Airey was staring above her head with icy blankness, and Cecilia heard no more, took the princess's hand automatically, and was whisked away by the Neihoffs.

"My dear." Mrs. Neihoff guided her across the room.

"I do not underst—" Dr. Neihoff began. Cecilia felt his wife's quelling look. "Miss Howison, I fetch for you drink."

"I…it's-it's very hot in here, isn't it?" said Cecilia.

"Indeed it is," said Mrs. Neihoff. "Too many people in such a small room. What was the director thinking? Men are never practical," and applied small talk while Cecilia took possession of herself. Dr. Neihoff returned with a glass. They stayed until persistent requests detached them, and she was finally alone.

Elbowed, jostled, she stood exposed on an empty plain. Was there another way out? How soon could she leave? Airey was an inescapable, blinding presence. Cecilia watched her covertly and saw that she never looked or moved in her direction.

The Neihoffs returned regularly to introduce her to other guests. Cecilia stood, snow sweeping through her, exchanging spritely conversation with a French-Canadian couple, with some naval officers, with one of Kehr's board members, who made it clear that he would be happy to stay beside her all evening. She moved to a more congenial older lady, who glanced at and then ignored her. Jurevič and Airey dominated the room like two suns, everyone turning their heads involuntarily to see them. The crowd thickened until the students, now waiters, had to wedge themselves through, and Cecilia was able to shift from group to group without effort, face fixed in polite interest. She stayed as far from Airey as the room allowed, yet was always too close, catching a glimpse of her profile, the line of her shoulder, the way she regarded a fierce-looking man asking why she had played those Goldmark triple stops in that outrageous fashion, the way she listened courteously to a woman enthuse, "*Votre performance était incroyable!*" and hearing her reply: "*Il le fallait bien, Madame, pour qu'elle soit digne de votre attention.*" The sound of her crow's voice roughened Cecilia's skin. Elegant, cosmopolitan, admired. Cecilia pushed through the crowd to study the massed bouquets and boutonnières heaped on a far table. *Sublime*, one card read. *Lovely beyond words*, said another. She smiled coldly. This was no help at all.

Jurevič called the room to attention. "My friends, tonight has overwhelmingly rewarded me, this night on which our soloist has triumphantly confirmed her mastery of the god of all instruments. No words of mine—"

Cecilia agreed. She needed no words of his. As the crowd pressed closer to him, she wormed her way to the tall curtains and edged an exploring hand behind. A French door, locked. She moved to the next. Unlocked. Jurevič asked Airey a question. Cecilia did not wait for her reply; she was behind the curtain, through the door, and out onto a long, narrow balcony.

The air was warm. Sunset had left a flush of peach across the sky. She heard applause through the half-closed door. Someone called, "Play for us!"

"Play? Tonight? After that?" Jurevič answered in mock outrage. A moment later, she heard the sound of a violin, a second violin: Jurevič and Airey playing together.

The city glittered around her as the sky steeped to black. A cross, outlined in electric light, hung in the darkness. On the river, a ship's horn, soft and low.

The music went on. The night went on. She heard clapping and laughter. She heard, faintly, Airey's voice. Airey was among friends, eminent and happy. Would be happier still when her intruder had gone. Cecilia moved away from the sounds of the party and leaned on the balustrade. The night remained pleasantly humid. She would wait out here. No one could see her in the darkness. At some point, the party would end and she would slip downstairs and find a taxi. She longed to be on the train to Old Waring, miles beyond this. Years beyond this. A violin sang again distantly. She listened to the indifferent city. Eventually, this night would be over.

"Cecilia."

She flinched toward escape. Stopped. There was no escape. She felt Airey approach. She did not turn around.

"What are you doing here?" Airey's voice was colder than ice.

Let this not happen.

"Why are you here?"

Cecilia turned her head away.

"Nothing to say? Why did you come?" Music drifted from the room. "To appraise your investment? I think we can agree it paid off."

Cecilia braced herself against the balustrade.

"Still nothing? I left home knowing I'd never see you again. Then tonight I look up and you're standing in front of me. I wanted to kill you. And you have nothing to say to me?"

Cecilia forced breath into her lungs. From somewhere, from long practice, came steadiness. "I came—I did come—to see what you had made of yourself. To hear you play. I didn't intend to meet you."

"Yet here you are."

"Because Mrs. Neihoff persuaded me to your soirée."

"What did you think I would do?"

"I didn't think."

"A mistake."

"Wasn't it?" Cecilia's fingers dug into the stone. "I took myself away as soon as I could."

"Out here is taken?"

"It was the best I could manage."

"There were other doors."

"I know."

"I wasn't sure what I'd feel if this ever happened." Airey made a harsh sound. "Now I do. I used to lie awake wondering. I used to lie awake wondering what a letter from you would be like. Sometimes, I'd pretend one was coming. I imagined tearing it open. Tearing it up. Sometimes, I'd lie in bed like blood was coming out of my mouth. Most of the time, I felt a coal mine burning inside me, and every breath I took was on fire. I raged till I thought I'd burn up. That you'd left me. That you kept on having left me. I got to hate the thought of you."

"You left me without a—you left."

"I left a place you'd already left. There's a difference."

"There is."

"It was hard on you."

"Yes."

"Not hard enough to tell you what I eventually realized you didn't know."

Cecilia watched windows turn dark in far buildings. "I know tonight."

"Is that so?" said Airey's cold voice. "For me, the fire keeping me on my feet finally burned out. It burned itself out at last. Then I went down. I went under. The Neihoffs thought I'd studied myself into a brain fever, but that was me breaking. If my Redeemer hadn't lifted me from the depths, if He hadn't given me my music, I would have—" Airey fell silent. "But I didn't. You were right. I survived. I built myself back together again."

"As I can see."

"You would if you turned around."

Cecilia looked down at the balustrade. At her hands bloodless on it.

"I built myself up brand new. I changed. I had to. You were right about so many things. Everyone's eyes were on me the minute I got here. But parts of me stayed the same. I couldn't change being mountain born or virtuosa. I wouldn't change being a saved soul or a standing woman. And I had every reason not to change being a lesbian."

Cecilia opened her mouth like a speared animal.

"Did you think I'd be otherwise?"

"You—wanted it hard. That cup is full."

"It's not why I'm telling you."

"Don't tell me. Don't."

"This one last thing."

"Let us be finished."

"I want you to know. Since you've come all this way. I looked at women—at how they looked at me. When I longed for comfort, when I hungered, it was for a woman's arms. Some were open to me." Airey's breath roughened. "I knew what I wanted. I passed them by. Turned out I'd built myself back up the same way I'd been built. I haven't changed. It could only be you. It will always be you."

Cecilia looked at the sleeping city. Every stone in her ramparts became pumice, powdering to dust when she needed them most.

"Cecilia, I—Cecilia—*Cec'ly.*"

Cecilia turned and looked at her. Airey's face was in shadow. Cecilia could see her stance, defiant and afraid. She stepped forward and came to rest against her.

After a speechless moment, Airey's arms swept around her. Cecilia heard Airey's heart beating against her ear, felt her lungs lifting under her cheek, felt her as tall and strong as a pine tree, and in the next instant was terrified that she was somehow in her room in Washington or Old Waring dreaming, dreaming again, of Airey. She put her arms around her, felt her body rigid under the silk jacket—*I'm awake*—holding her close, closer, growing frantic as Airey stayed real. Airey's breath was feathering her hair. "Cec'ly."

Cecilia pulled out words like strips of flesh. "We can't. We can't."

"We can."

"No." Cecilia pressed her face against her. *Let time stop.*

"We can."

"After tonight—now is exactly why we can't. Tom—you can't be endangered. I wouldn't then—I won't now."

Airey said, as if not hearing her, "I know we can."

Cecilia looked up to say *impossible*. Her lips said, "How can we?"

"Because what you told me back then was true, but not as true as you thought."

"You must have learned it is."

"I learned that you and I come from a narrow world. What you know is deadly true for back there. But it's not the only world. There's this one, which is perilous, I'm not saying it isn't, but it's different. And there's another, a bigger one, the one *Maître* Jurevič lives in. He said I'd—"

Cecilia recoiled. "He knows?"

"He was passing through Montreal on tour just after Easter, and Dr. Neihoff brought me to audition for him. He agreed to take me when he came back, but first he wanted to know why I'd played Bach's *Ciaconna* that way. I told him. And here I am, not condemned or locked up. He said that as long as I kept my wits sharp, I'll find better attitudes in the world I'm going to. We're going to."

"Is it really—can it be—so different?"

"In his world, he says that if you want the best and you give your best, nothing else much counts. But even if it's not like that, even if it's worse than back home, I'll take it."

Cecilia tried to push herself away. "We can't be tempted by one opinion. Tom still holds the chain. He can hurt you now as never before."

Airey held her fast. "Who's Tom Howison? Who cares? Nobody's heard of him up here. I asked."

"Then someone else. There's always someone else."

"Who's anyone, compared to Jurevič? Whatever Tom Howison or his kind will say, Jurevič will laugh at, and the world will listen to the *maître*."

"He's never lived our life. He can't know."

"He knows enough. He's got a lady accompanist who's one of our kind and a step-nephew that other way. And he knows tribulation. You met the princess. The *maître* calls her his wife, but she isn't, she has a husband living. Everyone knows it. Nobody says an evil word about her, she's welcome everywhere. The *maître's* fame protects her. It protects them both because fame is a shield."

"But you'll never, you mustn't, you won't hide behind a shield."

"You're right. I'm not looking for one. I'm thinking fame can be a spear."

"Do you want to be destroyed?"

"I think I won't be. I'm going to try. We should try."

"Why would I help you with this insanity?"

"You *know* why." Airey stopped. Her voice gentled. "Because you know why. You know why we're here. We've come from a far country to be here. I don't mean Canada, I mean here, to this unknown land. This new land. Just like those first Fitches. It's wilderness all around us. The forest is full of fierce things. But lift your head—see that up yonder, that clearing? That's our place. Up where all can see. We can get there if we want. It'll be hard. It's certain we'll be hurt. We can be too afraid to try, or we can climb up and stake our claim. We don't know if we'll live or die up there. Maybe we'll die. Dying up there would be better than living here. Let's go up there. Let's go there."

Cecilia heard her with every beat of her heart, every drop of her blood. That mountain was shining, golden, it was where she wanted to live and die, but the beasts of the forest were real, and they would rip Airey apart.

"Please," said Airey. "Don't be strong. *Please.* Go there with me. We can do this. Be with me."

I can't. Cecilia pulled away, fighting not to drown in her. "I won't."

"Stop being strong for me. Be strong for yourself. How strong are you? Show me. Cec'ly Howison, show me. I dare you."

"I wo—" The night vanished. Cecilia stood alone on an empty plain. She saw herself stifled, trapped, under Tom's cellophane. Tom, who had chosen to be a fossil when he felt the weight of the world. *But I'm not trapped.* Her body had shown her the truth. Her body had made her free. What greater revelation did she need? She knew why she was here. To battle the beasts of the forest. To walk the shining peaks above the pit. She lifted the hands of her spirit, and they were alight. To stand beside Airey and fear nothing.

Here is your sword. Take it.

Here is your spear. Take it.

Here is the crown of life. Take it. *Take it.*

Dare all.

Yes. Yes.

"I will. Yes."

She felt the words fall into Airey, Airey slowly hearing, slowly understanding, slowly closing her arms around her, slowly becoming still. Cecilia held her and stood on a high bright place looking at this new world she had entered as easily as stepping out of the woods.

She felt Airey's faint trembling, felt dampness dropping on her shoulder. "You're crying."

"That's so."

Cecilia tried to move, was held in arms of steel. She said at last, "Airey, my evening bag's on the floor. I have a handkerchief. I have two."

Airey laughed shakily and let her stoop for it. She wiped her eyes. "There goes Mrs. Neihoff's best face powder."

"What do we do? Do now?"

"First of all, rejoice."

Cecilia flung herself against her, desperate to speak. The grip of long anguish would not release her, the words would not be said. *Help me*. In stages, she became aware of the scent of cologne, of powder, of silk. Of rosin. Her heart shuddered, the chain around it fell away, the vault sprang open, and every moment of every day she had lived without Airey flew into the night. *I love you*. Time began again, and its direction was life. All things were given to her. "I love you. I'm in love with you. Airey, I love you."

Airey lifted her hands to her lips. They stood together above the multitudes of the silent city.

Cecilia said at last, "We have to be practical."

Airey's smile flickered. "That's you from the start."

"When do you come back from Europe? I'll return...I'll wait in Washington while you—"

"No. Your leaving days are over. I can't live through that again. The *maître* and the princess and I are sailing for England on the *Laurentic* this Saturday. You're going with us."

"But I—"

"You've got a day and a half to get ready. If you're short of money, I've," Airey took a quick breath, "I got ample. You're in Canada, so you must have your passport."

"I also have my maid and a lot of explaining to do."

"Send her home with letters to your folks. Tell them you're going abroad and you're staying for a little while. A long while." Airey smiled. "*Rise up, my love, my fair one, and come away.*"

"Buy a complete wardrobe, book myself a passage, and—go with you." Every cell was fizzing, foaming over, fountains were flinging her into the air. "Very well." No sanatorium would cure this. *I'm intoxicated by her. I always will be.*

"Gregorio will get you the ticket. He's the *maître's* factotum. That's secretary and foreman. He makes our arrangements."

"Then I can deal with the rest." She would call Elliott. She would call Trenton. That was what they were for. "If I can't manage it, it can't be done."

Airey sputtered. "You ain't changed a bit! I-I reckon I'm in heaven, hearing you say those things like you always—" She stopped with a shocked breath. "My talking's gone!"

"Your talking?"

"Mrs. Neihoff told me some of my ways should go, and how I talked was one of them. I haven't needed to think before speaking for nearly a month—then you come back to me and here I am, same as I ever was, falling over myself in love with you."

You, with your panther's grace? "Speak any way you please. Say anything you want. Read the voter rolls to me. Name every postmaster from the dawn of time. Talk to me."

Airey's laugh was dazzled. "You're here. I've got you. I've got you. Cec'ly, Cecilia, I—"

"*Cec'ly* is fine."

"No. Cecilia. I need to say it properly. I have to have it in my head."

"As long you have one or the other on your lips."

"You've been written there since you first kissed me."

"Airey." Cecilia felt a sting. "You've…you're calling yourself by another name."

Airey looked puzzled. "What name?"

"Ara Fitsch."

"That's not another. It's mine."

"What?"

"It's my name. The one I was born with."

"You—"

"It's Swiss. That's us. Way back, I mean."

"Fitsch."

"Or Fittes or Fitch, depending on how you spell it.

"And *Ara*? Oh, oh!" Cecilia laughed. "I'm a fool. As they say Sarey for Sara, or Poly for Pola."

"Folks back home."

"Your older brother—?"

"Freed? Friedrich. And Meretilda. Mrs. Neihoff showed me a photo of a town in the Swiss Alps called Saint Gall, which is more rightly said Sankt Gallen. It's near the place we come from. She said she should have known we were Fitsches when she saw our old clock."

"Swiss." Cecilia reoriented herself. "Ara."

Airey grinned. "You look hog-plugged."

"I'll need time to learn to say it. I'm not able to adjust to too many new worlds at once."

"*You* threw them at *me*."

"You took them in your stride." Cecilia ran her

hands inside Airey's jacket, feeling the ribs too close to her skin.

"That's 'cause I wanted to go where I was going."

Cecilia put her hands on Airey's shoulders and looked at her. She took her head in her hands and kissed her.

Sweet, shockingly sweet, sweet beyond anything she had ever known. Airey's lips were intent, wondering. Cecilia kissed her seriously, kissed her helplessly, kissed her, unable to hide her longing, not needing to. Kissed her, sought her, needed her, and Airey's lips answered.

They stopped to look at each other, kissed and touched each other's faces, kissed with soft sobbing breaths, kissed, electric under each other's hands, kissed, bodies hard together. Cecilia breathed flame against her mouth. "Airey—"

"Say the words again. Tell me."

"I love you. Airey. Ara. I love you. I love you."

"Cec'ly." Airey straightened. "Back then, you understood God's will. I didn't. What you done for me—I can't hardly bear what you done for me. You're constant, you're good, you're wise for my sake—you come from His furnace refined more purely than gold. Tonight, you would have walked away from me with all that's in your heart—would have walked away *for* me. And again on this new road. Cec'ly, you're that far above me, you're holy in my eyes. Strength and honor clothe you. Lord God, God my Savior, give me the grace to love you as you should be loved."

"As you do."

"As I'll strive to till I die."

Without moving, they had come to a new place. New, this rapturous high air. New, this covenant.

Cecilia linked her hands behind Airey's head and leaned back in the ring of her arms, looking up at her. Airey smiled down. This honorable estate. This union. They stood looking at each other as the world curved around them, sheltering and safe.

A line of light grew from the curtained door. Someone stepped through.

"Ara, I was told I'd find you here." Jurevič strolled down the balcony toward them. "Ah, em, good evening. I take it this is the Immortal Beloved?"

"It is," said Airey.

"Am I to ask Gregorio to book a new stateroom for both of you?"

"Yes, please, *Maître*."

Jurevič smiled. "Miss Howison, we met all too briefly. I'm delighted to welcome you into my household, as I'd prefer Ara to spend what little leisure time she has in a state other than stoic fury. If the two of you would...unentwine...and return to the party, we can assuage many feelings bruised over the extended disappearance of their newly anointed. Although it's clear I mustn't expect you to stay for long. Ara, you have many people to thank."

"I know, sir," she said, prince before a king.

Cecilia, having wrenched herself from her arms, found that she was still holding her hand.

"The young," Jurevič murmured. "Miss Howison, you may call me Monsieur or Herr Jurevič or Marus, whichever is more comfortable. The Princess Dražnaliska is always Madame. Ara, you needn't see me tomorrow, unless you want to attend my concert."

"Of course she'll attend," said Cecilia.

Jurevič smiled at the new management. "You will both enjoy it. Ara, I hope I need not say that, in spite of this reunion, you should try to practice tomorrow."

Airey lifted an outraged chin. "Cecilia needs time to arrange things anyway."

"I very much suppose so. You might also want to prepare for a visit by some gentlemen of the press. Now, shall we return to our guests?" He pursed his lips, considering them. "I'm confident you'll allow me to go in first, indeed by several minutes. Please do not linger." He left the door open.

Airey took Cecilia into her arms. "Where are you staying?"

"The Windsor Hotel."

Airey laughed. "The *maître* moved me there last week to be near him."

"My maid..."

"Then it'll be my room. First we have to go inside and stay maybe an hour."

"I know. At least an hour."

"No more than that."

They stood quietly. Cecilia finally said, "We must go in. You have a public."

"I do now." Airey smiled her slow smile. "I like it."

"You always did. Come one, come all."

At the door, she tried to slip her fingers from Airey's grasp. Airey would not let her go, and with a quick breath, she agreed. *We start now.* They walked into the party hand in hand.

Three hours later, drenched in sweat on bedclothes torn from the mattress, arms slack across each other, faces rough with tears, lips close to each other's lips, they lay tangled.

"Airey. Ara."

"My love?"

"You're beautiful." Cecilia's fingertip descended Airey's ribcage to the lowlands of her belly. "How can you be so beautiful?"

"Because I'm built by God for this place. The place that was always you. My rightful place." Airey kissed the corner of Cecilia's mouth. "He brought you here when He needed you to be here." She lifted her head. "*Why* are you here?"

Cecilia knew what she asked. "Lorimer sent me your poster."

Airey looked at her, stupefied. "He told me he was forbidden to write to you."

"He's also intelligent and brave."

"I never dreamed you'd see it." Airey looked away, out the window, into the farthest reach of night. She turned back. "Every time I learned a new piece, I'd think about how you'd listen to it. It was a way of keeping you in my life."

"The Bach tonight."

"I wasn't going to play him. Not tonight. Then, when they were shouting and calling for everything I had and my heart was full up, I felt God telling me to play it as if you were there to hear. So I played it. I played it—and you *were* there. You were there." Airey buried her face against her. Cecilia felt a pulse hammering through her body. To carry someone's love in your hands was power enough to daunt a queen. She ran her fingers through Airey's hair, thinking of the wonders beneath that delicate skull.

Airey eased slowly and kissed Cecilia's palm. "All the music tonight was for you. The *maître* let me compose the program. Didn't you hear it? The Mozart was the first record you played to me. The next piece I did is called *Lascia ch'io dica addio*: Let me say farewell. I thought I could, being that kind of fool. Goldmark, he was like me, growing up learning on his own, and tonight, he gave me what I needed to say."

"The opening Handel?"

"That's a piece he worked up from his own *Ode for St. Cecilia's Day.*"

Cecilia laughed in painful delight. "The encores?"

"I didn't know I'd play so many, but the first one I planned. It's the original slow movement from Tchaikovsky's violin concerto. He reused it as that *Souvenir d'un lien cher.*"

Cecilia brushed a fingertip across her mouth. "You speak French beautifully. I heard you at the soirée."

"That's not really me speaking it. Madame made me memorize a few polite lines in French. Those times she could, she'd give me a signal and I'd say the right one. Otherwise, it was *merci beaucoup*. You were close enough to hear? How didn't I see you?"

"You acted as if I weren't in the room."

"I knew you was there every single second, like I'd have known striked lightning." Airey rubbed her forehead with the heel of her hand. "There I go again. I'm learning German alongside lowlander English. Italian's coming soon. German's mostly easy, given I grew up with some, though the words are longer than a body could plow in a day with two mules and a boy leading."

"I *have* to kiss you."

Airey's answering kiss would have ignited her, had she not already been comprehensively reduced to embers. Airey gave a cocky grin.

"How am I to deal with you, Miss Fitsch?"

"Like you done from the first: by the grace of your heart."

Cecilia took her hand, kissed it, kissed each hard fingertip, the inside of her wrist.

Airey's breath caught. "Cec'ly, I want-I want all of last year with you now. I want every day of it right now."

"I hope the manager of this hotel understands."

Airey grinned, but said soberly, "You know we're going to be spending most of our time in places like this. Though the *maître* has two homes, in Geneva and Trieste, he says soloists live out their lives on the road. His suite here is bigger than the Neihoffs' whole house, but it's still a hotel room. He sometimes rents apartments for Madame when he's on tour. We could, too, if that's what you'd like."

"When have I ever wanted domesticity? I can barely cook and you not at all."

Airey ignored this with dignity. "Or if you want, we—"

"Madame appears to thrive on a nomad's life. So shall I. Does she mind your being with them?"

"Her and me—she and I—we don't talk much. I know she wasn't sorry to find out what I was. Most women in her place wouldn't be."

"Have they children?"

"Her husband's got them." Airey glanced southward. "Mam's expecting again. The pastor is sure it's a boy."

"I know. I-I've stayed informed."

Airey's smile was sweet. "Lorimer wrote me that you took him to that pay-for school on his first day. I know you did it to set him up in the eyes of the other boys."

"What's the use of being a Howison if you don't use it?" Cecilia remembered her dread of Tom all the way to Ruyerford. Tom, who had done nothing. "I'm fond of Lorimer. He's like his sister: one to watch. I'll ask Trenton to give him the monument."

"You still call it that?"

"You named it."

"That day. That day. Even in my lowest despair, I thanked God for it."

"I remembered it—all of it, over and over, every day, every hour. I couldn't bear to, couldn't bear not to, until I—"

"Went under, same as me."

"Fell to pieces in grand style. Poor Mother had to drop all her arrangements and take me away."

"Where to? Was you near?"

"I was in Cuba. Then back home, reconciled to a life in Washington. My trust isn't quite large enough these days to live on, and as it happened, I hadn't much interest in living. Oh," she said to Airey's sudden movement, "I accustomed myself to it again. In Washington, I even found myself noticing women—with a sort of dreary wonder. So many in the world, none of them you."

"We can't never be apart again, not from here on, not for one minute."

"What a whopper. You need to practice."

"And study. It won't be much fun for you."

"You don't know what I do for fun." Cecilia thought of the Orchestra Committee's accounts. "I've a few modest skills I can put to use. Did you earn a fee tonight?"

"An honorarium."

"What did you do with your share of the farm money? Are you living on it?"

Airey was silent. "I did when I first came north. I had to. Then, in October, I gave a recital and a man in the audience came round and promised me an allowance till I started earning properly. My other patron bought me my new violin and bow. I didn't need the money from back home, so your lawyer invested it for me."

"In long-term treasury bonds, I hope to goodness."

"Find out."

Cecilia shifted, but Airey held her. "Find out. You know what to do."

"You want me to handle all this for you?"

"The *maître* reckons that after four, maybe six, months of me studying with him in Geneva, he'll speak to his agent about getting me work over there. Then you and I'll swap. Your part will be to take my earnings and make us rich. Mine will be to spread the world at your feet."

"You already have."

Airey looked at her seriously. "What I've done is take you away from everything that's yours, everything you know."

"Which is what, exactly? Parties on the White House lawn? Such a loss."

Airey persisted. "I'm asking you—"

"I know what you're asking me. I've forsaken it all with a song in my heart. Whatever lies ahead can't harm me. I've been through the wilderness."

"Cec'ly—"

"This is the life I want to live." Cecilia sat up

and looked at her. "It began the moment I saw you sleeping in the meadow. I just didn't know who you were then."

"Who was I?"

"My Jerusalem." Cecilia leaned down. "My promised land."

She kissed her, they kissed, they turned to each other, they turned each other into fire, rolling in flames across the bed as they lit the night, laughing and tumbling, leaping to heights they had never been, rising in a rapture that circled the earth, flying above it, perfect and complete, shouting for joy as the world blazed below them, until they slept, until they woke, and they looked at each other in the first light of dawn that was creating the trees and the cross on the mountain from gold.

About the Author

Caro Clarke is a Canadian living in the UK. As a child, she moved around every few years from oil-town to oil-town, until the family settled in Calgary. From there, she followed an academic career until she ended up in England.

Having had all the fun of academia, she decided it was time for something new, mostly because she had fallen in love, and wanted to follow Her to London. Best decision ever.

She went through a variety of jobs: small independent publishing, carpenter, a short time in a bookshop, a shorter time as a bodyguard, freelance editor, copy-writing and, finally, designing and running websites, mostly for massive global companies.

Her first published novel was *THE WOLF TICKET*. She has written short stories for anthologies, and publishes poetry under a different name.

She has traveled extensively, including Antarctica, the Gobi, Iceland, southern Russia, and Patagonia. If it involves a desert, the sea, or needing oxygen, she wants to go. But London remains her home and favorite destination.

IF YOU LIKED THIS BOOK...

Share a review with your friends or post a review on your favorite site like Amazon, Goodreads, Barnes and Noble, or anywhere you purchased the book. Or perhaps share a posting on your social media sites and help spread the word.

Join the Sapphire Newsletter and keep up with all your favorite authors.

Did we mention you get a free book for joining our team?

sign-up at - www.sapphirebooks.com

Other books from Sapphire Authors

Broken, not Shattered – ISBN – 978-1-952270-22-2

Even when it seems hopeless, there can always be a better tomorrow.

Jill Bishop has one goal in life – to survive. Jill is trapped in an abusive marriage, while raising two young girls. Her husband has isolated her from the world and filled her days with fear. The last thing on her mind is love, but she sure could use a friend.

Alex McCoy is enjoying a comfortable life, with great friends and a prosperous business. She has given up on love, after picking the wrong woman one too many times. Little does she know, a simple act of kindness might change her life forever.

When Alex lends a helping hand to Jill at the local grocery store, they are surprised by their immediate connection and an unlikely friendship develops. As their friendship deepens, so too do their fears.

In order to protect herself and the girls, Jill can't let her husband know about her friendship with Alex, and Alex can't discover what goes on behind closed doors. What would Alex do if she finds out the truth? At the same time, Alex must fight her attraction and be the friend she suspects Jill needs. Besides, Alex knows what every lesbian knows – don't fall for a straight woman, especially one that's married…but will her heart listen?

Survival – ISBN – 978-1-952270-18-5

After surviving a school shooting, Mona Ouellet moves from Montreal to Peterborough, switches her PhD discipline from English Literature to Psychology, and tries to move on with her life. Unfortunately, her nightmares follow her--and so do a host of "bad men" who seem to appear around every corner to make her life difficult. Her only escape is to fall into her research completely, where she soon becomes obsessed with retelling true crime case studies and enamoured by a waitress at a local diner.

Kerri Reznik is a waitress by day and horror writer by night, where she turns elements of her two-month long captivity in the wilderness with her survivalist father into stories to scare others. Though over a decade has passed, Kerri is still haunted by her brother Lee's absence in her life and her inability to reconcile with it. She seeks camaraderie with Absalom Lincoln, a detective on Peterborough police's force, where the two bond over mysteries, both true and imagined.

As Kerri and Mona's connection becomes stronger, their past traumas begin to intertwine and both of their worst nightmares begin to evolve and intensify. Each character must struggle to negotiate how to live in a world where survival is never guaranteed, and even when it is possible, there is always a cost.

Talk to Me – ISBN – 978-1-952270-20-8

Claire takes a turn for the wild side when she chances into a job at San Diego's KZSD radio to work with Marly, the sharp-tongued lesbian shock jock of

Gayline. Under Marly's close tutelage, Claire feels the sparks fly as she learns to screen calls and handle board operations. It's enough that her formerly quiet life has been upended after separating from her husband, and at first, she keeps her feelings hidden. Even as bomb threats force the radio station employees to clear out, Claire's attraction to Marly's charisma, wit, and atypical beauty keeps her coming back. Meanwhile, she struggles to maintain a relationship with her teen daughter while her soon-to-be ex makes it clear he wants to try again. Its two steps forward, one step back as Marly and Claire grow closer and admit their feelings.

Will Marly's outrageous "anything goes" attitude be too much? As their on-air shenanigans and romance heat up, Marly's crazed plan to boost ratings threatens their relationship, and ultimately, their lives.

The Coffield Chronicles – Hearts Under Fire: Book Two – ISBN – 978-1-952270-30-7

1863 opens with a bang! President Abraham Lincoln issues his Emancipation Proclamation, freeing all slaves in the rebellious states. Independence Day is won twofold, when the Yanks win battles in Gettysburg, Pennsylvania, and Vicksburg, Mississippi. The Union Army is thoroughly exhausted by the time the siege at Vicksburg is won and the Stars and Stripes proudly wave atop the trenches they now possessed.

Melody Coffield, a.k.a. Lieutenant Melvin A. Coffield, survives battle, fighting even when the fear had threatened to overwhelm her. The Livingston Plantation in

Vicksburg is now a Union headquarters, where Melvin is an aide-de-camp to General John Robert Frommer. Still holding the secret of her sex, she meets the beautiful and intriguing Becca Chamberlain. The Southern belle possesses an air of mystery and a bit of arrogance that Melvin finds charming, even bewitching. Honoring her role as a soldier is becoming increasingly difficult. Hiding her true identity is detrimental, but with her feelings for Becca come carelessness and a need for love that was all but forgotten.

The Dragonfly House: An Erotic Romance - ISBN- 978-1-952270-14-7

On the outskirts of a small, picturesque Midwestern town, sits a large, lovely old Victorian house with many occupants. This residence, known simply as The Dragonfly House, is home to Ma'am, the proprietor, along with several young women in her employ. One such woman, Jame, is very popular among the female clientele. One such client, Sarah, fresh from a divorce and looking for a little adventure, as well as some gentle handling, becomes one of Jame's repeat clients. Once Sarah enters the picture, Jame and Ma'am, as well as the brothel, will be forever changed.

Printed in Great Britain
by Amazon

68813705R00222